Praise for
CLEAN

Written with **verve** and **wit** ...
it's **one to just enjoy** – STYLIST

An emotional freight train of a novel – HEAT

Addictive – THE POOL

As **bold** and **gritty** as it is **fabulously
glossy** and readable, it's a **provocative,
important read** – OBSERVER

Compulsively readable – GUARDIAN

Gossip Girl goes to rehab...
Clean **hits the spot** – i NEWSPAPER

Sharp, gripping and tender – ATTITUDE

Compelling – FINANCIAL TIMES

Hard-hitting and **unapologetic** – SUN

ALSO BY JUNO DAWSON

FICTION
Margot and Me
All of the Above
Under My Skin
Say Her Name
Cruel Summer
Hollow Pike
Clean

NON-FICTION
The Gender Games
Mind Your Head
This Book Is Gay
Being a Boy
What Is Gender? How Does It Define Us?

MEAT
MARKET

JUNO DAWSON

Quercus

QUERCUS CHILDREN'S BOOKS

First published in Great Britain in 2019 by Hodder and Stoughton

1 3 5 7 9 10 8 6 4 2

Text copyright © Juno Dawson, 2019

The moral rights of the author have been asserted.

A CIP catalogue record for this book
is available from the British Library.

ISBN 978 1 786 54038 6

Typeset in Adobe Caslon by Hewer Text UK Ltd, Edinburgh
Printed and bound by CPI Group (UK) Ltd, Croydon, CR0 4YY

The paper and board used in this book
are made from wood from responsible sources.

Quercus Children's Books
An imprint of
Hachette Children's Group
Part of Hodder and Stoughton
Carmelite House
50 Victoria Embankment
London EC4Y 0DZ

An Hachette UK Company
www.hachette.co.uk

www.hachettechildrens.co.uk

To the Dream Team: Sullyanne, Ivan, Marc, Samar and Max. Thank you for not being like the agents in this book.

'Fashion should be a form of escapism,
and not a form of imprisonment.'
Alexander McQueen

– OK, it's filming.

– What am I supposed to say?

– Well, why did you want to make this film?

– It's time, I think.

– Why now?

– I dunno. A lot of people have a lot of opinions about me. About who they think I am. About what happened. It's time to tell my side of the story.

– Cool.

– God. Where do I begin?

– Just start at the beginning.

– Erm . . .

– Take your time. There's no rush.

– 'Once upon a time, I was born . . .'

– OK, maybe not the *actual* beginning.

– I feel dumb.

– You're doing great, I promise. Go on . . .

– I guess . . . I guess it started that day at the theme park.

– So start there.

SCOUT

Why are men such trash?

I'm pretty sure we're being followed. I take another look over my shoulder, and, yes, sir, he's still there. What a creep. I first noticed him when we come out the loos and he's been lurking behind us all the way towards Stealth. Gross. Like, we're blatantly on a school trip. Fuck is wrong with you? Skanky bastards, honestly.

My phone vibrates in my back pocket. It's Ferd. They've gone to Swarm instead of Stealth.

'They've gone to get in the queue for Swarm,' I tell Laurel. The others went on ahead of us while we went to the loo. Laurel has a bladder the size of a pea, I swear.

Laurel nods. 'OK . . .'

We change paths at Tidal Wave – giving it a wide berth so we don't get soaked – and Laurel continues to babble on and on. I flick another look over my shoulder, pretending to play with my hair.

What the actual fuck? The lurker has changed route too.

OK. Little worried now.

'. . . I mean,' I try to focus on what Laurel's saying, 'why does she have to be so obvious? Like, I get it, she's seeing Harrison now, but the way she's always touching his hair and rubbing herself against him like a dog in heat. Has she never heard of dignity?'

I peek again. He's still following us. Shit. He looks about thirty. Not old enough to be my father, but not far off. We turn down the path that leads right to the queue entrance. It's supposed to look like an alien invasion: there's a burning ambulance, police sirens and a charred phone box. It's pretty cool but . . .

'Jana, are you listening to—?'

'OK,' I interrupt, pressing myself to her hip, 'do *not* look back, but I think we're being followed.'

'What?' Of course, the first thing she does is turn right around.

'Laurel!'

She turns back. 'Which one? The hipster guy?'

'Yes,' I hiss. 'Swear he's been right behind us since we come out the loo.'

'Really? Ew! What a freak.' This time, Laurel pretends to swish her waist-length hair off her face and sneaks another look. 'OMG, Jana, he's coming over.'

'What?'

'Hi there! Excuse me!' he shouts.

What fresh hell? 'Keep walking,' I say. Sometimes builders or whatever shout crap at us from off scaffolding and stuff, but I've never been actively followed before. Scary. You'd think you'd be safe at Thorpe-fucking-Park, right?

'Sorry to bother you, can I just have a minute?'

'Let's see what he wants. Maybe you dropped something.'

'Laurel, no . . .'

But it's too late. He strides right up to us. 'Crikey, you walk fast . . . I've been trying to catch up with you.' He talks directly to me. 'Hi, my name's Tom Carney and I'm . . .'

Swarm pelts by overhead and whatever he says is drowned out by the screams of the people on the ride. Ribbons of hair fly across my face. 'What?' I shout.

'I asked how old you are.'

Laurel grimaces. 'Too young for you, you skank.'

The man, Tom, smiles and slips a hand in his rucksack. He produces a business card and holds it in front of my face.

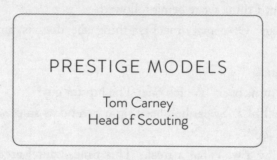

PRESTIGE MODELS

Tom Carney
Head of Scouting

I blink. The ride soars by again and all I hear are screams while his lips silently move. 'Sorry, what?'

'I said, have you ever done any modelling?' he repeats. He don't *look* like a paedo, although I figure only very unsuccessful ones do. He looks like a gay Shoreditch hipster: beanie hat, plastic glasses, lumberjack shirt and ginger beard. Bet he's got a fold-out bike.

'Seriously?' Laurel says. '*Jana?*'

I ignore the tone in her voice. Shade. 'No,' I mumble. I hate my voice when I'm nervous; it goes so deep. I sound like a giant man. Hagrid realness.

'Have you been approached by an agency before?'

'No.' Man voice. Is he for real? A modelling agency? Hold up, is this a porn thing? Cos literally *no one* wants to see my flat arse in porn.

'Wow. That surprises me,' Tom Carney says. 'How old did you say you were?'

'I'm sixteen,' I say. It's a scorching, factor-fifty day in June. My thighs are sticky in denim cut-offs, and I'm wearing a Nirvana T-shirt and filthy Converse that ain't been white for a long time. We've just finished our exams and school has brought us to Thorpe Park as a treat. The air is creamy with Hawaiian Tropic, candyfloss and hot dogs, mustard and ketchup.

'Don't tell him that,' Laurel says, tugging on my hand. 'He might be a paedo. We should find a teacher.'

'You're absolutely right to be wary – there are fake scouts out there – but I swear this is legit. Prestige is one of London's best model management agencies. You can call the office or visit the website. What's your name?'

I know nothing about fashion and stuff, but I've heard of Prestige. They represent Clara Keys. We love Clara Keys. She's our homegirl. 'I'm Jana. Jana Novak.'

'That's cute. Where are you from?'

'Battersea.' My name always solicits *that* question. 'But my parents are Serbian.'

'Awesome. Do you know how tall you are?'

Too bloody tall. 'I dunno,' I say with a shrug. 'Maybe five-eleven?' I hope. I don't want to be six-foot tall. I always hunch just in case.

5

Another train car of screamers flies over. 'Listen,' Tom says, 'take my card – the number is on the back. No pressure but, if you want, talk to your parents and we'll arrange a proper meeting at the office.'

Laurel sort of steps between us. 'Are you for real, mate?'

'Hundred per cent. This is my job.' He smiles and his teeth are like little Monopoly houses – too perfectly square to be real. 'I know, right? I go to festivals and theme parks or anywhere where there are lots of teenagers to find new faces.'

'Cool job,' Laurel says, eyes wide. 'What about me? Do you think I could be a model?'

Oh, Laurel, hon, no. Awks. Playing along, Tom steps back to get a look at her. Laurel is *much* prettier than me. She's got a little button nose and allergic-reaction lips that boys seem to bust a nut for. 'What's your name?'

'I'm Laurel Ross.'

'Well, Laurel, you're definitely a very pretty girl. But how tall are you?'

'Five-five.' Her voice drops. 'But taller in heels!'

He smiles sympathetically. 'To be honest, we wouldn't consider anyone shorter than five-eight.'

'Kate Moss is five-seven . . .'

Tom smiles. 'Kate Moss is Kate Moss.'

'Oh. OK.'

'But, Jana, I'd really love for you to give us a call. Seriously.'

Laurel's face changes. Her mouth hangs open and she frantically texts someone. I look to Tom. I shake my head. 'Me? You sure?'

He grins. 'Jana, frankly I'm *amazed* you haven't been scouted before today. Get your parents to give me a call, yeah? Enjoy the rest of your day. Wear sunscreen.' He walks away and gets sucked into a mass of Spanish tourists and I wonder if the whole thing was a weird hallucination. Country air, man.

'Oh my god, Jana! Did that actually just happen?' I guess if Laurel saw it too, it must have. She hops from foot to foot like she needs another pee. 'Quick! We have to go find Sabah and the others!'

I shrug. I look at the glossy little card in my hand. My thumb traces the embossed letters. It feels *expensive* somehow, and I think about that chocolatey bastard Charlie and his golden ticket.

- That was it. That was the BIG MOMENT.
- Why was it so big?
- Because . . . everything changed.
- For better or worse?

- Jana?
- Better. To begin with.

PRESTIGE

We are all proper tall in my family. Dad is tall, Mum is tall-ish, Milos is tall. I was always gonna be tall.

As such, I have to stoop a bit in front of my mirror because my bedroom is the attic room and it has stupid sloping ceilings. Swear I can only stand up straight right in the centre of the room.

I wonder if I'm going mad. I really can't imagine *anyone* would want me to model *anything*. Yes, I am mad tall, and I understand that fashion models, traditionally, are tall, but I also look like a big lanky freak. At school, I pretend I don't hear people calling me Giant, She-Hulk, Madame Maxime, Tranny, Goliath, Lurch, Slenderman (which even I thought was pretty funny, to be honest), Beanpole, Olive Oyl, Queen Kong. I've heard 'em all. If it's not my height, it's my weight: *Oh, she must be anorexic. Look how skinny her legs are! They're like twigs!* So I make a big song and dance of eating cheesy chips. *Maybe it's bulimia, then.*

I'm in the one bikini I own. it's violet with navy blue pin-dots. I wore it once – two years ago in Mykonos – but felt too naked to wear it in public and didn't take my T-shirt off all week. I came back as goth-lite pasty as I went. Today I will have to strip in front of strangers. I've been pre-warned. I guess it's fair enough that they'd want to see my body. It's such a weird body, though. It's not a *sexy* Kardashian body. I don't have boobs or a booty, I'm all bones and jagged joints, like I'm a walking bag of knuckles. I'm not even cupcake *pretty* – I've got Dad's beaky nose.

Boys at school fancy Emily Potter (D cup) or Tiana Blake (DD), not me, which is fine because I have Ferdy anyway and as long as he likes me, I couldn't give two shits.

Sigh. What the hell are you meant to wear to go to a modelling agency anyway? I have no nice clothes. Nice clothes don't fit me. I have to buy from the 'Tall' section or sleeves end halfway down my arms. I select some skinny jeans and my stripy black and white T-shirt because Laurel says it makes me look French and that's, I think, quite fashionable. I stick my grubby off-white Converse on my feet.

I trot downstairs for breakfast, although I'm pretty nervous and my stomach has shrivelled up like a raisin. I was the same during my exams. I got through them on Imodium and wishes.

'Look, it's the model,' says Milos. Sarky little twat.

I slap him around the head as I pass. 'Shut up.'

'Mum! Did you see? She just assaulted me.'

'You deserve it,' says Mum, handing me a bagel on a plate. 'Eat, please.'

'Probably got brain damage, but whatever.' Milos dumps his plate in the dishwasher and goes to get ready for school. For him, school don't finish for another two weeks. Too bad, asswipe.

I smear some Nutella on the bagel and wonder if my growling stomach is hungry after all. 'You want tea? Coffee? Juice?' Mum never sits still; she flits around the kitchen like a moth on crack. I wonder if that's why we're all so skinny – none of us can relax.

'Juice, please. Ooh, is there any apple?'

'Milos finish it. Just orange.'

'Mum, the apple is meant to be mine! Milos drinks it on purpose! He don't even like it!'

She throws her hands up. 'I get more later.'

'Where's Dad?' The door at the end of the kitchen leading into our little garden is open and I wonder if he's having his breakfast outside. It looks like another lovely day. Hottest June on record, so they're saying.

'He gone already.'

'Oh. I thought he was coming with us?'

'No, he has early shift.' He drives the trains on the Bakerloo line. Damn. At least he's on my side. Sure enough . . . 'Jana. Are you sure you want to do this?'

I roll my eyes and take a big gulp of orange juice. 'Ew, is this the kind with bits? Gross, why do you always—'

'Jana Katarina.' Oof. That's me told.

I sigh. 'Dad agrees . . .'

'Never mind your father. What do you think?'

'I think . . .' I choose my words carefully because Mum never forgets and will use anything I say as evidence at a future date '. . . it's worth going along and seeing what they've gotta say. Don't you?' She purses her lips like she's got a whole lemon wedged in her mouth. That's her NOT-HAPPY face. 'Mum?'

'I think if you want to be model, you can be in two years, after exams.'

11

She don't get it. I usually bite my tongue, but this is different. This ain't like when I wanted to play violin on a weird whim when I was twelve. She's got a point, though. It's not like this was my childhood dream or nothing. That was to be an air hostess or a dinosaur. But this has landed slap-bang in my lap and I can't pretend it hasn't. 'Mum. What if this is it? What if there's one shot to do this amazing thing and I turn it down and then it's, like – *poof* – gone for ever? What if this is something I can only do now? What if they don't want me in two years? What if I grow up with a load of what-ifs? I don't want to die with a load of what-ifs hanging over me. This is the only way to find out.'

Mum smiles. 'You know what is your problem?' She squeezes my chin gently. 'Much too clever.' I laugh. She goes back to loading the dishwasher. 'Is what your grandfather used to say to me.'

She so, so rarely talks about my grandparents. Milos and I know not to ask about the war.

I finish my bagel, shoving half in my mouth at once. 'They might not want me anyway,' I say. 'Maybe Tom Carney had sunstroke when he saw me.' He *was* wearing a beanie hat in twenty-five-degree heat.

From Clapham Junction, it's pretty easy to get to Oxford Street. After breakfast, and also after I've brushed my teeth and done a nervous poo, Mum and I cut through the Winstanley Estate to get to the station. Mum says when she and Dad first came to the UK this estate was a police no-go area and there was a stabbing or a shooting every week. Now, although the blocks are ugly as sin, I think it's a pretty nice place to live: there's the green to play on with some swings and a slide, there are trees on the sides of the road and the Caribbean café always smells like jerk chicken. What's not to like?

We catch the overground to Vauxhall where we switch to the Victoria line. I'm too anxious to even play with my phone so I stare out of the window while Mum reads the *Metro*. Mum don't like us coming into central by ourselves (even if it's with Laurel or Sabah or Ferdy or Robin) because she worries about terrorism and murderers, but I know how to get to Big Topshop on autopilot. Even after all these years, Mum ain't sure about London. She says it stresses her out. She still sometimes talks about 'going home'. I don't know any different.

Mum has had *many* phone conversations with Tom already and he's given us thorough, idiot-proof instructions to find the agency, even though it shows up on Google Maps anyway. She took some coaxing to even let me go meet them: I think she thought they were trying to sell me as a sex slave or something. It was only the phrase, 'Mrs Novak, we represent *Clara Keys*,' that convinced her they're legit. Even my mum has heard of Clara Keys. Of course she has; she's off the estate. At least she was, many moons ago.

We get off at Oxford Circus, ignoring a creepy man with teeth missing on the Tube who tells me I'm 'a lovely pretty'. London, innit. Never dull. The Prestige office is just a short walk from the Tube station down Marshall Street, which we find easily. It's not rush hour, but Londoners charge the pavements, hardly looking up from their phones.

I can tell Mum's nervous too. She looks like she's going to a wedding or something, wearing her floral summer dress, which she bought for her twentieth-anniversary party two years ago. She's even wearing make-up. She *never* wears make-up. I guess refugee care-workers from Serbia don't naturally mesh with fashion people. I don't think *I* do. I hope there ain't a test about clothes and designers and stuff. I'll fail.

'OK. I think this is it,' Mum says, stating the obvious. It says, PRESTIGE MODEL MANAGEMENT on an expensive-looking glass plaque above the door. It looks like any old office. I was expecting something more . . . nuts, I guess.

'Mum, I feel a bit sick.' Swear to god, I've never thought about being a model. Ever. But it feels like the sort of thing I *should* definitely want to be. Like, who wouldn't want to be a model? The clue, I figure, is in the name: you're a *model human*; what a human being is supposed to look like.

'You'll be fine. They ask you here, remember? They want you already.'

Good point. Let's get it over with. Why am I so nervous? I hope I don't have sweat patches under my arms. Not cute. I feel pure *embarrassed*, like me coming here is me saying, 'Hi, I'm Jana, I *definitely* think I'm pretty enough to be a model,' when actually I am fully aware I am a bit of a moose.

It was Ferdy, on the coach back from Thorpe Park, who made my mind up when I filled him in on what had happened. I'd pretty much ruled it out on the basis of it being fully ridiculous, but he told me: 'Models aren't supposed to be pretty, they're supposed to be captivating. And you are.'

Love that boy.

It got me thinking, though. From the top of Ferdy's tower block, you can see over the Thames to the posh side of the river:

Fulham and Chelsea, and the swanky glass apartments with the balconies and roof gardens. Shall I tell you who probably lives in them? Fucking models, that's who.

Rich and famous. Everyone wants to be rich and famous, right?

Mum enters the agency first and I follow her in.

I hold my breath. Beyond the door, it's bright, very bright; toothpaste-ad white. It's like I'm stepping into another dimension. Time stops and then . . .

Then it starts again. It's an office. Could be a dentist or a vet, to be honest. There's a little reception desk just through the door. The receptionist *must* be a retired model – she's about eighty-seven per cent cheekbone. That said, I guess a modelling agency probably ain't gonna hire a munter to sit in the threshold. 'Hello there,' she says with a warm smile.

'Hello,' Mum says, and I'm glad I don't have to talk. Bricking it. Mum uses her very best Queen's English; a voice she uses only on the phone or at parents' evening. 'We have an appointment. It's Jana Novak.'

I clock the recognition in the receptionist's face. 'Ah, yes. For Tom? Let me check he's ready for you. I think they're in a meeting. Just one sec.' She picks up the phone and dials.

They're expecting me. It's not a weird joke. I didn't daydream the encounter at Thorpe Park while off my tits on cherry slushie sulphates.

'He'll be down in one second. Just take a seat.'

It's well posh. As we sit on a minty-green love seat, I glimpse a busy office beyond reception. There are two large white desks like islands and both are hives of activity: phones ring and ring, staff babble away in French and English. There's a little coffee table in front of us, stocked with *Vogue, Elle, Tatler, Harpers*. A flatscreen TV on the wall scrolls through Prestige models' latest assignments. I don't recognise most of them, but every once in a while I'm like, *Oh, her*. Mostly they look alike – golden blonde, golden tans, golden legs, golden gold. None of them look a thing like me.

From nowhere, the most random memory pops into my head. I'm six and Year One has to do family assembly, where all the mums and dads come to watch us do a performance. Miss Skipsey, our teacher, made us sing 'English Country Garden' and we all had to be flowers and moths and hedgehogs. Except me. No. While Laurel was a daffodil and Sabah was a butterfly, I had to be a weed. I wore green tights, one of Dad's old jumpers in swamp brown and painted my face the colour of moss. A fucking *weed*.

Clara Keys – this month on the cover of *Vogue* Australia, apparently – pops up on the TV. She's like a black Barbie doll: impossible Disney eyes, full lips and famously flawless skin. I mean, it's the fairy tale that made her as much as her face (and legs): tragic foster child bounces around the care system until she gets scouted in McDonald's, Clapham Junction, while quietly enjoying a cheeky McFlurry, the same way I have a million times. Within weeks she's walking in London Fashion Week, with everyone saying she's the new Naomi. But, beyond her skin colour, she's not Naomi. She's Cinderella.

A girl sits on the other side of the coffee table in an armchair. Now *she* looks like a model. She cradles a Prestige portfolio in toothpick arms, racoon eyes peeking out from curtains of lank, sandy hair. She's tall but also somehow very tiny, sort of birdlike, as if she's just plummeted out of a nest in a very high tree. She looks about my age, but also like she ain't slept in a month.

If that's what they're looking for, I'm shafted.

'Jana! Hello!' Tom strides through the office, proper jaunty, arms wide. I stand to greet him and he gives me a hug. Hmm, no. I like my personal space. Not a hugger. 'How are you? Thanks for coming in.'

'That's OK,' I mutter. Talking to grown-ups who aren't teachers is weird. Talking to teachers is also weird. I try not to. 'This is my mum.'

'Hello, Mrs Novak. It's nice to meet you in person. Do you want to follow me? Everyone is dying to meet you!'

I want to ask how many people I have to meet but that sounds mental. I was hoping it'd just be him. Am I gonna have to stride around in a bikini for a whole room of strangers? I do not want to do that. Ever.

'This way. We're just in one of the meeting rooms upstairs.' I follow him and the rest of the office hardly looks up from what they're doing. A woman with blonde and blue hair is screaming in French down the phone, a million words a minute. Someone in France has fucked up big time.

At the next workspace, a young woman screeches at a stupidly beautiful guy with floppy ginger hair. 'I mean for crying out loud, Seamus!' she yells, grasping at her hair. 'I'm trying to make you money! The least you can do is TURN UP!'

Seamus, I reckon, is too stoned to care. He couldn't look less bothered.

Tom leads us up a narrow staircase to the first floor where there's another workspace with little offices off to the side. One looks like the boardroom off *The Apprentice*, but we go past that one and into a less scary meeting room with armchairs around another coffee table. Ooh, there's a bowl of decorative green apples I bet no one ever eats. 'Have a seat.'

There are already two women on a settee. One is a very cool-looking Asian woman with a turquoise pixie crop and the other is another retired-supermodel type. Her clavicle could have your eye out. 'Hiya!' says Pixie Crop, standing to greet us. 'I'm Ro, Head of New Faces. Nice to meet you, Jana.'

'Hi.'

'Hello, Jana, I'm Cheska DeBrett, Head of Women.' To be fair, she does legit look like she could be the actual Head of All Women. She's a goddess – about my height with flowing golden curls. 'Sit down. Can we get you tea or coffee?'

I shake my head but Mum asks for tea. Tom sends an intern to fetch it before joining us.

'How are you feeling?' Cheska purrs in a very sexy, husky voice. She looks one hundred per cent organic Chelsea. I'd put money on it.

I force my hands to sit still on my knee. I cross my legs like an adult lady. 'I'm nervous. Sorry,' I say, voice all thud.

'Don't be!' Ro says. 'There's absolutely nothing to worry about, hon. It's just a chance to meet you in person. We've already seen the pictures you emailed, so you're not on trial, I promise!' I see the portraits I sent – one face on, the other profile – are flat on the coffee table.

The intern returns with a jug of water and Mum's tea on a tray.

'Tom has not shut up about you since he saw you at Thorpe Park,' Cheska says.

'I really haven't! I'm sorry, Jana, I just can't believe you haven't been scouted before now. You're the find of the decade!'

I feel my cheeks burn.

'Tom! Don't freak the poor girl out,' Cheska says and pours me a glass of water.

'Jana, my love,' Ro says, 'you are quite special. Do you know that?'

I mean, fuck are you meant to say to that? 'Uh. OK. Thanks.'

Cheska smiles. 'Let me guess. At school, people make fun of how you look . . . right?'

Awkward. I avoid Mum's gaze. 'Sometimes. I get called Giraffe and stuff. And I'm not even good at netball.'

Everyone chuckles. 'Can you see that wall?' Cheska points through the glass to the wall opposite. There are rows and rows of glossy cards with faces on. 'Each and every one of those girls was called Freaky or Beanpole or Stick Insect . . . and nearly all of them Giraffe. And now they're making thousands and thousands of pounds with us.'

'Jana, you have, like, a super unique look.' Ro finishes her latte with a slurp and clatter of ice cubes. 'I'll be totally upfront – your face might not be a good fit for very commercial beauty campaigns, but for editorial and catwalk, OH MY GOD, the sky is literally the limit.'

She means figuratively, not literally, but whatever. 'You think?'

19

All three of them chant, 'YES,' in unison. There's a tap at the door. It BURSTS open, and a cloud of dyed-red corkscrew curls blows into the room. Immediately Tom, Cheska and Ro sit up straight in their chairs. 'Hello, hello, hello. Don't mind me.' She's older than the others . . . in her late forties, maybe. Her clothes are nuts but amazing: a pinstripe dress, with Gucci (it says on them) loafers and more jewellery than I've ever seen on one person at once. 'I just *had* to come get a look at Tom's new obsession.'

'Jana,' Tom says, 'this is Maggie Rosenthal, the director of Prestige.'

I catch a gasp before it pops out. She's changed her hair colour since I last saw her on TV. She pops up on the news talking about the fashion industry a lot. It was Maggie Rosenthal what was passing our Maccy D's while Clara Keys was eating her McFlurry in the window.

'Hello there, dearie. Is this your mum?' She shakes her hand.

'I'm Rita. Rita Novak.'

'Nice to meet you. Right, then, Jana. Let's get a look at you.' I'm brought back to earth with a clatter. What? 'Up you get. Stand up!'

I do as I'm told.

'Stand up straight, lovely. Good girl. Excellent height. Five-eleven?'

'I think so.'

She circles me, scanning me like one of those things at the airport. 'Marvellous. Have you got a hairband, sweets?'

'Um . . . no. Sorry.'

'Oh, here's one.' Cheska hands me an elastic tie.

'Can you tie your hair back for me, darling?'

'Sure.' I scrape all the hair off my face and secure it in a knot at the nape of my neck.

'Excuse my French, dear, but your bone structure is fucking immense. I've got a mouth like a sailor – sorry, Mum.' She gives Mum a theatrical wink. 'Ro. What do you think? Haircut?'

Ro nods sagely as if she had some masterplan the whole time. 'Exactly what I was thinking.'

'What size feet have you got, babes?'

'Six.'

'What's the intern called?'

'Nevada,' Tom says.

'Nevada!' Maggie screams out of the door. 'Heels, size six, please!' She gently takes hold of my chin and turns my face side to side. 'Don't take this the wrong way, sweet, but you're quite masculine. Brow, profile. I fucking love it. You're very androgynous. Androgyny is *very* fashionable.'

I've been told I look like a man many times, but no one has ever said it as a compliment before. Nevada scurries in carrying a pair of terrifying patent leather stilettos with a red sole. I know what's gonna happen next. 'Do I have to walk in those?'

'I'm afraid so.'

'I . . . I, um, can't walk in heels.' I don't wanna go into what happened at the prom, but it involved me, a pair of heels, and falling on a wheelchair user.

'Not yet you can't. Get 'em on your feet, babes, and give us a strut.' She squeezes my arm.

My face flushes again as I clumsily sit and pull my Converse off. My socks have little hearts on. State of me. I have faint pink rings around my ankles. The shoes say 'Louboutin' on the insoles. They have Louboutins hanging around the office for dressing up. Casual. Sabah and Laurel will weep when I tell 'em about this.

I slip them on and take a deep breath.

'Just give it your best shot,' Cheska says. 'I never wore heels until I started modelling. Why would we when we're so tall, right? The good news is, we can teach you to walk; we can't teach you to be tall and gorgeous.'

'Give us a little back and forth,' Tom says. 'Don't try to be model-y. It's easy: just walk.'

Another deep breath and I push myself out of the armchair using my arms to get upright. Immediately my toes are like, *Hey, why are you squishing us into a triangle? Your foot is not triangular.* I've seen fashion shows on TV and stuff. I've seen *Next Top Model.* I know models do not walk like regular humans do. When Clara Keys did Victoria's Secret, she did this leg-crossing thing as she walked. Do I try to do that? Or just try to not break a leg?

I turn around and walk towards the door. My ankles feel like they're wobbling. One shoe is a little big and feels like it might fall off. Suddenly, I'm at home, in my *Peppa Pig* nightie, aged four, wearing Mum's massive stilettos. I'm laughing my head off. The photograph is still on the mantelpiece.

'Look up, not at your feet, dear,' Maggie says as I get to the door.

I turn and make my way back towards them. My left ankle rolls in and I stumble.

'Unclench your fists, babe. You look like you're about to start a fight.' I didn't even realise I'd screwed both hands into balls. 'Let your arms swing. Relax your face.'

I do another lap and relax a bit. I even go a bit faster.

'All right, love, that'll do,' Maggie says. 'Jesus loves a trier.'

'Was it that bad?'

Tom smiles. 'It was fine. We've seen much, much worse.'

'Totally,' Ro agrees. 'Hundred per cent fixable.'

Finally Mum says something. 'Does this mean you want to . . . hire Jana?'

Tom, Ro and Cheska look to Maggie, who soaks up a dramatic pause. 'Mrs Novak. I don't say this very often, so let me enjoy the moment. I am not letting your daughter leave these offices until she's signed with us. I will barricade the doors, if need be.' Maggie smiles and her eyes twinkle. She leans over the coffee table and takes both my hands in hers. 'Jana, darling, we would be fucking *honoured* if you'd sign with Prestige Models. What do you say?'

DEVELOPMENT

'What does that mean?' Ferdy says. 'Oh, wait, no, we need to put the bonfire out or the police will stop us again.'

We're playing Final Fantasy.

I'm back in the real world. My world. Our world.

'Oh, yeah, shit. There you go.' I make Ignis run back to the campsite before he gets in the car. 'Development is ... I don't know ... development.'

'That's helpful, babe, thanks.'

I snort and pause the game so I can focus on filling him in. I've already recounted the whole day to Sabah and Laurel by group text and Milos at home, so I'm sorta over it. I swing my legs around to face him, not the TV. I reach out with a bare toe, to stroke his cheek with it, and he bats it away because he thinks feet are peak gross.

'Stop it!' he begs. 'I'll barf!'

I laugh, almost tumbling off the side of the bed. 'I suppose Development is like being in training or something. Tom says I'm actually quite old to be starting out.'

'You're sixteen.' Ferdy reaches past me to grab the bag of sweet chilli Walkers Sensations. Some people think other crisps are better than sweet chilli Sensations, but those people are scammers. Ferdy's mum and dad work pretty late most nights and his sister has a shift at Big Asda so we have the flat to ourselves. We're in his poky room, both cross-legged on the single bed, as Harley Quinn, Daenerys Targaryen and Deadpool look down on us from posters.

'I know, but they scout some girls when they're, like, twelve or thirteen.'

He grimaces. 'Skanky.'

'No, they wait for them to turn sixteen before they start booking them. It's not child labour.' He hands me the bag of crisps. 'Ferd, you have left me crumbs. You're the worst.'

He grins. 'They're not crumbs, they're fragments. There's a difference!' He gives me a sweet-chilli kiss on the lips. 'What happens next?'

'Well, I start training. Swear I could barely walk in a straight line. You would have pissed yourself if you'd seen me. I'm going in again next week to take some "digitals" for my portfolio too. And I think they want to cut my hair . . .'

His eyes widen. 'Really? Like what?'

'I dunno. Short, I think.'

'You gonna do it?'

'I don't mind.' I run a hand through my shapeless hair. At the moment it falls to my boobs, the ratty ends still lighter than the roots from where I begged and begged Mum to let me have an ombre dye job last year. She caved and I immediately hated it. Rather than 'bronde', it went as yellow as a pissy mop.

'Considering you just signed with an amazing modelling agency, you seem surprisingly chill.'

I shrug. 'If I think about it, I start to feel proper weird, so I'm not thinking about it.'

'Weird?'

I shake my head. I twiddle the silver skull ring he gave me on my sixteenth birthday around my index finger. 'I don't know. Like, it's a lot.'

'You know you don't *have* to do it.'

'Yeah. No. It's fine. It's just . . . last Wednesday the only thing I had to think about was if I'd chosen the right subjects for next year. And I was already thinking about binning off biology. It's all right for you and Sabs. You know what you want to be when you're grown up.'

He tilts his head to one side. 'You don't?'

I shrug. 'You know I don't.' I really, *really* don't and it scares the living shit out of me. People at school fall into two groups. Fucking clueless clones like Heather Daley, who want to go on *Love Island* and be famous for a bikini, and people like Ferdy, who seem to have it all mapped out: what uni, what course, what future.

I know *nothing*, and the nothing is so big it feels like it's crushing me sometimes. I can't see anything beyond playing Final Fantasy, making out with Ferdy, and sitting in the park with my friends. It's too bloody hot to think about the future.

'If I do this, everything . . . everything is gonna be different. It's scary. My head feels like it's imploding. You know what it is? I always thought something would randomly rock up like when I was twenty-two and be, like, "Hiya, I'm your job, hon."'

'What if this is that random job . . . just a few years early?'

I hadn't thought of it like that.

He takes my hand. 'And, hey, *I'm* not different. Whatever happens, I'll be the same.'

That does make me feel better. 'You promise?'

'I promise.'

And that's why I love Kai Ferdinand. Maybe he'll be my anchor. I put down my controller and lean over to kiss him. I sink my hand into his messy black hair, not quite as long as mine, but long. He pauses to take his glasses off and we kiss again.

There are two types of kiss: a kiss and a . . . starter gun, I guess. This one feels a lot like a prelude. It's serious and hungry. We lie back together, and I pull the empty crisp packet out from under my butt. Warm hands slide inside my top and towards my boobs. 'Are you wearing a bikini?'

I'd forgotten about that. 'Oh, yeah. For the agency.'

'Very Miss America.'

'The children are the future . . . something, something, world peace . . .'

We kiss again. He pulls my top off. I pull his top off. I undo the bikini top because it feels stupid. We press ourselves together, skin on skin. It's my favourite part. His fingers oh-so-gently trace my hips, my tummy, my nipples and it all feels shivery and amazing. I'm tingling in no time.

I unbutton his jeans and slide my hand into his boxers. He's hard and he's made a small damp patch. He groans as I give him a little rub. He shudders. 'You wanna . . .?' I ask.

'Yeah.'

Now this is the critical bit. He kicks off his jeans and I slide like a snake out of mine. He clambers over me and pulls the drawer of his bedside cabinet all the way out. He stows condoms under the drawer so his mum won't find them. 'Do you want to do it or shall I?' I ask. I'm on the pill, but we always take double precautions because babies are more terrifying than modelling. I have no desire to be one of those girls pushing prams around the Winstanley. At least, not for like twenty years.

'Maybe it's better if I do,' he says. He rips open the condom with his teeth and rolls it on. 'OK.'

I kiss him again and he rolls on top of me. I open my legs to let him in. I'm taller than him, but it hardly matters when we're laid flat. 'Are you ready?'

I nod. He slides himself in. It don't hurt like it used to, although it's still tight. I bite my lip. 'Are you OK?'

'Yeah.'

He lowers himself in further and we both moan. I reach down and cup his bum with my hand. Suddenly he seems to spasm, his butt muscles tense and his hips jut forward. 'Oh, fuck,' he hisses as he comes. 'Fuck. Jana. Shit. I'm sorry.'

His whole body trembles and goes limp on top of me. 'Hey, it's OK.' I cradle his face and kiss him, more gently this time. Just a kiss.

He pulls out of me and slides fingers up my thighs. 'Don't worry,' I say. It feels like the moment's passed.

'Are you sure?'

'Yeah.'

He rolls off me, pulling his hair off his face. 'Fuck, it's so embarrassing.'

'Ferdy, it's fine!' I prop myself up on my elbow to face him. 'I love that you get so turned on.'

'So turned on I jizz in my pants?'

'You got it in that time.'

'Big wow.'

'It felt nice.'

'For all of the five seconds it was in.'

'Ferdy . . .'

He looks into my eyes and I fix him with a no-nonsense *it don't matter to me* expression. At least I hope that's what it says. He smiles a little. 'I guess we'll have to keep practising . . .'

I smile back. 'I dunno, I'll be pretty busy trying to walk in a straight line . . .' He pulls me into his arms and I lie on his chest. I close my eyes and listen to his heartbeat.

I nod off for a bit. I wake up and I'm – one of my favourite words – discombobulated. 'Shit,' I say. 'What time is it?'

'Just after six.'

'Oh, god, I was supposed to be home for six. I promised I'd be there for dinner. Mum wants to discuss the modelling thing with Dad.'

I start pulling on my bikini and looking for my top under the bed. 'That sounds ominous,' he says, putting his glasses back on.

I roll my eyes. 'Mum's being a dick about it.' Ferdy makes a face. 'What?'

'Well, which would you rather? That she was looking out for you or she was a pushy, stage school, *Dance-Moms* mum?'

'Good point. I really have to go.' I give him a quick kiss.

'Give me a min and I'll walk you home.'

'I've got my bike. It's cool. See you tomorrow, yeah?'

'Yeah.'

Ferd lives in Brannigan House, one of the high-rise tower blocks the council is threatening to tear down after what

29

happened at Grenfell. The hallways and lifts are a bit choice, but Ferdy's flat is nice and big and has that sick view of the Thames and Battersea Power Station.

As I leave the block, I ignore a group of scary-looking girls loitering on the corner near where I chained my bike. I feel their eyes on me, and they go quiet, but I keep looking down and unclip my bike as fast as possible. I hop on and cycle away. That's the thing with the gangs round here: if you don't fuck with them, they don't fuck with you. As the scruffy indie kids, we have nothing to do with them. Luckily, I know this estate like she's my twin, all the alleyways and shortcuts. I cut down the side of Chicken Bucket and around the back of the laundrette and barbers – and I'm home in about five minutes flat.

I chain my bike up down the side of the house and tumble in through the front door. As I feared, the house smells thickly of some sort of casserole (because who don't want casserole in a heatwave?). I'm late. I'm sure that'll improve Mum's mood. 'Sorry!' I shout, wondering if I should add, *I fell asleep after I had sex with Ferdy,* just to really finish them both off.

'Hurry up,' Dad shouts back from the kitchen. 'Your dinner is going cold.'

I kick my trainers off and pad through the living room. They're already eating. Dinner time waits for no one in the Novak house. 'Oh, look,' Milos sneers, 'it's Cara Delevingne.'

'Is that supposed to be an insult?' I say as I slide into my chair.

'Stop it before you start,' Dad says.

I lean over and give Dad a kiss on the cheek. 'Hello, *Tata.*' Cliché, but I've always been a daddy's girl. Not in a creepy way.

'Hello, button, how did it all go today?'

I look to Mum, who is suddenly very interested in a bit of asparagus. 'They want to sign me.'

It was from Dad I inherited my 'icy' (Sabah's words, not mine) blue eyes and almost-black hair. His eyes burn out from underneath his heavy black brows. 'And what do you want?'

'Zoran,' Mum interrupts. 'She's sixteen . . .'

'She's old enough for an opinion.'

Mum says no more. 'They seem to like me. They think I could do fashion shows and editorial. I think that's like arty stuff in magazines. Ooh, potato wedges!' I shove one in my mouth. I'm Hank Marvin.

Milos is about to say something mean, but somehow Dad knows and holds up a finger to silence him. 'Do you want to do it?'

That's the big question, ain't it? A lot of girls would flog their granny for this opportunity. So why aren't I more excited? 'I think,' I say, 'it could be a really good way to make some money. That's what Maggie said.'

'Who?'

'The owner of the agency,' Mum adds. 'She was . . . a funny woman.'

'But she knows what she's talking about,' I throw in.

'What about school? And university?'

We don't know what I got in my exams yet, but I'm on a path towards university. I've always bossed school, if you take PE out of the equation, and if you do good at exams, you go to college, right? 'Well, I still want to go to college.' We're all due to start Hollyton Sixth Form College in September.

'Can you do both?'

I shrug. 'Yeah. Think so.'

Mum and Dad look to each other, psychically discussing the issue. I hate it when they do that. 'Ask them, please. Maybe I'll speak with them too. Education is very important, button.'

'I know. You always say how expensive university is . . .' I've heard Mum and Dad talking about student loans and tuition fees when they think I'm upstairs or whatever. They're proper worried. We're all worried. We don't have that much money. 'What if I did this for a couple of years and saved up for university?'

Something changes. Maybe I'm finally tuning in to my parents' frequency. That said, I don't have to be psychic to know that with both Milos and I heading off to university (my brother is a dick, but he's cleverer than me) in the next five years, money is gonna to be an issue. A massive one. Dad actually earns pretty good money from TfL, but Mum is on a part-time wage and zero-hour contract. Two lots of tuition fees, and a mortgage, and a car just ain't gonna happen, is it?

If I could pay for myself, well . . . that's a game-changer. Imagine being able to get my degree *without* the debt. Too good to be true.

I was probably gonna have to get a job at some point anyway. Can't say I'd given any thought to being a model, given how weird I look, but it's probably more fun than frothing milk in Starbucks like Ferdy does.

Mum speaks up, this time more softly. 'I don't want it to interfere with college, Jana.'

'Me either.' I'm actually looking forward to Hollyton. Like school, but without PE. What's not to like?

'It would be good to not have to get a job while you are at university,' Dad muses.

I strike while the going's good. 'So I can do it?'

'If you want to do it, yes,' Dad says and Mum nods, although looks less-than-thrilled.

Well, that's that, then. I'm signed to a modelling agency. Random. Funny, though, decision done, there's a little firefly in my tummy, underneath the potato wedges.

'Can I go to Corfu with Davey and his dad?' Milos chips in.

'No,' say Mum and Dad.

I can't sleep. Even with the Velux window tilted fully open, there's no breeze coming in at all. I lie flat on top of the duvet in a vest and pants, my skin tacky.

My head ain't gonna turn off, no way. Someone's switched a Powerpoint to slide show and I can't shut off about a trillion images. I imagine what my life might be like as a model.

Runway shows, photoshoots, pop videos, adverts. Fame and fortune. Like, MONEY. We never have any money. Mum and Dad bought the house off the council just before I was born and it nearly bankrupted them. London is expensive as fuck.

Don't get me wrong, me and Milos ain't never gone hungry; we always got food on the table and clothes on our backs. There's a lot a lot worse off than us. We try and have a family holiday every other year, but last year the car went so that meant a summer at home.

But we are absolutely, hundred per cent not *rich*. There's always a bill landing on the mat, always a school trip, always something breaking that needs replacing. Milos's feet don't stop growing. Mum spends half her life making packed lunches because none of us can afford to buy posh sandwiches at Pret.

What if I could, though? What if I could be one of those pedigree girls with big white teeth you see in Chelsea or on Northcote Road having avocados for brunch? Three quid for a coffee and fifteen for eggs on toast. Me and Ferd could get the Eurostar to Paris or fly to Berlin for the weekend. Nice hotel with a balcony and a bathtub in the room.

Like, imagine not even having to *think* about money because you knew there was enough in your account. The dream.

It's five to one in the morning. I flick my bedside lamp on and crawl to my record player. Dad found it in the attic a year ago and was gonna throw it out until I salvaged it. Yeah, I know it's uncomfortably hipster, but I love the scratchiness of the records. Dad had some vinyl in the loft too – Joy Division; The Cure; Roxy Music – and I've added to the collection.

Wish I was born in The Past because the music was way better. Blondie; The Runaways; Siouxsie and the Banshees; Kate Bush; Stevie Nicks. Not being funny, but where are women like that now? I select Fleetwood Mac's *Rumours* and drop the stylus. There's a familiar hiss and crackle before 'Second Hand News' starts.

I can't ever be a pretty girl, but a part of me wonders if I can be a *cool* girl like Debbie Harry, like Annie Lennox. Never was too keen on Barbies, to be honest. I remember what Ferdy said on the coach – models ain't meant to be sugarplum fairies.

I go back to bed and try to concentrate on the lyrics, Stevie's voice, instead of the tin-can racket in my head.

Next thing I know, the sun is coming up and it's almost dawn. The planes have started coming in to land at Heathrow. I don't remember falling asleep. I didn't even get to the end of the A-side.

I love London in the sunshine. The ties come off, grubby flip-flop feet, and everyone heads to the nearest patch of green just in case this is the last day of sun any of us ever see. We go hang out at Laurel's because she's got the biggest back garden. Her dad's a perma-tanned Essex-boy builder and she lives in one of the nice terraces by Battersea Park.

Now exams are over, Ferdy has picked up a couple of extra shifts at Starbucks but he says he'll join us later. Laurel has some little speakers for her phone so we're forced to listen to her highly questionable taste in music. I mean, I love her to death, but it's a lot of Ed Sheeran.

'Go on, then,' Sabah says, peeking over her sunglasses. 'Show us your best walk.'

'Really?'

'I can't *believe* they sent you home with a pair of Louboutins,' Laurel says, spraying her arms with factor thirty. 'Who does that? It's so extra!'

'They go so well with this outfit,' I say, wedging my sweaty feet into the stilettos. I'm wearing some cut-off shorts with a Rainbow Dash T-shirt. It's a look.

'The garden path can be your catwalk!' Sabah says. Today she's matched a pretty peach hijab with a simple cream top and skirt. She always looks wicked and her Instagram – hijabgirllondon – is getting pretty big. Well, she has more followers than me, Laurel, Ferdy and Robin combined, put it that way.

'Don't laugh,' I say. The paving slabs are harder to walk on than the carpet in the Prestige office. I feel stiff and lumpy as I clomp down the path. Can't shake the image that I'm goose-stepping. I try to style it out and pose in front of the hot tub, hands on hips, before I turn and start my walk back. 'Well?'

Sabah and Laurel look to each other.

'Shit, is it that bad?'

'No!' Laurel says. 'It's just . . . I . . .'

'She means we're just not used to seeing you in heels, babe,' Sabah quickly adds.

'Yes. That's totally what I meant. P.S. how freaking long are your legs? I had no idea!'

'Well, that's because I don't normally dress like a hooker!' I kick the shoes high into the turquoise sky. 'Will you please help me? I look like a proper dick!' I cry.

'We'll show you,' Sabah says. 'Laurel, have you got any shoes?'

Both Sabah and Laurel have dinky princess size-four feet so Laurel runs up to her room to fetch some heels. Laurel straps on a pair of silver strappy things from prom night and Sabah borrows some chunky black wedges.

'We need better music,' I say and switch Laurel's phone for mine.

'Oi! What are you putting on?' Laurel says.

'What else?' The opening chords of 'Fashion' by David Bowie start up.

'Perfect!' Sabah claps. 'Rest in peace, man.'

'What even is it?' Laurel asks, and we both groan.

Sabah goes first. With effortless grace she struts down the garden path, taking long confident strides. She's got junk in her trunk and jiggles in a way I never could with my flat arse. She poses at the shed, before starting her return. Laurel sets off and they cross halfway. Her walk has less chill than Sabah's; she's trying to be sexy. I remember what Tom said about *not* trying.

Still, both of them are making it look easy. It's not fair really. I bet they'd love to do this. They both love clothes and shopping; they spend hours roaming Westfield, whereas me and Ferdy tend to get all our shit at Beyond Retro or Rockit. Sabah has a fashion Insta for crying out loud; they can both walk in heels. All I am is tall and thin. I'm a genetic fluke.

As Sabah reaches the decking, I set off.

'That's so much better!' Sabah shouts after me. As we pass, Laurel gives me a high-five. Bit cringe.

'That's what they do at Victoria's Secret shows!' she informs me.

'Try to look more pissed off,' Sabah adds. 'Runway girls always look mad as hell.'

We take it in turns, our own little fashion show. With each pass, I get less wobbly, although my feet hurt more with every step. The balls of my feet burn. Sabah puts on 'Supermodel' by RuPaul as Robin arrives with a load of burgers, beers and some pot. 'The fuck are you doing?'

37

'We're having a fashion show! Duh!' Laurel says.

'Robin? What size feet do you have?' I ask.

'I'm a seven . . .'

I pull the Louboutins off my feet. 'Here you go! Your turn!'

'No way!' he laughs. 'I'm not wearing girl's shoes.'

'You have to or you can't play with us,' I say. 'Those are the rules.' We always make fun of Robin because he's a bit posh. He's not fully Rupert or Tarquin, but he's definitely posher than us.

He kicks off his flip-flops. 'Whatever. But don't tell anyone.'

'Oh, we're telling *everyone*,' Sabah says.

He wedges my shoes on. 'They're way too small.'

'That's like a real fashion show,' Laurel says. 'I saw it on *Top Model*.'

'Go on, Robin,' I laugh. 'You better work . . .'

Hands on hips and with a cartoon pout on his lips, Robin sets off down the garden path, wiggling his bum. We cackle with laughter. 'Oh, that's very sexy!' Sabah yells. Robin is more interested in Laurel – he's been in love with her since Year Nine, but she's not into him like that.

'Robin!' I shout. 'I swear to god, you're actually better than I am!'

He starts to walk back. He gets halfway down the path when he staggers on the grass and lands on his arse. We run over to help him up. 'I think I've broken my ankle! I'm gonna sue!' He's laughing so it can't be that bad.

'Aw, bless!' Laurel giggles.

'How do you walk in these things?'

'I don't!' I say. 'That's the whole problem!'

We all sit down on the cool grass. 'I can't believe Ferdy's gonna fuck a model,' Robin says and Sabah thwacks him on the arm. 'If you make a million quid, can I have a car?'

'I'm not a model yet,' I say quietly, squinting into the sunshine.

The others say nothing. They don't have to. They don't think I'm a model either. Because, honestly, I'm not.

- Looking back now, it's funny. I should have seen it. It was right in front of my face the whole time.
- What do you mean?
- Even at the very start, during Development, there were signs.
- What sort of signs?
- That things weren't right. That I, we, weren't . . . safe.
- Go on . . .

NEW FACES

Like a total boss I make my way to Poland Street all by myself. Mum ain't thrilled that I've come into central alone, but they were both working today so there wasn't much they could do about it. Also, I am seventeen in four months: I think I can get on a train by myself. London's not scary when you're from London: don't get your phone out when you leave the Tube, watch out for mopeds. Easy.

It's another scorcher. London smells like bins and beefy farts. Ro asked me to wear simple clothes because today they're gonna take some pictures. I asked Sabah over to help me pick something out and she *assures* me that a real model would just wear skinny jeans and a black vest top. So that's what I'm wearing. I'm in ballet pumps, the Louboutins safely stowed in my canvas satchel. Ro also told me to not wear any make-up – although I only ever really do a bit of mascara anyway.

I find the agency without any issues and everyone seems pretty happy to see me when I walk in. 'There she is!' Ro rushes over to greet me at reception and takes me to the booking table to meet everyone.

Cheska gives me a hug. She smells gorgeous ... sort of citrusy, but not like an actual lime. 'Hello, darling, how are you?'

'Yeah. Good.'

'We are SO excited you've signed with us. Seriously, the whole office is buzzing.' The rest of the bookers agree. Ro introduces me to the men's team and the commercial (Boobs and Bikinis) team as Tom comes out to greet me.

Tom's buzzing too, and their excitement is contagious. They're all so nice.

'Come on through,' Ro says. 'You want a drink or anything? Can we get you anything to eat? I'll send Nevada down to Pret.'

'No, thanks. I just had an almond croissant on the train.' Shit. I wonder if I'm not supposed to eat stuff like that any more?

'They are the *best* croissants!' Ro says. Phew. That said, it don't really make much difference what I eat. I've always repelled fat. Once, at primary school, the school nurse actually started sniffing around home because she was worried I was malnourished. Nah, I'm just a twiglet.

Tom follows us upstairs and this time I'm steered towards the conference room. I see there are already some girls in there. 'What we're doing today,' Tom says, 'is our standard induction. There's another couple of New Faces so it made sense to do you all together. I hope that's OK?'

'Sure,' I say, although imposter syndrome massively kicks in.

Ro shows me into the room and another two girls are waiting. The first is the miserable-looking troll who was in reception when I was last here. The second is a stunning red head with milky china-doll skin and perfectly symmetrical freckles.

'Jana, this is Arabella and Viktoria.'

Arabella jumps up out of her seat to shake my hand. 'Hello there,' she says in a ridiculously plummy accent. 'I'm so excited there are other girls here. It feels like the first day at a new school, doesn't it?'

'Yeah,' I say. I shake her hand, but I'm bad at handshakes. I never know if I'm doing it too hard or too soft. 'Hi.'

Viktoria looks up at me through hair curtains. 'Hello,' she says with a strong accent. Russian, maybe?

'Hi,' I say back.

'Viktoria doesn't speak too much English yet,' Tom says. 'We're practising. She came to us from one of our sister agencies in Paris. Not really a New Face, but we're very excited about her. About all of you.'

'Were you scouted too?' Arabella asks me.

'Yeah, at Thorpe Park.'

'No way! I love Thorpe Park! I was at the Hay Festival in May just minding my own business on my way into a Caitlin Moran talk when Cheska taps me on the shoulder. I was like, *Oh my god, how totally rando is this?*'

She's SO POSH, but seems really genuinely nice. I relax a bit. I'm glad it's not just me and Viktoria. She's pretty scary.

'OK,' Ro says, 'let's get the boring bits out of the way first. Can we do some measuring?' Almost like a magician, Ro whips a tape measure out of her back pocket. Arabella goes first. 'Hmm,' Ro says, face next to her butt. 'What dress size are you, hon?'

'An eight,' Arabella replies.

Ro stands and measures her chest. 'OK, that's cool. Poppet, maybe just watch how much bread and pasta and carbie stuff

43

you're eating. I don't know about you, but they really bloat me.'

'OK!' Arabella says enthusiastically and then it's my turn, Ro measuring up while Tom makes a note of everything. They do my height, leg, hips and bust. Viktoria is the skinniest – clearly – but I'm the tallest. Because I usually am.

'OK!' Ro says. All the measurements taken, she sits back down. 'Like, it's super important to everyone here at Prestige that all our models are healthy and fit.'

'*Super* important,' Tom adds, nodding.

'We *never* tell girls they need to lose weight. Like, ever. We *might* help you out with nutrition and fitness from time to time but that's very different. It's not about losing weight. It's about fitness. You're athletes.'

God, I hope not. I thought I'd left PE behind for ever.

'It's better for everyone if you're fit,' Tom says. 'You and the client.'

'Of course,' Ro says with an eye roll, '*some* designers or casting agents *will* tell girls to lose weight. But that's not what *we're* about.'

I don't really see how any of us possibly could lose any weight. We're all tiny. I know that I'm a freak of nature. Both Milos and I can eat like horses and never gain weight. It must be a genetic thing or something. In fact, all this food chat is making me hungry. I wonder what I'll get for lunch. Maybe a cheeky McDonald's cheeseburger at the station. They're only a quid.

'It's just common sense,' Ro finishes. 'It's not about *dieting*, it's about *diet*. Plenty of fruit and veg and water! Easy!'

Fuck that, I think. Vegetables are rank. I will tolerate sweetcorn, but that is pretty much it.

Ro runs us through 'strategy'. Apparently, as Viktoria and I are taller we're better suited to runway than Arabella who, at five-eight, is on the short side – in Model World. She will mostly be pitched for photographic jobs, or 'editorial'.

'Here's how it works,' Tom says. 'We get you booked for jobs. We send you out to castings in London, New York, Paris, Milan and, fingers crossed, you book shows or shoots. We hype you up as the Next Big Girls, the New Fresh Faces. The more shows you book, the more industry people see your faces and believe the hype. The hope is, once you've done enough shows and editorials, you might book a campaign – like adverts – and that's where you can earn some serious money.'

'What if we don't book stuff?' I ask quietly. Oh. That's the wrong question. Both Ro and Tom stiffen and I wonder if there's a dumpster full of rotting models out back, arms and legs poking out the lid.

'If we didn't think you could get work, we wouldn't have signed you,' Tom says with a grin, finding his composure. 'We sign, like, two per cent of the girls we meet.'

'We know what we're doing,' Ro agrees. 'You'll be fine. Better than fine! You'll be awesome. You're all stars.'

We then do some walking up and down the top floor of the office. Viktoria knows what she's doing; she stomps like she's on her way to murder someone. Arabella is told she's 'too bouncy'. She's a bit child-beauty-pageant. I'm told I've improved and I'm secretly glad I spent all week practising. I watch Viktoria closely and try to copy her.

'Just walk,' Ro tells us. 'Shoulders back, head straight, neck long, and imagine you're sitting back in your hips,' Weirdly, the last piece of advice seems to help. It's not like 'normal walking' at all, but I do feel more poised. After a while I ache from holding myself so stiff and upright. My usual posture is *rubbish*. I remember Miss Breen, our primary school dance teacher, squeaking at me: *You have a spine, Jana Novak! Use it!*

Next, we go down into the basement to have some photos taken. There are two big studio lights and a white backdrop rolled all the way across the floor. Arabella volunteers to go first and we sit on the sidelines and watch as Ro snaps millions of pictures. 'You smoke?' Viktoria eventually says, looking so bored she might die of it.

'No. But I'll come with you for some air.' I feel I should make an effort since she offered.

We stand outside the front of the agency, watching people go by for a while. 'So,' I say. 'Where are you from originally?'

Her eyes light up – I figure she must get asked that a lot. 'Belarus,' she says, sucking furiously on a Marlboro Light. Her teeth are gappy but in a cute way.

'OK. Is that near Russia?'

She nods, hugging her body even in the muggy heat. 'Yes. Near Russia and Ukraine. Is bad . . . life.'

'How long have you been a model?' I'm trying really hard not to do that offensive thing where you speak slow and loud to foreigners.

'Since thirteen.'

'Since you were *thirteen*?' I can't keep the surprise out of my voice.

'Yes. I go to Minsk to meet with agents. Agents go Minsk . . . look for girls.'

'What about school?' Viktoria looks confused. 'Erm . . . school?' I mime reading a book and writing.

She shakes her head. 'I, no . . . school. Make more money. I send money home to mother and grandmother.'

Oh, OK, that's nice. 'Have you done a lot of work?' I sort of point behind us at the agency.

'Yes. I go Japan and Paris when I am fourteen.'

'How old are you now?'

'Seventeen. I am old now,' she laughs, half-serious. I think.

I return her smile. 'Didn't you miss home?' She looks confused again. 'Erm . . . leaving home. Did it make you sad?'

'No,' she says emphatically. 'Was . . . not good.' Her eyes widen and I wonder what they've seen. It reminds me of the face Mum makes if anyone mentions Yugoslavia, the war. I make a mental note to google Belarus when I get home.

Ro pops her head out of the door. 'Who's next? Jana?'

We return to the basement and I take my turn. Ro directs me gently: 'Pull your hair back . . . chin up . . . nose ring out, please . . . chin down . . . look to your left . . . arch your back . . . relax . . . sort of go floppy.' After what feels like a thousand flashes, I'm asked to change into my bikini. Over the weekend, I went to H&M with Laurel and Sabah and bought a plain black one. My tiny boobs hardly fill it. My crotch is red, itchy and dotty where I had to shave it. I hope they don't see.

47

The pictures are going direct to a computer in the corner of the basement, which Tom oversees. 'These are really good, Jana. The camera loves you.'

'I'll be the judge of that!' Maggie says jovially as she bursts into the basement brandishing a ginormous strawberries and cream frappuccino. 'MOSCHINO' is displayed across her boobs. 'Hello, lovely girls, how are you doing?'

Arabella runs up to her and gives her a hug. Viktoria does not. As I'm standing in a bikini, a hug would feel a bit strange so I just fold my arms across my bare stomach awkwardly.

'I say, Jana, darling. These are wondrous. That neck! You're like a fucking swan, hon. Cheekbones!' She comes over to me and holds my hair back. 'Still not convinced about this hair, though. Does nothing for you. What do you think, Ro? Snip, snip?'

I doubt Ro would dare contradict her. 'Erm, yeah. Could do.'

'I just think it's not adding anything. I think the androgyny thing could be the ticket, you know?'

'Sure.'

Maggie grasps me by the shoulders. 'Jana, babe, do you trust me?'

I shrug. What am I meant to say to that? I barely know her. 'Yeah . . .'

'Get your kit on and come with me.'

I put my jeans and vest back on and follow her to the main booker's table. 'Jana, little one. Have you ever heard of Alexandra Holmes?' She flicks through some old Polaroids and holds one up for me. It shows a girl who looks a bit like Viktoria – long, straight mousy hair.

48

'I don't think so . . .'

'Of course you haven't. Now: who's this?'

She slides a copy of *Vogue* over the desk towards me. A girl with a bleached blonde pixie crop and a nose ring sticks her tongue out, the headline reads: 'The New Punk Revolution'.

'Oh, that's Lexx.' No surname, just Lexx. She was *huge* back when I was in primary school.

'Jana, Lexx *is* Alexandra Holmes.' She holds up the Polaroid again. 'This is Lexx before I got my hands on her. I saw something in her and . . . I just knew. You have to trust me. This is what I do. I find the diamond in the coal.'

I can hardly believe they're the same girl. I can't imagine Lexx without her trademark crop. 'OK.'

'Sure, sweetie?'

'Um. Yeah. If you think it's gonna help . . .'

'I don't think – I *know*.' She grins so wide I can see her silver fillings, and gives me a wink.

I smile back. 'OK. Please don't bleach my hair!'

'Wouldn't dream of it.' She picks up the phone and dials. 'Hello, dear, it's Maggie at Prestige. Can Remy fit one of my most special babies in for a restyle?' There's a pause. 'Sweetheart, can you tell him who's asking?' Another pause. 'Oh, that's wonderful. We'll be there in half an hour.'

Oh, how I've laughed at those poor bitches on *Next Top Model*, sobbing hysterically as clippers mow through their goldilocks. It's not so fucking funny now. I look at myself in the mirror, black Remy-Lopez cape secured around my neck. My lips are proper pale and pasty. Shitting bricks.

'Maggie, daaaaaarling!' Remy, a tiny little man with a neat black beard and tattoos all the way up to his chin swishes across the salon, and the two air-kiss like pantomime dames.

'Remy, my love, we need to create a supermodel.'

'*Dios mia!* Who do we have here?' He clamps his hands on my shoulders.

'I'm Jana.'

'You are exquisite. What are we doing for you?'

'Well,' Maggie says, 'we need something short, I think. Androgynous, but not butch. Enough to style still.'

'Yes! Cheekbones and chin!' He runs his hands through my hair. 'Hmm. You know what I think? Peter Pan, Liza Minelli, Stella Tennant, but edgy and messy and punk.'

What? Is he speaking in tongues?

'Oh, absolutely! Love it!' Maggie says.

'What? Who?' I say and they both laugh.

'You are adorable!' Remy laughs. 'You're going to look *fabulous*. Trust me.'

People keep saying that.

'You ready, sweetheart? It's for the best, believe me.'

You know what? It's a *haircut*. It'll grow back. 'Sure.'

'There's a good girl.' Maggie grins. 'Half of this game is about having a good, positive attitude, Jana, remember that. Just say yes!'

About thirty seconds later, Remy, whistling as he works, has gathered nearly all my hair into a ponytail and hacks it clean off. He lets go and my hair sits in line with my chin. My stomach lurches and I suddenly understand why the *Top Model* girls wail.

I get over it quickly, though. They bring me a cup of tea with two sugars and a super nice girl washes my hair and asks what it's like to be a model. I tell her I have no idea. She delivers me back to Remy with dripping wet hair, and he towel-dries it before starting to hack at my head with a razor blade.

It's all so fast. About three quarters of an hour later, Maggie returns to collect me as Remy finishes. 'What do you think?' he asks.

I hardly recognise myself. My neck feels *naked*. It's short short short up the neck before getting longer on top and spilling into a heavy mop of a fringe that falls around my ears and into my eyes. And, of course, Maggie was right. My cheekbones and chin are suddenly . . . *there*. You can really see them. I have nothing to hide behind. The haircut is like a picture frame for my whole face. I don't look like a boy exactly, but, without any make-up on, I don't look much like a girl either. Not sure how I feel about that.

Truthfully, I'm so not cool enough for this haircut.

'This is perfection!' Maggie claps her hands. 'Jana, what do you think?'

'It's so different . . . it's very . . . East London.'

They both laugh. 'That's the idea,' Remy says. 'You look like a model.'

I'm not sure about that. But I don't *look* like normal any more either. Tell you what, you'd see me coming.

'Do you still fancy me?' I ask Ferdy on FaceTime when I get home.

He laughs. 'That's a ridiculous question. I could never not fancy you. I'd fancy you with a paper bag on your head. You know I'm only here for your tits anyway.'

I cackle. 'Well, you're bang out of luck in that case!' I run my hand through my fringe. I have phantom hair syndrome – I keep trying to sweep imaginary hair off my shoulders. After the haircut, we'd gone back to the agency to redo the pictures. There was no point in keeping the ones I'd done earlier. I can't deny that, with the short hair, I look way more like a person who belongs in a modelling agency. In the black and white pictures I look like a massively pissed-off genderless alien. Everyone seemed very impressed with this.

'It's so weird.' I flop back on my bed, holding my phone aloft. 'I don't look like me.'

'You do. It's hot.'

'Is it?'

'Again . . . yes.'

'I think I look older.'

'You do a little. It's very hipster.'

'Might go hang out by that art school in Peckham. I'll fit right in.'

'Haggerston, Stoke Newington, Hackney. It's cool.'

I hear the front door close downstairs. 'Oh, god, that'll be Mum. I better go face the music.'

'Have you warned her?'

'Yeah. Well, I told her they cut my hair short. She's gonna die.'

'You gonna come over later?'

'If I'm not grounded, sure. Can we watch the new *Drag Race*?'

'Yeah, it should be on Netflix by now.'

'Aces. Be there about seven-thirty.'

'Good luck. And whatever you do, don't fuck it up . . .'

I laugh a little, hang up and take a deep breath. Reckon I'm more nervous now than when I was at the salon.

'Jana!' Mum calls. 'Is that you up there?'

'Yes!' I check myself over and ruffle my new fringe. I put a little eyeliner and mascara on so I still look like a girl. God, she's gonna go ballistic. Worse than when she found my prescription for the pill in my school bag. Here goes. I leave my room and slump downstairs. Mum comes out of the kitchen to greet me in the hall, still wearing her Green River Care overalls and Birkenstocks.

I wince.

Her hands fly to her mouth. 'Oh, my goodness me! Jana! What did they do to your hair?'

'Do you hate it?' This is the world's most unnecessary question.

She takes a breath. She sighs. 'Oh, Jana, is very . . . different.'

'Oh, god, you *really* hate it.'

'It . . . it's a boy haircut.'

'No, it ain't,' I say defensively. Milos walks through the door, skateboard under his arm. I brace for the inevitable insult. 'Go on, then, get it over with.'

'What?' he says. 'Oh, your hair. It's sick.'

Oh. OK. I wait a second to see if he's winding me up. 'You like it?'

'Yeah. It's all right.' He pushes past us to get to the fridge.

Mum shakes her head, exasperated. 'I don't understand you young people. I give up. I'm old.' She throws her hands in the air and goes back to getting dinner ready.

SHOOT

College starts on September the fifth. I'm quite excited. Hollyton College always seemed so far away, for the big boys and girls, and – somehow – now *we're* the big boys and girls. More importantly, I never have to wear the hideous Wandsworth Technology Academy diarrhoea-brown blazer ever again.

Results day came and went without drama, all of us did pretty good. I smashed it, actually. Laurel flunked maths but can resit in November so it's no biggy. She wants to be British Airways cabin crew, and always has, so she's gonna need that maths.

Because it's the first day, we all meet outside Starbucks and walk up St John's Hill together. Ferdy gets a staff discount so we all get coffees to go because that feels like a very grown-up thing to do. Robin, the wang, pounds two espressos in quick succession because he just can't stop trying to impress Laurel.

'How are we all feeling?' Ferdy asks, camera wrapped around his hand. It's his baby.

'Are you filming?' Sabah asks.

'Yeah, just testing out my new battery, this thing's on its last legs . . .'

'Man, I need a new video camera,' Sabah says. 'I wanna start vlogging again. Will you help me, Ferd? Like, if I could get as

55

many viewers on YouTube as I do on Insta, I could make some money.'

'Sure.' Oh, god, when Sabah and Ferd nerd out about tech stuff I tune all the way out.

'I'm psyched!' Laurel says, pulling Ferdy's arm around so the camera's on her. 'We can leave school for lunch ... free periods ... no more Mrs Fletcher spitting tooth foam on us all through English.'

'No more PE,' I add.

'I'll second that,' Sabah says.

'Rob? What about you?'

'I mainly just feel a bit sick, buddy. I think that second shot was a serious error.'

He asks us questions all the way up the street to school. Ferdy started a YouTube channel years back to discuss gaming, but recently he's been focusing on film-making. He made a really cute little film about his mum coming to London from Nagasaki in the eighties and I know he's keen to talk to Mum and Dad about what happened in Serbia back in the day. He's really good, but then, I would say that, wouldn't I, because I love him.

Hollyton College is shiny and new. The old building was knocked down a few years ago and replaced with a glass and steel design that looks a bit like the Death Star. We filter through the student entrance and loiter on the lawns waiting for the bell. There's a sort of terrace area outside the canteen with picnic benches. A hatch is open, serving coffee and croissants, although we're already caffeine-buzzed. It feels a lot more chill than school used to.

'OMG, Jana!' I see Heather Daley walking towards our table

with Lily McCoy and Emily Potter. I know it's not very sisterly or feminist, but I can't stand that bunch of fucking nasty bitches. Maybe if they weren't such fucking nasty bitches it'd be easier to like them. 'We heard about the haircut and it's true!'

Emily mutters something to Lily and sniggers. I ignore them. Most of the douchebags from school didn't get the grades to enter Hollyton, but to truly be an effective vicious bully, you also have to be *clever* so I guess we have to suffer these basics for another two years.

'Laurel told Harry that you're a model now.'

Laurel flushes. Harry is Heather's twin. 'We were just chatting on WhatsApp ...' she mutters. Laurel used to be proper good friends with Heather until they fell out about Heather not going to her twelfth birthday 'pamper party' or something. Things are pure dramatic when you're twelve.

I look up at Heather and blink. Her bleach-beige hair has been tonged into bouffant waves and she's wearing so much highlight, she looks like the Tin Man. 'And?'

'So it's true? *You're* a model?' Wow. Bitchy.

I shrug. 'I dunno. Sorta.' I slip into the extra Sarf Landan accent I use at school so I don't get my head kicked in. I have zero time for her. She's always been vile, and, like, there's no need. Heather and Harry's mum is one of the assistant heads at Wandsworth so Heather never once got in trouble, even when she was being a proper dick, and it boils my piss. Hopefully she won't have the run of this place.

'Have you met Clara Keys?' Lily says, loudly chewing gum. She's very blonde and very stupid. She once told Laurel that you can't get pregnant if you drink Diet Coke right after sex.

57

'No. But we have the same agency.' I slip that last part in real casual.

'No offence,' Heather says, 'but you sort of look like a boy. Is that what's in style or something?'

'Heather,' Sabah interjects with a cute, dimply grin, 'why don't you fuck off, yeah?'

'What? Rude. We were just coming to say well done.'

'You said I looked like a boy. A-buh-bye.' I turn away from her. If she starts on me, I'll just snap her fake nails off.

'Whatever. If you're going to fucking cry about it, I won't even bother. Jesus.'

They sashay away. 'I'm telling you,' Emily says plenty loud enough for us all to hear, 'she's a she/he. I saw her D in swimming that time . . .'

'Just ignore them,' Sabah says. We'll never know for sure who started the *Jana-Novak-is-a-hermaphrodite* rumour but it's a safe bet Heather helped it go viral.

Ferdy looks into his camera. 'As you can see, sixth-form college is a *huge* departure from Year Eleven . . .' He rolls his eyes. 'Are you OK?'

It's comforting really. I was worried things was changing too fast. 'Yeah. I'm good.'

Maybe it's my own fault. Maybe I should have worn more make-up or a big pink tutu to signal my gender. It happens again as we file into our big initiation assembly thing. 'Woah, is that a batty boy?' some gobshite mutters to his friends. Students from lots of different high schools come here. Lots of new faces.

Am I that manly? I'm wearing jeans and slouchy vest with a big plaid shirt over it. I wonder if that was a mistake. I feel my shoulders hunch further, trying to blend into the crowd. Ferdy takes my hand but I pull it away. 'What?'

'Everyone thinks I'm your boyfriend.'

He takes my hand and gives it a squeeze. 'And that would only bother me if I was a homophobic asshole.'

I could almost weep. 'You're the best.'

'No, *you* are.' It's a running joke. We've pretend-argued about who's the best for literally hours.

The head of the college, Mr Bennett, runs us through everything. It's not like school – we don't even have tutor groups, we just turn up as and when we have lessons. Instead of register, we scan ourselves in and out at the student entrance and then individual teachers make sure we attend all our sessions.

This morning is just orientation, he explains. Bennett is a giant Idris-Elba type. If Idris Elba let himself go a bit. Still, I wouldn't mess with him. All we have to do today is attend an IT suite at an allotted time, activate our school account and collect a personalised timetable. Then we're free to go.

'Amazing,' Sabah says. 'Shall we do something this afternoon? Robin, can you get us into a film?'

Robin works at Clapham Picturehouse. 'I only get two free guests per screening, but we could give it a go . . .'

'Can we get free popcorn?' Laurel asks.

'Sure!'

'I can't,' I say sadly as we file out of the assembly.

'Why?' Laurel moans.

'She's got her big photoshoot,' Ferdy explains.

'Oh, yeah! That's way more exciting, though! Your first assignment,' says Sabah.

'I'm so jelly,' Laurel adds.

'Yeah, I guess.' Because today was always gonna be a half-day, Ro asked if I could be free this afternoon. They have a studio booked all day and try to squeeze in as many girls as possible. Ro explained that because I haven't done any paid work yet they need something to start my portfolio off.

Ferdy looks down the hallway. 'Rob, I think we're supposed to be down there.' The first half of the alphabet has to go to the computer lab now. Me, Sabah and Laurel are in an hour.

'One sec.' Rob checks his phone. 'OK, this afternoon we have the new Marvel, the Pixar with the kittens, the street-dance one or the German musical.'

Everyone immediately says Marvel, except Laurel who votes for street dance. She's overruled. 'Aw,' I say, 'I wanted to see the Marvel.'

'I won't go,' Ferdy says. 'We can see it at the weekend or something.'

And that's just one more of the reasons why I love him so much. 'It's OK, you can go if you want. Dad might take me and Milos anyway.'

'Nah, it's cool.' He gives me a kiss. 'Hey, why don't I come up to Bethnal Green with you?'

I hadn't really thought about it. 'Erm, yeah, I guess that'd be all right. They said my mum could come, so I don't see what difference it makes if you do.'

'Awesome! You think they'll let me film it?'

'Don't see why not.'

'Cool. Right, we really better hustle. Rob!'

The guys dash off, following a procession into the computer lab. 'Shall we head to the canteen?' Sabah asks.

We make our way there, following the allure of bacon butties. 'Aren't you nervous?' Laurel asks.

'What about?'

'Duh! The photos!'

'Not really. There's a stylist and hair and make-up people. All I have to do is turn up and pose. They're even sending a car to pick me up from here. Zero brain power required. I'm a shop dummy, innit.'

I get a text message to tell me the licence plate of the Addison Lee that'll drive us to Bethnal Green where the studio is. We sit in traffic for AGES, and I can't help but think it would have been quicker to get the Central line. I'm glad Ferdy's here to keep me company. We both play a weird little game on our phones where you have to sort colours into the correct spectrum. It's soothing.

It's a sticky day, the air fluey. Boss-level black clouds crowd the skyscraper lids as we roll through the City and into East London. A little headache tells me there'll be thunder and lightning later. The first few splats splatter against the taxi windscreen as we arrive at a cobbled courtyard between warehouses. 'This is it,' the driver mutters, pointing out of the left window.

'Quick,' I say to Ferd, 'It's about to piss down.'

We run up a metal fire escape, following a sign labelled THE IMAGEWORKS. I hammer on the door and Ro answers. 'Hello, lovely! Come on in! Quick!'

'This is my boyfriend, Ferdy. Is that all right?' I figure it's too late now if it's not.

'Oh.' She don't look thrilled, to be honest, but it passes in a second. 'Sure. Nice to meet you . . . Ferdy, was it?'

'Yeah, Kai. Kai Ferdinand.'

'Hello, I'm Ro, Jana's agent.' Hearing that is fully weird, but I buzz a little. *I* have an agent. Random. 'You're lovely. Shame you're not a bit taller,' she tells him with a dismissive smile.

Ferdy grins and I roll my eyes. Ferd is a proper snack. He calls himself 'pan-ethnic'. His mum's Japanese and his dad's German and Argentinian and no one can ever guess what his ethnic mix is. He's a bit of every Disney princess: Jasmine, Mulan, Pocahontas, Moana.

We follow Ro through to the studio. Once again, it's like leaving the real world and going through the back of the wardrobe into Narnia. It's big, airy and brightly lit, although now rain pelts on the glass ceiling. The floorboards are stripped bare and it all feels very New York loft somehow. Not that I've ever been in one. At the far end of the studio is another, bigger roll of backdrop, surrounded by lights and fans. A photographer is kneeling down and, as a hairdresser steps back, I see she's shooting Arabella. 'Oh, that's Arabella,' I tell Ferdy.

'OMG!' she cries once she sees me. 'Hello, darling! I had no idea you were coming too!' She stays rooted to her spot, holding a creamy lily against her cheek.

'Yeah . . . you too. How's it going?' I feel less weird with someone else I know here.

'OK, I think. Do I look nice?' She looks *stunning*, her red hair curled into Renaissance ringlets, her skin Queen-Elizabeth white. She's wearing a flowing white gown, and she's serving elf-fairy-virgin realness.

'You look mad beautiful,' I tell her and she grins.

Me and Ferd loiter awkwardly at the edge of her backdrop. 'Don't move,' the photographer says, adjusting her stance slightly. She raises an arm and clicks her fingers. 'Look here for me, doll.' She's very East London with her nose ring and waist-length magenta-and-purple braids. 'Yeah . . . nice . . . dreamy. It's cute.'

'Jana,' Ro says, 'this is Layla Palmer, one of the most amazing fashion photographers in London.'

She looks away from her camera and smiles. 'Hello, darlin', how's it goin'?'

'Good, thanks.' I wipe my palm on my trouser leg and shake her hand. Ro has already told us how important it is to make an impression on industry people, so I try to cough up a furball of conversation. 'It was my first day at college today.'

'Huh?'

Oh, god, kill me. 'Um, you know, it's a big day.'

Layla grins. 'Ah, I see! You're still at school? No way! That's mental!'

I like her already. I love her gold tooth also. 'Sixth-form college. This is my boyfriend, Ferdy.'

'Ferdy? That name is sick, bruv. How you doin?'

'I'm good . . .'

'Jana?' Ro interjects. 'Let's get you into hair and make-up while Layla finishes with Arabella. Do you want anything to eat? We've got sandwiches . . . fruit . . . cake . . . tea or coffee?'

'Tea, please,' I say. The chocolate brownie looks great but I sense Ro is watching to see what I pick. 'And . . . that's it.'

'Ferdy?'

'Um, yeah, a tea would be great.'

'Cool, cool. Come with me and I'll get that sorted.' We leave the main studio and follow a little corridor to a tiny dressing room, thrumming with activity. It stinks of hairspray and burned hair – I'm guessing Arabella's. There are three rails of clothes, rows upon rows of shoes and a mad woman waving a steamer around. 'The good news,' Ro says, 'is that your hair will take about five seconds so you're my new favourite.'

'Is this Jana?' says a petite blonde lady.

'It sure is.'

'Gosh, aren't you a tall one?'

Be. Polite. And. Professional. 'Yeah. I, um, get that all the time.'

'Jana, this is Debbie, who's doing your make-up today, and this is Bethany Angst. Hot new stylist. Everyone is talking about Bethany.'

I've never heard of her. The mad woman hangs the steamer up. 'Oh, wow, you are stunning.' Bethany, honestly, looks like she coated herself in superglue and sprinted through Camden Market. She's wearing a psychedelic floral dress, metres of plastic beads, Reebok hi-tops and a purple beret on top of her Lego haircut.

'Thank you,' I say.

'Ignore this rail, that was Arabella's. These are yours.' She steers a different rail over. It's so stuffed my eyes struggle to make sense of it, but I see fur, leather, sequins and feathers.

'Take a seat, love,' Debbie says. 'Let's get you ready . . .'

Ferdy films us as Debbie and Jon, the hair guy, flutter around me. Jon blow-dries my hair out and styles it with some gunk while Debbie piles and piles make-up on my face – ironic, as the agency seems obsessed with me *not* wearing make-up. My blue eyes blaze out from a charcoal oil slick. I go to take my nose ring out again, but Bethany says to leave it in.

Bethany steadily steams while I'm getting ready. 'Does anything speak to you, hon?'

Mostly they're saying: *you wouldn't wear any of this mad shit in a million years*, but I'm not sure that's what she wants to hear. 'Erm, I hardly ever wear dresses . . . yeah . . . no.' I wore one to the prom and felt like *I* should be on *RuPaul's Drag Race*.

'What colours do you like?'

'I usually wear black . . . sometimes grey.'

'Ro!' Bethany screams and Ro comes running in. 'Is she shooting B/W?'

'Maybe. We do need some colour in there too.'

Bethany pauses. 'OK, try this . . .' My first look is actually pretty cool. It's a black tuxedo jacket with tight tight tight silver trousers. 'Bra off! Chop, chop!' Bethany commands. The room is full of people, including two men. 'Quickly! Let's see if it fits.'

I wriggle out of my bra, covering my nips with my arm. I look at Ferdy and he gives me an *I know, this is nuts* look. With no ceremony Bethany flings the coat over my shoulder. Fastened up, the jacket covers my boobs thankfully. 'That's last season Mugler,' she tells me.

'OK.' Never heard of him. Or her. 'I like it.'

'And put these on.' She hands me a terrifying pair of studded Jimmy Choos.

They're a little tight. I can hardly walk and I suddenly tower over everyone in the room. I suppose a five-foot-eleven girl in five-inch heels is six-foot-three. 'Shit, you're tall in those,' Ferdy says from far below in Lilliput.

'How do I look?' I ask. '*Honestly.*'

'Honestly . . .' He smiles. 'You look exactly like a model. I'm so proud of you.'

I know he means well but I'm not sure how to take that. I didn't do anything to be proud of. 'Thanks,' I say.

With Bethany on one arm and Ferdy on the other, I teeter back into the studio. 'Oh my days!' Layla says. 'You look sick, babes! Sick!'

'Jana, you look amazing!' Arabella rushes over, cupping a bit of brownie, now apparently done. 'Are those shoes killing you?'

'I can't feel my toes!'

'Won't take long,' Layla says. 'Let's get going so you don't have to keep them on for long.'

They steer me on to a fresh backdrop. They've changed Arabella's sky-blue backdrop to a stormy rose pink. Ferdy leaves my side to get out of the way and I suddenly feel very, very exposed. My arms feel freakishly, abnormally long, hanging like tagliatelle at my sides. Mrs Tickle.

Layla fires off a shot and the flashes boom in my face. 'Oh,' I say, taken aback.

'That was just a test shot, don't worry. Getting the levels sorted.'

Ro sits herself at a laptop to one side. 'Jana.' She summons me with a finger. 'Come see this.'

I weeble over. Ro twists the laptop around to show me the test shot. I blink, hardly believing it. I don't look like me. I look like a statue. Even standing front-on, gormless as fuck, pigeon-toed and mouth open, I look like a girl in a magazine. 'Oh. Wow. Is that me?'

'That,' Ro says, bouncing slightly on her stool, 'is a model.'

'Ro,' Layla says, standing behind us. 'This girl right here is a star. Mark my words. Never been wrong yet.'

'Oh, I know, babe.' I feel bad for Arabella. I hope they told her the same.

'C'mon. Let's do this thing.'

Layla helps me back to the middle of the backdrop. 'Do you want me to, like, *do* anything?'

'Just make interesting shapes with your body. Just go with it. You'll feel bonkers to begin with, but it looks amazing on camera. Don't be afraid to go over the top, I can always reel you in,' she says with a wink.

The suit – again using *Drag Race* as a cultural reference – says BUSINESS WOMAN REALNESS. I don't look like Jana Novak, aged sixteen, student at sixth-form college. I look like some high-powered mega-bitch. I'll go with that. I jam my hands on my hips and scowl at the camera. Layla takes a couple of shots. 'Chin down a bit, babe.'

She takes a couple more.

'Don't be afraid to move around, Jana,' Ro tells me.

I shove my hands in the pockets. 'Great. Hold that!' Layla orders. 'Arch your back!'

It goes on like this for a while. I make little changes and Layla snaps away. Ro keeps saying, 'GORGEY,' loudly and clapping so I guess I'm doing what she's after.

'I think we've got it. Let's get her changed.'

I pull the Choos off and my feet throb, feeling like they're expanding to twice their normal size. Bethany takes me back to the changing room and pulls off the jacket, leaving me topless. Ro says nude underwear is a model must-have; I need to get some. 'OK, slide the trousers off, hon.'

I don't see anyone leaving me to change in peace, so I guess I'll have to get used to be semi-naked around stylists and stuff. Oh, it's weird. The Novak house is not a naked house. The silver pants are so tight, I have to sit on the floor and wriggle out of them while Bethany pulls them off.

'Put these on.' She hands me a pack of beige tights. 'I thought the Republic of Deen dress?' She selects a leather dress off the rail. At first I think it's black but, on closer inspection, it's really a very dark purpley-blue. It has pointy shoulders and studs down one side.

I have no idea where I'd wear it, but I actually quite like it. 'Oh. OK,' I say.

'Do you know Republic of Deen? Very cool, very youth. It'll suit you.' Bethany slips the dress over my head. It's well short, but does look pretty rock and roll. She then wraps some strappy leather sandals around my ankles. They're not *quite* as deadly as the last pair and I manage to walk back to the studio unsupported.

Ferdy's eyes almost pop out of his head. 'Holy fuck.'

'Is that a good thing?' I laugh.

'You look insane.'

'You really do,' Arabella agrees, now changed into jeans and a stripy blouse. 'You are one foxy lady.'

I laugh again and take my place on another new backdrop – this one white. Debbie and Jon make slight changes to my make-up and hair and we're off again. This time, Layla lies flat on the floor and shoots up – the result being pictures that make my legs look inhumanly long.

By the end of the shoot, I don't feel *quite* so ludicrous. No matter how mad I feel *pretending* to walk on the spot, at least I can see the pictures popping up on Ro's laptop and they do look pretty cool. 'You can't take a bad picture, babes,' Ro tells me. I guess that's why Tom is good at his job – he knows who's gonna look good in pictures, however weird they look in real life. 'I think we're done, Layla. We have so many choices.'

'Yeah? Wicked.' She comes over and gives me a big hug. 'You're a trooper, babe. I wanna shoot you again. I'm serious.'

'Really?'

'Abso-fucking-lutely. You got it, babe.'

'Thank you.' I sense Arabella is waiting for the same feedback, but Layla don't seem to notice she's still here.

'You're a sweet kid. Hang on to that for as long as you can. Don't become a cunt, even if you can get away with it.'

Layla's assistant starts taking the backdrop down and it all wraps up in a flurry of air kisses. I mostly want the shoes off. As I change into my vest and jeans again, I can't help but feel a bit less special, like Clark Kent putting the tie and glasses back on.

– Who pays for all those things? The cars? The photographers?
– Ha! Good question! It turns out *I* paid for all of those things.
– Can you explain how that works?
– As a new model you basically go into 'debt' with your agency. Sure, they pay for the cars and shoots and portfolio and stuff, but it all goes on your account. They take the money out of your earnings.
– And what if you don't earn enough to cover it?
– Well, precisely. I guess that was Lesson One.
– What was?
– *Nothing comes for free.*

ATELIER

'Oh my god! You look well nice!' Sabah gushes.

Last night, Ro emailed over a few of the pics from the shoot last week. I hand my phone over the table. The canteen in college is way better than the one at school. They have a salad bar with all different kinds of pasta and they'll make you any sort of sandwich or panini you want. What a time to be alive. I had a fit tuna and cheese melt.

'Jana, you look *so* beautiful,' Laurel says.

'Which one?'

'The leather dress! I love it . . . very . . . well, I'm just going to say it . . . sexy. Not in a lesbian way, obviously.'

'Nice. Thanks for clarifying. That dress was cool.' Sabah hands my phone back. The photos, now polished, are incredible. I don't look like me; I look like some sort of gigantic Amazon warrior woman from space.

'Let me see the other outfit again,' Laurel says, and I give her the phone. 'Oh, you're ringing!'

I see it's Ro. 'It's my agent . . .'

Laurel 'ooohs' and Sabah laughs aloud. 'Get a load of her! *It's my agent!*'

I roll my eyes. 'What? It is!' I answer. 'Hello?'

'Hi, Jana, it's Ro. I've just had a *very* exciting phone call about you . . .'

71

I stand up from the canteen table and point to the terrace doors. 'Yeah?

'Guess who loved your pictures?'

'Erm . . . Maggie?'

'She *does* love them, which is amazing because she's hard to impress, but someone even better.'

I'm never gonna win this game. 'I have no idea.'

'Dermot Deen!'

I can tell from her voice I'm supposed to be thrilled but . . . 'Who's that?'

'Oh, Jana, what are you like? I told you to sit down with *Vogue* and *i-D*, didn't I?'

I want to say, *I've been kind of busy with actual school,* but I don't bother. Just because it's the first week back, they've started as they mean to go on. I have an essay on the role of law in society, I've got a ton of Brontë poetry to read *and* – worst of all – Sabah and I have to compose an original rap about immigration *in French*. Cringe – who comes up with this shit?

'Dermot is the creative director at Republic of Deen – you know, the leather dress you wore is one of his. Anyways, he's a friend of mine and I thought it'd be cute to send him one of the pics and he LOVES you!'

'For real?' That's actually really cool.

'Oh, it gets better.' It's starting to feel more like September now and I'm beginning to wish I'd worn more than just a hoodie as I stroll around the lawn. 'He loves you so much, he's asked to book you.'

My stomach flops up like I'm back on a ride at Thorpe Park. 'What? What for?'

'Fashion Week, babes! It's the week after next!'

The thought of being on a catwalk fills me with actual terror. I almost puke on the spot. Oh, shit, no. Fuck that. 'A fashion show?' I was told I'd be in development until at least Christmas.

'I know! Congratulations! Your first booking! And . . . he wants an exclusive! Yay!'

'Wh-what does that mean?' I see colourful spots. Is this what a panic attack feels like?

'It means you can't walk in any other shows before his. I mean, he's not one of the big designers, but the money's OK – five hundred for the show and another five hundred for the exclusive.'

'A thousand pounds? HOLY SHIT!' My voice rings out around the terrace and everyone stares at me. Awkward.

'I know, but it's a start.'

She's completely misunderstood. That's insane. Ferdy's on minimum wage. He gets about twenty-five pounds a shift *and* he comes home smelling of sour milk. 'I . . . do you really think I'm ready?'

A pause. 'I won't lie, we have a lot of work to do on your walk. You need to practise in heels every single day between now and the seventeenth. The casting is next week.'

I take a deep breath. The tuna and cheese melt has turned on me in a big way. Lil' bastard.

'Don't worry, Jana. Yes, it's sooner than we had planned. We weren't going to get you started this September, but this is a great place to ease you in gently. Dermot is a sweetie and he is obsessed with you, hon. I don't think I've ever known him to book an exclusive.'

I'm too scared to string together a sentence. 'OK.'

'Just go to the casting and see what you think. I'll come too, as it's your first.'

'Thanks.'

'I'll email all the details in a min. Love you, baby girl.'

She hangs up and I drift, *Walking-Dead* style, back into the canteen. I must look clapped because Sabah springs to her feet. 'Shit, Jana, what's wrong?'

I slide back on to the bench. 'Nothing. Well, I just booked my first show.'

Sabah's eyes widen. 'Runway show?'

'Yeah. For, um, Republic of Deen . . . he made that leather dress and liked my pictures. It's London Fashion Week . . .'

'OMG! Jana!' Laurel's hands cover her mouth. 'I ADORE Republic of Deen. They do these amazing handbags that look like little clouds but they're, like, two hundred quid . . . can you get me one?'

I shake my head. It feels like my brain has developed its own heartbeat and is currently throbbing in my skull. 'I dunno if I can do it.'

'Bitch, of course you can, don't be a dick,' Sabah says.

'I feel sick. I mean, how is it happening this fast? It feels like . . . it feels like my head is gonna fall off.'

'Should I ask for a bucket?' Laurel goes to stand.

'I think I'll be OK . . .'

'Jana, this is amazing. Fashion is fast,' Sabah says with authority. 'You'll get used to it.'

'It's your first time . . .' Laurel grins, almost visibly vibrating. 'You're losing your catwalk virginity!'

I manage a little laugh for their benefit. Who was it who fell off her shoes on the runway? Was it Naomi? The world never forgets.

'This is so nuts,' Sabah says. 'You're a real, live, working model. I'm so proud of you, babes. Oh, god . . . bitch, you is gonna make me cry!' She dabs her eye with a napkin.

'If you get famous, will you take us to parties and stuff?' Laurel says. 'What if you meet Clara Keys? Or Dido and Domino? Or Westley Bryce! Or . . .'

She ain't helping my spinning head. Shit just got real in a massive, massive way.

I am so lost.

I walk up and down Brick Lane and Google Maps is clearly directing me to a shut-down curry house. *You have arrived at your destination.* I fucking have not. A lady with a pram tries to mow me down. 'Hi! Excuse me, do you know where Unit 14b is?' I ask.

She ignores me.

'Thanks!' Cow.

Luckily, my phone rings and it's Ro. 'Hi, Jana, how are you getting on?'

'I'm so lost! I'm outside some derelict curry house and Google says this is it!'

'Bless you. The entrance to the warehouses is off Dray Walk. I'll come down and find you . . .'

I turn the corner just as Ro pops out of an inconspicuous gate to a mews courtyard. I walked straight past it about five times. 'Hi, lovely! It's just this way!'

I'm so relieved to see her, I almost sob like a goon. 'I'm so sorry! Am I late?'

'It's fine. Only five minutes – just don't make a habit of it. The myth about not getting out of bed for less than ten thousand dollars is a thing of the past, I'm afraid! Come on up.'

The downstairs unit is part of a little market and you wouldn't know there was a studio here unless you were looking for it – I was expecting a big flashy sign, but there's just a small logo next to the doorbell.

'His atelier's just up here,' Ro says, and I follow her inside and up a flight of narrow stairs. Once again, I'm in my uniform of black vest, skinny jeans and Converse, with some heels in a tote bag.

I hear the studio – or atelier – before I see it. Phones ring, footsteps clatter, Britney is on full blast. It's utter chaos. 'Where are the fecking gloves?' an Irish voice cuts over the din. 'I swear to Jaysus these gloves are going to be the death of me! How fecking hard can it be?'

'They're on a courier, Dermot. She says three, latest.'

'Yeah, well, you tell her I'm keeping one glove especially to shove up her prissy arse.'

It's like a beehive, worker bees swarming around their queen. In this case, the queen is a stocky, beardy man with awesome chunky glasses and *really* cool, furry teddy-bear Adidas high-tops. It's weird, ain't it? Sometimes you just like people the second you see them. I want to hug him.

Dermot Deen sees me and his eyes light up. 'Oh, wow! There she is!'

'Dermot Deen, this is Jana; Jana, this is Dermot!'

'You are a vision! Everyone! Stop whatever the feck it is you're doing and say hello to Jana!'

'HELLO, JANA,' the drones say in unison.

Remember your manners. 'Hello, I'm sorry I'm late. I . . . I . . . couldn't . . . find the door.'

'Oh, tell me about it, love, no one ever can. I keep saying we should put a sign on the gate. I expect my gloves will be delivered to the curry house down the street.'

He gives my hand a squeeze and I try to relax. I smile gratefully knowing I'm not the only one. The studio ain't as big as I'd expected, but it could just be that we're surrounded by dressmakers' dummies – all of them half-dressed.

'Excuse the mess,' Dermot says. 'Seven days until the show and this is the point where I start to truly believe I'm gonna have to buy a job-lot of little black dresses from Primark and just stick a logo on them. You want a coffee, darlin'?'

'Just some water, thanks.'

'Richie! Where the feck is he? Mary, mother of God, send me an intern who can vaguely function as a human being. RICHIE!' A frazzled young man runs up the stairs, carrying a huge cardboard box.

'I think it's the gloves,' he pants.

'Halle-fecking-lujah! Finally! Richie, run down the coffee shop. I'll have a wet cortado, a water for Jana – still or sparkling?'

'Um, still is fine . . .'

'Still water and then whatever anyone else wants. And quickly, please, before I go into withdrawal from the last one and get the shakes.' The poor boy scurries away. 'Oh, he's actually very sweet. Gives *excellent* blow jobs too.'

I honestly don't know if he's kidding, but Ro cackles so I *guess* he is. I hope he is.

I remember Ro's advice to seem interested and ask questions. 'How are the new . . . clothes . . . coming along?' I ask, hoping that's not a sore spot.

'I am so excited!' Dermot says. 'Top secret – it's called Deen Dynasty – inspired by the soap opera!' I must look really vacant. 'OMG, you have no idea, do you? Fuck, kill me now, I'm old. Alexis Carrington? Joan Collins?'

'Sorry!' I shrug.

'You're a wee baby, aren't you? Think the eighties, you know, twenty years before you were conceived!'

The pieces I see on the dummies look a little like they're made out of Quality-Street wrappers. Very shiny, metallic leather; big shoulder pads and ruffles. 'They're sick,' I say, although I would wear literally none of it. Unless you paid me, which if you think about it . . .

'You are such a sweetheart! You're adorable! Thank you so much for coming in, Jana. As soon as I saw your face I was OBSESSED. I said to my friend Rowenna here, I said that girl Jana is the new Lexx, so she is.'

'He did,' Ro confirms.

'Lexx opened my first show back in 2010. Love that girl. I think – and don't tell her I said this, she'll fecking skin me and wear me – I think you're even more special. Legs! Cheekbones! Gorgeous!'

'I never know what to say to that.' I fold my arms around myself. 'I'll pass it on to my mum and dad – they gave me the genes, I guess.'

Dermot laughs way more than the joke deserves, to be honest. 'Darlin', let's get you in some of the clothes. You know, this is the first time I've seen them on a model! Yay!'

'I hope I don't stack it . . .'

They laugh LIKE I'M JOKING. I'm not. Not even a little.

There's a folding screen for me to change behind, but once again, there's no chance of any privacy. As I strip down to my nude underwear – and wonder what dark-skinned models are supposed to do by way of 'nude' underwear – Dermot and his assistant, Chloe, hold different garments up to my body, discussing adjustments and changes. Tape measures coil around me like that snake in *The Jungle Book*.

'So . . .' I say as he measures my hips, 'did you always want to be a designer?'

'Oh, aye,' he replies. 'The first dress I ever made was for my wee sister Bronagh's Barbie doll! In fact, it looked a bit like this one, now you mention it. As soon as I was old enough, I knew I was gonna get the hell out of Galway and come to London.'

'And you did!'

'Sweetheart, it wasn't easy. One day, I'll write a memoir and it'll make your milk curdle. The things I had to do to survive as an intern in London . . . But, yeah, wee Dermot McLoughlin became Dermot Deen – because no fecker could say my name right – and then, out of the blue, Venus Ardito wore one of my T-shirts on stage at Glastonbury and that was it. That's what that's for . . .'

He nods to the enormous pop-art-style portrait of Venus in a bling gold frame that takes up almost one entire wall of the studio. 'Oh, I see!'

'I know! Insane! And here we are at the tenth anniversary of the Republic. Time flies . . . here, slip this over your noggin.'

He hands me a shiny purple metallic dress with one ruffle shoulder. I'm trying to figure out how it's meant to go when he eases it over me. 'It hasn't got a zip yet,' he mutters, pinning it shut. 'And the shoes are coming on Monday.'

'There's some in my bag,' I offer, but the assistant is already on hand with some last season ones – gold ankle boots. Thankfully the chunky heel ain't *that* high.

'You know what?' he says. 'The gloves are fecking vile, what was I thinking?' He tosses some turquoise leather gloves across the studio towards the trash.

'I'll be real,' I whisper to Dermot while Ro collects her coffee, 'I only got scouted about two months ago and my walk is shit.'

He laughs heartily. 'Well, that's a first! An honest model! Lucky for you, I like weird walks. I hate cookie-cutter girls. My girls are all freaks and weirdos.'

I zip the boot up and wobble. 'Well, you've come to the right place.'

'Just don't fall over. And if you do, for feck's sake, laugh about it and get back up. Right, then. Strut your stuff, darlin'.'

As if by magic, Venus Ardito comes on the playlist and I take that to be a sign. There are only about ten metres across the studio. I try to walk to the beat, remembering everything I've been taught. I sit back on my hips. I swing my arms. I pause by the door, turn and then walk back.

'See?' Dermot says. 'What was so hard about that?'

'Was that OK?'

'Babe, it was fab! I just wanted to make sure you could put one foot in front of the other. All this bollocks about having a "good walk"! If you can move to the beat, you're fine.'

'That was ace, Jana, you killed it,' Ro agrees, although there's a massive PHEW written all over her face in permanent marker.

I see myself in the mirror.

It's time to drop the coy, little-old-me bollocks.

You know what? I look like a fecking model.

FASHION WEEK

There's a lot to learn. The week before LFW – that's London Fashion Week – is New York Fashion Week, so Prestige goes into meltdown. I don't hear from anyone all week. It was decided there just wasn't time to get me acclimatised to New York so early in my 'career'. To be honest, I'm struggling enough with college without having to worry about trips to foreign cities.

THE DREAMS have started already. The dreams where I fall down and everyone laughs; the dreams where I get my period on the catwalk; the dreams where I sleep in and miss the entire show. I keep waking up at about five and not getting back to sleep.

College is a fucking struggle. I don't know how I feel about it so far. It's different to school. I'm lucky that I have Sabah in French and English, and Laurel, Robin and Ferdy in sociology – so there's always someone around, but I miss just hanging out. We never seem to be together any more. The work is *hard*, harder than last year, and there's way more of it. I had another fitting at Republic of Deen last night and had to do my French text translation on the train home at eleven. My eyes feel like they're full of superglue.

Worse, my reputation seems to have followed me to Hollyton. 'Hey!' Some spotty little weasel hurries to match my stride down the main corridor. 'Is it true that you're the transsexual supermodel?'

'Sure,' I say. 'Why not?'

At my other side Sabah cracks up. 'Asshole.'

'It's true!' The weasel runs back to his friends. 'She admitted it.'

'You should have punched him.'

'I can't be arsed.' I shrug. It's not just boys being boys. I'm very aware of girls – girls who didn't go to my old school – pointing me out to each other. *That's the model*, they whisper before pulling distasteful faces. Sometimes they follow up with, *but she's ugly*.

'They're just jealous,' Sabah tells me.

'There's nothing to be jealous of.' We head in the direction of English and I really can't be bothered with ninety minutes of *Tess of the d'Urbervilles*. Like, she got laid before she got married, get over it. I wonder if I can just write that for my essay.

'If you say so, babes.'

'I haven't actually done anything yet.' I feel at once both really superior and really shit. I got scouted, sure, but apparently I still look like a freak.

Sabah blinks her long lashes. She gets extensions glued to her eyes – which I find a bit terrifying – at Nailed It opposite the station. 'Are you high? Tomorrow you're in a Republic of Deen fashion show.'

'And today I have back-to-back classes and then a final fitting.'

'Stop! My heart is bleeding for you. Have you seen this?' She whips her iPad out of her bag and twists it around to show me something.

'What is it?'

'American *Vogue* named Republic of Deen *the* number one show to watch out for at London Fashion Week.'

I scroll down.

Increasingly wearable, but perennially playful, Dermot Deen's SS collection is set to be an instant sell-out. Previews of 'Deen Dynasty' suggest strong, yet stylish, eighties influences with a powerfully feminine aesthetic.

'Like, what does any of that mean? Is that even English?'

'Who cares? It's ranked above Burberry and Erdem. OMG, what if Anna Wintour shows up? What if you meet Anna Wintour?'

'Who?'

Sabah actually clips me around my ear. 'Wash your whore mouth out, heathen. Legend-in-chief at *Vogue*. You *need* to know these people, Jana.'

I rub my ear and smile. 'Why, when I have you?' I rest my head on her shoulder as we climb the stairs.

Suddenly Sabah stalls.

'What?'

'Look over there . . .'

On the other side of the mezzanine I see Laurel waiting to go into media studies. She's with Harry Daley – Heather's slightly less awful twin. He's all floppy boy-band hair and dimples. Girls cream over him. I think he's the human equivalent of ready salted crisps.

What's even more obvious is that she's flirting. Laurel has zero chill when it comes to flirting. Even now, watching her from ten metres away, she's clearly batting her eyelids like she has a nervous twitch and tossing her hair around. Laurel has a theory that boys are spellbound by the smell of hair, and she's wafting some in Harry's direction.

'God, she's blatant!' Sabah laughs.

'Laurel and Harry, though? Is it? Since when?'

'Random. Has she said anything to you?'

'No,' I say. 'You?'

'Nope.'

That's a bit weird. Normally Laurel is the most chatty in our group text. Now I think about it, she has gone quiet. With Laurel, you have to worry if it's something you've said. Whatever, I really don't have room in my frazzled brain to dissect everything I've said to her *and* do school *and* do Fashion Week.

Jana: Guess what?

Sabah: What?

Laurel: ???

Jana: Got message from agency and . . . CLARA KEYS is opening the show tom!!!!

Laurel: OMG! No way!

Sabah: FUCK OFF.

Jana: I KNOW.

Laurel: Please be her new BFF and invite her to things so we can meet her!!!!!!

Sabah: Literally dead bb. DEAD. Deceased.

CATWALK

I wake up at four, five, six o'clock, rigid with panic that I've slept through my alarm. When I do sleep, I have nightmares again, about falling over, about my legs not functioning, about Heather Daley spitting at me as I walk the catwalk.

Given that I only flopped out the back of an Addy Lee from the final, chaotic fitting at Dermot's atelier at one, I might as well have not bothered sleeping at all.

When my alarm *does* eventually go off, I reach for my phone. I dial his number. It rings and rings.

'Jana? Are you OK?' Ferdy croaks.

'I don't wanna do it.'

He doesn't have to ask what I don't want to do. 'Babe. That's just massive, hench, swole nerves talking.'

I squash my face into the pillow. It smells of night-breath. 'Yeah. And they're saying, "Don't do it."' He snuffles on the other end. 'Sorry, were you still asleep?'

'Yeah. But it's OK.'

'Sorry, bub.'

'I don't want to diminish what you do, but, Jana, all you have to do is walk in a straight line.'

'And not fall down!'

'True. You want me to come with you?'

I sit up in bed. 'Would you?'

'Sure. Why not?'

I think I could do it if I thought it was just for Ferdy. 'Are you sure?'

'Yeah. Just tell me what time to meet you at the station.'

We make a plan and I drag myself into the shower. I have no idea what waits in store for me today, but I know I should definitely turn my body over to Dermot Deen clean. *Of course* I nick my knobbly knee when I shave my legs. Why wouldn't I on the one day it matters? 'Fuck!' I hope they can cover the cut. It has the nerve to look like a tiny grin.

I think about Ferdy again to try to steady my jangling wind-chime nerves. I used the technique ahead of my exams too. I know it sounds wet but me and Ferdy are the most solid thing in my life – well, along with Mum and Dad, I guess. It makes sense that just thinking about him makes me calm. Nothing much bad happens with Ferd around.

We were friends first. We both did GCSE art and our old teacher, Mr Melvin, was proper laid-back. We listened to 6 Music in the cluttered, paint-splattered studio and were free to come and go as we wanted. The open door, weirdly, meant we all chose to stay.

I've been to school with Ferdy since we were ten, but we barely said more than five words to each other until our art classes. His first words, on that occasion, included 'vaginal'. For real.

We had to study the work of a famous artist, and me being a bit – OK, a lot – naïve, chose Georgia O'Keeffe. How was I supposed to know all those flowers could be interpreted as minges? Well, that afternoon Ferdy, as he passed my table, pointed out that some people saw the paintings as vaginal. He instantly blushed.

'They are?' I said, tilting my head at her *Inside Red Canna*.

'Well, that's what some people think,' he babbled.

'Oh, yeah. I see that now.' I smiled at him. It was like Eve seeing Adam properly after she'd had a cheeky nibble on that apple. I'd known him for years, but now I *saw* him. 'Well, this is awkward!'

'Should I go find a big phallic sculpture or something so we're even?'

I laughed. And laughed and laughed for the rest of the sunny afternoon. Even super-chill Mr Melvin told us to get on with our work. After that I just wanted to be around him all the time because he made me laugh. On a lunch break, I'd steer us towards wherever he was hanging out and I found myself looking forward to art as the highlight of the week.

I mean, thank fuck he felt the same or that would have been shit.

This time, I'm not trusted to find my own way there. Ferdy and I head to the agency where we check in with Prestige.

It's utter chaos.

It's like the last scene in a horror movie where the survivors mill about covered in blood, only here it's really tall, skinny girls chain-smoking outside and picking at a buffet. Trays and trays of pastries go untouched, bony fingers zeroing in on bananas and Pret yoghurts instead. Wheelie suitcases clutter the office as the phones ring and ring and ring.

'Jana, babes!' Ro runs over and gives me a hug. She looks like she was quite near the volcano when it erupted. 'Nice and early, brownie points for you. Have you had breakfast? Help yourself to croissants and stuff. Oh, and take water bottles with you, in case you're waiting.'

'Ferdy came with me,' I say, pointing back over my shoulder. 'Can he come to the show?'

Ro winces. 'Oh, hon, I don't know. Ticket only. If every model brought friends and family ... maybe we'll get him backstage.'

'I don't mind waiting outside,' Ferdy chips in.

'ROWENNA!' Maggie screams from across the office. 'Where is Viktoria?'

'She's in a car, coming from Wimbledon.'

'*Wimbledon?* Why is she in Wimbledon? I'm going to wring her scrawny neck. And has Clara landed yet?'

Ro sighs. 'I have to go find some girls. There's an Addy Lee outside to drive you to the show venue.' She nods wearily at Ferdy. 'Just take him and see what the producer says.'

A black car waits outside. I see the sign in the window is also for Viktoria, so I guess we're both in Dermot's show. Ro tells the driver to leave without her. 'I think she hates me,' Ferdy says as we drive away.

'She'll get over it. I'll say you're my guide dog or anxiety bunny or something.'

He laughs. 'I honestly don't mind getting a coffee over the street.'

'No.' I grip his hand for dear life. 'We'll smuggle you in. I want you there.'

I think it would have been quicker to walk. It takes twenty minutes to get down Regent Street towards the City. I see from the schedule Ro sent that Deen Dynasty is taking place in a derelict bank vault, which I think is pretty cool. The show ain't until one, but we have to be there for rehearsal at ten.

As we pull up, the nerves start to gurgle in my guts again. Luckily the driver knows where to go and follows a LFW sign around the back of the old bank. We get out of the car and an official person in a fluorescent tabard greets us at a fire escape. 'Hi there, I'm Jana Novak.'

She checks her list and hands me a lanyard. 'Who's this?'

'It's my personal photographer . . . the agency said they'd called ahead and that it was OK for him to come,' I blatantly lie. I figure everyone will be too busy to check.

She rolls her eyes. 'Whatever, just don't get in the way and –' she points to the camera around his neck – 'put that away right now. Official photographers only.'

'Sure.' He puts it in his rucksack and she gives him a lanyard too.

We follow Hansel and Gretel arrows that say ROD MODELS + CREW and take us deep below street level. The building smells kind of damp, and I wonder how long it's been vacant for.

'This is so sick,' Ferdy says, running his fingers along the chipped tiles on the walls. His voice echoes. Everything is a cool jade green; I think it's art-deco style. The floor has a seashell motif where it hasn't been smashed to pieces.

I hear a commotion ahead. We head down another flight of stairs and enter the old vault. 'Oh, wow,' I mutter. The huge circular door is wide open, and the catwalk juts from inside the vault. Neon strip lights hang – deliberately cockeyed – from tangled cables to the ceiling and the catwalk is flanked by hundreds of office fans of all shapes and sizes. Category really *is* businesswoman realness.

Intern Richie appears at my side and grabs my arm, dragging me through the vault door. 'We have Jana, over,' he says into his walkie-talkie.

A response crackles.

'Hi, I brought my boyf—' I say.

'Whatever. We need to get you into hair and make-up. We're behind.'

The backstage area is much less cool than the runway. Rails and rails of clothes are being steamed, creating a sauna, and fold-out tables are set up for make-up or food. Dermot, sweaty and ham-faced, necks a bottle of Pepto-Bismol.

I decide not to bother him. I wonder if there's a hierarchy of models because I don't see Clara Keys. Perhaps the last in is the most famous.

Richie deposits me at hair and make-up. 'Don't move,' he says and hurries away.

'Wow,' says Ferdy.

'I know,' I whisper. 'Who knew a few fucking dresses were so life and death?'

'Well, babes . . .' Dermot snaps behind me. I didn't realise he was so close. 'Did you know the fashion industry contributes sixty-six billion pounds to the British economy every year?'

The cringe is so strong I think it might snap my neck and kill me. 'Sorry . . . I just meant . . .'

'Yeah, I know what you meant. Six hundred thousand people

are employed by the fashion sector in this country, but, sure, it's no biggy.'

'Dermot . . .'

'And what bothers me the *most* is when *women* say that fashion is fluff, because it's only considered fluff because clothes are something we usually associate with girls. Fashion! It's fun, isn't it? It's frivolous! When did any cunt say that about football, and that's the most fecking frivolous thing in the whole fecking world!'

Oh, I could just die. 'I'm sorry . . .'

His shoulders relax. 'No. I'm sorry. I'm stressed out. Venus Ardito is half-confirmed. Anna Wintour is confirmed and so is Lucas Blo.' I must look confused. 'He's a big-fecking-deal photographer, I'll introduce you. It's not your fault that I CAN'T SMOKE IN THIS SHITHOLE. Thank you for being on time.'

I can see I've upset him, though. 'Is there anything I can do to help?'

He smiles. 'You're so sweet. The best thing you can do is get your hair and make-up done and hopefully we'll be ready for a rehearsal at eleven.'

I nod. 'Go have a cigarette,' I tell him.

There is a fleet of hair and make-up artists, or 'MUAs'. My one, a sweet Welsh girl called Lauren, tells me she earns as much during the four fashion weeks as she does over the rest of the year. She has three shows lined up today. Once again, I feel bad for saying Fashion Week was silly.

As Lauren focuses on my face, I try to get the hang of how it all works. A surly Viktoria skulked in a while back and nodded my way. She looked thoroughly over it and more than a little hungover.

Dermot returns with a blonde woman in a Burberry trench and she sits in the station next to mine. 'Jana, hon,' Dermot says, 'this is Alex.'

She shakes my hand and only then do I study her face. She looks *so* different without the bleach-blonde crop. It's only bloody Lexx. 'OMG, you're . . .'

She smiles and rolls her eyes slightly. 'Yeah. Don't worry, no one recognises me without the hair.' She has that lovely posh-Scot accent they have in Edinburgh – the same as Mr McFadden at school. I never knew Lexx was Scottish – I'm not sure I ever heard her speak. These days her hair is a messy off-blonde bob.

'Jana is walking her first *ever* show for me.' Dermot massages my shoulders, so he can't be too pissed off about what I said. 'Isn't she a babe?'

I feel my cheeks flush.

'Aye! Gorgeous! How old are you, love?'

'Almost seventeen.'

'You're a wee baby! Dermot, remember when we were that young? God, I feel old.'

'Al's coming out of retirement to celebrate ten years of Republic.'

'I'll show you the ropes,' she says with a wink.

'You're retired?' I ask.

'I'm thirty-two!' she gasps. 'I'm essentially a corpse in model years.'

'Oh, feck off! You're still a goddess!'

'I'm acting now, mostly. I was just in *After Miss Julie* at the Young Vic.'

Never heard of it. 'Oh, cool.'

Richie tentatively approaches. 'Dermot . . .?'

'Oh, feck, here we go. What?'

'It's Clara. She missed her flight at JFK . . .'

He turns white as milk. 'Feck.'

'It's fine. Prestige say she caught the red-eye and is gonna come here direct from Heathrow.'

There's a sudden commotion at the door and two *Incredible-Hulk* minders squeeze through the backstage curtain. Dermot and his staff suddenly flutter to life and attend to the new arrival. I can hardly see her through her entourage, but I see the red head of Dido Gant bob past us. I realise she's being taken into a private changing room. Fancy.

She's not as tall as the rest of us. I wonder if famous models don't have to be tall like us regular models do. It's weird I have no idea who Dido, or her sister, Domino are – or where they come from – and yet I know everything about them. It's like their whole lives were downloaded into my brain off Instagram. Between them they have seven million followers watching them flog 'tummy teas' and 'waist trainers'.

'Can we get some sashimi and turkey bacon for Dido?' I overhear one of the RoD staff ask another, who scuttles off at once.

Sashimi and turkey bacon? Gross. Turkey bacon has no right to sully the good bacon name. I turn to Viktoria in the next hair station and roll my eyes. 'Dido is bitch,' Viktoria says much too loudly. 'She never talk to other girls.'

I nod along, glad to be in on the gossip. There seem to be

about fifteen models, although it's hard to keep track because they mostly look *exactly* like Viktoria. So many languages criss-cross around the room, it's just noise. The Russian girls herd together and all look furious for no reason. Once again, the buffet goes largely untouched, aside from bananas, Haribo and Diet Coke.

A stylist grabs me after I've had a LOT of purple and blue eyeshadow applied. With magenta blush all over my face I look fully drag queen. I dunno, fashion, innit. I had pictures taken when I was at the fitting and now both are glued to the end of a clothes rail with all my bits and pieces on it. Each model has two looks. I have the metallic purple dress and a grey leather trouser suit. I'm buzzing when I see my shoes are a pair of slouchy silver ankle boots and some hot pink brogues. Neither have stupidly high heels. I'm so happy I could weep.

I hear a real honk of a voice just behind me. 'Rich, babes, don't suppose I can get six McNuggets and chips? And a strawberry shake?'

I'm hunched up in my hideous nude underwear, but turn to see Clara Keys towering over me. She's ridiculously beautiful. Her hair has been dragged into a messy ponytail and she's wearing a crumpled Keys-Loves-Adidas tracksuit but she's still gorgeous.

Dermot comes to greet her. His relief almost smells. 'Babes, you're here!'

'I'm so sorry I'm late. The traffic was fucked.'

'No worries, no worries. You're *here*.' He looks like he might legit weep. 'Let's get you ready. Do you want anything?'

'Yeah, someone's gone to get me a Maccy D's . . .'

Dermot guides her away and I'm still mute on the floor. I just met, or almost met, Clara Keys. And I didn't even take a picture. What a knob.

In various states of dress, we have a walk-through. It's really not rocket science. We walk up the right side of the runway and return on the left. An imbecile couldn't mess it up. Still worried sick, though. Three-Imodium day for real.

A scary, shouty lady will tell us when it's our turn, so all I have to do is a) be ready on time, and b) walk in a straight line. Dermot tells me to make sure I pause for photos at the end of the catwalk before I head back.

'Are you OK?' Ferdy asks. He's keeping a low profile, glued to the edges of the room. I squeeze his hand. Beyond the curtain, I hear the audience coming in. A DJ is playing a warm-up set. I feel the same way I felt before my last stage outing as the narrator in a junior school nativity play. The pretty girls got to be Mary and the Angel Gabriel. The clever girls had to do readings off bits of gold card. I stood up at the wrong moment and the teacher had to haul me back down.

'I need a nervous wee. But I wanna wait until the last minute or I'll have to go again.'

Ferdy grins. 'Treat yourself . . . go twice.'

'Five minutes, people!' The scary, shouty lady shouts.

'Fuck, Ferd.'

'Jana. Look at me. You got this.'

I try to exhale out the terror. I can't even kiss him because I'll fuck my make-up. 'Back in a sec . . .'

I sneak past the scary lady and slip into the loo. As I'm on the toilet, I become aware of a hideous retch and splat coming from the next cubicle. I wince as someone dumps their lunch in the lavatory. It's kind of depressing that the stereotype about models having eating disorders is true. Like, I'm naturally enormous and skinny; I just assumed the other girls would be too.

I'm washing my hands when the cubicle door opens and Clara Keys – in a gold lamé jumpsuit – steps out, dabbing her mouth with toilet roll. She catches me staring at her before I yank my eyes into the plughole.

'I know what you're thinking,' she says as she joins me at the sinks. 'But I think I ate some bad ribs last night in Brooklyn. I feel rank. Them McNuggets was a fuckin' error.'

Her famous skin – often compared to chocolate, which I always think is a bit racist – *does* look slightly clammy and grey *despite* all the make-up. Her eyes are metallic gold where mine are purple. 'Are you OK?' I ask.

She inhales deeply. 'Honestly, no. But don't say anything, yeah?'

'Sure. But why? If you're sick . . .'

She wrinkles her nose. Adorable. 'You're new at my agency, right?'

'Yeah.'

'Rookie tip: don't complain, don't explain. Just show up on time and smile.' She blasts me a fake smile. 'There's a reason I'm still getting work after all these years. Don't forget that . . . what's your name, babes?'

'Jana.'

'Nice to meet you, Jana, I'm Clara.'

'I . . . I know. I live on the Winstanley . . .'

Her eyes widen. 'No way! Big love to the SW11 massive!' She smiles again and this time it's dazzling. Even I want to give her money to take her picture. 'Well, here's tip number two – *always* introduce yourself, *especially* if everyone knows your name.'

'Got it.' I smile, although I can hardly look her in the eye. I worry I might go blind, like looking directly into the sun. This is so surreal. I'm in a loo with Clara Keys. And she slightly smells of sick. She seems nice, though. Bit stagey, but still nice.

'And number three: sharpie your name on your phone charger, because these bitches be thieves!'

I laugh.

'Come on, we're gonna miss the show.' Clara leads us out. 'Do you have any gum?'

I actually do. 'Yeah, well, my boyfriend has some.'

'Lifesaver. I won't forget this, babes.'

I have gum for Clara Keys.

The lights go down.

A hush falls over the crowd.

The music starts. I dimly recognise the song – a coldly electronic, bass-heavy remix of something I vaguely know. We all wait in line like cattle. I'm nervous. Some of the other girls yawn, totally over it. Others fiddle with shoes that are either much too small or large.

Is it the bass or my heartbeat?

Boom boom boom.

Thud thud thud.

Fuck, I'm dizzy.

'OK, Clara,' says Shouty Lady. 'Go.'

At the front of the queue, Clara launches herself down the runway. I see her profile only for a second, a glimpse of gold, as she steps into the spotlight and takes off. Her long hairpiece flicks like a whip. The queue moves forward. I'm sixth out. First look is the leather business suit. I've been told to shove my hands in my pockets, so I don't even need to worry about my hands.

Second girl, third.

It all happens so fast. Shouty Lady despatches a model every thirty seconds.

I'm on. Oh, god. My heart is going to explode out of my ribcage like the alien in *Alien*. And now *that's* all I can think about. Great.

'Jana. Go.'

Just do it, dickhead.

I step into the spotlight and I'm blind for a second. I adjust to the dazzle and see Viktoria up ahead of me and Clara on her return voyage. She gives me a wink.

Just walk.

Hands in pockets, I set off.

And I get it. At last.

I'm not meant to be Jana Novak off the Winstanley any more. I'm supposed to be . . . a goddess. I clench my jaw and walk with purpose towards the end of the runway. My pulse falls into rhythm with the bassline.

I'm dimly aware of a front row of smartphone faces. There

were rumours of actors, pop stars, and Anna Wintour, but all I see are iPhones. Camera flashes strobe ahead, reminding me to pause as I reach the end of the catwalk. Sabah's advice that models should look 'mad as hell' plays on loop. I pause, intensely stare down the photographers like I'm gonna nut them and head back. It's tempting to leg it for the return journey, I feel like I'm done, but I maintain Viktoria's pace until I'm past the RoD screen.

And then any sense of grace or decorum flies out the window as an assistant grabs me. 'Move! Second look! Quick!' Her hands are already unbuttoning the suit and a second pair of hands undoes the button on the trousers.

'Girls! Move it!' another voice bellows.

My feet don't hardly touch the floor.

The suit's pulled off, backstage cameras flashing all the time. I'm not wearing a bra. 'Can you not?' I ask a beardy photographer as he snaps me with my boobs out. He ignores me and takes my picture regardless. I see the flash even when I blink. I cover my nipples with an arm as I step out of the trousers. The metallic purple dress is already being lowered over my head.

It's dizzying.

I can't see Ferdy anywhere.

Where is he?

Someone shoves my foot into an ankle boot while fingers tousle my hair and a make-up brush prods my nose. Earrings clip on. I get a gobful of hairspray. It's like I'm being felt up by a giant squid. Hands, hands, hands all over my body. 'Jana, you're good. GO.' Someone slaps my arse to send me on my way.

I'm dragged back into line. There's no waiting this time, I'm pretty much on again in seconds. This time I'm in heels and I wobble as I step into the spotlight. I correct myself and set off. Nearly; fuck. One foot in front of the other.

I remember to pretend once more.

Can't even lie: this feels pretty cool.

A collective gasp from the audience snaps me out of feeling my fantasy. *Did I do something wrong?* Only then I see a girl on the opposite side of the catwalk stagger in her shoes. She's a tall Asian girl with pastel-pink hair. She lurches forward. Is she gonna . . .? Yep, she's gonna. She stacks it.

Her tangled limbs block the runway.

Oh, shit.

Girl down.

She tries to get back up, but one gold six-inch-heeled strappy sandal – thank god I didn't get *them* to wear – is hanging off her foot.

Ahead of me, Viktoria actually steps over her, like she's fashion roadkill. I guess Dermot *did* say to just keep going.

The poor bitch simply can't get up. What's more, she's getting in the way of the rest of us. It's gonna be a pile-up.

Oh, I can't. I can't leave her there.

As I reach her, I stoop down to help. The poor girl looks absolutely mortified, but takes my arms and I pull her upright. The problem seems to be that the shoe is attached to her ankle but not her foot. Hanging on to my shoulder, she manages to slot her toes back into the shoe.

The audience, to my astonishment, begins to applaud and cheer.

The model utters a quick, 'Thank you,' and continues on her

way with as much dignity as she can muster. The next girl has overtaken me, but I figure it's probably best to continue my voyage to the end of the catwalk so the photographers can get their picture.

My heart is beating so fast I swear I can feel it banging against my ribs. I feel electric. I don't even think about my feet or my walk. I pose, turn and head back just as Lexx emerges in the final look – a lightning-blue plastic trenchcoat – to a standing ovation.

Backstage, the Asian girl is being held by Dermot, visibly upset.

'Girls! In line for finale!' Shouty Lady shouts.

'Babes, it's fine! It happens!' Dermot tells her. As she gets in line, I see she's limping from where she went over on her ankle. Ouch.

'Clapping, girls, everyone clapping!'

We all walk in a procession, clapping as we go. Like a fashion caterpillar, we parade out to applause, Clara Keys leading the way. As we make our way back, Dermot and Lexx come on, hand in hand, and the crowd goes nuts. I guess it's job well done for Dermot.

And that's it.

Done it.

As soon as I'm backstage, all the adrenaline seeps out of me and I feel my body go limp. As the nerves ebb away, I'm suddenly starving. Shouty Lady is smiling, but still shouting. 'Great job, everyone! Great job!'

Dermot pulls me into a massive bear hug. 'You're a fecking lifesaver, you know that?'

I'm too exhausted to even reply. I just smile.

'I owe you one, girl.'

Another pair of arms wraps around me and I recognise the smell of Ferdy's fabric softener before I see him. 'You did it,' he says as I collapse into him. 'You did it.'

Later, a car drops Ferdy and then me back on the estate. I walk through the front door and Mum, Dad and Milos are all on the sofa watching *Pointless*. 'Oh, hello, love,' Mum says. 'I was just about to text and ask if you'd be home for dinner.'

'Nah, that's not right,' Milos tells the TV. 'She weren't in any Marvel films.'

Sure enough the contestant has got the answer wrong.

'How did it go?' Dad asks.

'Yeah, good.'

'Good? Good? Is that it?' Mum says.

'Yeah. I didn't fall over. In fact, I helped a girl up.'

'Oh, that's kind, well done. Do we want pizza or sausages?' says Mum.

We all want pizza. 'Ha!' Milos says. 'Look at your make-up! You look like a clown, sis.'

'Thanks.' I mouth calling him a dickhead so Dad won't get cross. I go upstairs and hop in the shower, scrubbing at my face with a flannel. I shampoo my hair, trying to get rid of all the gunk and spray.

When I'm done, I step on to the bath mat and the whole house smells of cheesy bread. 'Jana! Is ready nearly!' Mum calls up.

'Coming!'

I wipe the steam off the mirror and I just look like me again:

beaky nose, skin scrubbed raw, pink eyes, little yellow zit in the fold of my nostril. Reality. And I feel a bit disappointed somehow.

VIRAL

The next morning is Dali-level, melting clocks on shit, surreal. I have sociology first period on a Friday so my alarm goes off at seven. I thought I'd got it all last night, but my pillow is still somehow covered in glitter from the show.

It's mental that after everything that happened yesterday, I have to return to the stratosphere. I have to have Bran Flakes because Milos put the box of Rice Krispies back in the cupboard with enough cereal to fill a thimble. Bastard. On the other hand, if every day was like yesterday, I don't think my body could take the adrenaline. I'd snap.

I meet Ferdy at Starbucks. He gets a freebie coffee, I get a freebie tea and we head to school, both huddled under my *Miffy* umbrella. It's the devil's drizzle and my jeans are soon matted to my legs. Ferd's dad – a squaddie who ain't been a squaddie for, like, ten years but can't let it go – is giving him hassle. Again. He's such a haemorrhoid. I let him offload his rage as we stroll uphill together.

When we arrive at school, I know something's up because Laurel and Sabah come charging out of the student entrance to greet us. 'Did you see it?' Laurel screams. She looks pure wired, as if she's had a bowl of E-numbers for breakfast.

'What's up, Laurel?' Ferd asks.

'Baby girl, you've gone viral!' Sabah cries.

I'm very out of the loop right now. My legs are wet. 'What?'

We get in out of the rain and head to the canteen. The floors are slick with muddy footprints. Now: I'm usually pretty oblivious, but even I notice a hush spread around the cafeteria. 'It *is*,' a girl I don't know whispers. 'It's *her*.'

This ain't doing my paranoia much good. 'OK, Sabah, what the fuck is going on?'

She slides an iPad out of her Mulberry. I know it's Mulberry because she saved up her babysitting money for about a year to buy a handbag, which I thought was ridic. 'Check this out.'

She's connected to the Wi-Fi and on BuzzFeed.

You Won't Believe What Happened At This London Fashion Week Show . . .

I see there's a video. It autoplays and it's the moment the poor model went down like a granny on a frosty morning. Once more I hear the audience gasp and wince. Ooof. Her ankle bent all the way over; it must have really hurt. In her defence, Viktoria looks very professional as she continues past her. Then I stride forward and whoever was filming – a bit ghoulishly, if you ask me – zooms in on us. Wow: I look pretty fierce. I haven't actually seen any pictures from the show.

I guess I broke character to help her up. We look like a pair of gangly giraffes off one of them Attenborough things as I pull her up, but then the audience cheers and the video ends.

Sabah takes the tablet off me. 'Imma read it for you: *When Canadian model Lien Yim tripped during one of the opening shows of this year's London Fashion Week, Londoner Jana Novak* – babe, that's you! – *making her catwalk debut for Republic of Deen, came to her rescue.* How amazing is that?'

Laurel still looks like she might implode. 'It's all over Twitter and Facebook too. People are calling it a feminist triumph of female solidarity!'

'Is that all it takes?' I roll my eyes. 'I just felt sorry for her.'

'That other girl ignored her!' Sabah says.

'Someone else would have scraped her up,' I say. 'Ain't that Kanye West getting up from the front row to help her?'

'Uh,' Ferdy adds. 'I just read the comments. Big mistake. Everyone is all: *LOL fail.*'

'Internet people are always so kind and nice.' I take a sip of hot tea.

'What happened after?' Sabah asks. 'Was Dermot Deen cross?'

'God, no. He's cool.'

'Lien Yim is well famous,' Sabah says. 'Her mum is Anouska. No surname. Just Anouska. She was like *the* supermodel in the eighties. And her dad is some big fashion photographer. I guess it's in her DNA.'

'And if anything,' says Ferdy, 'this is all free publicity for his collection.'

I hadn't thought of that. I suppose more people will see the show. Good.

'Jana, tell us *everything*!' Laurel says. 'Did you meet Clara Keys? Is she cool? What's she like? Is she nice?'

'OK, you need to chill the fuck out. Yes, I did meet Clara . . .'

They both scream and I fill them in on everything: Clara's vomit, Dido Gant's sushi, Lexx. They hang on my every word. 'This is insane,' Sabah says once I'm done. 'Like, how can this be real? Here we are in a scummy canteen and yesterday you was giving chewing gum to an actual supermodel.'

I shrug.

'Oh, shit, here we go,' Ferdy mutters.

'What?' Only then I see Heather, Lily and Emily prowling towards us. 'Oh, joy.'

'Jana!' Heather says brightly. They're all wearing a variation on the same outfit with matching swishy ponytails. 'Saw your video on Instagram.' I brace myself. 'Just wanted to say, you looked sick, babes.'

I wait for the inevitable 'but'. After a pause, I realise she's finished. 'Oh. Cool. Thanks.'

'And did you meet Clara Keys?'

'Yeah. She was really nice.'

'Oh. My. God. Amazeballs.' The bell sounds. 'Sit with us in sociology, yeah?' Heather *smiles* and it's more chilling than seeing a cat eat its own skin off or something. They sashay away and we all look to one another, slightly stunned.

'What was that?' Ferdy says.

'You better not abandon us for that bunch o' cunts,' Sabah says.

'Yeah, that's definitely gonna happen,' I say with a huge dollop of sarcasm. 'You know all this will be worth it if I can sit with Heather Daley.'

*   *   *

When I arrive home, there's a huge bouquet of flowers on the kitchen table. I've never seen anything like them and I don't have a clue what they are: big, tropical orange and yellow flowers with spiky palm leaves. Somehow I know they're from Dermot before I even open the card. It reads: "Everyone is talking about the collection thanks to my baby Jana. Love, DD."

It'd be well glamorous if the kitchen bin didn't stink of rotting chicken.

I'm still reading the card when my phone vibrates with a message. It's from Sabah. *Shut the front door ur on Ellen bish!* There's a YouTube link. I sit on the sofa and click the link. The video starts with *The Ellen Show* logo before fading to Ellen in a trouser suit, standing in front of a wall of TV screens. 'Welcome to the show!' she says to rapturous applause. 'You know, they always say that fashion is cutthroat and full of backstabbers . . . and they're not wrong!' Big laugh from the audience. 'But just take a look at this clip that landed in my inbox this morning . . .'

They show the same clip from BuzzFeed.

'I mean, look at that! Some good, old-fashioned kindness. Am I right? I'm told the model who helped the other girl up is a sixteen-year-old schoolgirl from London called Jana Novak . . .'

This is just so weird. Ellen Degeneres just said my name. ON TV.

I'm still freaking out when I see Ro is calling, replacing the video. 'Hello?'

'Hello, sweetie! How are you, lovely?'

'Yeah, I'm OK.'

'Are your ears burning?'

'Huh?'

'The phone has been ringing about you *all day*. Everyone saw the Republic of Deen show, babes, and we need to talk . . .'

'Am I in trouble?'

'Oh my gosh, no! Darling, Riccardo Tisci just called Maggie.' That feels like a name I should probably know. 'Erm . . .'

'Burberry! He asked if you were available to come for a fitting tomorrow for the closing show on Sunday. Please say you can. I know we said we wouldn't send you on any more castings, but Jana . . . it's BURBERRY! It's as British as . . . scones and . . . racism.'

I have heard of Burberry, obviously. 'Erm, yeah, sure.'

'Consider yourself booked. This is a dream, Jana. Our sister agencies in New York and Paris have been calling too – it's more than we could ever hope for, seriously.' I sink into the sofa. My head is spinning. No, not my head . . . my *life*. 'Jana? Are you there?'

'Yeah,' I mumble. 'I'm freaking out.' I don't sound like I'm freaking out, I sound like a zombie.

'Why, sweetie?'

'I was just on *Ellen*.' I've split into two girls. One is me, fleshy, real and on the settee, the other is this . . . fictional thing what everyone's talking about. Holy shit, I'm Hannah Montana.

'I know! Isn't it amazing?'

'It's weird.'

She finally takes a breath. 'That's fashion, hon. It moves either painfully slow or stupidly fast. Sometimes a New Face just explodes.' Well, that don't sound ideal. 'Fashion Week is mental, it won't always be like this, I promise. I'm sorry you've been dropped in the deep end, but it'll all be worth it once you're established.'

'OK.'

'Yeah?'

'Yeah.'

'Lovely. I'm sending you through details of a car to get you to the Burberry fitting tomorrow. Don't be late.'

I hang up and sit on the sofa. I don't even turn the TV on, I just stare at the wall.

Burberry. Fucking *Burberry*. Shit.

Cara, Clara, Westley Bryce, Lexx, Adwoa . . . every model I can think of has done Burberry.

And now I am.

I knew things would change. I just didn't think they'd change so *fast*.

This feeling inside; I dunno if it's butterflies or terror.

RISE OF THE SUPER-SKINNY MODELS: HOW CLARA AND CO ARE A DANGER FOR OUR DAUGHTERS
Hattie Cope

Another London Fashion Week, and I dimly hear the tip-tap of stick-thin pins tottering around Somerset House. Is it just me, ladies, or do these emaciated husks get thinner with every passing year?

I fondly remember the glory days of curvy Cindy, Naomi and Claudia prowling like runway panthers. These days, my sweet eight-year-old daughter, China, has to witness a macabre trip to the abattoir with a parade of clavicles, ribs and hips grotesquely sold as aspirational by wildly irresponsible, often gay, male designers.

I mean, Industry darling Clara Keys looks like Naomi Campbell after a bout of particularly powerful chemotherapy. Much-heralded newcomer Jana Novak, who I had to explain to China actually is a woman (has anyone asked to see a birth certificate?), would look quite at home on an AIDS ward in the late eighties.

There is no way on earth that either of these girls, and many more like them, is eating healthily. I don't and won't accept it. To continually display these skeletal figures in magazines and on runways sends our daughters a dangerous message: that very thin bodies are achievable. They are, my friends, but only through starvation and anorexia.

Despite recent changes from the British Fashion Council, which supposedly forbid designers from using unhealthy models, I believe an industry-wide BAN on girls who are less than size eight should be implemented immediately.

SEXY LEXXY PROUDLY FLAUNTS CURVES IN BEACH BIKINI
Herald Online Team

Model-turned-actress Lexx showed off a somewhat fuller figure yesterday as she and her husband, Ric Paget of rockers The Wishes, holiday in Santorini.

Twice her former size, Lexx, 32, let her tummy hang out as she frolicked in the sea and surf. Displaying her ample assets, Lexx wore a blue itsy-bitsy polka-dot bikini from Marks & Spencer (£49.99). A far cry from her waifish modelling heyday in the noughties, Lexx was relaxed and happy, canoodling with Ric, 34.

We're guessing he likes having a little more Lexx to grab on to at night! Absolutely flabulous!

MODEL

Mr Bennett looms over me like some burly giant off *Game of Thrones*. We don't have much to do with him, but he seems cool. 'Let me get this right? You want four days out of college?'

I shrink in my chair. 'Yeah. Um, I need to go to New York . . . for work.'

'For work?'

'I'm . . . erm . . . I'm a . . . model.' The last word cringes all the way out of my gob.

He blinks, his head tipping slightly to the left. 'Ah! Yes! I heard staffroom talk of a supermodel in our midst.' I blush and say nothing. 'I wouldn't normally allow time off, but if it's important . . .?'

Jana . . . are you sitting down? Maggie herself actually called this time. *Sweetheart, what if I were to tell you the head designer at TANK Jeans wants you for a campaign?*

And then she told me what they were offering and I *did* need to sit down. It's crazy, stupid money. Mum's hand flew to her mouth when I told her. It's so much money, I might even suggest we go on holiday to make up for the cancelled one last year. How many brownie points would *that* earn me? A lot, I'm thinking.

'Yeah,' I tell Mr Bennett, 'it's important.'

Bennett nods and has a sip of his mint tea. 'How are your grades? I hope your *career* isn't affecting your school work too badly.'

I shake my head. Since Fashion Week, everything has pretty much gone back to normal. I have a lot more Instagram followers but that's about it. Layla shared one of my test shots on her Insta and everything went bonkers. Of course, with all the new likes comes all the new hate:

ILY JANA I LOVE U UR GORGEOUS GIRL
I SHIP JANA AND CLARA
Y IS THAT UGLY BITCH A MODEL SHE LOOKS LIKE
   MAN
THINSPO GOALS
I LOVE U JANA NO1 MODEL IN WORLD
ANOREXIA FOR SURE LOOK AT HER ARMS
SHE A TRANNY LOL

I'd delete it, but Ro says Instagram is as important as my portfolio nowadays, so . . .

'OK, then. I'll authorise the time off college. But don't make a habit of it.'

'I won't.'

I get the hell out of his office as fast as I can. I've never had to go to see a principal before and Dad refused to do it for me. He said if I was mature enough to go to New York by myself, I'm old enough to talk to the head teacher. Harsh, Dad, harsh.

I find everyone in the canteen. It's pizza day, yaaaas. 'Jana, we got you some!' Laurel calls and I join them, bypassing the queue.

'What did he say?' Ferdy asks as I give him a kiss.

'He said yes.' The pizza has gone a bit limp and sad.

'Oh, cool.'

'So that's it?' Sabah says. 'You're off to New York?'

I nod. 'Wow. Should I freak out now?' It's weird. I know I should be buzzing, but I can't even picture arriving at the airport without getting sweaty palms. Whenever I think about modelling stuff, my stomach screws up into a tight painful knot. Then I feel guilty for not being more hyped and somehow feel worse.

I really *want* to enjoy this. That's basically the same as enjoying it, right?

'No! But if I collapse to the floor it's because I have DIED of jealousy.'

I take her hand. 'Can't you come with me?'

She points at her hijab. 'Oh, yeah, hon, I'm just dying to go through customs in America right now.'

'Wait, when is it?' Laurel asks.

'I fly out next Tuesday and the shoot is on Wednesday. Then I meet my New York agency and some casting people and fly home Saturday.'

Laurel's eyes widen. 'But that Friday is my birthday party.'

Shit. I'd completely forgotten. Laurel's birthday seemed so far away. How can it be November already? 'Oh . . .'

'Jana! You *have* to come! My parents booked the whole restaurant. What if no one turns up?'

'Laurel . . . we're all coming,' Sabah says. Robin and Ferdy concur.

'I know . . . but . . .'

'But what?' Robin picks the mushrooms off his pizza and gives them to her. They're such a married couple and they don't even know it.

'I told everyone that *you'd* be there.'

I frown. 'That's a bit weird, innit?'

Laurel shrugs. 'Like, all my cousins saw you on *Ellen* and wanted to meet you. And Heather and Harry . . .'

Sabah grimaces. 'Heather and Harry are coming? Ew! Why?'

'My mum is friends with their mum!'

I smile and brush over that fact. 'Laurel, if I'm gonna be a model, I might actually have to go get some photos done, yeah?' I bite the pinnacle of my slice off. The cheese slides off and slaps me on the chin. Why does that always happen? I peel cheese off my face. God, I'm *so* sexy, I can see why I'm a model. 'It's a big deal.'

'It's TANK, Laurel, as if she's not gonna go,' Robin chips in seconds before getting a death stare.

'What are we doing *this* weekend?' I say. 'Maybe we could go bowling on Saturday or something. My treat.' I figure there's no point in getting all this money – not that I've seen a penny yet – if I can't buy things for my friends.

'You'd pay?' Robin asks.

'Yeah. I'm about to be . . . well . . . quids in.'

My friends look to each other. Did that sound like a brag? It wasn't meant to. Luckily, Robin breaks the stodgy silence. 'Well, if you're paying! I'm so skint I actually googled what rent boys make!' Everyone laughs before Sabah gives him a lecture on sex workers' rights.

And so that's what we do. I book a lane for two games for the five of us that Saturday evening in Kingston. I fully love the bowling alley. It smells of beer, vinegary chips and cheap, rubbery burgers. There's a steady *pip-pop* from the air-hockey table and the arcade games make bleeps and fanfares. The lane next to us is a couple on what I reckon is a first date. She's better at bowling than he is and I sense he wants to legit die.

For someone so petite, Laurel is weirdly amazing at bowling; she won the first game and is well on her way to winning the second. I am hopeless and the others wouldn't let us have lane buddies on, so most of my attempts wind up rolling down the gutter. 'I am so shit at this,' I say as I sit down. I take a slurp of my raspberry slushie. 'Is my tongue blue?'

'More purple,' Ferdy says. He leans in close. 'Hey, I'm home alone tonight, you know.'

'Kai Ferdinand, you kept that quiet, you shady bastard. How come?'

'They've taken Jen to a dance contest in Scunthorpe.' Ferdy's sister is a tap and jazz champion. 'Think you can convince your mum you're staying with Laurel?'

I grin. 'I think so . . .'

The rest of the night is sort-of foreplay. As we finish the second match (Laurel wins again) I keep catching Ferdy's eye and we both know what the other's thinking. Man, I'm nervous and excited and my skin buzzes. When Robin suggests we decamp to his 'man cave' (slightly damp basement) for a *Star Wars* marathon, we emphatically say no and I reckon everyone knows what's on our minds.

Ferdy's flat is strangely silent when we get home, although timed lamps have come on automatically. It's nice that we don't have to sneak around or anything. We have all night. What a luxury; half our relationship is trying to find places to have sex, I swear, and it's much more bloody difficult in winter. 'You want a drink or something?'

'Yeah, what have you got?'

'Well, Mum has a bottle of red wine on the go? That'd be very mature of us, I think.'

'I hate red wine. It tastes of cat piss.'

'We could share a cider? I don't think Dad would miss one?'

'Are you sure?'

He considers this. Ferdy's dad is scary. *Really* scary. I hate it if he's home, although Ferdy rarely invites me over if he's gonna be in, which is a lot. Ferdy hates his dad too. He told me once he thinks his dad hits his mum but can't prove anything. 'I think it'll be fine.'

I make myself comfortable in the lounge and stream some music to the speakers. I pick fairly obvious slow-jam-sex-music. I slide open the balcony door and look out over the Thames. Once again, I take a cheeky peek into the penthouses, that other world on the other side of the river, and remind myself why I'm doing all this: a place, one day, for me and him. Ferdy returns with two glasses of cider. 'Thanks.'

We sit at opposite ends of the sofa and it's like we're sitting on the rim of a cliff waiting to see who'll jump first. After an excruciating second or two – it feels more like an hour – we both laugh. It's stupid. How many times have we been here? Why does it still feel so naughty and taboo?

'Are you ready for Tuesday?' he asks, breaking the tension.

I shake my head. 'Nothing is happening on Tuesday. I'm not thinking about it. I'm pretending it ain't happening.' I sip some of the cider. It's dangerously like pop.

'Jana, it's an all-expenses-paid trip to New York!'

'It's big!'

'You're big!'

'What if I get lost?'

'You have Google Maps.'

'I wish you could come with me.' I shuffle up the couch to be nearer to him and swing my feet into his lap. There's a very sexy hole on the big toe of my sock.

'I have about sixteen quid in my account, babes.'

'But I'm about to get paid for the Fashion Week shows. I could pay.'

He scrunches his face up. 'I would feel so weird about that.'

'Well, that's not very feminist.'

He chuckles. 'No. I'd feel like I was in debt to you. I can't return the favour, can I?'

I hadn't really thought about this. I mean, what's the point in getting a load of money if I have no one to spend it with? I remind myself I'm supposed to be saving up anyway. I give Ferdy a cidery kiss. 'You can. When we get to New York you can buy me one of those big, greasy pizza triangles . . .'

'Deal . . .'

I put my cider down so we're free to make out properly. It feels extra scandalous to get it on right here on the sofa and it's honestly pretty hot. Ferdy lies on top of me and I let him nestle between my legs. Even through two pairs of jeans I can feel how turned on he is.

We kiss and kiss and I get out of my head, cluttered with stupid worries, and into my body. The mute button goes on and I focus on how good his hands feel on my skin.

We untangle momentarily because there's no sexy way to get out of skinny jeans. We both stand to wriggle out of them before collapsing on to each other again. I tentatively give his willy a rub through his boxers and he groans.

I take it slow, wanting to get him excited, but not *too* excited. His hand slips into my pants too and it feels awesome. My whole body hums and purrs.

'Oh, baby, maybe . . . stop . . . oh. Shit.' I feel a sudden hot wet on my hand.

Bollocks. 'Hey, it's OK.'

He looks embarrassed, but says nothing. Instead he moves down my body, kissing my tummy. He don't stop there and keeps going. I lie back and prepare to go there. Ferdy may have his shortcomings, but *this* he's very, very good at. No complaints here.

NEW YORK

Dad drives me to Heathrow. He can only come as far as customs. Ooh, it's big, and I feel little. Terminal 5 is like being in a space station, all glass and metal beams. Immaculate British Airways stewardesses with perfect buns and stressed-looking business people hustle and bustle past us and I feel about ten years old.

'You got your boarding pass and passport?' Dad asks.

I hold them up.

'OK, hang on to both of them. And you don't have no liquids in your backpack?'

I hold up the little plastic bag with all my liquids in. 'Dad, I have been on a plane before, y'know.'

'Not by yourself you haven't. Keep your wits about you, Jana. I'd rather not see you on the news.'

I nod. As it happens, I only have to manage until tomorrow when Maggie is joining me for the TANK shoot. They're a well important client apparently and she wants to be there in person. They probably don't trust me to not fuck it up, and who can blame them?

Dad hugs me for longer than he normally would and then ushers me towards the security gates. We're stupidly early, but Mum insisted in case there were long queues. There aren't and I'm through the scanners in about five minutes.

There's still two hours until my flight even boards. I have to read *Dubliners* for English, but that fills me with dread, so I decide to do what Ro's been banging on at me to do for weeks and buy *Vogue*, *i-D* and *Cosmopolitan* from the newsagent, along with some pickled onion Monster Munch and a Diet Coke.

At first I'm struck by how many adverts I have to flick past until I remember that I'm supposed to be the girl IN the adverts, and go back to the beginning. I guess, if I was into fashion and beauty, the adverts would sort of be the whole point. The next surprise is how many of the campaigns feature Clara, Domino or Dido. Are there only three models in the world?

The girls in *Cosmopolitan* look healthy, bronzed and outdoorsy. *i-D* is full of girls with their boobs out, while *Vogue* exists somewhere in the middle. The adverts are the same in all three. I wonder if I can do what these girls are doing. Viktoria is in a spread in *i-D*, squashed into a large cardboard box wearing only a pair of Gucci knickers and some fried eggs over her nipples. She looks like a very beautiful corpse someone is trying to dispose of.

Also: were they real eggs?

Fashion is weird.

I don't think I want egg boobs, thank you kindly.

There's a big feature on some photographer called Lucas Blo. I think he was at the Republic of Deen show. He has a new coffee-table book out to celebrate twenty years in the business. It's called *Some Photographs That I Took* and it costs ninety quid. Ninety quid! For a book! In the interview he talks about how he chose the pictures and his favourite muses . . . blah, blah, blah, I skip most of the text, boring.

There's an early picture of Clara, her nipples peeping through a sopping-wet vest as she stands in a shower, looking wide-eyed and confused. Another is of Lexx, naked, and covered in what seems to be treacle. At least I *hope* it's treacle. Gross.

Ping pong ping. 'Flight BA 177 for New York JFK is now ready for boarding at Gate A3. Will all passengers intending to travel please make their way to Gate A3.'

That's me. I feel a bit sick. Sabah told me that real models travel light so they don't have to wait for baggage at the carousels. She helped me pack a carry-on wheelie case with a capsule wardrobe. Feeling freakishly alert, I find my way to Gate A3. Look at me, I'm totally bossing this. I caught a plane all by myself. Adulting. Ish.

The gate lady checks my boarding pass and the nerves turn into something like excitement. Maybe I can do this after all. Plane smell – plasticky air freshener – reminds me of that trip to Mykonos a couple of years ago with Mum and Dad and Milos. Grinning cabin crew greet me as I stoop to board the jumbo jet. They direct me to my seat and I squidge my legs in. Wow, this is gonna be comfortable for *eight hours*. Plane seats are made for pygmy people. At what stage, I wonder, will I be famous enough to fly first class?

It feels a lot longer than eight hours. The idea of watching films for that amount of time *sounds* pretty fun, but three movies back to back was actually pretty excruciating. I was so bored I watched the last *Transformers* movie. And my arse went numb.

And I couldn't get comfy enough to sleep. The man next to me, however, had no trouble nodding off and snored like a giant walrus the whole flight.

My ears pop, and I go deaf, telling me we're coming in to land. This is it.

'Ladies and gentlemen, this is your captain speaking.' He sounds very quiet with my ears aching so bad. 'We have started our descent into New York JFK. The weather is cloudy with a minimal chance of rain. Local time is just after three p.m.'

We've travelled back in time. It's weird. It'd be early evening at home, but it's still the middle of the day here. I'm tired but I have a whole day to go before bed. The businessmen jostle to be the first off the plane. I take my time and walk past the nodding-dog stewardess and into the airport. Customs is crazy, way crazier than in London, *and* this one has fully scary armed guards.

Oh my days. I am in AMERICA.

After what feels like a billion years, and a grilling about my work visa, I properly enter America for the first time ever. I always thought America would have that hazy gloss that films and TV shows have, but, almost disappointingly, it's normal. From in here, it don't look no different to London.

As I walk into arrivals, I scan the hall for my driver. Sure enough, there's a little old man holding a 'JANA NOVAK' sign and I feel well famous, like a film star or the president. I wheel myself over to him. 'Hi!'

'Jana Novak?' he says in a Russian accent.

'Yeah.'

He takes my case and I follow him to his car. I hold my breath as I prepare for my first glimpse of the Big Apple. The doors slide open and I'm hit by a muggy humidity wave and nothing but concrete flyovers and chain hotels as far as the eye can see. Oh. Anticlimax.

'Is it far to New York?' I ask. He looks very confused. 'To the apartment? Is it far?' I point to my watch and mime driving.

'One hour,' he replies.

We drive down a drab motorway for ages. I have the email Ro sent and I'm staying in Brooklyn, not Manhattan, because that's where the shoot is tomorrow. I hope I'll be able to see some cool stuff while I'm here.

I needn't have worried. I'm half-dozing off when my eyes flicker open and I see *the* skyline. Oh. My. God. It's *real*. I've seen this in a million films and here it is in front of my eyes. This word gets bandied around way too often, but it's *iconic*. It's the Millennium Falcon, it's T. Rex, it's Mickey Mouse. I recognise the Empire State Building and Brooklyn Bridge at once. I hope to see the Statue of Liberty, but can't as yet.

Only then we turn off the . . . coastline or whatever, and down a side street. Even Brooklyn – if that's where we are – is *so* New York. The buildings are brown-brick with *Sex and the City* stoops and fire escapes zigzagging up the walls. Yellow cabs, man! Yellow cabs everywhere! Steam rises out of a manhole – why is that even happening? This is amazing. I feel like I'm on a film set. It's *Taxi Driver*, it's *Ghostbusters*, it's *Home Alone 2: Lost in New York*. I press my nose to the window to soak it all in.

The driver pulls up at one of the brownstones. 'We here,' he says and steps out to collect my case from the 'trunk'. I swing my 'sneakers' on to the pavement and see a slightly stoned-looking building. It's definitely the right address, but I was expecting something a bit, well, fancier. There are graffiti tags all over the door and metal grilles over the ground floor windows. Rusty air-con units jut out of the windows higher up. It's . . . ugly.

In my little instruction pack from Ro, she mentioned there's a safety box with the key in. I've got a code to collect it. The car pulls away – Sabah told me to tip the driver, so I did – and I haul my case up the stoop. When I go to the little box that should house my key, it flops open, broken. And it's empty.

Well, that's great, innit.

I look around but there's no one I can ask. Shit the bed. Instead, I press the buzzer for Apartment 4. It crackles and hisses, but I think it's alive. A broken voice stutters out. 'Who . . . is . . . it?'

'Erm . . . it's Jana Novak. I'm looking for the model apartment.'

The door honks like a goose and I hear the lock click. I push my way into the hall through a heap of takeaway menus and leaves from the street outside. There's no lift and I'm guessing it's the fourth floor. I sigh and start the climb.

As I clatter past Apartment 3, I hear a baby howling and I can only hope it's visiting for the afternoon. The fourth floor is the top apartment and I'm out of breath from dragging my case up. I almost collapse against the door to find it locked. I give it a knock. From inside, I clearly hear an exasperated sigh. 'Just push it! It sticks!'

I try again and this time it opens. I fall into a cramped kitchen and collide with another girl. 'Watch it!' she cries. 'Fuck.'

129

It takes me a second to recognise her because her pink hair is now silver-blonde.

It's the girl I helped up off the catwalk.

She clocks me at the same time I clock her.

And she don't look happy.

TANK

What's her name? What's her name? What's her name? 'Oh, hi . . . it's . . . Leanne, right?'

She actively scowls at me. 'Lien.'

'Sorry – there wasn't a key in the box.'

'There's one on the counter.' She has an American accent. No, Canadian, wasn't it? Yeah. I think I've woken her up; she has bed hair. 'I'm going back to sleep. I flew in from Tokyo and I'm jet-lagged. Don't wake me up.'

'Oh . . . just . . . do you know which my room is?'

She huffs again. 'You're in with me unless you want the sofa. The other room has two Russian girls in or something. They are a pair of thieving bitches. I swear they took my fucking granola bar.'

Shit, why are some girls so scary? 'Is it this one?'

'God, just hurry it up. I've got the top bunk.'

The apartment is long and narrow. The kitchen leads to a bare lounge containing a tatty brown sofa, one of them cheap, white, Ikea coffee tables and nothing else. At the far end of the lounge are two bedrooms. I glimpsed a bathroom off the kitchen. Lien leads me to the left room and it's pretty much a box. A metal bunk bed, the sort from Girl Scout camp, blocks the window and almost all the light. Instead of a curtain there's a towel stapled to the wall.

This place is a fucking shithole.

Lien's suitcase is open on the floor, clothes spilling out of it like lava. Too late, I realise I'm standing on a crumpled nude thong.

'Just step around my shit!' Lien snaps, climbing on to the top bunk.

'I'm gonna take a shower . . . I'll get out of your way.'

'Whatever. Just be quiet.' She tugs a leopard-print sleep mask over her face.

The bathroom is daffodil-yellow, and rank. An eggy hamster of matted hair clogs the shower drain and the torn curtain is patchy with mildew. Still, the pressure is good and the water's hot. I wash plane and taxi residue off my skin. I've decided – again on Sabah's advice – to stay awake. I'm told the only way to combat jet lag is to get on local time as fast as possible. If I have to prop my eyes open with matchsticks, I will.

A *filthy* towel hangs on the back of the bathroom door but luckily I brought one from home. I guess our Russian flatmates are out so I dry off and change into fresh jeans and Ferdy's 'LeviOsa Not LeviosA' T-shirt in the lounge. I see I have a message from him (wtf is AT&T?) and I instantly feel a mixture of glee and homesickness. *Yay! Glad u got there OK. Off to bed now.*

I fire a message back. *Sleep tight. Just gonna get some food and an early night. Love you.*

I know.

A pause.

Jk jk, love you too xxx

He's a dick, but I love him.

I look out of the grimy kitchen window at Brooklyn. I don't suppose I can hide away in this flat all evening. It don't look like Lien is getting out of bed any time soon and I'm guessing she ain't the hair-braiding, gossip girl, sleepover type. The agency gave me a hundred dollars in cash for expenses so I reckon it's time to venture into New York.

I put my phone and the cash in a handbag I've borrowed from Mum and grab a flannel shirt – it's too muggy for a jacket. I also make sure I take the apartment key. I do some Google-Mapping and work out that I'm in somewhere called Williamsburg. I type 'pizza' into the search bar and wonder what anyone did before this technology. There are maybe a trillion pizza places in Williamsburg so I just walk in the direction of the nearest, Sal's.

I soak up the street vibes: the cute coffee shops and 'drug stores'. I wonder if people think I'm a native or if I stand out like a selfie stick at Piccadilly Circus.

By the time I reach the pizzeria, it's starting to get dark and a neon Budweiser signs flickers in the window. I see there are booths to sit at and it don't look too busy, although a group of cool hipster types cluster around the door, vaping on the street. They all look alike: skinny jeans, rolled-up sleeves and beanie hats.

I shuffle past them and hover in the threshold. A chubby guy in an apron calls over from the counter. 'How many, doll?' He's got arms like hams and a rough blue chin.

'Just me.'

'Singles at the counter.'

Seems fair. I find a space at the counter and perch on a stool. The whole restaurant smells amazing and I realise I haven't eaten since the poxy chicken in sauce on the plane. The same guy comes over. 'What can I get you, dollface?'

'Oh. Erm, pepperoni, please.'

'Drink?'

Why not, I'm in America. 'Cream soda, please.'

He smiles as he slides a frankly ginormous slice on to a paper plate and places it in front of me. 'You English?'

'Yeah.'

'Hey, fellas, we got Princess Kate in!' he laughs. Some of the chefs wave past the pizza oven. 'You here on vacation?'

I shake my head, trying to angle the huge triangle into my gob.

'Lemme guess – model?'

I nod. 'How did you know?' I say through a mouthful of the best pizza I've had in my entire life. I'm almost embarrassed to admit I'm a model. Like he's gonna think *I think* I'm really hot shit or something.

'It's Brooklyn, baby. You see a tall, skinny, foreign girl – she's a model.' I smile and catch cheese as it slides off.

'It's my first time away from home,' I admit.

'That so?' His front tooth is missing. 'Hey, well, this one's on the house, then. Welcome to the American Dream, baby.'

Something unwinds in me and I feel my shoulders relax. It hits me. I'm in New York, all by myself. I did it. I actually made it.

And I ain't scared any more.

*   *   *

The next morning a car arrives to take Lien and me to the shoot. Turns out, she's also been booked by TANK, so stacking it on the runway can't have hurt her career too badly. Still, she basically ignores me as she falls into the cab, big sunglasses on and hair shoved into a baseball cap. Last night I bought some milk and cornflakes from the convenience store opposite the apartment, but Lien has tumbled out of bed and grabbed a banana for breakfast.

'Morning,' I say.

'God, it's early.'

It's actually not *that* early, but I ain't gonna argue with her. Within ten minutes we're at the location – a converted warehouse in Bushwick. It's basically East London, they're almost identical, same grungy vibe. I spot Maggie having a cigarette on the street and I've never been so pleased to see a familiar face.

'Hello, darling!' For the first time, I actually run over and give her a hug. 'Are you OK, little one? How was the flight?'

'It was fine.'

'Good girl! And what did you do last night?'

'Oh, I just got some pizza.'

'Pizza, eh?' Maybe it's just me, but I'm sure she casts a glance at my waist. 'Look at you, independent woman! So grown up!' Maggie turns to Lien. 'Hello, superstar. How was Tokyo?'

Lien sort of shakes her head to shut down the question. She bums a cigarette off Maggie and lights up, inhaling deeply. 'I'm not doing it again.'

'Oh, come on, darling. It can't be that bad?'

Lien holds up an overcome hand but I suspect she probably *does* want to divulge a lot more detail. Some people really fucking like to bathe in woe.

Maggie leads us up into the loft, and on the mad-o-meter, it rates somewhere between the chaos of LFW and the test shots. It's very New York, rusty steel girders holding up the glass ceiling. There are a *lot* of bodies in the loft, but it's a pretty chill vibe, Frank Ocean playing as they set up the backdrop. I see, with pure relief, that Layla Palmer is changing the camera lens.

'Hello, darlin'!' she says, coming over to greet us. Her braids are now silver, like Storm from *X-Men*. Hearing another South London accent is soothing. I feel less like an alien.

'Hey. I didn't know it was you!'

'Guilty.' She smiles broadly. 'What did I say, eh? I know a star when I see one.'

'First campaign,' I say quietly.

'First of many. I'm never wrong. Ask my girlfriend – I'm a cunt, but I'm a wise cunt.'

I grin as Maggie introduces Lien to Layla. I notice a none-too-subtle change in Lien's attitude. 'Hey!' she gushes. 'It's so good to meet you! I love your work!' Kiss-ass.

'Thanks, hon. Looking forward to today, it's gonna be fire, yeah.'

An assistant rounds Lien and me up and steers us towards hair and make-up. There's a small army of beauty people, already working on a pair of models. I sort of recognise both of them from magazines and posters, but don't *know* them. The first is a beardy, tattooed guy. He always looks like he's just stormed in from a Viking battlefield with intense, wolfish eyes.

'Matty, Astrid,' the assistant introduces us. 'This is Jana and Lien.'

Apparently Lien and Matty already know one another. 'Babes!' Matty springs out of his folding chair and embraces her. He's Scottish and his accent catches me off guard. 'I haven't seen you since the gala. How are you? Did you get into Brown?'

'Yeah, but I deferred. How's Guillermo?'

'Oh, you know Guillermo! He's good, on the yacht this week.' He turns to me. 'Hi, I'm Matty! Matthew MacDonald.' So much for wolf – he's more like a Labrador puppy.

'I'm Jana. I . . . I like your accent.'

'Glasgay, babes! I saw you scraping this wee hen off the catwalk!'

Even Lien manages a smile for the first time. 'God, don't remind me!' She seems to have loosened up a bit now. Thank fuck.

Astrid seems very sweet, chatting away in perfect English. She's from Norway and looks like she's come in straight from the fjords, all Daenerys hair and iceberg cheekbones.

The plan is to shoot individually and then do a group shot after lunch. There are stills and 'motion' to do. The hair and make-up people get to work on Lien and me, while Matty and Astrid go to work with Layla.

The brief is 'natural' so I'm done in what feels like minutes. They mess up my hair and put some shiny, oily stuff on my cheekbones to give them an almost metallic sheen. 'OK, baby, you're good for wardrobe.'

I spring off the chair and, distracted by the arrival of food, collide with a (very firm) chest. 'Ow! Sorry!'

'Hey, no stress.' His voice is a deep drawl and it sort of

booms through my bones. It's the most male voice I've ever heard. I look up. The face is as if Elvis and James Dean somehow had a baby. I can only name one male model, and it's Westley Bryce. It's rare I have to look upwards at anyone, but Westley makes me feel relatively short. 'Hi, I'm Westley.'

'I know,' I say before my twat-filter kicks in. 'I mean . . .'

'No sweat.' His very famous lips curl into a shy smile.

'I'm Jana.' I must look like a radioactive mutant next to him. He looks like a walking, talking Michelangelo sculpture. The light catches his face in all the right places, it's mathematical somehow – angles and vertices. All the sexy is in the eyes, though, something about the crease at the corners.

It's weird. A part of me thought people like Westley didn't really exist in real life; they're abstract, they exist only as an image or idea like God or Beyoncé. But here he is! And he's *real* – tall, sure, but pretty normal, really.

Mind. Actually. Blown. He's *gorgeous*, but also a mortal human male. It takes everything I've got to not reach out and touch him to check.

'It sure is nice to meet you, Jana. Cool accent. London?'

'Yeah.'

'I dig London so much, it's real swell.'

'Yeah. I love it.' What is wrong with my brain?

Westley must have crept in unannounced because the suits from TANK suddenly descend on us (well, him) fluttering, flapping and fawning. They coo at him like Furbies. I back away and he rolls his eyes at me. I smile, like I'm part of a private joke with him.

Once again, I haven't done a selfie. I'm a traitor to my whole fucking generation.

I do my shoot with Layla. I'm dressed in slouchy 'boyfriend' jeans and a skinny-fit white T-shirt. I'm the androgynous one, big surprise. I think I've got it figured out now: they just want me to look a bit drunk. I sort of half-close my eyes, let my mouth hang open like I'm catching flies and stand like I can barely keep myself upright. Everyone seems AMAZED by this. They do want you to move a *lot*, though. The idea that models stand around is bull. I'm knackered after twenty minutes – my calves burn from standing on tiptoes in bare feet and my back aches from overarching.

I take a break and pick at the buffet – BBQ chicken wings and salad – while they set up for the group shot. Another male model – Ziggy – with the most amazing Afro arrived just after me, so there are three boys and three girls. I'm gonna be pretending to be Matty's girlfriend which is pretty funny as anyone who has ever met him would know he's gay to the core of his DNA within a millisecond. If I have to cuddle up with a male model, I'm glad – for Ferd's sake – it's a gay one.

Just before we do the group shot, I see him and Lien emerge from the toilet, snuffling their noses like they have terrible hay fever. Oh. I wondered when drugs would pop up. I mean, it's a fashion cliché Ferdy and Sabah both warned me about, but I'm not sure I've ever seen people in real life do coke. Feels like something old, rich people do.

Matty was pretty extra before, but this is next level. He careers over to the food table and wraps his arms around my waist, lifting me clean off my feet. 'Are we ready, then? Look,

Jana is obviously my heterosexual girlfriend who I definitely enjoy putting my penis in every night.'

I laugh along, but I also want him to put me down. I guess he don't mean any harm. I scream as he carries me to set.

A camera runs around us on a little train track, capturing us from three hundred and sixty-five degrees. Ziggy, Astrid, me, Matty, Westley and Lien. The beautiful people all in a row. And I admit it, I wish Heather Daley could see me now.

And soon, I guess, she will.

BROOKLYN

The shoot all done, the suits from TANK have laid on a fancy dinner at Peter Luger in Williamsburg. I look at the menu and my eyes pop at the price of the steaks. Thankfully, it's not me paying. It all sounds so good and there's, like, twenty types of steak. I just thought it was 'cow meat' but apparently not. Chateaubriand, strip, porterhouse, ribeye . . . like, what do any of these words mean? Can't I just get 'beef'?

'Hey.' Lien leans in and whispers in my ear. 'Watch what you eat in front of Maggie.'

'Huh?'

'Trust and believe. You don't need the lecture. Order steamed fish.'

When the waitress comes, Matty and Lien order steamed fish and veg. Astrid orders a side salad to go on the side of her Diet Coke. Westley asks for a chicken burger without the bread. I guess I'm not having any species of steak, then. 'Erm. I'll have the same as her . . .' I nod at Lien.

On my left, Maggie gives my hand a pat. I think I made the right choice.

All through dinner, Maggie talks me up to various business people. I have no idea who they are. 'I'm telling you, our little

Jana is the real deal. I haven't been this excited since I clapped eyes on Clara. She's a star! A fucking star, I tell you.'

Luckily, Lien is outside having a cigarette with Matty and Astrid, or I can't imagine she'd have been thrilled at her agent saying that.

As the waitress clears our plates, I note Lien has hardly touched her fish and Astrid has pretty much just rearranged her salad. It's crazy but I feel sort of guilty for finishing my tiny piece of mahi mahi (nice, tastes like chicken) even though I was ravenous.

'Hey.' Westley returns from the 'restroom' and slides into Matty's vacant seat next to me. 'Not smoking?'

I have just shoved a huge mint in my mouth. It clatters against my teeth. 'Oh . . . I don't smoke.'

'A model who doesn't smoke? I thought I was the only one.'

I shrug. I don't really know what to say. *So, Westley, is it true about you and Dido Gant . . .?*

'How are you finding NYC?'

I dab my mouth with a napkin. 'Yeah.' *Answer his question, you fuckwit.* 'It's wicked. Well, I ain't really seen any of it yet. I'm going into Face First tomorrow so I'll see some of Manhattan then.'

'Need a tour guide?'

'You offering?' Random. Surely Westley Bryce has better things to be doing. Like . . . literally anything else.

'Sure! I pretty much live here now. I bought a little apartment in the East Village. I'm home for three whole days. Amazing, right?' Is it? Maybe it's because of the deep voice, or maybe it's because it feels like he's *been around* for ever, but I didn't realise how young he was. He's probably not that much older than me. 'There's New York ... all the tourist stuff ... and *real* New York. Don't get me wrong, the tourist stuff is cool, and you should do it all once, but I prefer real New York.'

'Are you from here?'

He smiles and it's almost stupidly gorgeous. I get a rush of blood to my head like I'm in a lift going up too fast. 'Aw, hell, no. I grew up in Nixa, Missouri.'

I nod like I know where that is. I wouldn't be able to point to it on a map. 'What's in Nixa?'

'A whole lot of nothing!' he says.

'Were you spotted there?'

'Naw, I was scouted walking through Miami airport coming back from vacation in St Barts.'

'Oh, wow.'

'Yeah, I was like fifteen, I think. God, yeah, five years ago. It sorta feels like I haven't been home since that day.' There's a bit of something sad in his voice. Maybe he's just tired; I know I am.

Matty, Astrid and Lien tumble in from outside, surfing a gust of chill wind. 'Guys!' Matty says, gleefully coked up. 'Astrid's boyfriend is in Hairpin 500!'

No way. Love them.

'Yes,' Astrid says. 'Jonny Elven is my boyfriend. We will go now to his loft if you want come party?'

'It's right around the block,' Lien adds.

Man, I'm so tired but Westley seems to light up. 'What do you think, Jana?'

'I was just gonna go to bed ...'

'I'll go if you go. We can always get you a car if you're beat.'
I wanna call Ferdy but realise it's already way past his bedtime.
I am tired, but I *am* in New York and might never be ever
again . . .

'C'mon . . .' Westley says. 'Loft party in Brooklyn . . . it
doesn't get much more Real New York than that.'

'Fuck it,' I say.

Outside the restaurant, a car pulls up for Maggie and
some of the TANK people. I slip a TANK denim jacket over
my shoulders – we all got goodie bags of clothes at the
shoot. Maggie gives me a hug. 'You take care, little one.
There's a car coming for you at nine . . . so don't party *too*
hard.'

'I won't, I promise.' She strokes the hair out of my eyes.

'I'll look after her, Mrs Rosenthal,' Westley says, flopping a
long arm over my shoulder.

'You do that. You're a good boy, Westley.' She squeezes his
chin-butt. 'Stick with him, Jana.'

'I will.'

The others are already halfway down the street so we have to
chase after them. 'I don't really drink liquor too much,' Westley
tells me. 'I always end up being the boring one who drives
everyone home.'

'Good friend to have,' I say as we catch the others.

'Westley?' Matty hollers down the road. 'Do you think
tonight is the night you'll go a wee bit bisexual?'

'You never know, my man,' he says with a broad grin.

'Och, you wanna watch him, Jana,' Matty says. 'He's a wee
tease, this one. Years he's led me on! Years!'

'Dude, you have a boyfriend!' Westley kicks him on the ass, prompting a chase around the block. I decide I like Brooklyn a lot. I think I could fit in here.

'Hey,' Lien says, pulling me behind the pack. 'I just wanted to apologise for being a total fucking bitch earlier at the apartment.'

I was not expecting that. 'It's OK,' I say. I was planning on keeping out of her way, but if she wants to smooth things over, I'm cool with that.

'Jet lag is a fucking killer. My doctor prescribed this melatonin stuff, but it does jack shit. Anyway, I owe you one for helping me in London.'

'No worries.'

She smiles. 'You're a down bitch, Jana. You remind me of me.'

'Really?'

'Like, when I was starting out and didn't know anything! No shade!' I don't *think* she's being a bitch, but it's hard to tell. 'All the other models were total bitches to me too. They all said I got a head start because of my mom. It's probably true, I don't know. But, anyway, I should know better. You know what it is, right?'

'What?'

'Every year there's a fresh batch of baby girls and you make us feel old!'

Dare I ask? No. 'You're not old.' Much safer.

'I'm twenty-two!'

I laugh so loud it echoes off the brownstones. 'That's so young!'

Lien pulls me closer. 'I'm actually twenty-four, but if you tell anyone that I'll kill you. Joking!'

I'm not fully sure she is.

The party has a pulse before we arrive. I feel the beat through my sneakers from around the corner. It really is a loft in an old warehouse and we have to ride a rickety old goods lift up to the penthouse. Ferdy loves Hairpin 500, he'll be so jel. They're a bit Diet Velvet Underground and I think they just won a Grammy or something. I had no idea Jonny − the singer − even had a girlfriend, but he's all over Astrid as soon as the lift arrives.

It looks like a party in a film. Not like at home, where 'a party' is me and my four friends hanging out in Robin's basement with a sad bowl of Doritos and whatever booze we can siphon out of our kitchens. Here, it's like a music video. There are maybe a hundred ridiculously beautiful people all dancing, waving those red plastic cups in the air. There's even some girl DJing. Why is there a mixing deck *in their flat*?

Westley recognises some guys he knows and goes to high-five them so I go with Lien and Matty to find a drink in the kitchen. As I walk through the doorway, some guy rubs up against me. 'Hey, baby,' he breathes beerily in my face. He's very skinny and wearing a top hat and no shirt. Like, why? I push past him and scowl. He smells like armpit.

'You want a beer?' Lien says, fishing a bottle out of the ice-filled sink.

'Sure.' I scan the kitchen and see it's that or tequila. Beer seems safer. I tell myself I'll just have a couple and then head home.

'Babes, have you got any more blow?' Matty asks.

'No, but we can score here, right?' Lien says. The drug chat makes me uncomfortable, so I slip away and leave them to it. I'll find Westley – at least he'll be sober.

As I weave through the crowd, people stare at me. I guess I look like a kid in an expensive jacket. I drink my beer and, weirdly, it reminds me how much I miss Ferdy – the taste of cider on his tongue when we kiss. It feels like a rubber band twanging in my tummy; homesickness, I guess.

Everyone seems so cool. They hang out in little groups, posing for selfies or making out on sofas. Some girl tattoos another girl with a buzzing needle which strikes me as a *really* bad idea. I don't see Westley anywhere. Suddenly the drunk guy in the top hat from the kitchen staggers into my direction. 'Hey, girl.'

I nod but don't catch his eye. He's gross and reeks of sweat and whiskey.

'You wanna dance, baby? I'm a real good dancer.'

He presses himself against my ass and grabs my hips. 'Get off!' I push him away.

'Whatever. Bitch. Dyke.'

I scowl at him and stride away. What a prolapse, honestly. I see an iron spiral staircase leading upwards somewhere so I go up it, for no particular reason other than I've never been up a spiral staircase before. The bass ain't punching my skull in quite so much up here. I peer down a corridor – looks like there's a bedroom and bathroom, but I hear some grunty, panty sex noises, so I avoid that direction.

At the other end of the corridor, a door flaps in the wind. I wonder if there's a terrace or balcony for a breath of fresh air. I stick my head out and see there's a fire escape leading on to the roof. Cool. This feels very Real New York so I head on up and find it deserted. There's a few sun loungers and a hot tub, but it's covered up tonight.

'Oh, wow.' *The* view. My eyes water.

How am I here? How is this real?

Very carefully, I sit on the edge of the roof, my legs dangling over the side. I take a picture on my phone, but it don't do it justice. Not one little bit.

'There you are.' Fuck. I shouldn't have come up here all by myself. I expect to see the drunk asshole in the top hat, but instead see Westley coming up the fire escape. I sigh and relax. 'What are you doing out here?'

I shrug. 'That's not really my jam.' I nod towards the party.

'Introvert?'

I wince. 'Dunno. *Everyone* always says they're an introvert even when they're being really extroverted, so . . . but, yeah, probably.'

'You're better with heights than I am.' He tentatively approaches the edge.

'I'll protect you,' I say with a smile.

'I'm supposed to be looking after you.'

It's sweet he went looking for me. 'What makes you think I need looking after?'

'You're a girl.'

'That's sexist!'

Clinging to the ledge for dear life, he steps over. 'It's fashion. It's bullshit for the girls sometimes.' He sits alongside me. 'Oh, god, that's high.'

'You don't like fashion?'

'Not really.'

'Then why . . .?'

He shrugs. 'It's OK for now. My mom always says I should be grateful for all the cool opportunities. She's probably right. But I figure some day soon I'll be done with the meat market.'

I finish my beer. 'The what?'

He grins. 'See that over there? Meatpacking district. We're the hired flesh. They ship us in, marinade us, fry us. And we just take it. In fact, I think they'd rather we were corpses some days; we'd be easier to manage.'

'That's not true. We have to *walk* too. And pout.'

There's a moment of peace. Sirens wail faraway in the distance. Our legs are pressed together and I wonder if I should remind him I'm not single, but then I remind myself that WESTLEY BRYCE probably ain't gonna waste his perfectly good sex on me. I actually laugh out loud.

'What?'

'Nothing,' I say. 'I mean. OK. Right. If *I* was Westley Bryce, I wouldn't be up here.'

His teeth are almost creepily white in the dark. 'What's that supposed to mean?'

'You're a superstar! Shouldn't you be . . . in the middle of an orgy or something?'

'Oh, my orgy is *tomorrow* night,' he says and I laugh. 'Is that what you think of me?'

I look at him, and moonlight hangs off his cheekbones just as much as daylight. 'I don't know what I think of you.'

He says nothing for a moment. He just looks at me and I can hardly stand the silence.

And then I hear footsteps clanging up the fire escape. 'Jana, babes?' It's Matty.

'We're up here!' I call back. I'm so glad he's here. I don't even know why. What *was* that, seriously?

He and Lien emerge on to the roof. 'Hiya! Oh, wow! Check out the view! Oh, shit, sorry, did you guys wanna be alone?' He makes an obscene gesture.

'No!' I shake my head and feel my cheeks burn. 'Matthew! I have a boyfriend back home.'

'Me too, babes,' Matty says. 'But what happens in New York, stays in New York. Guillermo is on a yacht right now with Brazilian twins called Javi and Ravi.'

'I'm more old-fashioned,' I say with a grin.

'Do you wanna come dance?' Lien says, attempting to twerk a non-existent butt.

I scrunch up my nose. 'I might head back to the apartment in a bit.'

'Me too!' she says. 'I have a casting for a Marc Jacobs perfume ad tomorrow . . . so why don't we dance until one and then I'll come with you?'

That don't sound so bad. 'OK!' I hop down off the wall.

'Wait,' Westley says. 'We should get a selfie "for social".' His voice is packed with sarcasm.

Lien and Matty groan. 'Come on, then,' Lien says. 'Let's get it over with.'

I suppose for people who get their picture taken as a day job, the pressure to do extra, unpaid, photos must be a little trying. Westley pulls me close and we all pack together, the Manhattan skyline behind us. 'Ready!' he says, stretching his phone out in front of us. Everyone else is pulling goofy faces, so I do the same.

'No way!' Lien screams. 'I look fucking hideous! Delete that immediately!'

'OK, one more!' Westley says.

He takes another and Matty almost tumbles over the side of the building. 'Matty!' I scream as Westley hauls him back.

'Fuuuuuck!' Matty says, clinging to Westley before howling with laughter. 'Shit! I almost fucking died!'

My heart settles and I throw my arms around him. I start to laugh and can't stop.

We all head downstairs to dance. We make our own little party of four and it ain't bad at all.

We dance.

And dance.

And dance some more.

Our Uber drops me and Lien back at the model apartment at a little after half-three.

REMITTANCE

When I saunter through customs back at Heathrow, I feel older.

Done it. Survived a trip to New York all by myself.

Mum and Dad wait nervously in Arrivals. I left JFK a little before midnight and somehow it's now an excruciatingly bright Saturday morning and I've lost a night in transit. Luckily Lien 'lent' me a sleeping pill so I've had a deep, black sleep on the flight home. Got a wicked crick in my neck now. Them neck pillow things are shit.

'There she is!' Dad says, rushing forward to greet me outside the Costa booth.

Mum has aged about twelve years in five days. 'Oh, Jana!' She throws her arms around me.

'Oh my god! I've only been gone five days! And I spoke to you last night!'

'My baby is so grown up!' She smiles. 'It makes me feel old.'

'Where's the car?' I ask, eager to get going. I think I'm still drowsy from Lien's pill. I should not operate heavy machinery.

'Wait! Have you eaten?' Mum says. 'Do you want breakfast?'

I guess nothing changed while I was away, then. 'I ate on the plane.'

I would love to sleep in the car, but Mum and Dad pelt a million questions at me as we pull on to the M25:

How did the shoot go?

Who did you meet?

Was everyone nice?

What was the flat like?

How were the castings?

I'm too tired to go into much detail. The rest of the trip was fine. I met with my New York agency, Face First, and they seem nice, but pushier than the gang at Prestige. They took their own 'Polaroids' and I had dinner with Maggie and Trent, my US agent, in Chinatown that night.

Trent didn't stop name-dropping for a single second. Exhausting. 'We've got to get you in front of some photographers,' Trent explained, brandishing chopsticks. 'Meisel, Knight, Liebovitz, Walker, Blo. We need to fill your book ASAP.'

On the Friday, I had 'go-sees' at Coda, DKNY, Fyona Tricks and Proenza Schouler. They seemed to go OK. It was not like *Top Model* and I was not disqualified for being late. They were for next year's summer campaigns. Maggie seemed excited because they're all big-money gigs.

The only bummer was that I couldn't see Westley again. He texted yesterday morning (god, was it only yesterday?) to ask if I wanted to see a gig in Brooklyn, but I had to tell him I'd have to get to the airport pretty much in the middle of the concert. I was surprised to hear from him. Like, he knows I'm with Ferdy and I'm not getting a c'mon-sexy-sex vibe from him, more big-brothery, if anything. It's sweet that I even entered his head.

'Maggie seemed pleased,' I tell Mum from the back seat.

'Good.'

'She even said it might be an idea to live in New York for a while.'

Mum's eyes almost pop out of her skull. 'What?'

'I'd get a lot more work and make more money. That's what she said.'

'No! No way! What about school?'

I rest my face into my travel pillow. 'Relax, Mother! I meant after exams.' But I dunno. What about Ferdy and stuff? I wonder how Ferdy would feel about maybe studying in New York. They have loads of colleges – Columbia, NYU – and I'm sure they all do film studies. I'm sold. I was only there for four days and I heart NY.

Mum glares at Dad. 'We'll talk about it next year.' Dad is a fan of shutting down conversations he don't like.

I feel grotsky – like my true essence is still somewhere over the Atlantic – for all of Saturday, so have a bath and head to bed right after *Strictly*. Feeling a million times better, I wake up to about six thousand WhatsApp notifications and I arrange to see everyone later that morning. I'm properly gagging to see them; it feels like I've been away a month, not a week. It's a bit weird. It's bugging me like a hair on my tongue. Like, what have I missed? It's making me paranoid. I don't want my friends to forget I exist. A week's a long time at school. Epic love affairs can start and end between Friday night and Monday morning.

Ferdy has a shift at the coffee shop so I head there. It feels properly wintery for the first time, and I wrap myself in the chunky-knit TANK scarf they gave me and – I think she'll love this – I take one of the sweaters in a gift bag for Laurel's birthday.

Lien told me that she makes a tidy profit from selling on 'gifted' clothes and not to be surprised if some brands try to 'pay me' with clothes knowing full well this is how models make a lot of their money. I suppose a Gucci dress is like ten, twenty grand, so it does sort of make sense.

I walk down the high street, almost skipping like a Disney princess. The air is fresh and crisp, and there are gold autumn leaves on the ground. New York was fit, but there are no place like home. And at home, I get to see Ferd. I swish into the coffee shop and the others are already there.

'You fucking bitch!' Sabah shrieks. Not the reception I was expecting. She barrels towards me, and some yummy mummies tut at her language. Little Hugo and Florence can fuck off back to Clapham. She thrusts her phone under my nose. 'Jana Novak, what the hell is this?'

I see it's Westley's Insta. He's posted the pic of us from the other night: me, him, Matty and Lien on the roof terrace. I grin at her. 'That's some of the other models,' I say, real coy.

'You running a scam, bitch?! That's WESTLEY MOTHERFUCKING BRYCE!'

'He's all right.'

Sabah drags me back to the table. 'Tell me everything. What does he smell of? What aftershave does he wear? I want to smell of him!'

'Oh my god! Give me a minute!'

Ferdy comes out from behind the counter. 'Welcome home. Guess what?'

'What?'

'I love you.'

I almost melt all over him. I nestle into his neck and take a big, deep breath of his shampoo. 'Missed you.'

'Really?'

'Yes, really. It would have been double fun if you'd been there. I'm taking you there, no argument.' I release him before Big Angie, his boss, catches him hugging a customer. I turn to Laurel before I'm punished for not acknowledging her birthday. 'And here's the birthday girl!'

'You remembered!' Her face lights up as she clocks the gift bag. If nothing else, Laurel is super predictable.

'Of course I did! How was the party?'

'Oh, it was fine. My mum got really drunk and my dad sulked. Standard.'

I take a seat and give Robin a hug at the same time. 'Here, I got you this.' I slide the gift bag to her over the table.

'What is it?'

'Only one way to find out . . .'

She reaches in and pulls out the rose-pink mohair sweater, 'TANK' in clashing acid-green text across its front. 'Oh my god! Jana!'

I beam. Her face is worth the trip alone. 'Like it?'

Sabah's mouth hangs open. 'No way . . .'

'Are you kidding? Jana, I LOVE it! Are you sure? This is too much! These are like five hundred quid!'

'We were given them. I'm giving you a freebie, don't sweat it.'

Laurel throws herself over the table, almost knocking her

latte on the floor. She pulls me into a tight hug. 'Thank you so much.'

'Happy birthday.'

I think I've just earned *major* points.

I don't even think about Westley's photo until I get to school on Monday. I must admit, going back to lessons after four days in New York is a bit of an anticlimax. First period is sociology and I've missed *so* much even though I only skipped two sessions. Ferdy made notes, but I can't follow what Mr Ellis is trying to teach us about Marxism at all. Everyone is talking about it like they know exactly what it is, and I don't wanna look like a dick. Everyone is like, 'Ha ha, that's so Marxist!' and I'm like, 'Ha ha, yeah?'

At break, all anyone wants to know about is Westley's selfie. I've never been so popular my whole life. It's weird. I suppose any lingering doubters *have* to believe that I'm a model now that I'm standing next to one. People I've never met crowd around our table at the cafeteria.

'Hi, I'm Phoebe,' one girl says. 'Do you think I could be a model? Like, I'm tall enough, right?'

She is tall. I shrug. 'I dunno, I think you can just send your picture to my agency . . .?'

'Do you think you'll see Westley again?' Laurel says.

I look to my right, to Ferdy. To his credit, he don't seem especially bothered by the Westley frenzy. 'I don't know. Maybe.'

'OMG – you *have* to introduce me.' Laurel looks like the heart-eyes emoji. 'Imagine if I was Westley's girlfriend.'

'What about *Harry*?' Robin asks with venom.

'He's too old for you,' I tell her.

'I read somewhere he's gay,' Sabah adds.

'I don't *think* he's gay. Matty MacDonald is, though.'

'The beardy one? Oh, wow.'

'It ain't a big secret or nothing.'

'Nor should it be,' Sabah adds.

At some point, Heather, Emily and Lily have joined the hive. 'So,' Heather says, reaching over and taking my hand, 'does that mean you have Westley Bryce's number in your phone?'

'Erm . . . yeah.'

'OMG, can I have it?'

Fuck that. 'I . . . I . . . no.'

'Why not?'

I look to Sabah who looks hugely amused by the whole exchange. 'Because why the hell would she?' she says, and I've never loved her more.

'Fuck off, Sabah, you bitch, who's asking you? Go on, Jana. I won't say you gave it to me.'

'Heather, I think that'd be, like, majorly unprofessional. Just . . . send him a message on Twitter.'

Heather scowls at Emily. 'I told you she'd be a stingy bitch about it.'

'Heather, I'm not . . . you know what? I'm not doing this. I'm out.'

Lily pouts. 'You ain't all that, babes, don't be acting like you're better than us.'

I decide to say nothing, because what's the point?

'Come on,' Ferdy says, 'I'll walk you to French.'

He takes my hand and, like a security guard, sort of clears a path through the cafeteria.

Emily cackles. 'Well, I guess he *must* be gay if he don't mind that she shagged Westley Bryce.' Heather and Lily fake-howl and a couple of others giggle too.

'Ignore them,' I mutter.

'I don't hear them,' he replies. 'They are noise I learned to filter in Year Two.'

'You know what you are?' Sabah says for everyone to hear. 'Jealous. Ooh, that jealousy is *real*.'

'I'm not jealous of *that thing*.'

'Sure, hon. This tea is scalding. Laurel, you coming?'

Laurel quickly gathers her things together and we flee the canteen. I feel my cheeks blush. Wow, I thought for about half a minute something might have changed. But I'm not gonna let Heather and her minions spoil New York. No way. Those memories are mine, and they can't have them.

'Jana!' Mum calls up the stairs. 'There is letter for you.'

Weird. I never get stuff unless it's my birthday – which it isn't until January. I am fully Capricorn. Early Christmas card, perhaps.

I trot downstairs and Mum hands me the envelope. 'What do you want for breakfast? Bacon and eggs?' It's a Saturday and I've slept in well past ten.

I push my moppy hair off my face. It's so greasy I can make it into a mohawk. 'Just eggs, please.' Sabah is always banging on about eggs and avocado. Is that something I should be into? I sit down at the table and open the letter. It's not a card. I peel the envelope open and see it's from Prestige. Maybe they've wised up and they're killing my contract.

'REMITTANCE ADVICE', it says at the top in capitals. 'The following will be transferred by BACS payment in the next three working days.'

And then there's a figure in a little box.

'Holy fuck!' I cry.

'Jana!' Mum actually clips me around the back of the head.

'Ow! Sorry, but look!' I thrust the letter under her nose.

'Oh my Jesus! Is that what they pay you?'

'Yeah . . . I think so.' Most of it's for the TANK campaign, but also the two shows I walked at LFW.

'Jana. This is a lot of money . . . Zoran! Zoran, come here!'

Dad trundles down the garden path from his shed. 'What's wrong?'

'Nothing! Nothing is wrong. Jana, show . . . show.'

I show my dad the statement. 'Gosh. Well . . . that's brilliant. It goes straight into your savings, yes?'

'Sure!' I grin. But also I'm planning what very expensive gift I can get Ferdy for Christmas.

My phone starts to vibrate on the kitchen table and I see Ro is calling. I snatch it up. 'Hi, Ro!'

'Hello, my little Jana, how are you?'

'Good! Great! I just got my first payment!'

'Well done, you! Don't spend it all at once!'

'I won't!' I couldn't. I wouldn't know where to begin.

'You'll like this, then. I had a very exciting email from New York overnight.'

'Yeah?'

'Jana, you star, you only went and booked the Coda summer campaign!'

'What? No way.' I didn't think that casting had gone too well. Coda is very mainstream, high-street realness and I'm . . . not.

'Oh, it gets better. Three-day shoot in Dubai in January!'

Bummer. 'I dunno if they'll let me have the time off college again . . .'

'Jana, it's forty grand.'

'FORTY GRAND?'

That gets Mum and Dad's attention. They crowd around me, trying to listen in. 'They're a massive global brand, sweetie. You'll get a buy-out for every territory they use it in too – you'll be looking at a lot more than that in the end. Anyway, enjoy your weekend, I just wanted to let you know the good news!'

She hangs up and I look at Mum. 'I got the Coda campaign. Forty grand.'

Mum's mouth falls open. She knows Coda. Of course she does. Everyone knows Coda. There's a Coda on every high street. Sometimes two. 'Gosh. That is big.'

'Is Coda the one on St John Street?' Dad asks.

'Yeah. Next to TK Maxx.'

He purses his lips slightly. His unimpressed face. 'Cheap tat.'

'Who cares?' I say, throwing my hands up. 'Forty thousand pounds!' It's more money than I could ever imagine. Dad just shrugs.

Christmas has come a little early.

We ain't poor any more. In fact, I'm rich.

*   *   *

Shepherd's Bush is four stops from Clapham Junction on the overground. Me and Sabah skive off college the last Wednesday before Christmas because we think it might be quieter. It ain't. It really ain't. It's *frenzied*. I think panic is setting in and people are looking well frayed, rolls of wrapping paper sticking up out of shopping bags.

'We gotta get gingerbread lattes!' Sabah says as we glide up the escalator into the Designer Village part of Westfield.

'Yes, queen. The eggnog ones taste like cat sick.'

We step into the mall by Louis Vuitton. I have never, ever been into this part of Westfield before – we normally skip it and go in by Topshop further down. I stop dead by the champagne bar. Prada, Burberry, Tiffany's, TANK and Gucci loom over me. 'Not sure I can do this, Sabs.'

She hooks her arm through mine. 'Bitch, of course you can. You know what you want, right?'

I nod and she steers me towards Mulberry. 'Yeah, Mum once slated a friend for spending so much money on a bag, so I figure she must have secretly been jealous.'

'Totally! It's here, look. Just act like you belong.'

I'm wearing double denim and a bobble hat. I do not look like I belong. Sabah practically drags me over the threshold into the store. 'Right. Which one is it?'

Immaculate shelves glow, each of the handbags like a precious relic in a temple. They all look alike. 'I'm not . . . sure . . .'

A man with a mahogany tan and a rod up his ass steps out from behind the counter. 'Hello, girls, can we help you?'

Sabah looks him up and down. 'Yes, boy, you can. She'd like a Seaton for her mum, please.'

His lips purse and he lifts a jade green bag off a stand. 'Are you sure? Honey, a Seaton is one thousand three hundred and fifty pounds.'

I step forward and pluck the bag out of his hands. I look him dead in the eye.

'I'll take two.'

– Would you say it was a Cinderella story?

– No.

– Could you try to repeat my question in your answer so we can edit me out?

– Oh, OK. Would I say it was a Cinderella story? Erm. I can see why people would think that. It looks like one. I guess Maggie was like a fairy godmother.

– Because she made your dreams come true?

– I dunno if they were *my* dreams. I knew it was what I was *supposed* to want. We all want to be rich and famous, right? Rich and famous *for nothing*. We want diamond watches and gold teeth and hotel rooms with flamingos in. Just . . . fucking money. And I got that.

– But you didn't want it?

– Not really, to be honest. I wanted . . . I wanted to . . . *like* myself . . .

– Actually, no. Cut that bit out. I'm grateful, I really am. It made things easier, for my family. I'm glad we were poor, in a way, because it meant we appreciated the money when we got it.

– But . . . ?

- It wasn't a rags-to-riches story is my point. More . . . reality to fantasy. And . . .
- And what?
- The magic only lasts until midnight.

CHRISTMAS

So full of food, I make my way to Robin's house on the evening of Christmas Day. It's bitterly, bitterly cold – it feels like my breath is freezing in my windpipe. Robin only lives the other side of Falcon Road, just past the mosque, and I'm feeding the cat while his family are at his grandmother's in Dartford.

As I pass each terraced house, it's like looking into different advent calendar windows. It's pitch black outside so I can see through the windows. One bunch are opening presents around the tree – perhaps a family ritual to leave them this late in the day; a family having a screaming row; a girl trying to snatch a remote control out of some guy's hand; some grandparents hugging their grandkids goodbye before getting in the car. Of course, evening prayers at the mosque don't stop for Christmas, and the men file in.

Our Christmas was low key. We slept late while Mum cooked; we opened presents; we ate a sort of mash-up of a Serbian and English Christmas dinner – roast pork and *esnica*; we watched *Frozen* and *Brave*.

This year, though, I was able to buy everyone decent gifts. As well as Mum's Mulberry, Dad got a new folding bike to get to work on and Milos got a satsuma. Well, that's what I gave him for about an hour until I relented and showed him where I'd hidden the Ted Baker coat. I swear he actually almost cried, the spoiled little shit.

Of course, Mum told me off for spending so much, but what's the point in having money if I can't buy nice stuff for the people I love?

And now it's Ferdy's turn. I promised I'd rescue him from his family Christmas and he said that was the only present he wanted, but I bought him something he can unwrap too.

He's already waiting at Robin's back door when I arrive, hands shoved in pockets. 'God, how long have you been out here?'

'About half an hour.'

'Jesus, Ferd, why didn't you call? I'd have come sooner.'

'Nah, it's cool. Dad passed out about an hour ago, so I slipped out before he could wake up and start picking at my hair again.'

I let us into the kitchen. 'That bad?'

'We've had worse. My Auntie Maria is here this year, so he mostly did the perfect husband bit. It's pretty creepy.'

'Well, let's get you warmed up.' His poor lips have a definite blue vibe to them. 'Shall I put the kettle on? We could have hot chocolate?'

'Sounds good. We going downstairs?'

'Yeah, I promised Robin we wouldn't shag in his bed.'

'Fair.'

I feed Samson and give him a cuddle before I carry the hot chocolates down to Robin's man cave. It honks of trainers and weed. How his parents don't know he smokes pot pretty much constantly is a mystery. Samson weaves between my legs, following me downstairs.

Ferdy is already playing Mario Kart. 'I feel more human already,' he says as I plonk a hot chocolate in front of him.

'Good,' I say. 'Merry Christmas.'

He pauses the game and turns to kiss me gently on the mouth. 'Merry Christmas. Thank you for rescuing me. I love you.'

'I love you too. So I got you something.'

He tilts his head. 'Jana, I thought we said . . .'

'I know, but that's what we said last year and then you got me Kate Bush on vinyl . . .'

He grins. 'And I did it again this year too!' He reaches into his bag and produces a gift box.

'You bastard!' I laugh, kissing him again. 'This year I'm ready for you!' I pull out Ferdy's present. God, I hope he likes it. 'You go first.'

He, like a boy, rips open the paper, tearing off the ribbon I spent ages doing. He freezes. 'Oh, Jana. You didn't . . .'

'I fucking did.' He ain't hinted at all, but I've seen him poring over the new Canon video camera online at school when we're meant to be doing homework and stuff. 'Is it the right one?'

'Jana . . . it's *exactly* the right one. I've been saving up my wages for months . . .'

'Well, now you don't have to!'

His eyes dip. He's about to say something but stops.

'What?'

'Nothing.'

'Ferd . . . ?'

'No, no, Jana, it's amazing. Thank you so much. But it's too much. My present cost, like . . . a fraction of this. Like, I can't even do the maths.'

Now I frown. 'It's not about cost. I got it because I knew it's what you wanted more than anything.'

He strokes my hair off my face. 'That's not strictly true, is it?'

I blush. 'Correct response, well done. So . . . do I get mine?'

'Yeah, although it's not quite on this scale.'

He hands me a little box and I carefully open it. It's jewellery, I can tell already. Inside the box is a teeny, tiny little J on an almost invisible chain. 'Oh, Ferdy – so cute! I love it.'

'I thought you could still wear it on castings and stuff without getting in trouble.'

It's very me. I hate feeling weighed down by jewellery. 'I really love it.' I put it on and press it against my collar like I'm pressing *him* into my heart. I give him another kiss. Then he hands me an envelope.

'What's this? There's more?'

'Yep!' He grins. 'I got you an all-you-can-eat international data bundle for your phone. You just need to activate it.'

I laugh loudly, almost falling backwards off the futon. I still haven't dared tell Mum about the hundred-and-five-pound bill I ran up in New York. Who knew Google Maps wasn't free? 'Amazing! You're amazing!'

We kiss again. 'And thank you for spending Christmas night with me. This is better than the camera. Honestly.'

'Liar.'

He grins. 'OK, *almost* as good as the camera.'

We have sex on Robin's sofa bed and Ferdy comes inside me. Neither of us mentions it; it don't need mentioning. We both know. Satisfied, we fall asleep all tangled up like headphone cables and I'm too happy to care that Mum will probably kill me in the morning.

Westley: jana its Westley . . . just saw the
tank campaign!!! u look AMAZING!

> **Jana**: Oh wow! Thanks!

> **Jana**: And Happy New Year x

Westley: hny from Hawaii xxx

Westley: hope ur goof

Westley: good

BILLBOARD

When Westley texts, I'm still in bed, on school-holiday body clock, but call Maggie immediately. 'Hi, Maggie, it's Jana.'

'Oh, hello, little one, happy new year! Are you all right?'

'I'm fine. I just wondered if you'd seen the TANK campaign? Westley messaged me.'

'Busted, darling, I have and you will SHIT YOURSELF when you see it. Are you sitting down?'

'I'm in bed.'

'Even better. I didn't email over the JPEG because, and you'll never believe this, the campaign is launching at Piccadilly Circus next Monday.'

'What?' No way. That's *insane*.

'Yep, you heard right. They're reopening the flagship store on Regent Street, so want to make a big splash. With *your* face all over it.'

I'm gonna need a minute. How can everything be happening so fast? I cling to the rim of my mattress.

'There's another thing, Jana, while I've got you.'

'Yeah?'

'How would you feel about me taking over your bookings? I know Ro does New Faces, and Cheska does Women, but with the big names, I oversee everything. I do Clara, I do Lexx. I think

– with the splash you've made – I should be steering you too, sweetheart. It's that time again, darling – almost Fashion Week – and there is so much buzz around you. Every year, one or two new girls – tops – go supernova. It's critical we get this right.'

I feel bad for Ro, but it's hard not to be flattered. 'Erm, OK, sure.'

'Marvellous. Now why don't we arrange to meet at Piccadilly next Monday morning to see your first campaign?'

That Monday is the first day back at college, but Sabah thinks that seeing my face as big as a building is more important than double French. We get the Bakerloo line from Waterloo and I swear she's vibrating with excitement. 'Honestly, Jana, how can you be so chill about this?' she asks as we pull into Embankment station and a load of tourists board our carriage.

'I dunno. It's weird.'

'Weird and COOL. God, I'm so jealous.'

I frown. 'Are you, though?'

'What?'

'Jealous?' I don't want my friends to be jealous of me. I don't want to be *above* my best friend at all. 'Seriously?'

Sabah takes my hand. 'You know what, babe, I think I *was* a bit jealous to begin with. Is that possible? To have two opposite but balanced feelings at the same time? I was as made up as I was jealous. Bitch, I'm a Libra.'

'But why?'

'Because you met Westley Bryce and Clara Keys! You went to New York! Next week you're in Dubai! Here we are stuck on an estate in Battersea!'

173

I quite like real life. I wonder if 'we' is her and Laurel? I've haven't seen Laurel all Christmas and I get the impression she's mad at me, as much as she denies it, and I don't even know what for.

I must look sad because Sabah continues: 'But then I chilled the fuck out. Jana, I'm so excited that I get to be here waiting for you when you get home. Just don't forget me.'

'I wouldn't *ever*.'

'And I know you're going to be super fucking busy and that's fine too. But I have one hundred per cent got your back.'

I love Sabah so much. You know, I can't even remember how we met, but we was in the same reception class and she's been there ever since. 'Thank you. I love you. And I need you. All these people are pure mental, Sabs. If I don't have you lot around, I'll go mad too.'

'Oh, I'll keep your feet on the floor, don't you worry.' We hug awkwardly, side by side on the Tube seat. 'And, from a very selfish point of view,' she says, 'if you get famous, you better plug my socials!'

I laugh. 'Well, duh.'

As the train pulls into Oxford Circus, we realise we missed our stop.

Rather than get back on a train in the opposite direction, we walk down Regent Street towards Piccadilly. We pass Burberry and see giant versions of Clara and Westley bounding towards us, their trenchcoats billowing in the latest ad campaign. Sabah stops to swoon.

There's a close-up of his face. He's smiling and I feel . . . a funny feeling, a glow in my tummy. That night in Brooklyn was . . . something special. But not like *that*.

I shake it off. 'Come on, we'll be late to meet Maggie. She's scary.'

Maggie is already waiting for us by the statue of Eros. She's wrapped in a blanket – it's far too big to class as a pashmina – and a furry hat. She's clutching a ginormous Starbucks. 'Hello, darling!' she cries, waving me over.

'Hi, this is my best friend, Sabah.'

'Hello, Sabah, darling. Isn't this just marvellous?'

'I'm, like, ten times more excited than Jana, I think!'

'You just missed it! It's on rotation, it'll be back around in a minute.' I look up at the giant billboard, currently carrying an ad for the new iPhone. 'Do you know this isn't actually Eros, it's his brother Anteros?' Maggie points up at the winged statue behind us, but I'm too nervous to listen.

Like, what if I look ugly?

'Oooh, here we go!' Maggie grabs my shoulders so I can't escape.

THE NEW JEANS, the display reads. First up is Westley (COWBOY); then Astrid in her miniskirt (MOD); Matty is PUNK.

And then I gasp.

It's me.

SKATER.

Thought process goes something like this.

1. I don't look like me.

2. I look really cool.

3. Is that my nipples?

4. Yes, that's definitely my nipples.

5. Why the fuck didn't anyone tell me the T-shirt was see-through?

'Oh my god!' Sabah shrieks, snapping me back into reality as Lien replaces me. 'Jana, you look sick! That is so sick!'

'Darling, I am speechless. Me! Speechless!'

I shield my eyes with my hand. 'Is . . . can you see my nipples?'

'Oh, maybe a little bit, darling, but nipples are very in right now.'

Ziggy vanishes and the billboard displays all of us standing in a row. THE NEW JEANS – EXCLUSIVELY AT TANK, LONDON REGENT STREET.

I mean, we all look great and very serious in black and white, but I know *exactly* what Milos will say and that's that I am 'smuggling peanuts'. Mum is gonna kill me. What? They couldn't have airbrushed them out?

'Oh, don't be worried, darling! It's your body! Your *gorgeous* body! Matty has his top off entirely, doesn't he? Gender balance and all that! Free the nipple!'

I smile meekly, already worried what Mum will say.

Fuck. I mean, I look AMAZING. If it was someone else's tits, I'd love it. But they're mine. Oh, well. At least they look good, I guess.

'Come on, darling, I said we'd pop into the store and say hello and take some pics for social. The window display should be up later today too!'

'Really?' Sabah is still so excited. The pair of them start to drag me back towards Regent Street.

I throw a look over my shoulder and there I am again: a giant – a giant with erect nipples – staring down at me. I wouldn't recognise myself.

*　　*　　*

The next day, I enter the common room during a study period. I said I'd meet Ferdy here. The room, which is all steamed up in the wet weather, stinks like damp compost and BO. It's gross. That might explain why it's more or less empty.

'Hi, Jana,' says some girl I swear I've never met. She's at the water fountain filling her bottle up.

'Hey,' I reply as she exits past me.

It's after morning break so there are crisps trodden into the carpets and the bin is overflowing with coffee cups and banana skins. Hanging out of the trash is a copy of this morning's *Metro*.

Of course, I recognise the advert right away.

It's the TANK ad, a full-page spread. Wow, that didn't take long.

As well as a moustache and a pair of glasses, someone has helpfully drawn a bra over my nipples with a biro.

Bit late for that, ain't it?

God knows where Ferd is so I head to the girls' toilet ahead of French next lesson. I'm mid-wee when I hear the door swing open and some familiar voices fill the room. The first is Emily: 'Like, I get that that's what models are supposed to look like, but I don't get it.'

'Totally!' That's Lily. 'Like, she is flat as a pancake.' Oh, I wonder who they're talking about? I sit very, very still on the loo.

'Boys don't fancy girls like that.' And, of course, there's Heather. 'Boys like curves. Like, literally, if a genie said would you rather look like you or Jana Novak, I'd stay like me.' They all mutter in agreement. I hear them rummaging in their make-up bags at the sinks.

177

'She's totally anorexic,' Lily says. 'Like, does she eat anything?'

'Well, she used to.' Oh. A voice I wasn't expecting. Laurel's. 'She might not now.'

'Maybe she's bulimic, then?' Heather adds.

'Maybe,' Laurel says. 'Like, I don't check on her after she eats. Why would I?'

Tears sting my eyes. *Laurel?* I know she's been hanging out with Harry . . . but Heather too? Something bubbles up inside me. Not sadness, but something red hot. That snakey fucking bitch. I button up my jeans and, with fire raging in my blood, step out of the toilet stall.

At least Laurel has the grace to look *mortified*. Even Heather freezes for a second before smirking. 'Awks,' she says.

'Jana . . .' Laurel begins.

'Save it. You know what? I don't care what any of you think. You're just *jealous*.'

That last word is a giant flat palm that sweeps through the bathroom, slapping each of them on their overly contoured cheeks. 'Jealous?' says Heather. 'Of you? Sure, babes.'

'Did I miss your billboard in Piccadilly Circus?' Lily's about to say something bitchy, but I steamroll over her. 'No, because you're ugly.'

All of their faces fall, and I can't lie. It feels delish.

'It's like Roald Dahl said: if you have happy, nice thoughts, they'll shine out of your face. And if you don't . . . well, maybe that's why you're such a bunch of rancid cunts.'

I smile sweetly and swish out of the toilets.

Wow, I don't know where that came from – and I'm sure I'll pay down the line – but that was pretty epic.

Laurel comes running out of the toilets, chasing me down the corridor. 'Jana! Wait! I'm super, super sorry! You weren't meant to hear that!'

I huff. 'Well, obviously not.'

'Look . . .'

I wait. 'Look, what?'

'I'm going out with Harry now and . . .'

'And so you're one of Heather Daley's little bitches?'

'No! It's not like that!'

'Funny, because you were pretty happy telling them I'm bulimic, apparently.'

'I just . . . look, you're never here and when you are, you're with Ferdy! And . . .'

I shake my head. 'Pick one, Laurel. Me or Heather. Choose. I'll leave it with you.'

I walk away, utilising everything I now know about walking. Somehow, I already know she'll choose Heather.

SEVENTEEN

'I'm afraid it's a no, Jana.'

'Huh?'

Mr Bennett glowers at me. 'I said no. I won't authorise the absence.'

I blink, trying to process the information. 'But I *have* to go.'

He sits back down at his desk. 'Do you? It seems to me you have a choice. Your A-level courses are full-time, you knew this when you enrolled. It seems your work as a model is also full-time, if chaotic. You might have to make a choice, Jana.'

Oh, god.

I need a Time-Turner.

Mum is gonna kill me. She's still pretty pissed off about the nipples.

'I can do both, I swear! A lot of the time I'm sitting around . . . I could work while I get my make-up done and stuff,' I plead.

He smiles. 'Jana, I can't ask my teaching staff to use their free time prepping materials for students who are out of school. I just can't. If that's the way you want to work it, I can recommend some online home-schooling courses.'

I shake my head. 'But . . . I don't want to leave college.' True fact.

'Then don't. I don't want you to leave either, but I won't be authorising any more absences. If you choose to go on work trips, your parents may face legal action.'

Man, this sucks.

I'm fucked.

After English, I relay the meeting to Sabah, Ferdy and Robin in the common room.

'Wow,' Sabah says. 'Harsh.'

'What am I gonna do?'

Ferdy gives my hand a gentle squeeze. Today is the worst. I've also just discovered that what I thought was a satsuma in my lunchbox is actually a clementine. Vile.

'You have to go!' Robin throws his hands up. 'It's forty grand. FORTY GRAND. That's almost enough to stick a deposit down on a flat or something, Jana. A HOUSE.'

He's right. I wonder if, in my head, that's the exact amount of money you can't walk away from: house money. 'I know.' It comes out very quiet.

'You'll quit college?' Sabah's eyes pop. Ferdy gives my hand another squeeze.

'Maybe for now.' Well, that's a lie. Even I'm not that deluded. It means for ever. I know I'm not coming back here once my friends have moved on. I'd rather die. No. Modelling was not THE PLAN, but the thing is, there was *never* a plan. Like, I don't even know what I was heading for. I changed my mind every single day. I suppose this has . . . made my mind up for me.

'You'll quit school before I do?' Robin says. 'Wow. Didn't see that coming.'

'And to be a full-time model! Who knew?' There's a stodgy silence. None of them will look me or my great big mistake in the eye. 'You all think I'm dumb, right? Giving up an education to do something really shallow.'

They all protest. 'I don't think you're dumb,' Ferdy says softly.

'Fashion is *not* shallow!' Sabah prods my arm.

'Ow! Sabs, c'mon . . .'

'Fashion *is* important and you are speaking from some white privilege there, girl.' She points at her jade-green headscarf. 'Like, why do you think I run my Insta? This says so much to so many people. I don't *have* to wear this. My sister don't wear one. I choose to wear this because I know what people think when they see it. *Ah, she's a terrorist, Bride of Isis, poor little repressed Muslim girl.* Fuck that shit. I wear this because I want to, and because it's beautiful.'

I look to Ferdy and Robin for about a second before we burst into applause. 'OK! I'm sorry!' I say.

'Where did that come from?' Robin laughs.

'The children gotta learn.'

'Consider me taught. Fashion is not shallow. Anyway, this ain't a job I can do after uni. It's depressing but I'll be too old.'

'Speaking of which,' Ferdy says, 'what are we doing for your birthday?'

I love him for changing the subject. 'I dunno. Pizza?'

'I support pizza,' Sabah says and discussion switches to where in Battersea does the best pizza.

But I got a bigger decision to make. Am I really gonna do this?

*　　*　　*

There's a spare seat at the table in Il Molino, like one of us has fallen in battle. I did invite Laurel; she didn't even reply. She chose, then. I suppose I *did* call her a rancid cunt.

I want to treat my friends for my own birthday. It sounds the wrong way round, but they don't have much money and I do, so buying them pizza makes me happy. Now we can all enjoy a night at Il Molino without them having to watch what they're ordering.

'It's weird,' I say, motioning at the empty seat. 'Maybe I shouldn't have said what I said.'

'She called you bulimic,' Sabah grimaces. 'If she wants to hang out with Heather, Emily and Lily, she is dead to me. Cancelled. In the sea. And, anyway, a friend who can't handle another friend's success ain't even a friend.'

Still sucks. 'We've been friends since Year Six.'

Robin says nothing; not like him at all. I wonder if he really fancied Laurel or if he fancied the *idea* of Laurel.

'We're not eleven any more,' Ferdy says.

'Well spotted,' I say, confused.

He sips his beer. 'What I mean is, we're not the same people we were in Year Six. Laurel is becoming who she's going to be. We all are.'

'And Laurel's becoming a full twat,' Sabah says.

'Do you have Tourettes?' I ask.

'Fuck, man, that's deep,' Robin says.

'He's right, though,' Sabah agrees. 'It's just growing up shizzle. Next year we're all out of here. Jana's already out of here!'

'I'm not!'

'Hello! New York! Dubai! You're an International Hon, hon!'

'We have to grow up sooner or later,' Ferdy says and I note an undertone of sadness. No one else would hear it, but I know him too well. It's like a dog whistle. He's right, though. I sense it too. We're dangling on a knife-edge: everything is about to change and a part of me wants to bottle this moment for ever. The four of us, around a table, eating pizza, buffalo wings and cheesy garlic bread. Why we gotta change? We're perfect the way we are.

'Fuck growing up! Who wants ice cream?' I grab the dessert menu. 'Get whatever you want. It's all on me.'

'Are you sure?' Sabah asks.

'Yes! It's a double celebration! You can pay me back when you're a super famous fashion blogger.'

'I can't believe you just left college,' Sabah says. 'You have a job! Babe, you're already a grown-up!'

'Hardly!' I laugh. 'I might actually order the ice-cream penguin for dessert.'

The waitress comes to take our orders. Every couple of hours, the reality of the fact that today was my last day of schooling, maybe ever, kicks in and it feels like the earth is splitting apart. There was no fanfare, no going-away party, no word from Bennett. The bell went and we just walked out as normal. *What am I doing?*

It was actually Ferdy who made my mind up last week. We were in his room after school and he said, not once looking up from Final Fantasy, that we're only still at Hollyton because we don't have anywhere better to be. I'd never thought of it like that. Everyone (well, everyone who gets the grades) from our high school *automatically* goes on to Hollyton. I never made a choice. I'm not sure I've *ever* made a choice my whole life, not one that counts.

'But if I quit school, I won't see you as much.'

Ferdy paused the game and looked me square in the eye. 'Babes. As if. We'll see each other all the time. Like, here we are, not at school.'

I rolled my eyes. 'Valid, I guess.'

'The only thing that's gonna change is I won't see you between nine and three, and that would have changed in eighteen months anyway.'

My stomach lurched as I failed to picture any sort of future beyond my timetable. It's a black blob filled with whispery demon words like *UCAS* and *responsibility*.

I can make some serious money, and I can only do it now. It's a no-brainer. Right?

Weirdly, even Mum and Dad – although not exactly jumping for joy – were pretty chill. Mum wasn't aware of online schooling, so I think explaining that took some of the sting out of my decision. That and forty grand.

I'll model while people want me to model, then I'll go to college and think about what I want to do when I'm a proper grown-up. Right now I am *definitely* not one. My ice-cream penguin is yum.

Mr Bennett seemed a little disappointed when I told him I wanted to quit, but said that he totally understood. 'My daughter was a model in her teens,' he said. 'She had fun while it lasted.'

He shook my hand and wished me luck.

I'm seventeen today and self-employed. Random. No more school and Laurel ain't speaking to me any more. This is . . .

different. I wonder if that means *I'm* something different. This ain't where I was gonna be, if you know what I mean.

'I think we should do a toast,' Sabah says, holding her Diet Coke aloft. 'To my dear friend Jana, I wish you all the best on your new adventures but please don't forget us mere mortals taking the slow route.'

We all chink glasses. 'I promise I won't. Not ever.'

– That's the problem with promises, ain't it?
– What is?
– You make 'em, you break 'em.

CODA

Coda pay for me to fly first class. It is FANCY. It's like I'm a goddamn queen or something. The snotty cabin crew woman was all like, 'Dearie, are you sure you're in the right place?' And I was like, 'CHECK THE TICKET, BITCH.'

Now they're all falling over themselves to bring me food and drink and I have my own little pod thing to sleep in. The meal – a creamy salmon bake thing – is one of the best things I've ever eaten, in the air *or* on the ground. Definitely beats a sad plastic tray with chicken in sauce. I'm just a little bit – OK, totally – out of place in my jeans and skanky fisherman jumper, like some sad stray Daddy Warbucks has plucked out of the orphanage. The only other First Classmates might genuinely be the Sultan of Dubai and his family – they're giving off that vibe, but then, wouldn't he have his own jet?

The flight takes about seven hours and I try to watch more sensible films this time to compensate for being a college drop-out, although give up and watch *Thor: Ragnarok* instead after about twenty minutes of some drama with subtitles.

Dubai airport is EXTRA, gold palm trees everywhere. Once again, I'm collected by a driver waiting for me after customs and driven through what looks like desert at dusk. Arabian nights. I'm tired, but force my eyes open. The sky is on *fire*. I've never seen . . . nothing . . . nothing like it, ever. 'Oh, wow . . .'

'First time?' the driver asks, looking over his shoulder with a grin.

'Yeah. It's incredible.' It's all very galaxy far, far away, like Tatooine or Jakku. It's beautiful, desolate and, well, sandy. I try to get a video to send back to Ferd, but it looks like an orange blob; it don't do it justice. I stop, put down my phone, and just see it with my eyes.

I am such a lucky girl.

All of a sudden, up ahead, it looks like a very different, much more futuristic *Star Wars* planet is jutting out of the landscape. 'That's the Burj Khalifa,' the driver tells me. 'The tallest building in the world.' It's like a shard of steel stabbing far into the clouds. I think it's a bit silly, to be honest. What's the point? Size don't matter, as we all well know.

'Cool,' I say.

He drives me to the Atlantis on the Palm and it's certainly a *lot* more impressive than the grimy flat in Brooklyn. It's how I imagined models lived. 'Welcome to the Atlantis, Miss Novak,' says a smiling butler-man in white gloves. 'Can I collect your suitcase?'

'Um, yeah, thanks.'

'Right this way, ma'am.'

Ma'am? What? This is batshit! The lobby is held up by huge white pillars and the floors gleam. There's a giant glass sculpture a bit like the one at the V&A – like, loads of blue glass tadpoles – and I'm quite impressed with myself for recognising it. But, seriously, any second now, someone is gonna realise I'm a massive fucking fraud and I do not belong in a place like this. I feel I should probably take my Converse off and leave them by the front door.

All checked in, a fleet of bellboys shows me to my suite for the next three nights. I hold my breath all the way down the spotless corridors. 'This is your suite, Miss Novak . . .'

'Thank you, Coda,' I mutter. The bellboy opens the door and I gasp. Everything is either a) gold or b) marble. It's like a Barbie Dream Room. The hotel room is bigger than our whole house pretty much. Fuck it, the *bed* is almost as big as my room.

'Is the room acceptable, Miss Novak?'

I turn to him, my face aching from grinning. 'For real? Yes, mate, yes, the room is acceptable! Thank you so much.'

I tip the concierge – like Dad told me I should – and pelt around the room. Oh, wow. It's ridiculous. The view of the sunset from the balcony; the bath is like a swimming pool; fluffy white robes. There's a *huge* Coda goody bag already waiting on the coffee table.

I do what any rational person would do.

I bounce on the bed, laughing my head off.

But I take my shoes off first, I'm not a monster.

My alarm goes off at 5.40 a.m. Ungodly. No human should be awake before seven. But my call-time is stupidly early – six a.m. in the hotel lobby. I drag my body downstairs, my head very much still in bed.

Outside, a people carrier waits to ferry me back into the desert. We leave the skyscrapers behind us as the sun rises, although I nod in and out of snooze mode. We drive for about

190

thirty minutes, I think, through swirling golden sands, and then I see an oasis of trailers, vans and tents some way off the track. The car swerves off-road, and we disappear into the eye of a sandstorm. *What is my life?*

I step out of the car and pull up my hoodie. My hair is still wet from the shower and it's pretty chilly, although I've been told it'll warm up later. Ro told me I should be lucky we're in Dubai. All the summer campaigns are shot in winter, she said, so half the time you're modelling skimpy bikinis and stuff in the freezing cold.

'Hi, Jana, sweetie!' A man in a jazzy tropical shirt comes over, also talking on his phone. 'I'm Simon, the brand manager from Coda.' We've spoken on the phone and he seems nice. 'Come on, let's get you into hair and make-up.'

I'm the first model to arrive and the glam squad get to work on me. I think I'm perfecting the art of sleeping while sitting. After a while another car arrives with the other models: Viviane, a very striking girl from Senegal who don't speak much English, and Kami Brennan. I didn't know Kami Brennan's name until about ten minutes ago, but I definitely know her face. She has a mane of massive blonde hair, a golden tan and more white teeth than I'd have thought could fit in a mouth. I've seen her in a million adverts and never realised it was the same girl. 'G'day!' she greets me in an Australian twang. 'I'm Kami, how's it going?'

'I'm good, thanks, I'm Jana.'

She plonks herself into the fold-out chair at the make-up station next to mine. 'Nice to meet you, Jana. Gonna be a long day, right? I hope you know some good jokes!'

'I'm crap at jokes.'

'You a pom? From England?'

'Yeah.'

'OK. Here we go. Why was the Aussie Sheila disappointed when she visited England?'

'I don't know . . .'

'Because she misheard when someone said Big Ben was a *clock*!'

The English-speaking crew laugh. I smile and relax. Kami's attitude seems to change the mood in the make-up tent as everyone realises we're in a diva-free environment.

Hair and make-up takes AGES and I see why they brought us out so early. Kami and I are covered in greasy fake tan, and there's a hold-up because no genius thought to bring make-up suitable for Viviane's dark skin *and* the photographer decides he don't like her buzzed hair after all, so someone has to fetch her a bouncy Afro wig. Viviane looks broken before we've shot a single picture.

Coda's summer look is flowy and gold – a lot of kaftans and beads and feathers and accessories. As I walk to set, I feel like Buckaroo, weighed down with sunglasses, bangles, dangling earrings and pendants. My hair has been spiked up into a sort of mohawk. The 'creative' is we've all survived a plane crash in the desert and are now waiting for rescue in a variety of strange poses.

I'm starting to think everyone in this business is on a fuck ton of drugs.

They've dropped part of a burned plane fuselage into a hillside and artfully scattered suitcases and airline chairs around. I can't decide if it's insensitive to crash victims or not. The photographer, Roberto, is a chatty Italian and is clearly about quantity over quality: he snap, snap, snaps a hundred frames a minute.

I follow Kami's lead. She's obviously old-hat at this malarkey. She twists, moves and shifts her body constantly. It's more like contemporary dance than posing. Roberto has a whole team of assistants who move us around; literally grabbing and dragging us across the set as he shouts instructions in Italian. I sit, stand, lie, crouch.

And it would all be fine if the sun weren't getting hotter and hotter with every passing second. 'Eyes open!' Roberto screams, but it's almost impossible in the glaring sunshine.

'Darl,' Kami says, 'keep them shut while he fucks around and open them when he shoots.'

'Thanks.' It actually helps.

We break for lunch when the sun is too unbearable. Roberto seems happy he's got what he needs. The next scene is us trekking through sand dunes at dusk, so hopefully it won't be as hot.

'Shit.' Kami inspects her cleavage once we're in the catering tent. 'I've got freckles.'

So have I. 'At least we didn't burn.'

'No, darl, you don't get it. My agent will kill me. You can't get a tan before Fashion Week. You'll get dropped from shows like *that*!' She clicks her fingers.

This is when I again notice the difference in what I've selected from the buffet table and what she has. I went for some tuna pasta with some crusty bread and butter. Kami has an apple.

She must catch me staring at her near-empty plate. 'Oh, you do you, darl!' she says. 'When I was your age I could eat what I wanted too! I'm strictly on the apples until after Fashion Week. Apples are great because they have some chemical that make you feel full or some shit. God forbid I'm old *and* fat!'

'You're *so* not fat,' I say, picking at the tuna. Maybe I'll leave the bread. White bread is bad, right? 'And you're definitely not old.'

She flicks her artfully beachy hair over her shoulder. If you look too closely, you can see where the extensions are glued in. 'Strictly between you and me, I'm twenty-seven in a couple of weeks. This is it for me, Jana. Last Fashion Week before my tits start to go.'

'You're stunning,' I tell her. 'I mean this as a compliment: you're like Barbie!'

'That's what everyone calls me!' She nibbles on her apple. 'You know what? I've been doing this since I was fifteen. I've had a blast.'

I say nothing.

'Look, Jana, if you can stomach this fucked-up world, you get ten years, tops. Ten years of travel and parties and money. Milk it while you can, but not everyone can take the heat . . .' She nods towards Viviane, who's in the make-up tent, crying to someone on her mobile phone.

'Is she OK?'

Kami shrugs. 'I don't know. She's probably homesick. And hungry. Aren't we all? That's the thing with modelling . . . none of us actually *want* to be models. We're just tall and thin. Unlike any other job in the world, you can't *want* to be a model, and you can't work at it. You either are one, or you aren't. I'm counting down the days until I can go back to New York. For good.'

'You're not going back to Australia?'

She laughs. 'Back to Wagga Wagga? Fuck, no.' She waggles her left hand at me, and the light from the diamond ring on her finger is even more blinding than the midday sun. 'Sorted out my retirement plan a couple of years back. Daniel Winters the third. Investment banker. He worships the ground I walk on.'

I can't work out if she's kidding or not.

'If you're smart, Jana, you'll figure out what you're gonna do when it all starts to sag. We can't all be Elle or Naomi! Get yourself a nice, rich man and pop out his sprogs.' She grins and tucks into her 'lunch'.

Wow, that might be the single most depressing conversation I've ever had.

We shoot until we 'lose the light'.

I'm so tired, my *bones* are tired.

Every crease and crack in my body is full of sand.

I want a shower.

Kami, Viviane and I are put in a minivan to run us back to the hotel. We have another day of this starting at five a.m.

We drive into the glittering lights and skyscrapers of Dubai. As we hit the outskirts of the city, we overtake shabby-looking buses heading in the same direction.

'Slaves,' Kami says.

'What?'

'Well, basically. They ferry immigrants into the building sites to build all the shiny hotels and stuff. They take their passports and papers off them until they've worked off the cost of shipping them here, which they never do, so in effect they're slaves . . .'

I stare at the faces of the men – who look South Asian mostly, some Thai, perhaps, too – on the bus. They look grim. 'Oh my god . . .' I say.

'They don't want the tourists to see how Dubai was made.'

'That's awful,' I say, gazing out of the back windscreen.

'Fucked up, right?' Kami says.

She's got that right. I'm not in Kansas, or for that matter Battersea, any more.

As I doze on the back seat of the van, I half-remember what Westley said on the roof terrace in Brooklyn.

Human meat.

Hardly able to keep my eyes open, I see the glass towers of Dubai glitter with laser lights. *All that glitters . . .*

My body battery hits zero per cent and I must fall asleep, because the next thing I know Kami is shaking me awake outside the Atlantis.

- So, yeah, Dubai was a downer.
- Was it good to get home again?
- It's funny. I remember the first time I didn't have to set my alarm on a school night. That, truly, was the best feeling in the world . . . probably the highlight of this whole experience. But after that, my feet didn't touch the floor. It was full on: back-to-back meetings; test shoots and editorials for magazines; and then, before I knew it . . . February Fashion Week rolled around.
- Introduce the concept of Fashion Week.
- Well, for starters, it's actually *four* weeks – New York, London, Milan, Paris, in that order. I don't know why they call it Fashion Week. It's Fashion Month.
- What's it for?
- Twice a year, all the designers exhibit their new collections to, erm . . . buyers and journalists and stuff. A lot of shows. Hundreds. More, maybe. You go on castings. The more shows you book, the more money you make.
- Did you enjoy Fashion Week?

- Jana?
- Well, you know what happened next.

LHR > JFK

Trent hands me a very confusing piece of paper. I've come straight from the airport to the Face First offices on Park Avenue. I hardly slept on the plane. Back to economy this time and a baby screamed the whole flight, I swear. I feel like crap. 'OK, Jana, here are the deets for your castings.'

The office is packed with jet-lagged girls pushing little wheelie suitcases. Everyone – models and agents alike – seems frayed and aggy. A lot of snapping, sighing and flouncing about.

'What I've done is highlight the ones you absolutely *have* to get to. If you're booked for Marc Jacobs, that's an exclusive, and TANK have you on retainer.'

I don't know what any of these things mean.

'If you *can* make the others, that's great but not essential. The buzz is insane, Jana. For a new girl, this is freaking incredible.' He hands me an envelope. 'Here's some day money for cabs and stuff. Don't be late, take water and be prepared to wait. Now go, you've got Calvin Klein at ten-thirty. Go!'

I've been in the office about ten minutes. I want to go to the model apartment and change, but there's not time. I turn to leave.

'Oh, Jana?'

'Yeah?'

'Did Maggie talk to you about food?'

Huh? What does he mean? Do I get a food allowance? 'No.'

He steers me down a corridor next to the photocopier where we're alone. 'For campaigns and editorial you can afford to carry a little more weight. What are you? A four?'

'What's that in UK sizes?'

'An eight.'

'Yeah . . . usually.'

Trent chews his lip and looks me up and down. 'For catwalk, you really want to be closer to a UK six.'

Am I hallucinating? I am pretty tired. The punchline is that Trent is a tubby Baby-Bear type, his tummy bulging over the rim of his jeans. 'But I'm, like, five-eleven.'

'I know, I know, it's *crazy*. But clothes just hang better off bone than they do fat, what can I say? It's only two months a year, baby, just stick to your diet and you'll be fine.'

Let me guess. 'Steamed fish and vegetables?'

'That's the one!' He slaps me on the arse, sending me on my way like a pony. 'Go knock 'em dead. Don't gain a single pound, Jana, I mean it.'

Oh, he can fuck right off.

I guess the good news is he put me in such a bad mood, I aced the Calvin Klein casting and booked the job on the spot. They must have loved how pissed off I looked.

After Calvin Klein, I visit Marc Jacobs before meeting Lien for supper. To be honest, I was kinda shook she made the effort and asked if I was in town, so I figure I should go along. I meet her in the West Village – apparently she's just bought a studio apartment here. It's neat and prim, with definite Chelsea vibes. 'Is this bar OK?' she asks, sipping a vodka and soda.

I got 'carded' so I have a Diet Coke. 'If I'm drinking Diet Coke, it don't really matter,' I tell her. To be honest, I need the caffeine. The jet lag struggle is real. I overheard the casting director at Minky Monky make a jab about my dark circles. Bitch.

'I'm sort of dating the bartender,' she whispers. 'The one with the tattoos ...'

I look over the room and see a wasted-looking hipster type in a beanie hat. 'Yeah, he's cute.'

'Right? My mom would *kill* me if she knew. She's always trying to set me up with fucking preppy trust-fund assholes on the Upper East Side. As if. I'd rather die.' The bartender looks over and gives her a grin. 'Man, he's hot. I'm trying to play it cool, though. Are you hungry?'

'Yeah.'

'OK, let's finish these and then head around the corner. There's this great vegan sushi place I've been dying to try.'

'Great,' I smile. 'So not even steamed fish? I got a lecture from my agent earlier.'

'Uh, fuck him. It's like I *know* I have to watch what I eat, but I don't need you assholes to tell me that. Right?'

I shrug. I don't see how either of us could possibly be any thinner.

'OK,' Lien says, leaning in, 'last season in Milan, I swear to god a girl *dropped dead* backstage at Allonqué. It was a huge cover-up. Honestly. She was Brazilian or Portuguese or something. So sad.'

'For real?'

'On my grandfather's life.'

'That's awful.'

200

'And we all say we eat. All of us. Like, find me a model who tells the truth about how much they really eat. If we were honest, we'd all say we survive on Diet Coke and cigarettes, but then our agencies would fire us for making them look bad, when it's them telling us to lose weight.'

But . . . I do eat. Like multiple times a day. Maybe I should be more careful with what I'm eating. I hate myself for doing it, but I compare my arms to Lien's. Both skinny; hers maybe a *bit* skinnier. What does she want to hear? That starving yourself is normal? I change the subject. 'It's crazy. The whole Fashion-Week thing. It's nuts.'

'Baby! It hasn't even started yet.'

'I know.' I take a deep breath. 'I'm freaking out. I was reading an interview with Clara in *Vogue* and she was saying she walked, like, fifty shows last year. How?'

'Oh, it's different if you're Clara. You don't even have to go on castings.'

Ah, I see.

'Do you know her? Clara?'

'No. Well, I met her once properly. Is she nice?'

Lien leans in again, like she's about to say something especially juicy and she don't want it to drip. 'How much do you know about her?'

'Huh?'

'She's so private. Like, I've met her loads of times and she's real nice and everything, but none of us know, like, the first thing about her. Dido Gant thinks she had a secret baby when she was like thirteen and that's why she's so goddamn cagey all the time.'

'What?'

'For real! Her mom, or foster mom or whatever, is always with this mixed-race kid. Like, who is he?'

'Another foster kid?'

The look on her face says Lien hadn't even considered this. 'No way. There's something. I'm never wrong about these things.'

Clara seemed so nice, I hope that's not true. Not that she has a kid, but that she's ashamed about it. I dunno where Lien grew up, but where I'm from, there's nothing shocking about teen mums. You just get on with it, or you don't. It's no biggy. I once thought I was pregnant when I was a few days late. I wouldn't have kept it, but no judgement on girls that do.

'What castings have you got?' Lien asks. 'Let's compare and I'll see if my agent isn't doing her job.'

I reach into my bag and present the list that Trent gave me.

'That's interesting,' she says, chewing a nail. 'You've got Fran Tulip. That bitch never uses Asian girls. Racist.'

'Is that still a thing?'

Lien shrugs. 'Two seasons ago, you couldn't move for Asian models. They finally figured out China is a huge fashion market. But this season and last . . . not so much. Guess we're a trend.'

'That's depressing.'

'We all are. But this is *your* big season, Jana. You've got the look.'

'You think?'

Lien nods, almost begrudgingly. 'Everyone is talking about That British Girl. Work it. You're gonna be busy. But next year change your hair or everyone will get bored of you. Ask Lexx.'

'Fuck.' My stomach turns. I don't know if I'm ready for it.

'What? Don't be nervous!'

'I am. It's all . . . it's all just so quick, you know?'

'It'll settle down.'

Suddenly I feel queasy.

'Hey, are you OK?'

I don't know. 'I'll be fine. I'm just . . . I'm just tired and jet-lagged, and I don't like being away from home so much.'

'Oh, at first I was the same. But then I got my ass on Xanax. Are you on Xanax?'

'What?'

'Oh, baby. I'm gonna change your life.' She reaches into her purse and thrusts a little orange bottle in my face. She shakes it like a rattle. 'You're welcome!'

'What are they?'

'Just Xanax!'

'What's Xanax?'

'They chill you out. Every teen in America is on them. I don't know how I coped before I started taking them. Here! You can keep those.'

'Don't you need them?'

'I have, like, a million back at the apartment. I use them to get me through Fashion Week.'

I take the bottle and give the pills a rattle. ALPRAZOLAM 0.25MG. There's maybe twenty, twenty-five left. 'What? I just take one a day?'

'You're meant to take three a day, but I forget sometimes.'

'And they work right away?'

'No,' she says. 'But start taking them today and you'll be good for the shows. Seriously. Trust me!'

Hmm. Lien was right about the Zopiclone she gave me to sleep on the plane that time. Worked like a dream. Maybe she's the model pharmacy or something? I shake a white pill into the palm of my hand and knock it back with some Coke.

'Bottoms up!' Lien smiles.

Three pills a day, easy.

Castings go like this: I turn up at some dingy loft, warehouse or office. If you're nice and early you can get seen pretty quickly. You don't meet the designer. It's usually a casting director. A couple are nice. The others are fucking insane power-trippers who must really hate models.

You wait.

You wait for *hours*.

Sometimes, if you're lucky, there's a chair.

Usually, you sit on the floor, on the stairs, in a corridor. It's February in New York. It's fucking freezing. FREEZING. Not once do I see food. More often than not, you're seen in the order you arrived. You take in your 'book' – portfolio – and hand it to the casting director.

'Walk,' they bark.

You walk backwards and forwards a few times.

You might get to try on some clothes, you might not.

Sometimes, I see someone I know. Lien and I are sitting on a cold stone floor outside the casting for Fabrizio Harman, wondering if it's true you can get piles from sitting on cold surfaces when Domino Gant (the brunette one) swishes past us. I guess the Gant sisters don't wait for anyone.

'She's a fucking cunt,' Lien says. 'And her sister's even worse.'

At Proenza Schouler, I see Viktoria clustered into a smoky corner with a group of virtually identical Russian girls. They're not all *actually* Russian, I've learned that's become shorthand for pretty much any girl from Eastern Europe: Latvia, Lithuania, Estonia, Ukraine, Belarus – like Viktoria – as well as Russia. It sounds *awful* but there's *always* a group of 'Russian' girls, they only ever talk to each other, and they are basically Heather Daley Mean Girls, but without subtitles. Ah, well, at least Viktoria gives me a nod and (I guess) tells the other 'Russians' to stop scowling at me. So that's nice.

Wait, walk, wait.

On repeat.

Weirdly, though, I feel the Xanax doing its thing. After a few days, I start to just *care less*. I turn up on time, if I'm late I don't sweat it. If one designer makes me late for the next, I just call and say I'm running behind. And I *hate* phoning people more than going to the dentist. I always get Mum or Dad to do it.

I meet about a hundred new people. I pretend to be friendly. I make small talk. I eat food by myself in restaurants; there's a Vietnamese place opposite the model apartment that stays open all night and does Trent-approved brown rice and broccoli. All those things would send me spiralling normally. Not any more. I know I *should* be stressed, but I just can't get it up.

I feel fine.

Maybe I can do this.

I've been waiting outside Young York for three hours. I didn't even realise. I've been trying to read a book but keep reading the same page over and over again. The casting directors – a loved-up couple called Vanessa and Vito who can't stop touching each other in a very TMI way – seem to be running some sort of dictatorship where they emerge from a room and seemingly call girls in at random.

I'm about to walk out (even though it's one of the castings Trent highlighted) when I get a message from Westley: *U in town yet?*

Wasn't expecting that. I reply at once and tell him I am.

Wanna get a drink later? What time you done?

Oh, I'm done. And the thought of going back to the freezing model flat on the Upper West Side – with its mildew, and mice, and miserable Russian girls – fills me with dread.

'Jana Novak!' Vito calls my name. Fml.

I'm supposed to have another casting at ten, but fuck it, it's not a highlighted one. I'll tell Trent they kept me at Young York for four hours instead of three.

Westley has texted me the address of a bar in the East Village but I can't find it. To make matters worse, thick, feathery snowflakes are swirling all around in a blizzard and I can hardly see. A cab drops me off but then I circle the block on foot twice before I see Westley waiting at the top of a tiny staircase. Oh. I didn't realise I was looking for a *basement*. He looks great, his cheeks rosy red from the cold, all bunched up in a puffa jacket and fur-lined hat.

'Jana!' he calls. 'I was starting to think I'd been stood up.'

My feet hurt, I'm beyond hungry, and I've been up since five-thirty.

I burst into tears.

'Jana? Jana, what's wrong?'

He holds his arms wide and I sort of flop against him. 'I don't know!'

'You don't know?'

'I'm really tired.'

'Welcome to Fashion Week.'

'I'll be fine.' I wipe my eyes on my sleeve.

'Listen. Do you have fake ID?'

'No!' I start to cry again. I can't even get a cheeky beer in this fucking country.

Westley laughs. 'Hey, it's not a problem. My apartment is on this block, no ID required. What you need is a big drink.'

He's not wrong. I'm not supposed to drink on the Xanax, but fuck that jazz.

We run around the corner, Westley pulling me through the snowstorm by the hand. It turns out even the biggest male model in the world can only afford a fairly dinky apartment in the East Village. It's in a shiny modern block and smells brand new, unlived in.

The lift announces we're on the fifth floor and Westley lets us into his apartment. It feels like a pretend Ikea-showroom flat. I guess that's because he's so rarely in it. Everything – the crisp white walls, the black marble kitchen units – are pristine. But, on the plus side, it's warm, and out of the snow, and I can't hear a mad Chinese woman screaming at her husband like I can at the model flat.

'I keep meaning to buy some art,' he explains as he takes my coat. 'Like, proper art by a real artist. I think that's something a grown-up would do. But I don't really know any artists. Like, what's good?' He fetches me a beer out of a gleaming Smeg fridge.

I laugh. 'Just go with what you like.'

'In my room in Nixa I have posters of Ferraris.'

'Whatever tickles your pickle . . .'

Now he laughs. 'What? Speak English! I bought a Ferrari last year but sold it. I looked so dumb. Red Ferrari, what was I thinking? Cliché or what? Make yourself at home,' he says as we enter a long, slim lounge, again a bit bare and cold. His TV is almost as big as the entire wall. He's such a boy – who needs a screen that big?

I take off my wet Adidas and put my socks on the radiator to dry them, before tucking my bare feet under my bum on the sofa. Well, he did say to make myself at home. Westley brings a bowl of 'potato chips' from the kitchen and I grab a handful. 'Thank you. I needed this.'

'I was really worried about you for a second there.'

I feel more normal now. 'I'm fine.'

'You sure?'

I don't want to tell him I'm popping crazy pills. That sounds like something a crazy person does and I'm not crazy. 'I am sure.'

'Shall we –' he leans in to whisper and I feel his breath on my ear – 'get *pizza*?'

My hand flies to my mouth. 'Westley Bryce! Blasphemy! Do they even *do* a steamed fish pizza?'

He laughs. 'Fuck it.'

About twenty minutes later, we sit either side of the coffee table, sharing a Pop's Pizza salami and pepperoni. I grin at him. It feels like a quiet rebellion.

He sticks *Next Top Model* on the giant screen and we howl with laughter at how little like the fashion industry it really is. At one point, Tyra tells a girl to eat *more*. I drink one beer, then another, then another.

'I better think about getting home,' I say. I stand to collect my coat but the room seems to capsize and I stumble into the coffee table. 'Whoa.'

'Are you drunk?' Westley grins. He only had one beer.

'No!' I say, but then remember I mixed the beers with Xanax. The room is spinning. 'I'm fine.'

He swoons in and out of focus. 'You don't seem fine.' He rises off the sofa and steadies me.

'I'm just a little woozy. I'll get a cab.'

'Why don't you stay here?' I let go of his arm. Is he . . . trying something? 'Oh! No! Not like that. I'll take the sofa. I know you have a boyfriend back home.'

Tempting. As mentioned, Westley's place has no mice, no mildew and no miserable Russians. It's warm and clean. 'OK,' I say, 'but *I'll* take the sofa.'

'No way. That's not how my mom raised me. I insist.'

It's a no-brainer. 'Do you have a spare toothbrush?'

He smiles. 'I do.'

'Sold.'

Teeth cleaned, I sort of collapse on to his crisp grey bedsheets. They smell of whatever fragrance he wears – sort of oaky. It's lovely. I'm pretty tipsy, but my fuddled brain keeps strolling back to what he said . . . *I know you have a boyfriend back home.* What does that mean? If I didn't he'd . . .?

No fucking way.

I *must* be out of it, because that shit is pure fantasy land. Yeah, Westley Bryce, American god, wants to shag Winstanley Jana. Sure thing.

I slide into a swampy sleep, but before I do I think I might not tell Ferdy I stayed here.

- So why do it?
- Stay at Westley's?
- No! The Fashion Weeks.
- The money.
- It can't *just* be that . . .
- I've thought about that a lot.
- And?
- OK. There's a moment, when everyone stops faffing with your hair and clothes and the person with the headset says, 'GO,' and it's just you. You walk down that catwalk and the lights are flashing and the music is pumping, and you become this . . . fantasy. It's like being on a rollercoaster. Yeah, exactly like that. For about sixty seconds your heart is in your throat. You stop at the end of the runway and I'd be lying if I said it didn't feel good. You bathe in it. They love you and you feel *beautiful*, even if you're wearing something insane. You're not even human, you're a goddess. Then it's all over and everyone breathes again and you feel this insane rush, this high, and everyone is falling over themselves to tell you how amazing you are and it's all fun and champagne for about half an hour.
- And then?
- Then it's over. But that don't stop you from queuing up for more rollercoasters, does it?

Naomi! Kate! Lexx! Cara! Clara, and now Jana! London is the fashion capital of the world when it comes to edgy, unique beauty, and teenager Jana Novak is the latest face taking the fashion world by storm! In the space of a few short months, hot debut Jana has shot campaigns for TANK and high street giant Coda.

The true break-out star of New York Fashion Week, Jana walked for Marc Jacobs, DKNY, Proenza Schouler and Calvin Klein. As she gears up for London Fashion Week, we caught up with the androgynous beauty backstage at TANK.

Jana! Welcome to Fashion TV!

'Thanks for having me.'

Jana, this is a fantastic first season for you! You are IN DEMAND!

'It's been . . . busy.'

What was it like walking for so many amazing designers?

'To be honest, I've been so busy, I'm just focused on walking in a straight line and not falling down!'

Favourite show?

'They've all been great, but it's fun to do TANK with my friends from the ad campaign.'

And next stop, London!

'I know! I'm so tired! At least I can sleep in my own bed!'

And you're in the new Coda campaign?

'Yeah. It's a big deal. It launches in the spring all around the world, I think.'

Of course, we're all still reeling from the disaster in Bangladesh . . .

'I'm sorry?'

Didn't you hear? Last week, three hundred workers died in a deadly fire at the garment factory in Dhaka that produces clothes for Coda. Some people are saying poor working conditions in the factory were responsible for the tragedy. What are your thoughts on that?

'I . . . I'm sorry . . . I didn't know. But I'm sorry, that's awful . . .'

JFK > LHR

How did I get here? I'm at Prestige. Was there a taxi? I don't remember.

'Absolute fucking bullshit!' Maggie slams the laptop shut. 'Who did you speak to at Fashion TV? I'll get them fucking fired!'

I'm slumped, almost asleep in a chair. I'm jet-lagged, my skin has gone to shit and my hair is so dirty it actually aches. I think I'm still under the influence of the sleeping pill Lien gave me backstage at the TANK show. It was amazing. I took it as we taxied at JFK and the next thing I know, a stewardess is shaking me awake at Heathrow. 'I don't know. They just grabbed me before the show.'

'Unacceptable!' Maggie rants. 'What the fuck has it got to do with you what happens in Pakistan?'

'Bangladesh,' I mutter.

And it happened, it really did. It wasn't on any news bulletin or front page that I saw, but two hundred and eighty-seven textile workers couldn't get out of the building. The stairwells collapsed, burying them alive. I googled it and it looked *horrific*.

Coda are *deeply sorry* but claim no responsibility for the conditions in outsourced factories. They *trusted* the safety standards were suitable. So I guess that's OK, then. WTF? I was paid forty grand for the photoshoot in Dubai. I wonder what those poor people in Dhaka were getting. Just thinking about it makes me want to vom in my mouth.

Dirty money.

I feel grubby. I try to shake it off.

'Jana, little one. We need to get into castings for next week. A lot of designers want to book you after New York . . .'

No! Not more castings! Did I say that out loud? Fuck. My eyelids are so heavy. What if this is a dream and I'm still on the plane?

'You're already booked for Dermot and Burberry, hon, but they want to see you for Heritage, Pam Hogg and JW Anderson. How exciting is that?'

Cheska seems about as worn as I do. The whole office looks like they've been up all night; there's a blatant tinge of Red Bull in the air. London Fashion Week starts tomorrow. 'Maggie, we can't send her to Veroniqa Heritage like this. She looks stoned.'

Maggie chews her lip. 'They might quite like that, but you're right.'

'What?'

'Jana, go home. Sleep, for fuck's sake. Wash your hair. You have a fitting at Republic of Deen at five. Don't be late . . .'

Cheska bundles me into an Uber and it's the last thing I remember until I'm home on the estate.

'Jana, hon? It's Sabah. Me and Ferdy at are Nando's. You on your way, babes? Give me a call when you get this.'

Shit. I accidentally slept through lunchtime. I was meant to meet them on Northcote Road.

After I call her back and grovel, I have a very, very long bath. I feel like shit. I've told them I'll meet them tonight after my fitting instead. From under the water, I watch the light dance across the ceiling and count how long I can hold my breath. I wash my hair, my scalp sore from the torture my hair's been through in New York. Mum fusses around me, bringing me a bacon sandwich. 'Here. Eat. You are too thin.'

If I have lost weight during New York, it's not by design, it's because I haven't sat still for five days. Being taxied from fitting to runway left no time to eat, and I wonder if that's what they bank on.

I saw a lot of very thin girls eat a lot of apples last week. There was one girl at Jayden G who was so skeletal I was genuinely worried her legs might buckle under the weight of her torso. I hope I don't look like that.

That said, I do have another three weeks of this shit left. But I doubt one bacon sandwich will kill me. As I eat it – oh, god, it's good, smothered with butter and HP Sauce – I have a sudden terror that I won't fit into Dermot's clothes, and vow I won't eat again until after the fitting.

'Hey, baby, where are you?'

'Ferdy, I'm so, so sorry, I can't come.'

'What? Why? Are you OK?'

'I'm still at House of Holland. I booked the show and they want to do the fitting now.'

'What? It's almost midnight.'

'I know. I'll be here for a while yet.'

'Oh, OK. Well . . . no worries.'

'No! I wanted to see you!'

'Jana, don't get upset! I'll see you tomorrow.'

'But I wanna see you now! Ferdy, I miss you.'

'I miss you too. You OK? You sound miserable.'

'I'm just tired.'

'Then go straight to sleep when you get back. It's an order.'

'I love you.'

'Cool. I'll see you tomorrow.'

He hangs up.

Well.

It ain't a good fucking sign when they don't say it back, is it?

– That week I think I did Dermot, Burberry, Veroniqa Heritage, House of Holland, Burdock & Rasputin, Pam Hogg, Vin + Omi, Ashish and Topshop.
– Fun?
– Sure. Mum and Dad came to see me walk for Heritage. That was cool. Although you could see my boobs. The dress was see-through. Beyond caring, tbh.
– What do you think they made of it?
– The show? I think they were proud. In a way.
– You think?
– Well, their only daughter had the word SLUT written on her face in black pen, so . . . sorry! It's just so absurd, ain't it? Poor Mum! She was like, 'Oh, you look nice . . .' and my tits are out and I have rude words literally on my face!
– Were *you* proud?

– Jana?
– I must have been doing something right.

CLARA

Tomorrow I fly to Milan and I really don't want to go, but tonight it's the British Fashion Council party. They always hold one to celebrate the end of Fashion Week, although it pretty much looks like everyone just wants to collapse. Or cry. Or both.

Apparently I *have* to be there.

Anyone who's anyone is going and now I am an anyone.

An Addison Lee takes me from the Topshop show in Old Street to the party at Café de Paris in Leicester Square. Really can't be bothered, to be honest.

On the way in there's a Pap Board I also *have* to do. The photographers all know my name now, which is a bit weird. I'm in a denim skirt, fishnet tights and Docs with a Spice Girls T-shirt. My hair is still full of clay from Topshop and my eyes are black like a raccoon's. I must look insane. I pose awkwardly, given I do this professionally, for about a minute before ducking into the party.

I grab a sugary cocktail thing, down it, and then swipe a handful of tiny chorizo canapés before I collapse. I'm so hungry I feel hollow. I see Arabella talking to Cheska on the other side of the room and head over to join them. 'Hey!'

'OMG, Jana!' Arabella throws her arms around me. She smells lovely, like strawberry shortcake. 'You are totally smashing it, babes! You are everywhere!'

I roll my eyes. 'Thank you. How are you getting on?'

'Oh, not so great,' she says. 'Just one show booked for London.'

'Hey,' Cheska interrupts, 'don't be down on yourself. You're not really a runway girl, so anything is a bonus.'

We compare notes from castings. Arabella too has experienced the weird sex-couple casting agents, Vito and Vanessa, and their strange power trip. She didn't go to New York, but she is going to Paris the week after next, so I hope I'll see her there. She's still in school, still trying to get her A levels, so she couldn't take the whole month off. I ain't even thought about Hollyton really. It ain't entered my head. After Fashion Week, I swear I'll sit down with the online college stuff, but I so haven't had time.

Maggie and some guy sidle up to us. 'Hello, Jana, darling.' She kisses me on both cheeks. 'Don't you look cute? There's someone I'd like you to meet. Jana, this is Lucas Blo, Lucas, this is my new baby, Jana.'

The man is short and chubby with a flaming ginger beard, a baseball cap and a gold tooth. A thick chain sits on his Minky Monky T-shirt. Lucas Blo . . . it rings a bell. In the nick of time I remember reading about him at Heathrow. The photographer. 'Oh, hi!' I'm smug with my fresh knowledge. 'I saw your pictures in *i-D*!'

I sense Maggie's relief.

'Oh, that's real cute!' He pinches his nostrils. 'And congrats on everything. Fuck, bitch, you're everywhere right now.'

He looks me up and down. I feel my cheeks burn. 'Thank you.'

'Maggie, she's fuckin' A-Star.'

'Oh, I know, Lucas, darling. We'll have to get her over to Portland some time.'

He rubs his nose again. 'Look at her! Of course! Let's set it up. Excuse me . . .' Lucas Blo sees who I think might be Lil 69er and bounds over to join him.

'Oh, well done, darling!' Maggie grasps my arms. 'I think a Lucas shoot could make your season! Good work! Oh, look! There's Kate Moss!' And like that, she darts away.

As Café de Paris fills up, I recognise more faces: Lien, Lexx, Dermot, Viviane, Matty, both Dido and Domino Gant, various other models I've seen at castings and shows. It's funny. I don't know if it's the tablets I'm taking or just how tired I am, but everything has a fuzzy gloss over it, like my eyes are smeared in Vaseline. I don't quite feel like I'm here.

I'm in the loo washing my hands – they have little face cloths for hand towels, which I find very decadent – when I hear a familiar voice. 'Hey, it's Jana, right?'

Clara Keys emerges from a cubicle, looking like an utter goddess in a slinky chain-mail dress that scoops all the way down to finish a millimetre above her bum crack. 'Hi. Wow. Sorry. I'm shook. I can't believe you remember my name.'

'Of course I do, hon! For one thing you are KILLING IT and two, you're the girl from the Winstanley who gave me gum when I had puke breath. You don't forget your saints, babe. How the hell are you?'

'Good! Good. Tired. Like really, really tired.'

'First season? You'll get used to it. We can't just be toilet friends, c'mon. I'm on Edward Enninful's table. You wanna join us?'

I'm suddenly more nervous than I was before the first catwalk. 'Erm, yeah, sure.'

I follow Clara upstairs on to a mezzanine overlooking the

dance floor. It seems there's a VVIP area within the VIP party. We pass Dido Gant (the red-haired one) sitting talking to Jared Leto and Sienna Miller.

My life is *really* weird.

Vogue have a table, so it seems. 'Jana Novak, this is Edward Enninful and Anna Wintour.'

Oh, shit.

I am wearing a Spice Girls T-shirt.

'Hello, Jana,' Edward says, shaking my hand. 'Well done on New York.'

'Thank you.'

'Pleased to meet you, Jana. Congratulations on a very impressive season.' I shake Anna Wintour's hand, hardly daring to breathe near her.

Clara takes my hand and we slide past them into the booth. 'You want champagne?'

'Sure. That was terrifying.'

'They're pussycats.' We clink. 'You off to Milan, babes?'

'Yeah,' I say. 'But I don't really wanna go. I'm thinking of asking Maggie if I can have a week off . . .'

'Do *not* do that. She'll do the *look*.'

'I don't think I've seen that yet.'

'No and, believe me, you don't want to. Just me, maybe, but Milan and Paris always seem to go quicker. Like, you're past halfway or something. Or maybe you're just too tired to care.' She downs her champagne and pours another. 'You want some more unsolicited advice?'

'From Clara Keys?' I should really stop referring to her in the third person. 'Yes!'

222

'Just go with the current.' She rolls her eyes. 'Don't try to swim against the tide or whatever. This is my seventh season. I've seen a lot of skinny white girls come and go. You either give in to how mad everything is, or you go mad too. Just don't forget what all this is. It's selling clothes to rich-as-fuck people. Nothing else. Someone's always trying to tell you it's art or some shit, but, nah. Remember what this is.'

She's right. She's exactly right. Back at Thorpe Park, there's a white-water rapids ride where you're in this dinghy thing. I feel like that dinghy – tugged along by the current, crashing and banging and bouncing off the rocks. And it don't matter how much I try to cling on, the river is pulling me away from my life: away from Ferdy, away from home. Away from me. Maybe I should just stop fighting and let go.

LHR > MXP

This is happening. This is my life now.

Milan is noisy: mopeds zip up and down the narrow streets like wasps. Horns and sirens scream at each other as they try to get through the clogged alleys. It takes about an hour in traffic to reach Prestige's sister agency Pantera and they make a fuss of me. I get my castings, and they assign me Rafael, a tubby little guy who will be my guide for all of Milan Fashion Week. I squeeze my legs into his tiny Punto and he drives me to yet another model apartment in Porta Genova.

As I drop my bags off, I run into Viktoria. She's crouched like Gollum in the corner of the kitchen, eating cashew nuts. 'I charge phone,' she says, possibly explaining why she's crammed next to the washing machine in her underwear.

'Hey, how are you?'

'Is shit,' she says.

I kinda like Viktoria. In a crazy, crazy world, at least she's predictable. She will swear a lot and chain smoke. 'I'm going to the Gucci casting. Are you going to that?'

'Gucci? Yes.'

'You want to go with me? Together?'

'Yes. You wait.'

Viktoria has zero shits to give about personal grooming and shoves on a pair of jeans and a jumper before dragging her greasy hair into a topknot. We both squish into the back of the car and set off for the casting.

As we whizz through the backstreets, Milan looks fully Italian – pizzerias, chapels, gelato, cute coffee shops, although a fine drizzle spoils the picture-postcard moment. As best as he can, in broken English, Rafael points out the *Duomo*, a big, spiky cathedral thing and some of the museums and restaurants we should try to get to. Yeah, like that's gonna happen on our schedule.

After Gucci, it descends into New-York chaos once again. Casting after casting after casting, only the Milan fashion people are even more horrible than the New York ones. The old hag from Mancari is particularly bad. She's a leathery lizard woman and she actually slaps me on the ass as she passes. 'Hate,' she says simply.

It's no big shock when I don't get cast for Mancari, look at it that way.

I do however get Gucci, Moschino, Fendi and Versace, so Madame Mancari can fuck right off. I keep taking the Xanax and it makes the whole thing doable. It's like there's this little voice in my head telling me to get stressed, but the pills give me this chemical barrier keeping my body safe from the little voices. My brain is in a goldfish bowl, protecting me from the terror on the outside. The only thing which *is* starting to worry me is the fact I'm running out. I'll have to ask Lien how I can get some more.

The night before the first show kicks off, Hotel Italia Style throws a glitzy party and the Pantera people ask me to show my tired face. I'm so far past exhausted from my late fitting at Moschino but I figure I can do a quick circuit and then slip away.

The party is *insane* and I'm glad Jeremy Scott let me steal a sweater dress especially. There are so many famous people underneath the chandeliers I don't know where to look. Would it be awful to ask for a couple of selfies? I swear to god, actual Beyoncé just smiled right at me. If I die right now, I'm OK with that.

I do a couple of laps and say hello to some people from my agency, but can't find Clara – or anyone else I know – anywhere. The nibbles are stinky fish bubbles in jizz, and I'm not eating that. God, I'd kill for a McNugget actually. I decide that's the best plan of action, when I see Viktoria. She beckons me over. 'Jana! Hello! Come sit!' She's seated at a table with a whole bunch of men in suits. They all look rich – rich but greasy, smoking fat sausage cigars. Chunky gold chains and bracelets catch the light. 'These are my friends, *ja?*'

'Hi,' I say, shaking their hands to be polite. One of them lowers his shades and scans me over. All of a sudden, I'm reminded of *Little Red Riding Hood. What big eyes you have.*

'English? Loooooove English girls,' one of them leers. I think they're Italian, but I'm not sure. They all have deep, wood-varnish tans.

'Here, pretty girl, drink,' says another. 'Is good.' He pours me a glass of Dom Pérignon and pats the seat next to him. I perch, one foot in and one foot out of their booth.

I have a sip, but I don't wanna stick around. The vibe is not good. The men grin to one another and there's something

226

animal about them; they're a pack. The men are forty or fifty, and me, Viktoria and the other blonde girl look like creepy jailbait. They're all old enough to be our dads. Not a good look.

What white veneers you have.

I scan the room and it's like being at the MTV Awards. I see a hundred faces I recognise and not a single person I know. No escape in sight.

One of them, a big swollen thumb of a man, pulls Viktoria close and growls into her ear. I give them a wave as I walk away from the table, but she chases me down and grabs my elbow. 'Jana, stop. My friend . . . he like you.'

'I said I'd meet Domino Gant . . .' Not true, but I see the brunette one on the other side of the room.

'Just wait. My friends,' she whispers, 'they have *money*.'

'Yeah, and?'

Viktoria looks deep into my eyes, waiting for me to understand. I say nothing. 'Three thousand euro for each to . . . *party* with them.'

Is she saying what I think she's saying? 'Party?'

'Is fun. Is good money. Pretty girls.'

I look back and see one of them rub the blonde girl's thigh with a hairy hand. I've seen her at a couple of shows . . . Anja something, from Lithuania, I think. She's about my age. The hand vanishes up her skirt. 'Viktoria! No! I'm not a . . . no!'

Viktoria scowls. 'OK. You choose. Is easy. Is money.'

'No.' I say it like I mean it. I walk away. I cast a look over my shoulder and see Viktoria slide back into the booth alongside one of the businessmen. They pop another bottle of champagne and she cheers and claps ecstatically. She's quite the actress when she wants to be.

I feel sick. I cover my mouth with my hand.

It's Viktoria's choice. I know that. But there's this little stone in my shoe, a niggle that makes me question if it really is. I know how much she needs money. I know she sends it home to her mother in Belarus. Three thousand euros is a lot of money.

So, really, how much choice is there in her choice?

I look back again and see Viktoria massage one of the men's shoulders. I want to go home. I walk straight past Domino Gant and out of a fire-escape door.

MXP > CDG

Paris.

Last week of this shit and then home. If I let my brain think about Mum, Ferdy, *London* for more than a minute, tears start to push at my eyeballs. Paris is like Milan only I don't have a Rafael ferrying me from casting to casting. Instead I have to rely on cabs crawling through traffic, or – the faster option – catching the Metro. My GCSE French is being tested to the absolute limits.

As pretty as Paris is, like Milan, I'm seeing it all from street level, with barely enough time to look up at, let alone appreciate, the skyline. Sure, I've passed the Eiffel Tower, like, a gazillion times, but I'm so tired right now, it might as well be a glittery telephone mast.

Worse still, the hotel my Paris agency has put me in – a hostel above a delicatessen – looks like a crack den. The only thing going for it is that it's handy for some of the show venues. It smells of *le pain et le fromage*, which is fucking cruel when I daren't eat either of those things.

I've already booked Chanel and Alexander McQueen, which is cool, and now, if I can find it, I have Caesar's Bones. I emerge from the Metro at Place d'Italie and try to get my bearings. Luckily, I see a trio of super skinny tall girls clutching their books on the other side of the street so I figure following them is a safe bet.

The casting is in what looks like an old school building or something. It's sad and cold, the wind somehow rattling through the long corridors. I see there are already girls queuing down an endless gloomy hallway waiting to be seen. I pass them to check in. I recognise the girl at the desk. She works with the sex-couple Vanessa and Vito. Oh, great. These two are the worst, and there's never a system. I'm gonna be here a while.

I check in and the assistant takes my book – a sly move which means I can't give up and leave. I'm trapped.

On my way back down to join the back of the queue, I hear someone call my name. I turn and see Arabella already squatting on the floor. 'Arabella! Hello! How long have you been waiting?'

'Uh, like an hour. This is the couple . . .'

'Who just randomly pick you as and when they feel like it? Yeah, I'm familiar. Can I . . .?' All the Russian blondes push in with each other so I don't see why I shouldn't. It's not as if we'll be seen in any logical order anyway, is it? I squidge in alongside Arabella to a scowl from the girl behind us.

'How's it going?' I ask.

'Oh, not so great,' she says. 'I booked McQueen, but that's it so far.'

'McQueen, though! That's amazing.'

Arabella's big blue eyes turn watery. 'I know, but . . . I just wish I knew what I was doing wrong.'

'Nothing. You're not doing anything wrong. I guess they

either like the way you look or they don't.'

And now her eyes widen to anime-proportions. 'What's wrong with the way I look?'

'Nothing! That's not what I meant. I just . . . Clara told me that we have to step back and just see this for what it is. We're . . . mannequins, innit? Moving mannequins. There is nothing we can say or do to convince these people. It's not personal.' Phew, think I dug myself out.

Her shoulders sag a little. After a minute she says, 'I spy with my little eye something beginning with A.'

'Apple,' I say.

'Your turn.'

One hour rolls into two. The corridor is freezing. A couple of girls start crying or calling their agencies. They're told to wait it out. I guess, in the grand scheme, Caesar's Bones are more valuable to our agents than we are.

How are they allowed to do this? I'm not having a *DON'T-YOU-KNOW-WHO-I-AM?* moment, I'm having an *IS-THIS-LEGAL?* moment. I ration out half a bottle of water between me and Arabella, but that's all we have. I'm so hungry I feel a bit weird and dizzy.

After *three and a half hours* of sitting on my arse, me, Arabella and two other girls are summoned. We stand, pose and walk. I'm too cold and hungry to even try to be charming or charismatic. I put on the giant Bones clown shoes and strut up and down a few times.

Both Arabella and I are asked to try some clothes on. I've stopped actually *seeing* the clothes most of the time, to be honest, but even I clock that these outfits are stupid – exactly

231

the sort of thing I'd have expected to see on a catwalk this time last year. Everything is made of semi-opaque rubber plastic, sort of like what you'd wrap burn victims in. The material is so tight I kind of scuttle along like my legs are bound together. Because, you know, they are.

Across the room sex-woman Vanessa is trying to zip Arabella into a rubber pencil skirt, but the zipper won't close over her bum. I don't catch all of what she's saying, but I *definitely* hear her say *grosse vache*. She's calling Arabella a fat cow.

I'm struck by a sudden urge to stomp over there and rip her fucking stupid fedora off and shove it so far up her arse it pops out her mouth. How *dare* she? How dare she say that with Arabella standing right *there*? Only good thing is that Arabella don't speak French as well as I do.

Anyone with eyes can see that Arabella ain't fat. She's tiny as a sparrow. She just has a bum and hips like human women are meant to. I'm the freak; she's perfect. 'Get off,' I tell the man currently trying to squish my boobs into a corset. He protests, but I push him off. 'I said get *off*, I'll do it.'

I have no intention of walking for them. I'll turn it down if they offer it. They can fuck right off. This whole thing can fuck off. For something all about beauty, it's so bloody ugly.

That night I sink into the bath at the fleapit hotel. It's a tiny tub and my long legs jut out. I catch sight of myself in the shaving mirror and flinch. I look fucking awful. Make-up runs down my face. My skin is covered in acne from all the crap it's been caked in for the last three weeks. Emerging from the soapy water, I honestly look *monstrous*.

I bury my face in a flannel and cry.

'Hi. It's me. Are you asleep? Can you call me when you get this?'

'Hi, Ferdy, it's me again. I'm in this really crappy hotel and I can hear people fighting outside and it's just properly fuckin' scary. I just wanted to hear your voice. I hate it here. I hate it.'

'Ignore that last message. I was being a baby. I'm fine. I'm just really tired. I know it's only one more week, but I really want to come home. I'm gonna have a bath and go to sleep. I love you.'

– There's a difference between *fear* and *danger*.
– How do you mean?
– Fear is imagined, danger is real. Problem was, I hadn't learned to listen to my gut.
– Can you expand on that?
– Well, *now* I know that anxiety, that knot in your stomach, is just your 'fight or flight' mechanism kicking in. And a lot of the time, yeah, it's all in your head, and that's when doctors give you medication. But sometimes, your body's telling you to run away *for a reason*. I should have listened to my body. It was talking to me, telling me something was wrong. But instead of listening, I just kept taking them pills, numbing myself, but . . . I knew, y'know? Seriously. I *knew*.

BLO

I somehow drag my body down the necessary catwalks. It's fine. I take a little stumble at Dior but I don't think anyone really notices. Hurt my ankle, though. Tomorrow I have the closing Chanel show and then it's HOME.

Oh my god, I'm counting down the minutes.

I get it now. The reason models always look mad as hell is because THEY ARE. I don't think the Xanax is even touching the sides any more. I sent Lien a message and she said you get used to them pretty fast, so I should take an extra one every day. She also sent me the details of a doctor where I can buy some more online so I don't run out. Apparently you can't get Xanax in the UK for some bullshit reason, but the online pharmacy will deliver. Boom. Easy.

I've reached the stage where if I'm motionless for more than about three minutes, I fall asleep. My body shuts down. I'm half-snoozing in the back of a rowing boat on the Seine, a photographer standing over me. I'm shooting an editorial for *Elle* France in my 'spare time'. I'm in a huge, gauzy Chloé dress the colour of sunshine. I'm supposed to look 'dreamy' so I'm hoping it's OK that I'm half-asleep. Honestly. I'm so tired at this stage, it's like I'm a ghost, floating about three metres above my body, looking down at some other girl, some cuckoo, living my life. She looks great.

'Someone's ringing!' the assistant says.

'Oh, that's me,' I say, waking up. It's Prestige. I groan. 'Sorry, I better take this.' The photographer nods and changes lenses. 'Hello?'

'Hello, little one, it's Maggie. How are you getting on?'

'Good.' I rub my eyes, forgetting they're covered in thick, greasy, green glitter.

'Wonderful, me and Cheska will be at Chanel to see you tomorrow. We're so proud, you know.'

'OK, great. Maggie . . . I'm on that shoot . . .'

'This'll just take a minute! I have good news.'

'Yeah?'

'Lucas Blo has asked to see you for a casting session.'

I dimly remember the ginger guy from the party in London. 'What? Sorry, I'm half-asleep.'

'That big photographer, sweetheart. He's casting a new campaign for Burdock & Rasputin and I said you'd meet with him while you're in Paris.'

'When is it?' I ask. I sit up and push my hair out of my eyes. It needs a cut.

'Friday. We can change your Eurostar and get you a hotel, don't worry.'

No. Oh, no. 'Maggie . . . I just want to go home.' I'm so tired tears sting my eyes at once. I was so close, this seems really fucking cruel.

'Oh, sweetheart, I know you're tired, but it's just another day and we'll get you a nicer hotel, I promise.'

'Maggie, can't it wait? Seriously, I'm so exhausted and I look like shit. No one in their right mind would cast me for anything.'

'Jana, sweetheart, you don't ask people like Lucas Blo to wait. He's someone who can make or break careers. He's a big deal, a really big deal. I wouldn't ask you to do it if I didn't think it'd take your career to the next level. You know he was one of the very first photographers to work with Clara, and look what happened!'

'Is it in the morning?'

'I'll see what I can do, I promise. And we'll get you a first-class ticket home. This could be massive, darling, and open huge doors in America. I think a lot of people know your face now, but we need them to know your name . . .'

She witters on and on. I think I nod off while she's still talking.

The Chanel show is super extra. There's like a hundred girls (OK, slight – but only slight – exaggeration) and the theme is *Alice in Wonderland*. The catwalk, if you can even call it that, is a winding pathway through a botanic garden with little monkeys and tropical birds and butterflies all over the place.

I'm so tired, I legitimately get lost as I try to follow the 'whimsical' route. I don't think anyone notices. We were told to, 'Be more Alice,' so it probably works. I must look confused, if not curious, in my stripy tights and backcombed blonde wig.

After the show, we all pose backstage in big fluffy Chanel robes as Annie Leibovitz takes 'candid' pictures. Maggie and Cheska come backstage to congratulate me. So I guess I done good.

'Right, young lady,' Maggie says. 'You're all booked in at Le Meurice. Go have a big bath. Early call-time tomorrow, as promised.'

'Thank you.' I want room service. I want a burger. A CHEESEburger. WITH FRIES. And I want to call Ferdy and Mum. There are screens for us to change behind. I slip off the robe and wonder if I can burn the nude underwear I've been walking around in for four weeks. I wash them in the sink every night, but they still smell rank. It's well glamorous, modelling.

Maggie checks her phone. 'Right. Our cars are here. Knock 'em dead tomorrow. Tell Lucas I say hi, won't you?'

'Sure.' I pull a T-shirt over my head and look around for my jeans.

Maggie chases off after one of the casting directors, leaving me with Cheska. She looks as thoroughly done with Fashion Week as I am. 'You need anything, Jana? I've got a car outside for you to take you to the hotel and they'll pick you up in the morning too.'

'Thanks.' I find my jeans and start to pull them on. I have one leg in and one leg out when I suddenly go light-headed. It's like all the fluid in my head swooshes forward and the rooms goes very bright. My legs feel like wet sponge and . . . Cheska jumps towards me and steadies me.

'Jana?'

It passes. I blink and shake my head. 'Oooh, that was weird.'

'You OK?'

'Yeah. Yeah, I'm good.'

Cheska don't look convinced. 'When did you last eat?'

I actually can't remember the last time I sat down and ate proper non-buffet food. 'I had a banana before the show.'

'Jesus, Jana. Don't forget to eat, for god's sake. Look after yourself. We need you fit and healthy.'

I nod and finish zipping my jeans up.

Cheska goes on. 'Thank you so much for all your hard work, Jana, you've absolutely smashed it. After a couple of nights in your own bed, I hope you think it's all been worth it. You've made an absolute fuck ton of money too.'

I smile up at her as I tie my shoelaces on the floor.

'Hey, Jana?' Cheska looks back as she makes her way out.

'Yeah?'

'Just . . . watch yourself with Blo tomorrow. He's . . . a funny one.'

I look up at her. She's like a mighty Amazon towering over me. 'Funny?'

'He can be a bit of a prick. Don't take anything he says personally.'

Frankly, I'm too tired to listen or care.

I think it'd all be water off a duck's back at this stage.

It's funny how much difference a bath, a burger and a very big bed make. The next morning I wake up refreshed. I look out of the window and see Paris in the springtime. It's absolutely gorgeous, like I'm seeing it for the first time. The Seine, Notre Dame, the Eiffel Tower, the Arc de Triomphe. *Très jolie.*

As requested by Blo's 'people', I shower and wear absolutely no make-up. I googled his work last night. It's pretty weird stuff. I can see why he wants me. His models are often androgynous, flat-chested, almost extra-terrestrial looking, so I guess I fit the bill.

He often does nude or semi-nude stuff – like that one of Clara in a shower – but if this is for a Burdock & Rasputin campaign, I can't imagine I'll need to get my boobs out because I'll be wearing their clothes. Nipples *are* very fashion, I've noticed. I wore that semi-opaque blouse thing at Veroniqa Heritage and didn't mind so much because it made sense in context and all the other models – including the boys – were wearing them too.

With the shows over, I *think* I'm allowed to eat like a normal human again, so grab a chocolate croissant to scoff in the car on the way to the studio.

We crawl through heavy traffic for about fifteen minutes when the driver pulls up outside a big fancy hotel. 'Is this it?'

'*Oui, mademoiselle.*'

'Oh, OK.' I step out of the car while the driver fetches my bags. I'm heading straight home after the casting. We're at another swish hotel: Le Palais. I suppose it is only a casting, not a shoot, so that makes sense.

I wander into reception and try to figure out where I'm going. 'Jana?' a voice says. I look around and see a tiny hipster girl in a beanie hat and tent-like plaid shirt.

'Yeah.'

'Hi, I'm Suzuki, Lucas's assistant. Do you wanna follow me? We've got a suite.'

'Cool, sure.'

I follow her into the lift and we ride up to the seventh floor. There's a labyrinth of corridors until we arrive at a penthouse with grand double doors. 'Just wait here and I'll see if they're ready.' I do as I'm told and Suzuki returns a minute or so later. 'OK, Jana, come on in.'

The suite is pretty swish, but reeks of cigarette smoke, weed and whiskey. The curtains are all drawn. Prince is playing from the stereo. I wonder if they've been up all night.

'Hey, hey, hey!' Lucas is dancing on the sofa. Without his trucker cap, his red hair is braided into cornrows. Ugh, this guy is truly the worst. He's wearing only tiny red shorts, gold chains and sneakers. 'So great to see you, Jana, come join the party! You like Prince? "Raspberry Beret"! What a fucking tune!'

There's Lucas and two other guys, although one looks essentially comatose in an armchair. 'Yeah. Love him.' Who don't love Prince?

'I knew you'd be cool. You want some coke?' Lucas says. 'Where'd you think I got my name from? Blo? Geddit? Well, my name is Blomfeld too, but it's pretty cute, right?'

'Yeah,' I put my bags by the door.

'Line, baby?'

'It's a little early in the day for me . . .'

He does a fat line of white powder off Clara's face on a magazine on the coffee table. 'God, you kids! You're all vegan, clean-eating, detox freaks! I've been up for three days straight and I'm old enough to be your daddy! You want a beer or anything?'

I wasn't sure if I liked him when I met him in London, and now I know I don't. I don't know why, I just don't. I just want to get this over with and get the train. But I guess I should remember my manners. 'A coffee would be great, thanks.'

'Suzuki! Coffee for Jana.' She scurries off to fetch a coffee.

'Brody, move your fat ass, let Jana sit down, she's our guest, for fuck's sake.' A chubby guy not much older than me scoots over to make space. I perch alongside him.

'Hey, I'm Brody.'

'Jana.'

Blo does another line of coke and pinches his nose. 'I have the best dealer – this guy who delivers anywhere. Finest Bolivian marching powder in the world. What's wrong, Jana, babe? You look so uptight!'

I'm uptight because I'm the only sober person at a three-day bender. I'm dying to get home, but decide against telling him the truth. 'I'm just tired off the back of Fashion Week.'

'Got it.' He lights a cigarette and grabs a beer out of the fridge. 'Well, relax, babe. Listen. You gotta understand. When you work with Lucas Blo, it's a party. I don't take pictures, I capture a motherfucking vibe. Now answer me this: you gonna bring the party?'

I force a smile and hope it don't look as fake as it feels. 'I'll try my very hardest.'

'YES, GIRL, JANA!' Lucas cries at the top of his voice. 'We are gonna PARTY! I fuckin' love this bitch already.'

Suzuki returns with my coffee but then wanders off again. I wish she'd stay. I don't like being the only girl. Lucas and Brody share a joint, and try to pass it to me. It's nine-thirty in the morning. 'Come on, Jana, bring the party,' he says. I take a tiny toke, not really inhaling.

'Nice, babe, just relax. Where's your sense of humour? Don't be so stiff. What we're gonna do is just a few test shots . . .'

'Here?'

'Yeah. I prefer locations to studios. In studios you have to fake everything. Like, why construct a fucking fake pile of fake garbage in a studio, when you could take some girl to the city dump? Know what I mean?'

'Sure.' I actually don't, but whatever.

'This'll work. I like the natural light anyway. I'm just gonna do some test shots and see who works best.'

'And this is for Burdock & Rasputin?'

'Yeah. Autumn/Winter campaign. It's gonna be real. I want it dirty and fucked.' He picks up an old-fashioned camera and fires off an unexpected shot.

'Oh. I wasn't ready.'

He takes another. 'I despise ready.'

'OK.' What a thundercunt, honestly.

'Erm . . .' He looks around the room. 'Here, put this on.' He thrusts a massive fur coat into my hands.

'Is this real?'

'Yeah, mink. But it's vintage.'

God, this guy *is* a prick, Cheska was right. I don't wanna wear fur. I think it's beyond needless. Still, I'll just wear the coat and get the fuck out. I start to put it on.

'No, honey, *just* the jacket. No T-shirt. Bit of skin-on-fur action! Hot, right? Like you're a fuckin' animal.'

Great. 'Give me a minute. I'll change.'

'Cute! You British girls! I love ya!' He takes a shot of my back. 'Say, Jana? Do you shave your bush?'

'What?'

'You European girls are real nasty, right? You rock a full fucking bush, right? Love that.'

244

I am speechless. Actually dumb. Gobsmacked. Am I hearing this right?

'Well? You got a hairy pussy, baby?'

My mouth opens but I can't speak. I'm frozen.

And then Blo laughs. 'Oh, Jana! You're too cute! Come on through and change.'

The suite is in two halves. One half is like a living room, the other is the bed area. I move through the partition wall and pull my T-shirt and bra off. I slip the coat over my shoulders.

There's a flash and Blo is behind me with the camera. 'Hey!' I say.

'Sorry, couldn't resist. You look cool as fuck. Shall we make a start? Go sit by the window in that chair.'

I do as I'm told.

'Do you smoke?'

'No.'

'Pretend for me. Brody! Give her a smoke.' Brody comes in and hands me his lit cigarette. 'That's fucking hot. Cover your tits, though, yeah. Good.' He has no fear there. I am covering my tits.

He takes another couple of shots and I relax. Now we're working, it feels less weird. I sink into the chair and find my light out of the window.

'You are fucking living!' Blo yells. 'You're so dirty. You're like . . . a boss! You're a pimp! Yeah, that's it, you're a pimp.'

I put the cigarette between my lips, figuring that'll look good. Ash rains down on to the mink.

'Fuck me, that's hot. Love it. She's good, huh?' He takes another few shots. 'Hey, Brody, take over, will you?' He hands the camera to his assistant.

245

'Sure,' Brody says.

'Imma jump in with you, Jana. That cool?'

'Sorry . . . what?'

He must pick up on my stone-cold tone. 'Oh, I do it all the time. I'm my own fucking muse.' He grabs a brown leather belt off the bed and slips it around his neck like a leash. 'Here, I want you to tug on this, like I'm your bitch. I fuckin' love that.'

'This is so weird . . .' I say.

'No! It's cool! I'm your bitch and you're the pimp.'

He kneels down on all fours and barks like a dog. I take hold of the belt. Well, this is odd.

'What are you fuckin' waitin' for?' he snaps at Brody. Brody takes a camera and I do my job. I strike a fierce stance, posing like I'm dominating him. *This is my job, just do your job. It's a job.*

'This looks sick,' Brody says, looking at the screen.

Blo hops up and joins him. 'Fuck, yeah!' He bounds back over. 'Oh, wait.' He stops and wriggles out of his shorts. He leaves the sneakers on and kicks the shorts to the other side of the suite. He's not wearing underwear.

The actual fuck?

I flinch, raising my hand to avoid a clear view into his hairy butt crack. 'Oh, god . . .'

'What?' he says. 'My dick? C'mon, don't be so British, it's just a dick!' He gives it a waggle and I look away, mortified. I don't even wanna see it. 'Jana! I'm, like, being a dog!' He drops to the floor again. 'OK, have you got my lead, pimp? Let's do this, Brody! Go!'

Brody fires off another round.

Blo stands up and shoves his dick right in my face. I can smell it.

'Stop!' I bleat, almost like a reflex.

'What?' he says. 'Is it too much?'

'It's . . . you're . . . *naked* . . .' I say.

'It's cool, right? It's just a body. Here.' He grabs my hand and holds it over his soft, shrivelled dick. It's warm and damp against my palm. 'There, now I'm not nude, Brody?'

Brody takes the picture before I can snatch my hand back. 'Jesus!'

'Fine. Whatever.' He dismisses me with a wave of his hand. 'Then I think we're done. I can't work with that shitty attitude.'

'I'm sorry . . . I just wasn't expecting . . .' Why am I apologising? I guess because I've ruined the shoot. God, I'm gonna be in so much trouble with Prestige.

'No,' Blo says, padding away. 'It's cool. Not all models get it. It's supposed to be a *party*, Jana. You didn't bring the party. It's not a biggy. No *hard* feelings.' He waves his flaccid cock at me and both he and Brody fall about laughing.

'I'm sorry if . . .'

'You can go now.' He's utterly disinterested, strolling away to get another beer. 'Keep the coat if you want it.'

I slip it off and cover my breast with my arm. 'Do you mind?' I say to Brody, who's just standing there, watching me change.

'Oh, sure.' He goes back into the lounge. I stoop to pick up my T-shirt.

* * *

247

I hold my breath as I leave the suite. I don't say goodbye, worried they won't let me leave. I hold it in all the way down the corridor until I get to the lift.

I press the button.

I look over my shoulder to see if I've been followed.

The lift arrives with a *ping* and I step inside. I can't even face myself in the mirror.

The doors slide shut.

I burst into tears.

– Do you want to take a break?
– No. No, it's OK.
– You sure?
– Yeah. It's why we're doing this.

AFTERMATH

I keep bursting into tears on the Eurostar. It's stupid. On the train, it's light and bright and smells of pine air freshener, and I don't know why ... but my whole body shakes, convulses, and I can't stop. Another passenger, a glam older woman, peers over her cat eye specs at me and asks if I'm OK. All I can do is laugh it off and say I'm being silly, hormonal. The steward, also clearly concerned, brings me a cup of sugary tea but my hands won't stop trembling.

It's all through my skeleton. Electric shocks. My bones rattle and my teeth chatter.

Emotions, all of them, strobe through my head:

1. *Angry* that he got his dick out.

2. *Repulsed* because it's been on me. I feel soiled.

3. *Worried* I'll get shouted at for fucking up the shoot.

4. *Scared* Ferdy might dump me, or think I slept with Blo to get cast.

5. *Confused*. Like, how did that happen?

I'm a fucking mess.

In the end I go and sit on the floor in the vestibule between carriages because it's cooler and I feel nauseous. Here, there's a cold draught that keeps me from throwing up.

The poor old woman must think I'm insane.

*   *   *

By the time I get to St Pancras I don't feel hysterical any more. Just seeing London makes me feel more human. I'm nearly home; I'm safe.

Only now do I realise how much worse it could have been. I guess I'm lucky. If Suzuki, or Brody, or that other unconscious guy hadn't been there, god knows what Blo might have done. I got out. I'm not hurt.

It was fucked up.

But I'm fine.

I think.

So why is my skin screaming? Why do I want to tear it all off and bleach clean the flesh underneath?

I make my way to Vauxhall and eat a chocolate muffin with gooey filling. It helps me feel more solid, like my feet are in contact with the floor. I take the overground to Clapham Junction and then walk through the Winstanley, wheeling my big suitcase behind me.

They're ugly as sin, but I've never been so pleased to see the grey tower blocks and pebbledash walls, the rubbish bins and garages. I've missed the scribbled tags, the abandoned Asda trolleys and peeling posters for reggae or gospel nights. A filthy fox, more black than red, struts down the centre of Ingrave Street, bold as tits in broad daylight.

I'm *home*.

As I walk up the garden path, I almost start to cry again. It feels so good.

Mum appears at the front door. 'There she is! Come, come, give me your case. You must have so much dirty laundry. I'll put a load on now.'

A little sob breaks free and I fall into her arms.

She rubs my back. 'Jana? Are you OK?'

Tell her.

But my brain can't make the sentence. It stalls halfway up my throat. She's my *mum*. I can't tell her about what some sleazy fucking asshole did with his dick. I can't say *dick* to my mum. She'll keel over and die. And she already feels guilty about me leaving school and . . . oh, god, I can't.

'I'm fine,' I say. 'I'm just really tired.'

'Aw, poor girl. I worry about you.'

'I'm really glad to be home.' And that is the truth.

The hallway smells of *home*. Of socks drying on the radiators; of Milos's stinky football boots on a piece of newspaper; of the hideous blue cheese only Dad eats and keeps in the fridge. It's home. I'm home.

Mum insists I have a ham sandwich and some tomato soup, and I tell her what I can remember about the shows: about *Alice in Wonderland* and almost taking a tumble at Dior. 'And how was your . . . shoot, was it? Today?' she asks, pouring some tea into a faded *High School Musical 2* mug.

'Fine,' I say, suddenly unable to touch the soup. 'It was just a casting.'

I take a very long, very hot shower. It feels a bit clichéd, but it helps. I wash the whole day off my body. My hair reeks of that smoky hotel room. I can't forget the wet tip touching my hand. Gross. I shampoo my hair twice. The water is so hot I feel like it's scouring the top layer of skin clean off. I feel like a blacklight would show up his grubby fingerprints all over me. The room fills with steam like a sauna.

My shoulders go down.

I'm home.

I'm fine.

I think.

I hardly recognise Ferdy when we meet outside Starbucks later that night. My body is almost dragging me towards bed, but I haven't seen him in weeks. His hair is tied back and he's wearing a skinny tie with his plaid shirt. In his hand is a bunch of peonies, my favourites. 'Oh my god! What's this?'

'I wanted to welcome you home!'

'You look so cool!'

We kiss, but I feel . . . odd. It's *Ferdy* not Blo, but . . . oh, it's weird, like I've forgotten to do something. Like déjà vu, but awful. I'm on red-alert for no reason. 'I booked us a table at Alessandro's for seven-thirty.'

'Alessandro's?' I try to smile brightly. 'Fancy! OK!'

He takes my hand and leads the way towards Battersea High Street. 'How was Paris?'

My feet stop. My stomach bucks and I almost vomit right there on the pavement outside the vape shop.

'Jana? You OK?'

And it passes. 'Yeah. Yeah, I'm fine.'

His brow furrows. 'Sure?' I nod. 'OK. Shall we?'

I feel underdressed for Alessandro's. It's one of those that does 'tasting menus' and a chef comes running over every five minutes to explain what you're eating. Places like this make me feel about eleven years old. I'd have been fine with Nando's, but Ferdy's made an effort, so I need to try for him.

I'm famished *until* my carbonara served in a coconut (?) arrives and then it feels like my stomach shrivels up like a raisin. Ferdy fills me in on everything that's been going on while I was away. 'So Laurel is fully one of the pretty girls now. You should see her, she looks totally different, like she's been assimilated by Heather. Jana?'

'Yeah?'

He smiles. 'Are you listening to me?'

I stop poking the spaghetti around in the coconut. 'Yes.'

'What did I just say?'

'Erm. Something to do with Heather?'

'You're a million miles away.'

'I'm sorry.' Nearly all of my brain is saying that, if I tell Ferdy what happened, he'll believe me wholeheartedly. But one rogue brain nubbin is saying that I agreed to go into a hotel room and did a nude photoshoot with a man old enough to be my dad. What if he's upset? What if he dumps me? There's no way I'm losing Ferdy over that *pervert*.

Also, I keep telling myself that I'm being a crybaby. Like nothing *really* happened, did it? It's not like he did anything to me. I'm *fine*. I'm back home with my boyfriend, who I love, and I can't even hear a word he's saying.

'I know, theoretically, you can't get jet lag from Paris, but I feel pretty gross,' I say. 'I've heard Maggie talk about Fashion-Week flu, maybe it's that.'

'Hey, don't worry,' he says, although I know this boy. He's annoyed and trying to hide it. He's made an effort and I'm serving lobotomy realness. 'I'm just glad to have you home.'

I try to focus on my food and what he's saying. We finish

dinner and then share some tiramisu. On his way to the bathroom, Ferdy asks for the bill and the waitress drops it off at the table on a silver tray with some mints. Wow, the bill comes to eighty-five pounds. Ferdy don't have eighty-five pounds. I reach into my bag and get my purse. Although most of my modelling money has gone in a trust fund for when I'm eighteen, I'm paying myself an allowance so I can afford to eat and stuff when I'm working.

The waitress takes the card away as Ferdy returns. 'Was there a problem?' he says as he slides back into his seat.

'No,' I say. 'It's my treat.'

'Jana!' He seems pissy. 'I wanted to treat *you*.'

'You did! We get to spend a whole night together!'

'That's not the point and you just shat on my big romantic gesture.'

And now I'm pissy. 'Jesus fucking Christ, did you go the toilet or the TARDIS? We're not in Victorian England. Girls can buy their boyfriends dinner.' Some of the other snotty diners look over. I scowl back at some woman glaring at me over the top of her merlot. Cow. Bet I make more money than she does.

He swallows his words and sits down at the table. 'That . . . that's not what I meant. I wanted to do something special for you.'

'It *was*. But I can afford it and . . .'

'And I can't because I'm the loser boyfriend,' he mutters under his breath, but plenty loud enough for me to hear. He can't even look me in the eye.

I sigh. Could today please just fuck off? I'm gonna cry. I can feel the tears trying to push out. I'm gonna scream and never stop. 'No one thinks that.' I just about keep my voice on the rails.

'You have to let me be a part of your world, Jana, or we're screwed.'

'Ferdy.' A tear runs down my face. My throat has glass in it. 'You *are* my world. Please don't leave me.'

His face changes from pissy to concerned. 'What? Jana? That's not what I'm saying? Are you OK?'

'Yes. Yes, I'm fine. I just don't wanna fight over a bloody bill!'

'I'm sorry,' he says. 'You're sure that's all it is, right?'

'Yes.' I dab my eye with a napkin. 'What else would it be?'

'I don't know. You've been away for a month pretty much. Like, maybe you've met someone . . .'

'Ferdy, no!' My voice goes weirdly loud and even more diners look over. The merlot woman tuts. I lower it again. 'That's not what's happening. I swear.'

He looks relieved. Is that what he thinks of me? That I'm shagging a whole bunch of people behind his back? 'If you say so, I believe you. It's just . . . god, I don't know if there's a way I can say this without sounding like an ass . . . you have a new life now. And I'm not a part of it.'

'You are. When I was away, all I wanted was to be home with you. In Dubai I met this model called Kami and she was saying that none of us actually want to be models. It's not something any of us chose.'

He sighs. 'I know. I know all these things. I just missed you.'

'I missed you too. I don't know if I even like it that much.'

'So . . . stop.'

It seems pretty obvious when he says it like that. I've made a fuck ton of money over the last few months. Maybe it's like going to Las Vegas: the trick is in knowing when to cash your chips. 'Yeah. Yeah, you're right.'

He seems surprised. 'Really?'

'Yeah. I mean, if I hate it, why keep doing it?'

We head back to Ferdy's. His mum, dad and sister are away again on a dancing competition. We have the whole flat to ourselves.

I'm already a little tipsy from the beer we had at the restaurant. Luckily for us, we didn't get ID'd. Ferdy's tie must have fooled them. 'You want another beer?'

'Yeah.'

'Do you think you can stay over?'

'I don't think so. Mum wants to have a big family day tomorrow.'

'No worries.'

He sticks the fire on and I cuddle up to him on the rug as we watch *The Exorcist*. 'Is this supposed to be scary?' I ask. I'm being over-nice to make up for the shittiness at the restaurant. I'm trying too hard and I know it, and he knows it, but he plays along.

'She just came down the stairs on her back. Didn't that freak you out?'

'No! You know this stuff don't scare me.' I grin and kiss him.

I turn back to the film, but he turns my chin to his lips. He wants to make out. Maybe he's forgiven me? It feels so lovely to be in his arms at last. I melt on him like butter on toast.

We lie side by side on the rug, and I'm nicely drifting into it, feeling the blast from the electric fire on my face, when his fingers graze my hips.

It feels alien.

My spine arches.

I go cold.

I freeze.

I open my eyes, and just for a second, Lucas Blo gurns down at me, slobbering. I feel prickles spring up all over my skin like I'm a porcupine. His touch almost hurts.

I push Ferdy off and sit up.

'Jana?'

He looks so wounded. 'Sorry.'

'What was that?'

'Sorry. That . . . that tickled. Not in a good way.'

'I . . . I'm sorry . . . I didn't mean to.'

'No. I know.' I cuddle up to him again and we kiss, but I've chased the moment right out of the door. I follow it out as soon as the film ends.

Home, and back in my bed, I can't stop thinking about that fucking hotel room. My body aches with tiredness and my eyes are sore, but my mind is whirring. I just want to sleep, for this day to be over, but I can't switch off. All the different things I could have done.

I *could have* laughed it off and told him to put it away.

I *could have* threatened to tell my agency.

I *could have* walked out of the hotel the second he took his pants off.

I *could have* screamed for help.

I *could have* punched him in the face and kneed him in the nuts.

I *could have* pretended to feel ill and made an excuse.

But I didn't do any of those things. I just sat there like a twat in a fur coat while he rubbed his dick in my face.

I roll over and bury my face in the pillow. I want it to stop. Something is wrong. I can feel it in my marrow. I wish there was a way I could get out of my body.

And just be somewhere else.

Sabah: Heya! You home?

Sabah: You alive hon?

Sabah: ???

Sabah: Hey. Have u remembered it's Mo's wedding this wkend?

       Jana: Of course! Soz! I'll be there.

Sabah: K x

DENIAL

Sabah's big brother got married today and I'm invited to the evening party. It's a noisy, colourful affair with a live band and dancing in a huge marquee. Mo, Sabah's brother, and Farah, his new wife, look sick and seem properly, blissfully happy. It's pure Bollywood and I wish I could dance the way Sabah's family seem to be able to, but I don't think I can, because I dance like my dad at the best of times, and I think if I tried, it'd look like I was taking the mick.

Since I got back, I've mostly slept. I think Mum and Ferdy think I'm sick. It's weird: I don't really have a life any more. I don't have school and I don't want to go to the fashion parties I get invites to. I can't be arsed. Perfume launches; fashion lines; beauty brands. There really is something every night. I just ignore the emails in my inbox. I feel badly dubbed, with my life a few seconds behind everything that happens.

Still. Now that I'm here, I'm glad I couldn't wriggle out of the wedding – as much as I would have preferred to stay home and watch Netflix in bed. Mo's wedding has been in my diary for months. Last night I went over to Sabah's place and her cousin did the most beautiful *mehndi* on our hands. Sabah has lent me a gorgeous silk scarf – violet with golden embroidery

– to cover my head. I feel very Arabian-Nights, Princess-Jasmine realness right now.

I pick at the buffet, letting the party flow around me. The food is FIT. I sample stews and curries and little delicious lamb thingies. I'm told it's a mixture of traditional Somali and Gujarati food to please both Mo's and Farah's families.

Sabah's family history is *complicated* and I don't like to pry, but her dad was killed in the civil war when Sabah was a baby and that's why they came to London as refugees. Only then there was some sort of a scandal when her mum remarried outside of the family. I dunno. I remember them having to move a lot when we was about nine. Things have calmed down now, though. Her stepdad, Abdi, is lovely and she's always just called him 'Dad'. Right now he's dancing with Farah.

I'm fully full, but I might just have a tiny bit more of the spicy lamb . . . I scoop another spoonful on to my plate.

I feel hands on my ass.

Blo.

I yelp and spin around, ready, fight or flight. 'Get off!' I blurt out.

It's just Sabah, eyes wide in her pretty peachy-pink bridesmaid dress. She holds up her hands in surrender. 'Sorry! I thought you saw me coming!'

'Well, I didn't!' I snap, my heart settling back into its normal rhythm. What a stupid fucking thing to say. *Tell her*, I think. *Tell her what happened. She's the one person you can tell.* 'Sabs . . .'

Only then Sabah's expression hardens. 'Bish, there's no need to bite my head off! Fuck! You know what? You've been acting like . . . actually, no, never mind.'

What? 'No. If you got something to say . . .' I dump my plate on the buffet table and face her.

She holds her hands up. 'I'm not gonna get into it here, OK?'

'Get into what? Sabah?' I can't. I can't fall out with her on top of everything. It'll kill me.

'Jana,' she hisses, 'it's my brother's wedding . . . can we not?' People are looking over at us.

She turns to leave the buffet, but I grab her arm. 'Sabah, please? Have I done something wrong?'

She sighs. 'No, no, no. It's just . . . you're never here.' Her eyes roll back and her posture slumps. 'Laurel is cancelled, you're a fucking supermodel, and I am here. Same place as before, same old Sabah, all by myself.' On the last word, her voice wobbles. Sabah – *Sabah* – almost just cried. Fuck.

And now I can't tell her about Blo. It'd be like I was trying to one-up her or something. 'Look, I am properly sorry. Now that Fashion Week is done, I'll be around more, I swear.'

She looks like she's gonna argue but then nods. 'Cool.'

'Are we good?'

'Yeah, we're good.' I think she means it, but I'm not sure she *believes* it. Something in her voice. Fake nice. Like sweetener.

I pull her into a tight hug and squeeze. She don't really squeeze me back, though.

I want to, I want to tell her everything.

But I can't.

I need us to be good.

If I can't tell Sabah, I'll tell Ferdy. The morning after the wedding, he's working at the coffee shop but I go to see him anyway. When he can, he comes over and joins me in a booth, wearing a hoodie over his Starbucks shirt. He leans over and gives me a kiss. 'Hello! This is a nice surprise.'

He smiles and sits opposite me with an iced mocha.

Tell him.

'Ferd . . .'

'Yeah?'

Ferdy, I went to a hotel room in Paris to meet a man called Lucas Blo. I took my top off and he got naked. He made me touch his cock. I felt it on my skin. I have felt sick ever since. I can taste battery acid in my mouth. It burns my throat. I didn't want to do it, I swear I didn't . . .

Oh, god, I can't. I can't do it.

Lucas Blo has changed me. I'm bruised and dented, like rotten fruit.

I don't want Ferdy to know I'm rotten.

I need him to love me the way I was when I was still good and nice.

'What is it?' he says.

'Nothing!' I force a grin. 'I just wanted to tell you I had a really hot dream about you last night!'

He smiles with dimples. 'Really? Hot. What did we do?'

'Oh, it's too filthy. You'll blush.' I lean in for a slow, iced-mocha kiss. 'And I've also been thinking about what you said about my job. It sucks I'm never here. I'll try harder to be a good girlfriend.'

Big Angie glares over at our table. 'Kai!' she calls. 'It's not your break time.'

'Well, look.' He takes my hands. 'Whatever you wanna do,

I've got your back. It's funny. *The Devil Wears Prada* was on E4 the other night and I was thinking how I never want to be her dickhead boyfriend. But . . . your job . . . you know, I think your job might be bullshit.'

I manage a smile. '*You* watched *The Devil Wears Prada?*'

'My sister was watching it,' he says with smile as he heads back to work.

I swallow down the taste of battery acid.

I'm on my own.

On Monday I receive another remittance statement from Prestige. It's for a hundred and twenty-five thousand pounds. Everything I earned in New York, London, Milan and Paris.

It feels like hush money.

Or maybe I'm no better than Viktoria and those men in Milan.

Maybe I'm a whore.

They pay me, so I lie back and let them do what they want with my body.

I just have to take it because it's not my body any more, it's theirs, they own it. My mind got divorced from it.

I'm theirs completely.

I'm a body.

I'm flesh.

I am meat.

She looks *so* young.

A baby.

Did I look that young?

A New Face waits with me in reception at Prestige. She has

impossibly big Disney eyes, like a human Bambi. Her hair falls in thick chestnut ringlets almost to her waist. She's proper thin, baby-bird bones, and almost as tall as I am. I've seen enough to know she'll do very well in this business.

As I flick through the new *Vogue* – Domino *and* Dido on the cover – I catch her staring at me. The poor girl looks away, blushing.

'Hi,' I say.

'Hi.' She blushes more. 'You're Jana Novak, right?'

Still weird. I'll never get used to it. 'Yeah.'

'Maggie was showing me your pictures. You're, like, really cool.' She has train-track braces on her teeth.

It's mad that after less than a year, she already knows my name. It's flattering, sure, but I hang on to what I'm about to do. I have to break up with Prestige, regardless of – well – the prestige. 'What's your name?'

'I'm Elyssa. Elyssa Sayers.' She has a gentle Brummie accent.

'New Face?'

'Yeah. Tom spotted me at Winter Wonderland, but I had exams right after Christmas so I couldn't come in until February. I just signed with Prestige last week! I'm so excited! I can't believe I'm going to be a model!'

'You look *exactly* like a model.' I smile.

'Do you think?'

'Yes!'

Elyssa beams. 'There's this horrid boy at school called Jake Kirby and he's always calling me Stick Insect and stuff. I can't wait to see his face when I book my first job.'

'How old are you?'

'Oh, I'm fourteen. I'll be fifteen in May.'

'Fourteen?' I can't mask the horror in my voice. She's in Year Ten!

'Elyssa's in Development until she's sixteen.' Cheska appears in reception, apparently picking up on my tone. 'It's good you've met. Ely, you could learn a lot from her. Jana, we're ready for you.'

I follow Cheska to the conference room. It smells of coffee and Maggie's slightly overbearing perfume. Ro and Tom are present too. We're here to discuss My Future. Or at least that's what they think.

'Well, Jana,' Maggie says, after gushing for ten minutes about how well Fashion Week went. She's wearing a hot-pink metallic blouse that clashes with her hair. 'We've got to get you moved to New York for a while. It's where the work is, but also you're going to get taxed to shit, babes.'

Apparently I'm poised to be a supermodel.

I'm actually here to quit.

'No,' I say. 'I don't want to go to New York.'

'All the campaigns are there,' Cheska says.

'And if you spend less than a hundred and eighty-three days in the UK, you're not a tax resident,' Tom puts in.

The idea fills me with dread. I don't want to live abroad for half the year. Also, I don't actually mind paying tax, because I'm not a cunt. 'No,' I say again.

The three of them look confused but move on.

'OK. If you prefer, we can put you in a model flat while you're in New York,' Maggie says. 'It'll be fine, and you're there and back in eight hours.'

'No,' I say for a third time. 'I've had enough. I don't want to go *anywhere*.'

OK, that gets a response. 'What?' Maggie says.

I can't quite look them in the eye. 'I'm really sorry, but I . . . I think I've had enough. I . . . I really hated Fashion Week. I don't want to do it again.'

The temperature in the room drops about a hundred degrees. There's a horrible silence. '*Every* new girl says that after Fashion Week!' Ro finally pipes up, but Maggie silences her with a glare.

'Jana, darling, the catwalk shows are important for showing you off, but they aren't for ever. Once you get bigger you can pick and choose what you do and you won't have to bother with castings.'

'No.' A fourth time. Was it Peter who denied Jesus three times in the Bible? Apparently fashion is more hardcore. 'I'm really very grateful for what you've done for me and everything, but . . .'

'But nothing!' Maggie says, her smile now slightly forced. 'By all means take a break but there are some *really* exciting things coming up, Jana.'

'Tell her,' Tom says.

'Tell me what?'

The four of them share a smile. 'Jana, little one,' Maggie grins, 'you've only gone and booked *Vogue* China! The cover! Your first *Vogue* cover!'

Oh, wow. That's pretty cool. 'China?'

'Yep. We wanted to keep it a secret but . . . well, anyway. Beijing is a *huge* market. While you're there for *Vogue*, we can sort you out with castings for the Asian market. Very, *very* good money, Jana.'

'Thousands,' Cheska adds.

'Oh, *and*,' Maggie says absentmindedly, 'I got a message from LA this morning. You booked that Burdock & Rasputin campaign with Lucas Blo. Fab or what?'

'NO!' I shout so loud the people outside the conference room turn and stare. His name is like a bomb going off. My ears ring.

'I beg your pardon?' Maggie gasps.

'I said no, no way.' I stand, the palms of my hands flat on the table.

'Jana . . .?' Tom looks worried. 'What's wrong?'

'That pig . . . that pig was disgusting. There's no way. No way I'm going anywhere near him ever again.'

'What happened?' Cheska asks cautiously. She pointedly catches Tom's eye.

'He got totally naked and, and waved it in my face . . . and he made me . . .'

'OK, little one, OK, we get the picture, sit down.' Maggie looks to the others. 'Have you told anyone about this?'

'No,' I say, interested to see what their response will be. Reluctantly, I return to my seat.

'Maggie . . .' Cheska starts, but Maggie holds up a single finger, her red nails talon sharp.

'Can I talk to Jana alone, please? *Now*.'

Tom, Ro and Cheska file out of the conference room.

Maggie walks around the table and sits right next to me. 'Tell me again what he did.'

I tell her the full story from the beginning.

'Oh, Jana, Jana, Jana. What's he like, eh?' Maggie buries her face in her hands. 'He's *such* a bad boy. I've told him about this before.'

'So you *knew*?'

She rubs my back. If she's trying to soothe me, it's not working. 'No! How could I? But he's something of a ladies' man, what can I say?'

'But he—'

'Try not to take it personally. When I was your age, I did a bit of modelling too and *all* the photographers had busy hands. It was just the way it was and you got on with it.'

'But, Maggie, he—'

'He's a provocateur, darling, that's what they do! But you're fine, aren't you? He didn't really *do* anything?'

'Well, he—'

'Oh, but that was just him messing around, wasn't it? Look, little one, if you're not happy I'll turn down the Burdock campaign. That's fine. Lucas isn't for everyone. No hard feelings, I'll make sure of it.'

'But . . .' I struggle to get a word in edgeways. 'What he did was . . . Shouldn't I tell someone? If he's done this before we should . . .'

Maggie slides out of the chair and closes the door. 'Listen. Oh, little one. I *know* Lucas and he meant no harm, and you have to see the bigger picture. We're all a . . . big fashion family. Everyone knows everyone and we look out for one another. I'll have a word with Lucas, don't you worry. And it won't be the first time I've given him a slap on the wrist.'

I look at my scuffed cherry-red Docs. 'He gets a slap on the wrist?'

She tuts. 'It's better than what you'll get if people start to see you as a troublemaker. Girl to girl, I'll tell you now, Jana, that if you get a reputation as a whiner . . . well.'

'I honestly don't care.' I shrug. I don't.

'You should, Jana. Do you know what people are saying about you?'

I shake my head.

She crouches to be on my level. 'They're saying that you're the new British It Girl. The new Lexx, the new Kate, the new Clara. You could be the biggest model in the world, Jana. We are talking millions and millions of pounds. You'll never have to worry about money ever again. But more than that. This morning, in the *Metro*, they had a hairdresser telling readers how to ask for the "Jana" at a salon. You made it. You're a star.'

Oh, god.

I'm a haircut.

'Do you know how rare that is? For a generic model to be known by *name*? Rare as fucking hen's teeth, babes. Think about it.' She walks to the door and holds it open for me. 'Don't blow it now.'

When I arrive home, there's a British Gas van parked outside. The door's on the latch so I enter and find Dad looking utterly flustered in the lounge, hands on hips. 'Dad? What's up?'

'Boiler, ain't it? Went for a shower and there is no hot water.'

'Oh, shit. Aren't you supposed to be at work?'

'Yes, yes. I call in and tell them emergency. Boss wasn't happy but what can you do, eh? And don't swear, please.'

I nod through to the kitchen where I can hear the engineer banging and clattering around. 'Can he fix it?'

'Says the boiler is completely broken. Will need new one. God knows how much it will cost. Thousands.'

I shake my head. 'Well, I'll get it!'

'No! Jana! That money is for your future. For college.'

'Don't talk shit. I owe you, like, seventeen years of rent.'

'Language . . .'

'Sorry,' I say. 'I'll pay. Seriously. As if I'm gonna have you and Mum struggle.'

Dad pulls me into a hug. 'Oh, Jana. You have your mother's warm heart. Is very strange thing when your child starts to earn more money than you do, let me tell you.'

'It's just money.'

'Easy to say when you have it.'

I laugh a little.

'How was your meeting at the agency?'

And suddenly I can't bring myself to tell him I want to quit.

- So you went to Beijing?
- Yes. I didn't want to, but I did.
- Why?
- Can you think of a different job where a seventeen-year-old girl with zero qualifications can make a hundred and twenty-five thousand pounds in four weeks?
- Nope.
- Well, there you go.

LHR > BJS

No one on the whole shoot speaks English. Why would they? I'm in China. Well, there's someone from *Vogue* and she speaks a little. She acts as an intermediary between me and the crew, but it might as well be semaphore for all the good it's doing. The studio, a basement in a district called Fengsheng, is set up like a cherry-blossom garden, and I'm at the centre of it in a giant ostrich-feather coat in pastel pink. It's all very Hello Kitty, and I know I look wicked, but the jet lag feels like I've had liquid cement poured in through my ears.

I've been in China less than twenty-four hours. I'm huge here and I mean that literally. I'm like a metre taller than anyone else. I've only been from the airport to the hotel and everyone openly gawps at me like I'm a freak. I feel like Godzilla. What's worse is that everything is blocked by the state: no WhatsApp, no Google Maps, no Instagram. I'm totally cut off from home. I've been away a day and I'm already over it.

The photographer, Lin Jing, is apparently very famous, and seems very nice and all that, but it's like playing charades. He can only signal and gesture and I have to signal and gesture back. If he wants something complicated, Soo, from *Vogue*, has to try to translate. In the end, it's easier for Lin to come and just twist my body the way he wants it, like I'm a fully poseable action figure. And we have two days of this; we're shooting the cover and a fashion editorial. I have a feeling it's gonna be a *long* two days.

And the stupid thing is, we're in a *room*. This studio could so easily be in London. Why couldn't we just *email* the pictures over?

Still, Prestige and my Chinese agency have paid for a nice hotel room and, with *Vogue* wrapped, I have some time off between castings and shoots. I visit the Forbidden City. It's pretty cool, and at least I can see over most people's heads. Good thing too; it's packed full of tourists. It's beautiful and I take loads of pictures for everyone back home, but with no one to enjoy it with, I'm done there in about an hour. What next? Time passes weirdly slowly when you're alone.

As cool as Beijing is (playing pot luck with the street food is fun – I have potentially eaten some highly questionable meats), it's so smoggy, I can hardly see past my nose. It even clogs the hotel corridors. I get now why the Chinese tourists in London wear face masks – they're used to it. I get myself one on my second day in town to be on the safe side. After a few days, the tall thing gets real old. On the train to a go-see, an actual queue of locals comes to get their picture taken with me. I guess to them I might as well be Godzilla.

I try to make my way to castings by foot so I actually see some of China. The streets are thrumming. Once upon a time this would have stressed me all the way out, but on Xanax everything feels manageable. Play-Doh brain. When I start to feel the seasick, panicky feelings returning, I just up the dose like Lien suggested. I didn't have any trouble getting a prescription from an online pharmacy.

I'm cruising on autopilot. All I have to do is wake up on time and shower. If they need me, someone will collect my body from reception and get it to where it needs to be.

When traders see me, they assume I'm American and scream 'iPHONE' or 'GUCCI'. I've been warned about scammers, so I ignore them. Apparently, it's called the Tea Trap. They see tourists and take you to a lovely touristy tea shop, only then you get stung with, like, a two-hundred-pound bill.

I could be on an alien world, for all I understand. The subway trains have posters warning you that westerners are spies – or at least that's what my agent here tells me, maybe he's kidding, who knows? I know it's really Brexit, but I'm mostly just going to McDonald's or Starbucks, because at least I know what to ask for.

I shoot for catalogues. Outfit change after outfit change. The clothes are . . . functional, and I'm often pinned into them with clips and pegs. I shoot a cereal commercial in which I have to milk a big pink plastic cow directly on to some cornflakes. I'm dressed as a farmer girl. Am I on glue right now? It's pure *Zoolander. Think of the money, think of the money, think of the money.*

After the first few days, I end up spending the nights in my hotel room. I eat my McDonald's Happy Meal on the big, king-size bed and watch badly dubbed films on the hotel TV. Tonight, the toy is a little hamburger with googly eyes. I place it on the bedside table with all of my other Happy Meal pals.

BJS > ICN

Seoul is kinda like Beijing but with way more western stuff. It's more high-tech and modern and everyone is a lot friendlier, thank fuck. It's funny how fluent we are in branding and logos without even knowing it. I mean, I speak not a single word of Korean but recognise Coca-Cola, Adidas, Nike, Starbucks, Burger King and the rest in the gleaming shopping malls. Makes life easy. But boring. If I didn't know I was in Korea, I could be in London, except for the massive billboards that, weirdly, display more pretty *boys* in make-up than girls. They're beautiful and androgynous, pouting down with pastel-pink or baby-blue hair, glossy lips and smoky eyes.

I think it's pretty cool.

More's the point, my phone works again. Without WhatsApp, China was *hell*. I've missed a week of group-chat action. Fuck knows what's going on back home, I'm so out the loop. I can't remember when I was last in the loop. The loop is a distant circle.

My schedule in Korea is pretty full-on. I have five days to shoot editorials for Korean *Vogue* and *Elle* and then I'm doing a video for a musician called K-Boy who I'm told is one of the biggest K-pop stars in the entire world. It's a long two-day shoot. For the most part I have to walk up and down pretend back alleys. It's gross and grungy, but it's all on an indoor sound stage.

In the video, I'm supposed to be a runaway model and K-Boy is a detective trying to find me and get me home. Or something.

Worst of all, K-Boy, real name Koen, has a complex about his height and insists on standing on a box when we're in shot together. Like, you knew my height when you cast me? I'm in a claret Burberry trenchcoat and insane Heritage platforms so, to be fair, I am about six-foot-three at present. Predictably, the detective falls in love with me (well, who wouldn't?) and we have a big kiss at the end. I'm too tired to care. At one point, the director tells me off for yawning.

Tomorrow I have a five a.m. wake-up call to fly to Tokyo so, when we're wrapped, I return to the hotel and order room service. All the Korean food at the video shoot was *insanely* spicy (who knew that was a thing?) so I order a turkey burger. While I wait for it to arrive, I sit on the window sill. My room is on the seventeenth floor and I see out over Seoul by night. It's very *Blade Runner*.

Seoul is nine hours ahead of London. I look at Sabah's feed and see they're all at the cinema. Is it Saturday? I don't even know what day of the week it is any more. She's made a video of everyone mucking about in the foyer: Robin is trying to get some pick 'n' mix, but Ferdy keeps shoving extra sweets in his bag. 'Stop it, you fucker!'

Sabah laughs raucously. There's some other girl with them. Who's she? She's got long blonde hair with mermaid pink and blue streaks. A vinegary sting of jealousy fills my mouth from nowhere. I know I shouldn't – I don't even know her – but I irrationally hate her. Great, they're all on a double date. Without me. Seriously? Who the hell is she? She's every internet boy's manic pixie wet dream.

I bet she just loves retro vinyl and has a nose ring. I bet she wears band T-shirts and plays video games. Fucking cliché. Try-hard.

She's the new me. I've been replaced.

Stop. Just stop.

My eyes sting and a tear rolls down my cheek.

I rest my head against the glass, and the reflection is distorted, like a gargoyle.

There's a polite tap on my door.

Room service.

Jana: Who is the girl with
the long hair?

Sabah: Well hello to u too

Jana: Sorry. Early start. Cranky.

Sabah: She is Amber. Does
English with me. I told u about
her. She cool. But she not you ;)

Jana: Did I sound like a
crazy person?

Sabah: Yes. But we'll
forgive u. Where r u?

Jana: Airport. Flying to Tokyo.

Sabah: BISH GIT ME
HELLO KITTY SHIZ.

Jana: Hahahaha yes.

Jana: Are Amber and Ferdy . . .?

Sabah: Bitch no, u crazy!

Jana: AM I THO???

Sabah: hahahaha yes you are. Oh I'm
fine btw

Jana: Sorry.

Sabah: xxx

ICN > NRT

I'm gonna be in Tokyo for a couple of weeks, so they put me in a model apartment. The block is bleak from the outside, a grey concrete cube with narrow balconies running all the way around. Inside, it's *tiny*, but clean and – for now – I don't have to share it with anyone else. The peach bathtub is so dinky I have to sit with my knees under my chin. It's chihuahua-sized. I can't even deal with the remote control next to the toilet . . . there are, like, fifteen buttons. What do they even *do*?

On the first evening, I have to go grocery shopping, which is a *trip*. I pass a crazy, massive seafood market filled with squid and octopus and swordfish hanging from hooks. I dimly remember something Robin once said about sushi so potent it can kill you.

I get a *lot* of instant ramen from a supermarket. Seems safer.

Tokyo is extra. Zero chill. It's like being in space or the distant future. *Everything* is different here, nothing is easy. Everyone moves so fast. Everything is electric, neon, even the air seems to glow magenta. It's cool, but again, there's no one to *show* it to, no one to share it with.

I take selfies, I pull faces. They get likes. Looks really fun, I guess.

I meet with my Japanese agency and they've set me up with an interpreter, a really nice woman called Aiko, who will come with me on castings and stuff. Thank fuck for translators, honestly. I'm shooting a huge campaign for Fujitsu phones the day after tomorrow and the money is really good, so the trip is worth it even if I don't book anything else while I'm here but, even though everyone at the agency is mint, I still feel so alone.

In the evenings, I mostly go to Club Sega in Akihabara. It's fucking nuts – part-museum, part-arcade for serious gamers. They have a mixture of classics – Tekken, Virtua Fighter – and brand-new exclusives. The cramped club is smoky and noisy and plastered in sexy manga pin-ups. Little crowds gather to watch the super-nerds destroy each other. I keep myself to myself, and when guys try to chat me up I just try to explain I don't speak Japanese. A couple get the hump; I ignore them. Can't a girl kick the shit out of stuff in peace?

I spend a few days at castings. Half the time I don't even know what they're for. As ever, the Mean Girls from Russia clique together and largely ignore me. A lot of them look really, really young. I get thoroughly lost about a trillion times and no one speaks English when I ask for help. At one casting I just sat on the pavement until Aiko came down to find me.

The Fujitsu campaign is two days. One for the print campaign and one for the TV advert. It's some sort of swinging sixties retro vibe and I'm done up like Twiggy. It's pretty cool, but the day we film, the advert don't wrap until two a.m. and I have to attempt lines in Japanese. The director ends up screaming at me and storming off when I can't do it right. So that's good.

Just dub me, you ass-hat.

I get booked for a lookbook shoot so I have to stay a couple of extra days, but get a day off. I plan to see Japan, find a blossomy temple, do the tourist bit, though I'm so tired I sleep for almost all of Sunday. My alarm goes off at nine, but I ignore it and pull the duvet over my head. I just want to go home.

I eventually rise at about one and get dressed. I promised I'd bring Sabah home something cool and Japanese and I desperately want to get back in her good books. I grab a coffee and take the subway into the Harajuku district. A pair of giggling school girls in their *Battle-Royale* school uniforms take sneaky pictures of me on their phones. I should start charging.

Harajuku is as bonkers as I hoped it might be. There ain't really anywhere in London where loads of young people hang out, because just leaving the house costs about twenty-five quid, but if there was a comparison, I suppose it's Camden Market. Harajuku is like a cool shopping market with shops and stalls and music. It's candyfloss pink with blazing magenta and jade lanterns. It's cool and I wish with every bone in my body that Sabah or Ferdy was here too.

The style is off the hook. There are different types of Harajuku Girl, it seems. I know about the Lolitas, but there are different types – goth ones, baby-doll ones. I'm not sure how I feel about girls dressing as some jailbait fantasy from a novel about a paedophile. I tried to read *Lolita* once, but got bored shitless and read a *Squirrel Girl* comic instead. Oh, well, they look awesome regardless.

I wander one district over, looking for Kiddy Land to hunt for Sabah's gift. The toy store is ginormous – like nothing I've ever seen – and very, very Japan. It's like my brain is suddenly filled with kawaii bubblegum glitter. I could quite happily spend the rest of the day with Hello Kitty, to be honest.

'Jana Novak. Well, how random is this?'

I almost snap my neck, I spin around so fast. It's so weird to hear English, and even weirder to find Westley Bryce, disguised in Ray-Bans and a Lakers cap, standing right behind me. My hand flies to my chest to catch my heart. 'Oh my god! Are you real?'

He grins wonkily. 'I was the last time I checked.'

I launch myself into his arms. I've never hugged anyone harder.

'Jana, are you OK?'

'I'm so bored! I haven't seen anyone in four weeks! I thought you were a hallucination!'

'What?' He probably thinks I'm drunk.

I let him go. 'Westley, I've been to Beijing, Seoul and now here. I'm going out of my mind! What are you doing here?'

He looks around, probably checking I've not drawn attention to him. Presumably everyone just thinks we're a couple of nice, normal western tourists. 'I have a big shoot for Toshiba and, weirdly, I'm opening a new Apple Store.'

'Sure you are. Why wouldn't you be? And you just love Hello Kitty?'

'Ha! I always pick something up for my kid sister.'

'Aw, that's cute.'

'No, this is cute! I was going to have a boring night in my hotel tonight, but can we get dinner?'

'Yes!' I practically scream. 'I feel like I'm losing the ability to form sentences! OMG, Westley! It's so good to see you!' I hug him again. Zero chill.

'Told you so. It's a lonely life, right?'

I nod, feeling a little embarrassed to admit that.

'Well, I know this insanely good sushi place. You like sushi?'

'Of course!'

'I'm staying at the Mandarin, and Sushi Sora is ridiculously good, plus it's on the thirty-eighth floor so you get *the* view.'

He could have offered me mangled fish gizzard from a bin and I'd have said yes, just for the company. 'Sure!'

'Cool! You know where the Mandarin is?'

'No.'

'Where are you?'

I try to describe where I'm staying, near Ochanomizu station.

'OK, I'll send a hotel car to get you.'

'Really?'

He shrugs. 'Of course!' His phone buzzes and he sighs. He plucks a stuffed Kitty off the display at random. 'OK, I better motor. I have to go meet with the Apple team. But shall we say, like, eight?'

'Absolutely!'

He sort of gives me a salute as he walks away and I beam back at him. Suddenly Tokyo is a lot more fun.

I got to keep some clothes from the *Elle* shoot so, after a shower, I change into a silver Saint Laurent dress and boots. It's not like I'm gonna be going for Michelin-starred raw fish any other time soon, is it? Also, I'm excited to talk to someone. In English. At length. And it's Westley! I haven't seen him since NYFW. There's *something* about Westley. Maybe it's that you'd expect him to be a douche, but he's not, or maybe it's that we both seem to be in on the joke that is fashion. I can't tell. But I can't wait to see him.

I got given some MAC freebies before I left the UK, so I dig out a deep plummy red lipstick called Sin. It's funny, I think – while seemingly catatonic, I've been picking up make-up tips from all the artists who've been attacking my face for the last year. I do a pretty good 'smoky eye' now. It's all about the blending. I look, if not feel, like a grown-up.

The car, a gleaming Merc, arrives a little before eight and it's about a fifteen-minute drive to the Mandarin through insane traffic. 'Is this it? Mandarin?' I ask the driver.

'*Hai.*'

The Mandarin is a glass blade, stabbing into the night sky. I can't even see the tip of it. 'Oh, wow.'

The concierge directs me to the thirty-eighth floor, to Sushi Sora. The lift shoots up unnervingly fast and I grip the rail for support. The restaurant is everything I expected. Luckily, the Saint Laurent creates the illusion that I belong somewhere so stylish. There's a single sushi bar for just eight diners with two chefs preparing the sushi right in front of us.

Westley waves from his stool at the furthest end of the counter, but I'm too busy being in awe. 'Oh my god,' I say, making my way over. 'Look at that . . .'

The view is just breath-taking. I know because I'm having trouble breathing. We're *so* high up. I can see the entirety of Tokyo, or at least it feels like it. 'I know, right? I sometimes come here just to look out.'

'Wow, that's deep.'

'Not really,' he grins. 'You can watch the planes fly real close. Got me like *woah!*'

I laugh. Adorable.

'You look amazing,' he says. 'Saint Laurent?'

'Thanks, and, yes, well spotted. So do you.' He's wearing a mint-green Ralph Lauren shirt and smart chinos with Converse. All-American Boy Next Door.

There are four other diners, but we're on the end of the counter next to the windows. Westley is getting the VIP treatment and we seem to have a chef all to ourselves. I sense now is not the time to say I don't really love raw fish *or* that my experience of sushi has mostly been the Westfield branch of YO! Sushi. I can always pass myself off as a vegetarian.

I am, however, a fan of the saké. It tastes a bit like wine, but it's so dry it's almost like drinking air. I love it.

Westley fills me in on his adventures. He's close to being cast in a big Hollywood movie. Although he's twenty-one now, he's down to the last two to play a closeted gay jock in an adaptation of some YA novel I've never heard of: *Our Hearts Are the Color of the Sun*. 'It'd be cool to do something that'd push me. I don't think there's anything left in modelling to challenge me any more. And it's a great script.'

'Yeah?'

'Yeah. I'd be "Colby", this quarterback who tries to kill himself and then falls for a guy he meets at a "gay cure" camp.'

'Sounds heavy.'

'It's great. Also my agent thinks gay stuff always does really well at awards season.'

I almost choke on some tuna sashimi, which is actually delish. 'Classy.'

'Right? Have you been to LA yet?' I shake my head. 'It's like great white sharks crawled up out of the ocean, sprouted legs and went to work in Hollywood. They're all crazy. And deadly.'

'What do you mean?' I'm determined to persevere with the chopsticks, although I'm making a mess of it.

'God. Like they all sold their souls to work in the movies. I won't tell you some of the shit I've seen . . .'

'No! Do!'

'It's not good.' He shakes his head and sips his saké. He don't normally drink, but it seems when in Japan . . . 'There was one agent a couple of years ago who basically said if I let him . . . you know . . . he'd get me in some big comic book movie.'

My stomach turns. I put my chopsticks down.

'He, like, cupped me . . . down there . . . so I just stood up and got the hell out of his office. I still see him at parties sometimes and he always gives me this *look* . . . Jana?'

I snap out of it. 'What?'

'What's wrong?'

'Nothing,' I say too quickly.

'C'mon. I know it's a cliché, but you look like you've seen a ghost.'

'What? No. No, it's nothing.'

He frowns. 'It's clearly *something*.'

I'm already a little woozy from the saké. I guess I'm mixing it with five pills a day now. Probably not ideal. 'Oh, god. I don't want to make what happened to you all about me.'

'Please do. I'm sick of talking about me. It's all I ever do.'

I sigh and look to the ceiling. 'It's just . . . well, I had a similar thing happen to me.'

'With an agent?'

'No.' I pause. 'A photographer.'

His eyes narrow a little. 'Wasn't Lucas Blo, was it?'

I don't know whether to laugh or cry. A mix of the two pops out of my mouth. And finally, just like that, it's out. Fuck, I feel lighter. 'Yes. Jackpot. How did you know?'

'Oh, the guy is a fucking wang. I've heard other girls say he's been less than gentlemanly.'

'That's one way of putting it,' I say quietly. Just the thought of raw eel now turns my stomach and I push it aside. I already feel like I have raw eels slithering inside me, thanks.

'Do you wanna talk about it?'

I shake my head. 'Not really.'

'When did it happen?'

'Paris Fashion Week.'

'Just now? God, I'm sorry.'

About a month's worth of bottled-up thoughts start to spill out like an oil slick. 'You know what the worst part is? After I got away, he offered me the campaign so I'd have to go back. I think . . . he *knows*. He knows he has all the power.'

Westley grimaces. 'He's a pig. Actually, that's not fair on pigs. I got nothing against pigs.' He tentatively takes my hand over the table. It's warm and soft. 'Are you OK? Do you need me to do anything?'

'No. I don't think so.' I sip more saké. 'Apparently we work in an industry full of pigs. Are *you* OK? I just hijacked your story.'

'It was a long time ago. I make sure I tell every new male

model and actor I meet to avoid him like the plague. Helps me sleep better.'

It feels like a fog has lifted. Here we are, both OK. I think it's gonna be all right after all.

Somehow, before I know it, it's half-one. We've been chattering away for hours and clearly the poor chef wants to go home. But I don't. The thought of going back to the draughty little apartment all by myself is too depressing for words. Worse, as it seems to do three or four times a day in Tokyo, the heavens have opened, and rods of rain pelt the neon city.

Westley and I wait in the foyer for it to stop. 'What time's your shoot tomorrow?' he asks.

'I think the call-time is eleven.'

'Oh, in that case, you're more than welcome to stay in my suite. There's plenty of room. I'm happy to take the sofa. It's huge.'

A sleepover sounds a million times more fun than going out in the downpour, and I'm not yet ready for the night to end. 'Sure,' I say, 'let's get another bottle of saké. Slumber party!'

Westley is staying in the Presidential Suite and it's, well, presidential. Another sweeping view out of the city through floor-to-ceiling windows. The room is divided in two and, instead of saké, we drink bottles of beer from the mini bar on the sleek leather sofa. 'Thank you,' I tell him.

'What for?'

'This is gonna sound tinfoil-hat crazy, but I think you were sent by the universe, Westley Bryce.'

'Or we just happen to have the same job?' he says with a very sexy smile. He's only had the same amount as me to drink, but

I don't think he's used to it – his eyes look a little glassy and his words are slurred.

'No. No way. Just running into each other in the Hello Kitty shop? What are the odds? You saved me, Westley. I was going out of my mind.'

He finishes his beer. 'It's ridiculous, isn't it?'

'What?'

'How lonely it is.'

'How can *you* be lonely?'

'I got a theory,' he says, and I tell him to go on. 'You know when people wanna be famous? I think they're really looking to be loved. People think fame is like love, but it's not at all. I'm very, very famous and very, very lonely. A million people "like" my posts but none of them have my number, none of them are my friends.'

He looks so sad. He's not playing. 'West,' I say, trying to lighten the mood, 'you're just saying that because you're drunk.'

'Nope.' He gazes up at me with impossible blue eyes. 'You saw my place in Manhattan. I'm never in it. I have no roots. I'm rootless. I'm a tumbleweed. It'd make more sense to have my mail delivered to an airport. Couple more years and I'm done. I swear. I'll move to LA, get a beach house in Malibu or something. Surf. Get a dog. Being famous . . . it's like you *get* a lot more love than you *give*. And it doesn't sit well with me any more.' He picks the damp label off his beer bottle idly. 'I wanna put down some roots, see what kinda tree grows. And I can't . . . date . . . while I'm living like this. I miss people too much. Call me old-fashioned, but I just want that one girl I can spend forever with.'

You could sink your fingers into the silence between us.

'Well, I guess that answers those *Is Westley Bryce Secretly Gay?* rumours,' I say, because the silence is too dangerous.

He laughs. 'I know, right, what's that about? If I was gay, I'd be out. And also married to Matty! That's another reason I want to do that movie. I'll break the internet. But I guess he's not my type.'

'And what is?'

Dimples. 'I don't really have a type. This is going to sound . . . what did you say? Tinfoil hat? But it's about a feeling, a warmth, security, trust. That's what I need. It's like fashion. We're surrounded by fakes. I can always spot the genuine article.'

He looks me in the eye.

I think of Ferdy. He has it. He has that warmth.

My life ain't felt real, I ain't felt real, for months, but *he* is real.

But he's a million miles away.

I ain't seen him in over a month.

I have to stop.

'I think it's time for bed,' I say, getting up abruptly. 'Are there some spare blankets?'

'I'll take the sofa.'

'No!'

'I insist . . .'

Westley has the concierge send up a toothbrush and a fresh white robe. I brush my teeth, thinking about his eyes, his lips. *Stop.*

I wash my face as best I can, thinking about his skin, his arms. How he held my hand. How real, solid and flesh it was. It made me feel real again, just for a second.

You have to stop.

I see a parallel world where I'm with Westley. What if I was his girlfriend? It's pure ego talking shit in my ear, but we'd be the most famous couple in the world. He'd make me a household name. A power couple. Westley and Jana. Westa or Janley. How the world would blaze with envy. We'd be #goals. Every other girl in the world would see us on Instagram and feel like crap. It would actually kill Laurel and Heather dead.

If I'm with the most beautiful man on the planet . . . what would that make me?

Maybe it's time . . .

Time to stop pretending I'm the same girl that Tom Carney found at Thorpe Park.

That's not me any more.

That's not my life.

This is.

My insides feel like they're buzzing with nervous energy and I don't think it's the booze. My skin is humming. I head into the bedroom and click off the bathroom light. I perch on the end of the giant bed. Neon blue bleeds through the blinds and I see Westley's silhouette through the paper screen that cordons off the lounge.

He's tall and muscular, just perfectly male.

Oh, god.

My heart is in my throat.

'Westley?' my voice squeaks.

He slides open the screen and pokes his head through the gap. 'You good?'

Even at model height, I'm dwarfed by the super-king bed. I don't *know* what I'm doing, but I'm doing it. Runaway train. 'It's a really big bed. You don't have to sleep in there.'

He steps fully into the bedroom. In the blue light, I see he's wearing just a pair of Calvin Klein briefs. As he was in the billboard for the exact same underwear. The light ripples over his skin, making him glow silver, as if he don't already look enough like a Greek god. 'Are you sure?'

'Yes.' And I am. I want to feel the warmth of him. I want to feel his skin on mine.

'Cool.' His smile is Hollywood-white even in the gloom. 'Move over, then.'

I shuffle over and he flops down next to me. 'It's weirdly important to me – after everything we talked about – for you to know I didn't ask you up here for . . . this.'

'I know. That's why I came.'

I touch his cheek to make sure he's real. He is. I run my hand down his neck, across his chest and stomach. Harder than Fer— *(don't even think it)* —but still soft. Just when I'm about to turn back, he reaches for my face and kisses me.

And it is good. I *know* this is wrong and that's why my heart is pounding. It's gonna crack my ribs. I'm not sure if I've ever been this alert. This is, at the same time, a new high and a new low.

How low can you go?

I pull him close and his hand snakes inside my dressing gown. I shiver. I lie down flat on my back. I switch my head off, and it's like I'm connected to my body again for the first time in *weeks*. I let myself feel everything that's happening: where his hands are; where he's kissing; the tingle in my skin.

The kisses become hungrier and faster, and I don't think I can stop.

I don't want to.

It surprises me, this feeling, but I want him *in* me.

I don't think. I just do.

CONFESSION

Everything and everyone is different when the sun comes up. The room don't look sexy and decadent any more. It looks like a heap of bedding and discarded clothes and it smells like come and morning breath. I lie awake for about twenty minutes without moving. Westley's arms and legs are wrapped around me and I can feel his morning glory pressed against my butt cheek.

Oh, fuck.

What the fucking fuck was I thinking?

I have a headache and my mouth feels like cat litter.

I make a move and Westley stirs. 'Oh, hey.' He snuggles closer. 'Morning.'

I wriggle away. 'I've got to go.' I grab the robe and my dress and head to the en suite. I lock myself in. I sit on the toilet and bury my head in my hands.

Fuck.

I feel so bad, this guilt might kill me. Has anyone ever died of sheer guilt?

A few moments later there's a gentle knock on the door. 'Jana? Are you OK?' he says.

'Yeah,' I say, although I think I might vomit. My stomach's wedged right up in my throat. 'I . . . uh . . . need to go back to my apartment. I can't go to the shoot in Saint Laurent, can I?'

'Don't see why not.'

I turn the taps on full blast to drown him out and lean over the sink until the urge to puke subsides. I'm such a dickhead. I'm on the pill, but we didn't use a condom. I actually giggle like a psycho imagining the fiasco of getting the morning-after pill in Tokyo, but then the thought of taking chlamydia home as a souvenir sobers me up.

What a total twat.

And where are my knickers? Great. This is all really, super dignified. I slip the dress over my head.

I see myself in the mirror. I look like shit. I did an awful thing and it's made me ugly. I'm wearing it all on the outside.

How am I gonna tell Ferdy?

Because I will.

I have to.

This is gonna be the end of us, ain't it?

I feel it, an actual pain under my ribs, like I've been stabbed. A whimper pops out of my mouth before I can stop it.

It's funny, they say love hurts, but I always thought it was an abstract, emotional kind of pain. Nope, just the regular sort. I start to cry. I slump down next to the toilet and try to cry silently, muffling the sobs with my hand.

'Jana? Are you coming out? You got me worried,' Westley asks again after I don't know how many minutes have passed. I dry my eyes with some toilet roll. I emerge from the bathroom and start searching for my knickers. I don't look him in the eye.

'Sorry,' I say.

'No worries. You want breakfast?'

I finally look at him reclining on the bed like some sort of Renaissance art. He seems crumpled, but as Westley as ever. This is his life. It's not mine. 'I . . . I'm gonna head back to the flat. Can you get me a car?'

'Of course.' But first he hops off the bed, now in his Calvins, and tries to hug me. I pull away. 'Hey, hey, hey, take a minute.' He steers me back to the bed. I sit awkwardly on the edge, feeling cactus-prickly. 'Jana, it's OK. It . . . happened. I know you have a guy back in London, and I'm not trying to make trouble. Although you should know . . .'

'No.' I stop him. 'Whatever it is you're about to say, don't say it, West. It won't help.'

Now he looks hurt. I've made a mess. I didn't for a second think that someone like Westley would *ever* be into me, so I wasn't careful with his heart. You shouldn't ever juggle with hearts. Reckless. I should go. 'I'm sorry.'

'No, it's good. I knew you had a boyfriend, but if . . .'

'No buts or ifs . . .' I smile.

He smiles too. 'Can't blame a guy for trying. I like you a lot, Jana.'

I shake my head. 'Why?'

He tilts his head, apparently seeing something I don't. 'Because you're real.'

Well, that's a gag because I feel less real with every passing day. Ain't there some myth that a camera steals part of your soul picture by picture? I'm being whittled down to a toothpick if that's true.

Westley waits for my response. I search for the right words. 'If things were different . . .'

He clamps a warm hand over my mouth. 'Oh, god, don't you say that either.'

'So let's just not say anything else?'

'Maybe for the best.' We sit apart, both absurd. Suddenly he hops up. 'I'll get a car for you.'

I feel sick for the next five days. It don't matter if I eat or not, I feel nauseous. It's the hangover that just keeps on hanging. Because I know what I have to do. And it's going to be horrible. So horrible I don't deserve the comfortable distance of telling him what happened by Skype or text. I deserve the horror of telling him in person.

Telling him is the first part of the sentence and the only way the sentence could potentially be reduced. Manslaughter instead of murder.

I phone it in for the last two jobs and scrape my life back into two enormous cases. My flight home has a stopover in Rome, but I'm too out of it on Zopiclone to care. It's late when I arrive back at Heathrow and Prestige have sent a car to get me.

'Are you OK, miss?' the driver asks.

I didn't even realise I was crying.

It's somehow become spring. While I was in Tokyo, the blossoms have sprouted and the trees between mine and Ferdy's look like candyfloss. I cycle over to his. I have a vague idea what I'm gonna say, and I know how I would *like* him to respond, but hope is cruel.

I slept for most of yesterday, trying to stave off jet lag, but I had such hideous dreams about what the morning would bring,

I don't feel even slightly rested. My brain has played out this scenario many times over. I've gone up to two Xanax tablets, three times a day.

His sister opens the door and scowls at me. She's never liked me, and I don't think the fact I'm about to be on the cover of *Vogue* China especially impresses her. 'He's in his room,' she says, and I hurry past her.

Ferdy is on his bed, in his *Rick and Morty* boxers, playing Final Fantasy, same as he ever was. I'm something else.

It's weird, ain't it? The urge to ruin perfect things. I remember once I was a little girl and Battersea Park was covered in a blanket of thick white snow. For whatever reason, I just couldn't hack it. I had to get on there, stomp around and mash it all up with my wellies. Only then it was a dirty, muddied mess and I cried and Mum couldn't understand why I was upset.

I couldn't *stand* the beauty of it.

So I spoiled it.

'Hey!' His eyes light up. He pauses the game and bounds over. 'I didn't hear the door!' He throws his arms around me and I squeeze him back because it's very possibly the last time he'll do so. I allow myself this last one. 'I missed you so much.'

'I missed you.' And I start to cry. My whole body folds in on itself. I shake with sobs.

'Jana?'

Now I'm here, I can't talk. I've been holding this inside for six days and I've rehearsed it in my head, but I got nothing.

'Jana, what's wrong?'

I crumple to the floor. I can't hold myself up. I'm kneeling at his feet. Mary Magdalene.

'Jana?' Ferdy's voice changes. There's a hint of panic. He crouches to my level. 'Jesus. What's wrong?' And then it changes again, lower, deadly serious. 'Jana? What did you do?'

And like that, he knows. I should have known. I've always wondered if he was slightly psychic.

I can't look at him. I load the gun. 'I slept with someone,' I fire.

He says nothing.

It feels like he says nothing for a really long time. I dare to look up. He's sitting with his back to the radiator.

'Ferdy?'

His face is chalk white, his empty eyes stare at the wall. 'I knew. I knew it. You were weird on the phone.'

How could I have done this to him? 'I don't know what I was doing.' My throat is so tight it hurts. 'It was . . . I don't even know what it was.'

He closes his eyes. 'I don't know you any more.'

Not the reaction I was expecting. He's so cold, so robotic. 'Ferdy! You do! It's me!'

He slowly shakes his head. 'No, you're different.'

'I'm not!' I start to crawl over to him, but he holds out a hand.

'Don't come anywhere near me,' he says. 'You are. And you don't even see it. We all stayed the same and you changed.'

'Ferdy, please. I am the exact same person. I still love you, I just . . .'

'Just what? Just stop, Jana.' He picks up a copy of *GQ* magazine and flings it in my direction. The TANK ad is on the back page. 'They made you into someone new.'

For a second, I'm red-hot-lava mad. How can he do this? It's right on the tip of my tongue. *Blo*. I'll tell him, I'll tell him what happened to me in Paris and maybe then . . .

Maybe then what? He'll feel as bad as I do? What happened with Blo is no excuse for what I did. Westley looks up at me from the magazine. I feel sick.

'It's like –' he drags his hands through his hair – 'we're still kids and you're a grown-up.'

'Please, Ferdy . . . I *know* I did a stupid thing, but I still love you more than anything in the world.'

His shoulders sag inwards. He looks so dejected.

And I know.

For him, it's over.

There's nothing I can say.

'Ferdy . . . no.'

'I can't do this any more. Do you know what it's been like? Having a telephone girlfriend? It's too hard.' I can't reply. He goes on. 'Maybe this is just what growing up is. Sooner or later we had to. We got together when we were *fifteen*, Jana. We were kids to think it was for ever. So stupid. So naïve, it's embarrassing.' He spits out the last word.

'Don't say that.' I'm properly crying now. I can't breathe.

He wipes a tear away too. 'I . . . I don't match you any more. You're hardly even human.'

And what the hell does that mean? 'I'm not *human*?'

'You're so much bigger than I am.'

'That's bullshit.'

'No, it isn't.'

'Then you don't know me at all.' I stand and grab my jacket. 'I can't believe we're doing this.'

He looks up at me, eyes red. 'You already did it.'

I look around his room. The posters; the action figures; the PlayStation. It couldn't be more different to the hotel rooms, to Westley's apartment. But this box room was our whole world. I don't want to go. 'Is this it? Really? This is how it ends?'

'I think it is.'

I shake my head. 'I . . . I'll go, then.'

He don't say anything, or even look at me.

And so I go.

CATALYST

'Are you sure?' Cheska asks. She's wearing big geeky glasses and somehow, inexplicably, she looks even more gorge.

I shrug. 'Might as well.'

'It's a big step.'

Without Ferdy I don't really see the point of staying in London. If there's money to be made in New York, I may as well move there. And it's nothing to do with Westley. He messaged me yesterday to see if I was OK. He also told me he got the part in that film and he'll be filming in Vancouver for the next six months.

'I'll try it for a year and see.'

'But your family . . .' We're in the reception area. I'm here for a meeting to discuss the next 'phase' of my career. I know Maggie was angling for me to make the move to NYC so I think she'll be delighted.

'I'm rich now,' I say flatly. 'I'll fly them over or fly home to see them.'

Cheska shakes her head. 'You seem really down, Jana.'

'I am.' I manage a rueful half-smile. I'm still taking my pills, but I don't think they're doing much. I feel like I've been ironed flat by a steamroller.

She smiles. 'I lived in New York when I was working. I loved it. You will too, but there's nowhere like home.'

I shrug again.

'Oh, there she is!' Cheska is in reception waiting for Arabella and now she walks into the agency. Well, about two thirds of her does. I do a double take. She's lost a *lot* of weight, and she didn't have much to lose in the first place. She looks *ill*, her cheekbones jutting out and her eyes sunken.

'Oh my god,' I mutter under my breath.

Arabella goes to hug me but there's nothing to hug. 'Hello, darling! How are you?'

'I'm . . . well . . . I'm OK. Are you?'

'Yeah, I'm really good . . .' But she don't look good, she look like she's suffering from a biblical plague or something. Her eyes are glazed, almost zombie-like.

Maggie breezes in behind her. 'Hello, sweet darlings,' she says. 'Bels, sweetheart, you are looking magnificent. Is the juice diet working out for you?'

'Yeah,' she says, misty-eyed, vacant. 'I'm down to fifty kilos.'

'Great! Well done, you! Keep going! Let's get you down to the bone for Fashion Week!'

I perch on the sofa, hardly believing what I'm hearing. Did she just say that? Really? I feel sick. A juice diet? What sort of fucking bollocks is that?

'Jana! Little one! Come give us a love!'

I stand and Maggie hugs my breath away. 'Some great news for you . . . Dermot has asked if you'll be his date to the Met Gala in May.'

He texted me about it a few days ago, but I'm still too numb to care. I ignored him. 'Sure. Why not?'

305

'Jana!' Cheska says, aghast. 'It's the *Met Gala*! People *kill* to go to that!'

'So send one of them instead, then.'

'Turn the attitude into gratitude, young lady!' Maggie slaps me on the arse and we start to head towards the meeting room.

'Maggie, wait!' Ro slams the phone back into the receiver from where she's working on the booker's desk. 'Great news . . . Elyssa Sayers is confirmed for the *Fashion and Art Vol Four* editorial with Lucas.'

'Oh, wonderful! Wonderful!'

'Lucas Blo?' I say. The last word catches in my throat.

Cheska, Ro and Maggie freeze and look to one another.

Maggie clears her throat. 'Yes, that's right.'

Arabella looks confused. I haven't seen her since Paris.

'You can't,' I say quietly, not wanting to cause a big drama. 'Elyssa's, like . . . what, fourteen?'

'She's fifteen now,' Ro chips in.

I can't help raising my voice this time: 'And Lucas Blo is a—'

'Jana! That's enough!' Maggie snaps before composing herself. 'Darling, I'll go with Elyssa myself to chaperone. Everything is fine.'

Ro looks embarrassed. Cheska looks at her feet. Maggie smiles, but her eyes are ice-cold.

'No, it ain't,' I say. 'I can't do this any more.' The fog finally lifts and I can see for fucking miles.

'Jana . . .' Cheska starts.

'I gotta get outta here.'

I turn on my heel and march out of the agency. If nothing else, they've taught me to walk with conviction.

Cussing at tourists as I storm down Oxford Street towards the Tube, it takes me a second to clock my giant stupid face gurning out of Coda on the corner of Regent Street. Oh, the S/S campaign must have launched. Great. I'm the fifty-foot woman in a dental-floss gold bikini.

My flawless ass is the size of a house, my long legs like sizzling wieners, my breasts perfectly pert. I'm airbrushed to within an inch of my life: every pore, every freckle and fold gone. I stop and stare up at myself. I look so unlike me, I can evaluate it as if I'm a stranger: I look like a goddess; an Amazon; a bronzed superhuman.

I don't even feel proud.

That's not what I look like.

That's not what any human woman looks like.

I wonder how many thousands, millions of women, how many little girls, have walked past me so far and felt like shit? How many women have looked at the sandwich in their hand and thought, *Ooh, bread's an error, better get on the juice diet?*

And that's when it really hits me: I'm part of the problem.

Coda seems to lean drunkenly to one side, like it's a block of butter, melting. What the . . .? My feet stumble to the left. My head feels like it's got air whooshing through it. People swarm around me like wasps. When did I last eat?

I don't . . .

I don't know . . .

My enormous face looks down at me with sheer fucking hate in her eyes.

I don't feel very . . .

My legs are like spaghetti. Wet spaghetti.

I stagger, crashing into a small woman in a beret. 'Hey!' she snaps.

Too late. I try to say sorry but I can't.

And that's when I see him. He's coming out of Topshop, walking straight for me. Ginger beard. Gold tooth. Baseball cap. It's him. Blo.

No.

Did I say that out loud or in my head?

Everything is going dark.

I'm going . . .

I'm going down.

AWAKE

It wasn't Blo, of course. It was the security guard from Topshop. They look similar, I guess.

He saw me wobble and came out to help me. He scooped me off the pavement and brought me inside for some water. I'm pretty sure everyone thinks I'm drunk or on drugs.

There's no way anyone would recognise me from the billboard outside Coda right now, so I think I'm OK.

By the time the ambulance comes I'm fine. Well, better.

'Jana,' says the paramedic, a handsome man with a goatee, 'what have you taken?'

'Nothing,' I say. He thinks I'm on drugs. He looks at me like I'm lying, and then the penny drops. I am lying. I am on drugs. Sort of. 'Oh, I'm on medication for anxiety ... and sleeping pills.'

He nods. 'Riiiight. We're going to take you in. We need a doctor to check you over. Is that OK?'

Uh, really? 'Do we have to tell my mum?'

'No. Not if you don't want to.'

I nod. She'd only worry.

I've never been in the back of an ambulance and the short ride through London to University College Hospital would be pretty exciting in different circumstances. As it is, I feel as dizzy as hell, like there's fluid sloshing about my skull. I'm still light on my feet, so they wheel me into A&E, which is actually embarrassing when I consider how many real emergencies there must be. Shameful.

They park me in a little bay, hidden away behind some minty green curtains, holding a kidney-shaped cardboard thing to hurl in if the mood takes me. I'm woozy as fuck. Again, I feel like I'm hovering a couple of metres outside my body, watching this sad, skinny figure, legs dangling off the gurney. From nowhere, I imagine Elyssa Sayers, in her school uniform, waiting in a similar position to see Lucas Blo. Will he ask her about her pussy, I wonder?

I squirm. My whole body aches.

God knows how long I've been waiting when a doctor pushes his way through to see me. He looks not much older than Milos and thoroughly knackered. 'Hello, Jana. I'm Dr Davies. Let's see . . .' He consults his notes.

'It's nothing,' I say. 'I just fainted. No biggy.'

'Hmm.' He shines his penlight thingy in my eyes. I do as I'm told: look up, down, left and right. 'You're a model? Now, Jana, I want you to be honest with me. Are you eating healthily?'

'Yeah,' I say and it's true. Without show castings hanging over me, I'm eating pretty much whatever I want.

'Are you sure?'

I nod.

'OK. Now you told the paramedic that you've been taking anti-anxiety medication and sleeping tablets?' I nod again. 'Can you tell me what?'

'Xanax and Zopiclone.' I know where this is headed, I'm not stupid. 'But I only take Zopiclone when I can't sleep. Not every night.'

He hm-hmms. 'What dosage of Xanax are you taking?'

'Like, six a day.'

Dr Davies fixes me with shrewd eyes. 'Jana. Who prescribed you those medications?'

I say nothing. I'm not gonna lie to his face. Done enough of that these last few weeks.

'Online?'

I nod.

Dr Davies pushes himself up to sit on the gurney alongside me. Classic *I'm not a doctor, I'm your buddy* move. 'You know what I'm going to tell you, don't you?'

'That I have to stop?'

'Bingo. Jana, the NHS doesn't prescribe Xanax in the UK for a reason. It's a powerful tranquilliser and can be really addictive. Did you know that?' Oh. Lien left that bit out. 'And as for Zopiclone, it's hugely habit-forming. It's for short-term use, and probably not for someone your age at all.' I didn't know that either.

'I don't take them if I'm at home – the sleeping pills.'

'OK, good. Listen. I think you're dehydrated and exhausted, you're underweight for your height, but the tablets were probably a contributing factor. You're not the first model I've treated after a "fainting spell". I don't know, maybe you do have anxiety, maybe it's just work stress. What you need to do is to see your family doctor. If need be, we can get you on a prescription and talk about getting you some therapy, perhaps. But let's not get any more pills off the internet, please.'

'OK.' I didn't really know what I was taking. Honestly. What a dick.

'I'm going to discharge you,' Dr Davies says. 'But please take it easy, Jana. Have you been under stress? Is anything else bothering you?'

I could tell him, couldn't I?

But he's not the person I need to tell.

DISCLOSURE

I wait until I'm on the train. I've had a chocolate chip cookie and some tea and I feel fine.

I feel ready.

It's time to get back inside this skeleton.

Time to take back a body they took off my hands.

And make it into a missile.

The phone rings four times before she picks up. 'Sabah?'

'Hi. You OK?'

'We need to talk,' I say. 'I know things between us are weird. Where are you?'

'Free period. I'm in the library.' Her tone softens. 'Bored off my tits, tbh.'

'Is Ferdy there?'

'No. Why?'

'Can you meet me?'

'METROPOLITAN POLICE', says the sign, 'WITH YOU, MAKING LONDON SAFER'.

We stand in the little reception area at Lavender Hill Police Station waiting for a homeless guy to finish arguing with the desk sergeant. Apparently the police cleared away his sleeping bag and he wants it back.

Another sergeant appears at the next window over. 'Hello, girls. Can I help?' She's an older woman with short silver hair.

'Go on,' Sabah says, giving me a nudge.

'Hello,' I say, keeping my voice low. 'I need to report a crime.'

I did agree to take my T-shirt off, but nothing else.

No, I wasn't told to expect nudity.

He didn't ask before he got naked.

He grabbed my hand.

I didn't have a choice.

Why does it matter if he was hard?

No, he didn't touch me.

Um, yes, he did, to grab my hand.

He didn't touch my breasts.

No. He didn't touch my crotch.

Why would it matter if we had sex?

No, we didn't have sex.

No, we never had sex.

Yes, there was witnesses.

Yes, they heard me say no.

I felt like I didn't have a choice.

He said he couldn't work with me if I wasn't willing to touch him.

I thought it would affect my career.

I didn't consent to touching him.

He forced me.

I didn't. I didn't have a choice.

* * *

It's exhausting and takes *hours*. I go over and over the story. They pour what feels like gallons of piss-weak tea down my neck. Sabah sits silently next to me the whole time, gently holding my hand under the desk in the interview room. The police officer, a nice woman called Kate, is actually calm and friendly, but I still feel like her questions are trying to trip me up.

Kate leaves us alone. 'You did so good,' Sabah says, looking around as if she's worried we're still being recorded.

'How long did that take?'

'About an hour and a half.'

'God, it felt like double that.'

'I'm sorry that this is taking up *your* time and not that asshole's.'

'Yeah, well. Hopefully he'll get what's coming *before* he can get his hands on anyone else.' I pause. 'Thank you for coming with me.'

'Bitch, please.'

She gives me a wink and a tear pops out of my eye. I've got my Sabah back. 'I'm sorry I didn't tell you right—'

'Shut the front door. Don't you dare apologise when I should be.' She squeezes my hand. 'I shoulda known something was up.'

'But . . .'

'No. Me and you ain't doing this. We good.'

I rest my head on her shoulder.

Kate returns about half an hour later with another woman in a grey trouser suit who introduces herself as Detective Trish Affra. 'Hello, Jana, Kate has taken your statement so I won't ask you to go over everything again.'

Thank god for that.

'I want you to know that we take sexual assault very seriously indeed. I'm on a taskforce especially dealing with sexual offences. Now, Jana, I need you to understand this is potentially a really difficult case. We have a British girl accusing an American man in a French hotel. See what I'm saying?'

I nod again.

'But we will open an investigation. Here's what we're going to do. I'm going to speak to our partners in Paris and get them to talk to the hotel. I'm sure there's CCTV that can support your case. I'll also do everything I can to track down the accused and the witnesses you mentioned. You might not hear from us for a while, but rest assured we're trying to build a case that'll stand up in court. Last question: would you be prepared to see this all the way to court? And understand it could well be a court in Paris.'

I look to Sabah. 'Yeah. I think he's done this before. And I think he'll do it again.'

Trish nods. 'I think you're very brave, Jana.'

I look to Sabah and then back to Trish and feel like I'm absorbing strength from them. 'Let's get him,' I say.

When I get home, I'm greeted by that brick wall of stifling central-heating heat that tells me Mum's home, but Dad isn't. The new boiler is definitely doing its job. 'Hello?' I say as I close the front door.

'Hello, darling,' Mum calls from the lounge. I walk through and she's on the sofa, watching *Holby City*. 'You OK, my love?'

'Yeah,' I lie. 'I'm fine. Where's Dad?'

'Milos has a match near Twickenham. He's gone to pick him up. Have you eaten?'

'No.'

She sits up. 'You want me to make you sandwich or something? There's pasta bake in the fridge . . .?'

I clamber on to the sofa and give her a cuddle. I can't remember the last time we had a cuddle for no reason. I don't think I was taller than her the last time we did.

'Aw,' she says, stroking down my unruly hair. 'What's this for?'

'Do I need a reason?'

'No. I wish you do it all the time. Hugs are nice.' I just lie on top of her for a while, smooshing her into the sofa. 'Still my baby girl,' she whispers.

MET

The flashbulbs are *blinding*. They flicker like constant sheet lightning. 'DERMOT!' they call. 'JANA! OVER HERE, JANA! SMILE, BABY! GIVE US A SMILE!'

The theme of the Met Gala this year is 'Great Britain', celebrating British style. There's a lot of Heritage, McQueen and Galliano, but – of course – I'm dressed top to toe in Republic of Deen and Dermot is my date for the night. He begged me and I felt I couldn't say no. Inspired by Britannia herself, I'm wearing this slinky, floor-length cobalt-grey dress with insane armour over the top. It weighs a ton and I just pray I'll be able to sit down once we're inside. I have to be very careful of the deadly-looking spikes jutting off my left shoulder. Dermot convinced me to cut my hair too. I now have a lobotomy fringe and a very short 'Louise Brooks' bob. If only I knew who Louise Brooks was.

Worse still, the GP took me off Xanax (obv) and gave me sertraline instead and it's giving me a dicky tummy. I've had like three Imodium but I don't feel a hundred per cent. I imagine crapping myself on the red carpet at the Met Gala and chuckle to myself. I was a little ball of nerves long before I was scouted. My job just made everything a hundred times worse. Well, now I can fix it. I hope.

Dermot has recommended a really good therapist too – she apparently helped him loads – so maybe I'll make an appointment to see her when we get home, although I don't know how I feel about telling a perfect stranger all my issues. I guess she wouldn't be a stranger for long.

I try to enjoy the gala. I've already seen Leonardo DiCaprio with Dido Gant, and Clara Keys gave me a wave from the other side of the red carpet with her chaperone for the evening, Tom Ford.

We are 'muses'. Imagine that being your job. A girl whose sole purpose is to inspire a man to create things. Who the fuck is supposed to inspire me?

I look around and see men in their forties, fifties, sixties, each carrying a skinny model down the red carpet like we're handbags. These men, I think, could change the world. Dermot squeezes my hand and I smile, but he could fix this. He has the power. Sounds obvious, but he could make his clothes bigger. Instead of building them around girls like me, he could base them on girls like Sabah. These men could change what beautiful is.

While Dermot talks to Fashion TV about being 'at the forefront of the new wave of Brit Pack designers', I look behind me.

I hear the photographers call his name before I see him.

'WESTLEY!'

And there he is. In his tux, he looks like a fifties' film star. Just for a second, everything is black and white, and he's Marlon Brando or something. I allow myself to remember that night. I've been blocking it out, like reliving even the memory is cheating on Ferdy all over again. I remember him between my legs, I remember the curve of his spine sinking into me and . . .

Then the flashes start and it's technicolour again.

He's with a girl I recognise. The girl from that Netflix series. Oh, what's her name? Estella something? Her silver braids are twisted into a knot on top of her head and she looks super cool in oxblood-red vintage Heritage.

It's weird, a part of me wants to run straight over and give him a kiss. And that's exactly why I won't.

Our eyes meet and he smiles. I smile back.

We had what we had.

One night.

And I think that's it.

'And you're seventeen years old?' She scrutinises me over the top of her glasses.

'Yep.'

'That's awful young to be looking to buy property, doll.' The *real estate* agent is an uppity woman with a perm and a skirt suit the colour of Dairy Milk wrappers.

I shrug. 'My dad says it's a good investment.'

That seems to make more sense to her. 'Ah, I see. He's absolutely correct.'

'But I earned the down payment myself.' That shuts her up.

I do love the apartment a lot. It's in Williamsburg overlooking the bridge and is kind of how I imagined all New York apartments to be based on a binge-diet of *Friends* on Netflix. It's a big open-plan lounge and kitchen with a spiral staircase that leads up to a balcony bedroom. It's big and airy and light.

Just for a second, I imagine walking through the door, my portfolio under my arm. Ferdy looks up at me from the sofa, where he's playing with his camera. 'Hey,' he says. 'How was the casting?'

'Terrible,' I say, flopping down next to him. 'Shall we get takeout?'

And then it's gone.

Ferdy's gone.

I thought *he* was my future. I know. I know time will pass and there'll be other guys, but right now I can't see them. I can't see anyone else, even Westley, waiting for me on that imaginary sofa.

I'm still so torn. I don't want to be in London, it just reminds me of Ferdy. I definitely don't want to be in Paris. Similarly, I'm not sure about this any more. By *this* I mean modelling. It's like a bee is trapped in my skull, buzzing around telling me that everything I do is fundamentally gross and wrong.

But what else am I gonna do? After everything I've done in the last year, all the things I've seen and places I've been, how do I go back to real life? I have this nightmare where I go back to Hollyton and a bunch of strangers stare at me as I walk through the halls. This time, I'm not just an anonymous 'beanpole' or 'tranny', I'm 'failed model Jana Novak'. Worse somehow. Ego.

Maybe it's just Maggie and Prestige I'm sick of. After I walked out of Prestige last month, I checked my contract. They own my ass *in the UK* until August – I signed a one-year deal – but I can still work with other agencies overseas. I wonder if I'm here, being solely managed by Face First, if things might be better.

Who am I kidding? They'll probably be worse. Trent is a premium douchebag.

As if by psychic magic, my phone vibrates and it's him. 'Sorry, I better take this.'

'Take your time.'

'Jana, doll. Great news!' They always say this just before something awful happens, so I've become wary.

'Yeah?'

'Are you ready? You. Your face. AMERICAN *VOGUE*! November issue! THE COVER!'

OK. 'What?'

'I know! A certain editor-in-chief was very impressed with a new haircut – can't think why – and wants to book you!'

'Seriously?' Even I know that girls, especially models, wait *years* to be on *Vogue*. Usually it's big Hollywood stars.

'I know! It's a British theme or something! Cool, right?'

I wonder if this is a sign. It's *Vogue*. I could forever say I'd been on the cover of the most famous fashion magazine in the whole world. And then retire on a high. Yeah, that sounds like a plan.

I tell Perm Melanie I'll think about the apartment and take a cab back to my hotel in Manhattan, looking over all the paperwork she's given me. The doorman opens the taxi door and I stride into reception, head down, checking my emails on my phone. I've come to hate this thing. There always used to be a message, sometimes even just an emoji, from Ferdy. Now, more often than not, the screen is blank. It's like carrying a tiny square corpse around.

'Ms Novak?'

322

I look up and see a man and woman, both in sharp suits and trenchcoats. They block my path. 'Yeah?'

'Agent Richard Deichmann and Agent Ana Perez of the Federal Bureau of Investigation,' says the man.

'What?' I say, suddenly very worried about the visa forms I filled in last week while I was half-asleep on the plane.

'We were wondering if we could talk with you privately,' Perez says. 'About Lucas Blo.'

They drive me to the local police precinct in a normal-looking car. They assure me I'm not in any trouble, but we have to go somewhere we can talk privately and they can record the conversation. We go to a grimy interview room that smells of BO but does have a great view over Central Park.

Perez waits with me while Deichmann fetches us all coffee. When he's back, they finally explain. 'Sorry to bother you, Ms Novak,' Perez explains. 'Your accusations against Lucas Blomfeld were passed to us by the LAPD as part of an on-going investigation.'

I let that sink in for about five seconds. LAPD? That's nothing to do with me. 'He's done it before. I knew it.'

The agents look to one another, but say nothing.

And it says everything.

- So I told them everything.
- And then what?
- And then . . . god. And then everything just . . . imploded.
- Talk us through it.
- Well, I guess it started with SX9.

**LUCAS BLO QUESTIONED BY FBI Reportedly
Over Model Assault Claims**

SX9 has exclusively learned that controversial
fashion photographer Lucas Blo, real name
Lucas Blomfeid, was arrested last night on
landing at LAX and taken in for questioning
over multiple claims of sexual assault.

It's alleged that the FBI has taken
possession of CCTV footage from a Paris
hotel and photography OF THE ASSAULT
HAPPENING from a former assistant of Blo.

SX9 understands the most recent claims
were made by seventeen-year-old British
model Jana Novak, but that various historical
allegations are being investigated.

Rumours about Blo's alleged misconduct
have been an open secret, and the subject of
blind items, in the fashion world for years but
no formal charges have ever been made.

Speaking outside his West Hollywood home
this morning, Blo (41) denied all wrongdoing.

SX9

Two worlds collide.

My home. The one where I live with my mum and dad and brother, surrounded by *them*. Photographers, reporters, news channels camped out on the Winstanley Estate and there ain't even been a stabbing. Is this legal? Are they allowed to do this?

Apparently so.

Mum called the police and they did send a car, but the officer told us that if they're not blocking the road and they don't enter our premises, there's nothing they can actually do. They're just vultures on a pavement.

I watch them from behind the net curtain in Mum and Dad's bedroom.

'JANA!'

'JANA, IT'S THE BBC.'

'JANA! WERE YOU RAPED BY LUCAS BLO?'

'JANA, DO YOU HAVE A STATEMENT?'

I don't know who leaked the story to SX9. It could be anyone really, I suppose. It could be Blo himself.

All I know is that the FBI have told me to say nothing at all because it could jeopardise the case they've been building against him for years.

'Jana,' Mum says. 'Come away from the window.'

'This is bullshit . . .'

'Do not swear in the house, please.'

'It is. How are you gonna go to work?'

'I called in. I'm staying with you.'

I shake my head. 'Mum, you don't have to do that.'

'Yes, I do. Is very scary for you.' She pauses and sits on the edge of the bed. 'And I want you to tell me what happened with this man.'

'Mum . . .'

'No. No more, Jana. I am your mother and I have to know everything.'

I laugh. I'm not sure if that's her struggling with her English or if she's pretty much described the purpose of being a mum: omnipotence.

'OK.' I join her on the bed.

When Do We Pull The Plug On Trial By Media?
Monty Pearce

Another day, another innocent man has his name and reputation dragged across social media. I pointedly use 'innocent' to describe photographer Lucas 'Blo' Blomfeld because I live in the United Kingdom where I was raised to believe people are innocent until proven guilty.

No court of law has convicted Blomfeld of a crime, and yet so-called Social Justice Warriors have taken to social media in their droves to 'virtue signal' their support for a teenage fashion model who is seemingly more credible than a father-of-two simply because she is pretty, young and female.

I'm sorry, but simply tweeting #IBelieveJana isn't going to stand up in court, is it? And nor should it. When will these children of the broadband generation learn that they are neither judge, jury nor executioner. The laws of our land stand to protect innocent men from egregious accusations of rape and sexual assault. In fact, I'd hazard that such histrionics about a pat on the derrière, a wolf whistle, or even a simple glance, so it seems, will deter real victims of rape and sexual assault from speaking out.

On the day, should it come, that Lucas Blomfeld is found guilty of rape in a court of law I shall join the baying crowds at the gallows, but until then, he must remain an innocent man.

Is It Time For Some Uncomfortable Truths About Sex, Ladies?
Hattie Cope

Yep, I'm going there. For years now, us girls have had our cake and very much eaten it. We can wear, say and do what we want, and no one is allowed to challenge us on our behaviour, or we cry sexism. And maybe it's time we have to admit that we can't have it both ways.

The curious, and ongoing, case of Lucas Blo and teenage model Jana Novak is presently being played out on social media. She alleges she was sexually assaulted in a Paris hotel room, he claims they were doing a photoshoot like any other. Provocative, certainly, but par for the course in the fashion industry.

Novak, 17, is a prime example of Generation Snowflake. She's been taught she can bare her erect nipples for a billboard campaign and yet is fully entitled to a lawsuit when someone later asks to see those same breasts. A girl who parties in New York, Dubai or Tokyo, and cavorts half-naked with male models, later cries rape when a man somehow gets the message she might enjoy this sort of thing.

I mean, is this what it's come to? Next, perhaps, we could bring back chastity belts and issue 'consent keys' to prospective partners. It strikes me as odd that all sexual power has now been devolved to women. I remember when gallantry, the responsibility to 'woo' or 'romance' was the domain of men.

I am a woman who wants a man, a real man. Deep down, don't we all? If we continue to play this absurd cat-and-mouse game whereby we appear sexually available, but never really are, how are men ever meant to learn the art of seduction?

Oh, tweet me your worst, snowflakes, but deep down, you know I'm right.

Matty: Cavorting?!?!?!?!

      Jana: Yeah. I know. Sorry.

Matty: Don't be insane. I don't
know where they got those pics from.

      Jana: Insta I guess.

Matty: I've tweeted the website and asked
them to take them down. Everyone
knows I'm gay anyways.

      Jana: Thank you xxx

Matty: How are you?

      Jana: It has to blo over soon.

      Geddit?

Matty: The guy is a ducking ass-hat
I fully believe you xxxxx

Arabella: Jana, I am sorry this is happening to you. I love you and fully support you.

> **Jana**: Thank you. Love you too xxx

Arabella: I'm starting to think we don't work in a very nice business . . .

> **Jana**: Ha! What was the first clue?

Westley: Jana, I'm so inspired by
your strength and dignity in the
middle of a shitstorm. If you need
to get away I can charter a private
jet from Heathrow to anywhere
in the world. I'm still in Canada
on set and you are more than
welcome to visit OR my NYC apartment
is all yours. Whatever you need.
Let's fry the bastard. x

MATRIARCH

Through Mum's bedroom window again, I see Maggie pose for the photographers on the driveway. Her zippy little Maserati is parked just outside. I suppose she wants to be seen coming here, what with all the stories in the press. The *Observer* ran an exposé over the weekend about the reality of life as a young model following the Blo scandal. Prestige did *not* come off well. 'That's enough!' she barks and struts to the front door.

'Jana!' Mum calls up the stairs. 'She's here!'

Oh, I know. I head downstairs as Mum lets Maggie in. 'Gosh! That is a circus!' Maggie declares. 'You poor things!' And then she sees me. 'Fucking hell, Jana. What did you do to your hair?'

It's now bleached peroxide-blonde. I didn't want people to recognise me as the girl on the news, but I think I've only succeeded in drawing more attention to myself. I can't decide if it looks cool or stupid.

'Well, I suppose we can fix it before *Vogue* comes around. How are you doing, little one?'

I stand halfway up the stairs. 'How do you think?'

'I know. This must be beastly.'

I say nothing. I just glare at her.

'I'll put the kettle on,' Mum says. 'Why don't you go to the lounge?'

I show Maggie the way. In her orange faux (?) fur, she looks comically out of place on our flumpy sofa. It's like we've invested in a piece of abstract modern art and hung it in our former council house in Wandsworth. 'Darling, this will all blow over . . .' she starts.

'What do you want?' I cut her off.

'Jana . . .'

I'd love to be a frosty power bitch, but it's not really me, is it? 'Maggie, I'm sorry, but I really am done. How can I go back after this?' I motion to the jackals prowling the drive. I'm not *just* in media hiding. I'm plotting. I need a plan. In the meantime, I'm doing my A level modules online – French and English. It feels nice, stretching my brain again.

'Darling! There's more interest in you than ever! Now you're a *star*! Everyone's talking about you! You're the name on everyone's lips.' I swear, if I look really closely, there's dollar signs in her eyes, spinning like a fruit machine.

Mum enters with the teas on a tray. She's in her uniform, ready to go to the night shift. 'Biscuit?' she asks.

'No, thank you, darling, not with Fashion Week just around the corner.'

Mum wanders back to the kitchen. 'Maggie, I told you what happened to me in Paris and you told me to forget it. I don't know how much you knew before that, but you were *still* gonna send Elyssa to a casting with him.'

I note Maggie's hands are shaking slightly as she takes a mug of tea. 'Sweetie, I told you, Lucas is a bad boy, but . . .'

'But nothing.' I look her dead in the eye. 'In a choice between me and him, you chose him.'

'That's not true at all!'

'Yes, it is.' I'm back in the room now. I'm sleeping like a normal person, free from jet lag, and exhaustion, and the drunken effect of Xanax. The sertraline gives me a little dry-mouth, but I can handle it. I'm ready for the fight.

'Jana, please ... be reasonable. Look. If this is about commission ...'

'You're not listening to me!' That shuts her up. 'Maggie. I saw the Broadly piece about you. About all the women who covered up for Blo.'

Her lips purse. 'I don't know what you mean.'

'I mean, this – me – it all looks *really* bad for Prestige, don't it? You sent teenage girls to a man who—'

'Jesus fucking Christ, Jana, do you want me to beg?' She actually falls to her knees in the middle of the lounge. 'My mother started Prestige in 1967 and this sort of publicity could finish us.' My face must look super impressed with that comment. 'I'm sorry, that was out of line. I care deeply about my girls, Jana, you know that.'

I tilt my head. 'I think you *think* you do.'

Maggie is about to protest when Mum comes back from the kitchen. 'Mrs Rosenthal?' she asks. 'Do you have a daughter?'

Maggie stiffens. 'Yes, I have a grown-up daughter. Why?'

'Would you have let her be a model?'

'Well, that's neither here nor there ... it doesn't work like that.'

Mum cuts her off. 'I trusted you, and you put my daughter in harm's way.' Her jaw clenches. 'Now please leave.'

I feel such a swell of love for her, I actually go a bit dizzy. My vision goes all sugar-rush pink at the edges. 'Listen . . .'

'Now.'

'Very well.' She gathers her Birkin and scarf. 'But I think this is a mistake, Jana.'

I shrug. We'll see. But already I feel free of her.

Old Jana is dead and gone. I don't know what the future holds, who I'll become. For now, I'm . . . waiting. And I'm not sure what I'm waiting for.

I get my answer a couple of days later. A knock at the door. The press have mostly given up, but there are still a couple of photographers in cars outside.

I'm home alone. I hide behind the sofa and hope whoever it is will think the house is empty.

Another knock.

And another. They're not gonna stop. I crawl through the hall on my hands and knees. 'Who is it?' I ask through the letterbox.

'It's me,' says a very familiar voice. 'Ferd.'

I've hoped for this so hard, I wonder if I'm dreaming it. 'Ferdy?'

'Yeah.'

I unlock both locks and slide off the chain. 'Quick,' I say, hustling him in before one of the photographers sees him. I close the door behind him and lock it again.

'Your hair . . .' he says.

I blink. 'Never mind my hair, look at your hair!' He's shaved his head. Gone is the shoulder-length mop, replaced with a fuzzy buzzcut. It takes everything I have not to reach up and stroke it. That wouldn't be right.

'Yeah. I finally had enough of Dad nagging so . . . you like it?'

He looks so much older. And, without any hair to hide behind, you can see how handsome he is. 'I really do.'

'Yours is cute.'

I finger my hair. It feels dry, brittle and straw-like. 'Yeah. I wanted to be someone else for a while.'

'I bet your mum loves it.' A smile thaws his face. I grin back. *He's home.*

We can't just stand in the hallway talking about hair. 'You want a cup of tea or something?'

'Tea is The One.' I nod and we go through to the kitchen.

As I make the tea, we do banal small talk: college, his course, his application for film school next year. I carry the tea over and we sit on either side of the little breakfast table, hands cupping our mugs. 'Thank you,' I say.

'What for?'

'For coming over.'

He shrugs his left shoulder, just a centimetre. 'Jana, I . . .' He stops. 'Look, I'm gonna square with you. I made Sabah tell me *everything*. And you can't be mad at her . . .'

'I bet I can, but go on.' I'm not admitting anything until I know what Sabah's said. She knows *everything*, including Westley.

He stares into his tea. 'How are you doing?'

I love you, and I miss you so much it feels like it's killing me. 'I'm fine.'

'Jana . . .?'

'OK. I'm a prisoner in my own home and my hair's in the witness protection programme.'

He half-smiles, but he looks in pain. 'I am so sorry.'

Now I frown. 'What for?'

He looks up at the ceiling and takes a sec. I think he's on the edge of tears. I want to reach out to comfort him, but feel like I can't. 'Jana. With this Blo guy, I . . . I should have been there for you. The fact you felt . . . you felt like you couldn't tell me. I know this isn't about me, but I feel like I failed you.'

No. No, no, no. 'No. Ferdy . . .'

'Let me finish. I . . . you'd been through this awful thing, and then I gave you such a hard time about what happened in Japan.'

'Ferd. What I did in Japan was fucked. It has nothing to do with what happened with Blo.'

He looks right into me with a look that says, *Really?*

'I dunno. Maybe. I was a fucking mess.'

'I remember the night you got back from Paris. I was such an asshole at that restaurant, seriously, and I could tell something was wrong and I made it all about me,' he says. 'I'm meant to know you better than anyone. I got it all so wrong.'

I say nothing for a moment. 'What do you mean?'

'When I said you were someone else. I was wrong. Sabah told me everything. About Westley Bryce.' Fuck, I will *kill* her. 'And that Elyssa girl and why you went to the police. It all made a lot more sense. It was very *you*.'

'Me and Westley . . .'

'No, it's cool. OK, cool is a reach, but it's . . . *understandable*? I've tried, but I cannot imagine what the last year has been like for you. None of us can. But someone like Westley Bryce does get it. In a way that I can't.'

My eyes sting. 'That's not an excuse. I did a shitty thing.'

He blinks back tears. 'You must have been so lonely.'

If I speak, I'll sob. I just nod.

'And I wasn't there.' His voice wobbles too. 'And I wasn't helping.'

'You *were*. Ferdy, you were. *You* were my reason to come home. Every time I stood in a freezing cold studio, wearing some fucking stupid dress, I thought of how many days, hours and minutes I had until I saw you again. I swear. The notifications on my phone. Your name. That's what kept me going.'

Neither of us speaks for a minute. The tail on the kitchen cat clock swings back and forth.

'We need to forgive each other,' he says very quietly.

'You haven't done anything . . .'

'I need you to. I feel . . . so shit. I let you down.'

'You didn't . . .'

'Jana, please.'

'OK,' I say. 'If you need to hear it, I forgive you. I just want things back the way they were.'

He nods and takes a sip of his tea. 'I dunno if things can ever be the way they were before. Too much has happened. But I think things can . . . go on. Different, but good. You and me, we're not gonna be goodies or baddies.'

'Ferdy, stop!' I hold a hand up. 'You don't need to say anything else. Honestly. If you can forgive me for . . . what I did in Tokyo, I . . . I just want you back. I have missed you so much. And not just because of all this . . . fucking shit . . . I feel like I lost half

340

of me. I've been drifting around the world like a ghost. It's like I'm not even solid any more. I don't know if you can trust me again, I dunno if I would, but if you could just give me a chance to . . .'

'I love you.' He looks up at me and I remember how much I *adore* the shape of his face. No. It's not gonna be on a billboard, but it's warm and kind and gorgeous and wise. And this new hair. This new hair is . . . fit. He looks like a proper man. 'I know we used to say we loved each other all the time, but now I mean it. It sounds nuts, but I didn't really feel it until I let go. Then I fucking felt it.'

'Love hurts?' I allow myself a tiny, hopeful smile.

'Mate, they aren't kidding. It felt like I'd been . . . kicked in the chest. Hard. A lot. By a fucking giant. In boots.'

I laugh. 'Can we try again? Please?'

'Yes.' He takes my hands, and I just stop myself from cheering. 'Yes, times a hundred. I said you weren't Jana any more. But you are. You're just *more* Jana than you were before. And I love that.' I squeeze his hand tight. 'And now it's me who has to grow to fit with how . . . freaking glorious you've become. Fully evolved Jana. I'm so proud of you. I need to fucking keep up.'

A tear runs off my cheek and splatters on to the table. 'I haven't done anything, Ferd.'

'Jana. You single-handedly brought a sexual predator to justice. Don't you see how huge that is? You saved god knows how many other girls from going through what you went through.' He lifts my hand and kisses it.

As his lips touch my skin, I feel something at my core unwind. A low-level wrong has been righted. I know we're young, but I also know my heart feels pinker when Kai Ferdinand is near. Every minute of every day, I tolerate a nagging background hum of nervous energy, and when I'm with him, just for a few hours, the buzz mercifully stops.

'You're incredible,' he says.

I shake my head and another tear trickles down my face. 'I've done *nothing*,' I admit with a sob.

'What? You have . . .'

'No. Ferd, you don't understand. I heard yesterday. The French police say there ain't enough evidence to push for a conviction. He's gonna get away with it.'

– And then?
– Well, you know what happened next.
– Tell the viewer.
– A friend. A friend helped me out.

SUPERMODEL KEYS:
I WAS VICTIM OF BLO
by Shawna Sands, senior reporter

Following explosive allegations made by fellow Brit model Jana Novak, global supermodel Clara Keys, 23, tells her story exclusively to the *New York Herald*.

We meet on the first hot day of summer at the Plaza in Lower Manhattan. Keys contacted me through a mutual friend and said she wanted to speak to a trustworthy female writer. She waits for me in the bar, nursing a large glass of Malbec. She seems nervous, but routinely stunning in a black Calvin Klein dress and Louboutins.

'I want to talk about Lucas Blo,' she begins. 'I've never told anyone this, but I can't sit back while Jana Novak gets crucified in the tabloids.'

I ask her if she knows Novak personally. The two share a UK agency, Prestige Models. 'I've met her a few times. She's very young – just a baby – and so sweet. I feel so protective of her right now.' Keys has lost none of her London accent or charm, although she now mostly lives in Manhattan.

What unfolds is a case of finally putting some names on scurrilous rumours and tabloid blind items. 'I'd just been scouted,' Keys says. 'I'd just walked in my first Fashion Week and it all kicked off. I met Blo backstage at Mancari, I think, and he asked to photograph me while I was in New York. My agents obviously said this was a wonderful opportunity and that I shouldn't turn it down.'

Keys agreed to meet him in a hotel, the same MO he allegedly used six years later with Novak. 'Sometimes you do go to castings in hotels,' she explains. 'They have conference rooms and stuff and they can be professional spaces. But this was different.' How so? 'It was just us in a suite. I felt vulnerable straight away. I was only just sixteen at the time and very new to everything. He asked me to try on some clothes but they were, like, kids' clothes . . . tiny sizes. I felt stupid, but he took pictures, so I thought it must be normal. But then he was like, "Oh, I have this crazy idea, let's get you in the shower." Obviously I said no, but he assured me I'd look beautiful, that it'd make my skin look great.

'He told me how rare it was for black girls to break through and become stars, and how he wanted to make me a star.' Even now, Keys is one of only a handful of black models who have the clout to book magazine covers. 'And what he said properly tapped into real fears I had. My agency had said the same thing: that only a few girls of colour reach the top.'

I ask Keys if she felt she could walk away from the job. 'No. I mean, how could I? I'd been told that this man was one of the most important photographers in the world. He could make or break my career. And there was no way I wanted to go back to my foster homes, you know.'

Keys's childhood in social services is well-documented. I ask if she did consent to the photoshoot. 'Yes, but that's *all* I consented to. I'd also argue that when a man has all the power, and you have none, is it really even consent? Like, I was in a position where saying no was almost impossible. And he knew that. He banked on it.'

And what happened next is truly sickening. 'So I got in the shower in the T-shirt and shorts and socks and got wet. He was taking pictures, but he was also wanking himself off [masturbating]. "I do this all the time, baby," he said. "It's how I know it's all working . . . if I'm jerking off, so will the client."'

How did she feel? Keys shakes her head, the memories obviously difficult, even now. 'Scared. Disgusted. Embarrassed.' Did he touch her? 'He didn't touch my body, but he touched my mind, you know what I mean? Like, I've replayed that day in my head every day for the last six years.'

I have to ask the difficult question. Why didn't Keys speak out at the time? 'I did! I told my agency and they laughed it off, told me that's just what Lucas Blo is like. Other models rolled their eyes when I told them. They were his friends! They'd say, "Oh, you get used to it," or "That's Lucas." There was this feeling that we owed him. He'd turned us into supermodels, so we kept our mouths shut.'

Does she think it's happened to other models? 'I know it has.'

Is this sort of abuse endemic in the fashion industry? Keys sips her wine and considers her words. She is, I admit, more composed and wise than I'd have anticipated prior to meeting her. She may have left school at sixteen, but Keys speaks with the authority of someone older than her years. 'I think there are people in this business who do not treat the girls as well as they could. There are a lot of us and so I think they forget how young and how vulnerable we are. Often we're miles away from home, without our parents, for the first time. You get manhandled; left waiting in corridors; working all night; you stay in cockroach-infested flats [apartments].

'And I'll be honest, no one is encouraging you to eat. I've had designers and agents tell me I'm too fat, too ugly, too black. I've had hairdressers rip my weaves off my scalp. It's brutal. That's not everyone. I've worked with absolute sweethearts, and I'm blessed

346

now because I've reached a level where everyone treats me like I'm made of diamonds. But I don't forget the way certain people was [sic] in the beginning. And that's why I gotta speak up for Jana.'

But why reach out to the *Herald*? Why not go to the police? 'I can't go into details, but I did go to the police a few weeks back. They were nice but there's nothing they can do because it happened so long ago and there's no evidence. Jana did tell the police and Blo is still a free man. I told the police and he's *still* a free man. At first I felt really powerless, like I couldn't help Jana, but then I realised that I do have power. I'm Clara Keys! People listen to me! If I tell people to try a new type of moisturiser, millions of people do it. So I figured I had to do this. Maybe if I say something, other people will say something too.'

A spokesperson for Lucas Blo denies any inappropriate behaviour took place. NYPD did not respond to my requests for comment.

Unknown: Hi Jana, it's Clara K. Got your no off Cheska, hope you don't mind. How u doin?

> **Jana**: Hey! I'm good! Just saw the NYH article. Thank you so much for doing that. It must have been painful but it means more than you can ever know.

Clara: Any time, babygirl. Now let's get that fucker.

SNOWBALL

It feels like the first time in a long time I've had the sun flat on my face. I got sent some super cool Republic of Deen sunglasses so, between them and the bleached hair, I feel fairly incognito as we sit on Clapham Common. I lie on my back, head resting in Ferdy's lap. Robin is rolling a joint and Sabah is playing on her phone. New girl Amber is here too with her dog – an elderly chihuahua with no teeth called Gizmo.

I feel more normal, more me, than I have all year. I went away and came back.

'You fired them?' Robin asks, licking the Rizla.

'Yeah. Officially. When Maggie gave that statement.'

'Sorry? Who's Maggie?' Amber asks. She's actually fully nice and I now feel like a megabitch for being so suspicious about her while I was away.

I'm bored of explaining. Luckily, Ferdy takes over. 'Maggie runs Prestige. She gave a statement saying no one at the agency had any idea that Lucas Blo was a predator.'

'She lied through her teeth,' I finish. 'So I fired them.' OK, my contract expired and I didn't renew it, but saying "fired" is way more extra.

'So that's it?' Robin asks. While I've been in my drama-hole,

Robin has apparently discovered the gym. He's looking good. 'You're done?'

'I still have my overseas agencies. I still want to do my *Vogue* shoot next month.' I do. I reckon in fifty years when I'm old and grey I'll be well proud of a *Vogue* cover.

'And,' Ferdy says, 'it's not like you don't have offers.'

'Models 1, Premier, IMG and Elite have all offered to represent me now I'm out of contract.'

'Get her!' Sabah prods my leg with her toe.

'I dunno.' I prod her right back. 'I'm sort of done with hiding out. Now that I'm not so tired I could weep, I sort of miss the adventures. I got used to the speed, y'know? I know Dermot wants me to do a campaign too.' Also, and I'll admit this, I'm bored. I've been doing my online A levels, keeping one eye on the Blo case, helping out around the house, but I'm starting to go a bit nuts. That said, the thought of plunging myself back into Fashion-Week madness stirs up a lot of shit. I vividly remember how I felt last February and never want to feel that way again. But I do want the high. I want that catwalk high. I do.

'Well, you look insanely good in the window of Coda,' Amber says.

Robin cups his chest with his hands. 'Your boobs . . .'

'Photoshop,' Ferdy and Sabah and I all say at the exact same time and fall to pieces laughing.

'Fuck,' Sabah says quietly. She's looking at her phone.

'What?' I say.

'Do you really want to know?'

'Do I really want to know what?'

Sabah chews her lip. 'More Blo stuff . . .'

I sit up. 'Go on, then.'

'Another two models have come forward.'

'Who?' Ferdy asks.

'Erm . . . Rosanna Brujas and Kami Brennan.'

'I know her!' I say. 'She's in the Coda campaign.'

Sabah scans the item as quickly as she can. 'Um. Says Blo groped her in a Jacuzzi . . . like, eight years ago.'

'Gross,' I say.

'Oh. This is interesting. Turns out this Rosanna Brujas actually took him to court in 2014 and settled for "an undisclosed figure". Part of the deal was that she wasn't allowed to talk about it.'

'See, how can that be OK?' Ferdy asks. 'America is so messed up.'

'So what?' I say sadly. 'Everyone knows Blo is a pervert. They knew it before, they know it now.'

'Apparently magazine publishers have said they won't work with him any more.'

'Oh,' I say. 'That's good, I guess. At least there's *some* consequence.'

We fall quiet. I'm so sick of Blo. The incident in the hotel room lasted about an hour, and it don't seem fair that he's stolen the following four months from me too.

I check my phone and see I have a new message from Clara. 'Huh.'

'What?' Ferdy asks.

'It's Clara.'

'Keys?' Sabah asks.

'Yes.'

'Sorry, can we just pause and reflect on the fact that you have Clara Keys's number?'

'She's asking if I want to meet her. She says she has a smoking gun.'

'Woah!' Robin says, puffing on his spliff. 'Like she shot someone?'

'No, you dick,' Ferdy says. 'It's a metaphor. Like she has evidence.'

'What is it?'

I shrug. 'Let's find out.'

I take the Northern line to Chalk Farm and pretend to ignore a group of girls who clearly recognise me despite my clever disguise. Could of course be because a tabloid papped me having that picnic the other day. 'BLONDE JANA PUTS ON A LEGGY DISPLAY.' No, you shit rag, I was wearing shorts because it was warm. I don't get how men hiding in bushes with cameras is any different to stalkers. How is it legal?

It's about a ten-minute walk from the Tube stop to the address Clara sent me. 'Holy fuck.' I check I've got the right place and I do. Clara legit lives in a mansion. *Real-Housewives* realness. I have to buzz before scary, spiky gates screech open. It's a mini White House with a zippy red convertible sitting in the drive.

Clara greets me at the door, dressed in her own branded athleisurewear. 'Hey, baby girl!' Her fluffy little dog yaps and yaps, circling her feet. Clara scoops her up into her arms. 'Come in, come in!'

'This house is huge!' I say as I enter a *Gone With the Wind* entrance hall with sparkling marble floors.

'You want it?'

'Huh?'

'Didn't you see the "For Sale" sign?' she says. 'Come through to the kitchen and I'll sort you a coffee. You drink coffee, yeah?'

'Sure. Why are you selling it?'

She rolls her eyes. Without a weave in, her natural hair is scraped back into a tufty little ponytail. She looks so young, so fresh. 'Have you seen the state of this place? Like, does it look like me . . .?'

There are already boxes piled up in the corridors as we head through to the kitchen. 'Honestly? Not really.'

'Jana, I never even unpacked. What? Yeah, I know. I must have been outta my tiny mind when I bought this place. You know what I think it is? When you come from a foster home, I suppose it makes sense that you'd want a big fairy-tale castle, but I swear down, yeah, we only ever used one little room upstairs because everything else just felt ridiculous. And so fucking cold.'

I wonder who 'we' is. Surely not the mystery baby rumour?

'Nah, girl, I'm selling it. I got my apartment in Manhattan and I think I'll get a cool crash pad south of the river for my mum to live in. Gotta keep it real. Primrose Hill? What the hell was I thinking? And, god, the neighbours' little white faces when I moved in!'

The kitchen looks cellophane-new, like she's never once slopped spag bol over the gleaming stove. I see towers of takeaway cartons piled up on the side like the New York skyline.

353

Domino's, Nando's, McDonald's. I smile to myself. We have so much money, but we're kids. We live like kids.

A girl I recognise with bright pink hair pads barefoot into the kitchen from the back garden. She's wearing a bikini top and harem pants. OMG, it's . . .

'Jana, this is Mik – Mik, this is Jana.'

'Hey.' She extends a hand.

'Oh, wow,' I say. 'Sorry . . . I . . .'

'Don't sweat it,' she says in her Baltimore accent. I've seen *The Wire*, I'd recognise it anywhere. 'Hey, I just wanna say . . . what you did, speakin' up against Blo, that was dope. You're my heart, girl.' Mik is Mikita Flame. I saw her once supporting a band at the O2 and she is incredible. She raps faster than anyone else I've ever heard. Now, she turns to Clara. 'Baby, imma take a shower before my car comes, OK?'

'Sure.' They kiss fleetingly on the lips, Clara about a head taller than Mikita, before she heads out of the kitchen and up the sweeping staircase.

Clara tries to figure out a Nespresso coffee machine a bit like a caveman using tools for the first time. I go to help her. We have one at home. 'Thanks,' she says. 'OK. Look. I know what you're thinking. *OMG, secret lesbian Clara Keys!* What? Big scandal.'

'I really wasn't.' I was. A bit.

'It's about Miki. I don't care what people think about me, but she's surrounded by assholes and her ex-husband is trying to take her kid away. Everyone kinda knows. It's an open secret.' She pauses. 'Another one.'

I realise the issue is that she ain't plugged the Nespresso machine in. 'I . . . I never really thought about who you were dating really.' It's true. Like, what mortal man could ever measure up to a goddess like her? Answer: only another goddess. It makes sense.

'It wasn't something I planned. I was only nineteen when we met, and she was twenty-eight. Love just gets you, right?'

I chuckle. 'I hear you. I think I might end up with a guy I met in Year Ten.'

'Don't fight it, babe. Why would you? If it's love, lock it down, I say.' She smiles and I'm reminded why a lot of people think she's the most beautiful woman on earth. 'You want something to eat? I could heat up some pizza? I like cold pizza, personally, but Miki says it's gross, so . . .'

'I'm good,' I say, sipping the bitter – and very strong – coffee. 'I just wanted to say thank you – again – for speaking up.'

Clara shrugs. 'I felt guilty, to be honest. If I'd said something six years ago, we might not be where we are now.'

'It's OK. Lucas Blo is not your fault. People keep apologising for him. Everyone *except* him, in fact.'

'I know. The weirdest thing happened a while back.' She propels herself on to the work surface and crosses her long legs. 'I did an interview with Victoria's Secret and they were surprised that I had, like, a London accent. I realised it's because in seven years, I've barely spoken. I mean, "Because We're Worth It" is hardly Shakespeare, is it? How is it that the whole world knows what I look like, but no one knew what I sounded like?'

'Be seen and not heard?'

'Yes! So fuck it! I'm fully famous and people are listening now. And I had something to say.'

'You did it,' I say. 'You brought him down.'

'Hmm. Not yet we didn't.'

'What do you mean? Lots of magazines have said they won't hire him any more.'

'For now. It'll all BLO over – lol, etcetera – and then some dick will hire him to be all like, "Ooh, look how edgy and provocative we are." A lot of men are on their fifth second chances, know what I mean? Nah, sis, we need to get him locked up. And I think I got the missing piece of the puzzle.'

'What?'

Clara grins. 'What are you doing tomorrow? Fancy a trip to France?'

CELINE

The rain drums against the roof of the car, and all I can see for miles is shifting grey skies. Doomy. We left Paris behind us about an hour ago and seem to be driving into oblivion. 'Is this the right way?' I ask Clara under my breath.

'I dunno. Ask the driver.'

We established at the airport that Clara's French is non-existent. *'Excusez-moi? On est bientôt arrivé?'*

'Oui, oui, mademoiselle.' The driver looks exactly how you'd imagine a French driver to look. Sandpaper jaw, flat cap, smells like an ashtray. *'Cinq minutes.'*

'Five minutes,' I tell Clara.

She smiles. 'Thanks, babes, I got that bit.'

I thought long and hard about coming with her. I was in no rush to come back to France, but then I thought, fuck it. Like, a) not like I've got anything better to do, and b) I started this. I should finish it. 'Do you know what it is she's supposed to have?'

'Not a clue,' Clara says. 'But after I did the *Herald* interview, Lien Yim – you know her, right? – gets in touch and says I need to give Celine Marchand a call. So here we are.'

Sure enough, the Lexus turns down a concealed dirt track towards a farmhouse half-hidden by trees. In better weather, it would be pure *Beauty and the Beast* fairy tale, but in the gloom, it's menacing somehow. The pale blue shutters over the windows screech in the wind. A weather vane on the chimney stack whips around. If this was a horror film, I'd be telling the driver to turn the other way. The car crunches over the driveway and gets us as close to the door as possible.

'Let's run for it,' Clara says.

The driver tells me he'll wait in the car. I think. With a cry, Clara steps out into the downpour and I follow her, running for the front door as it opens. An older woman with wild grey hair beckons us in out of the rain. ''Ello,' she says. 'Welcome. Come inside.'

My hair is dripping even from the dash from the car and she hands me a towel. '*Merci*.'

'I'm Clara, and this is Jana.'

'Darling! I know who you are! I am Marie, Celine's mother.' They share a resemblance and Marie must have been stunning back in the day. 'Let me make tea. Celine is in the salon.'

We're both too tall for the twee farmhouse and duck through doors in the direction she points us. It's a lovely, homely home, with knick-knacks and flowers and wooden beams in the low ceilings. Mum would love this. In the lounge there's an easel in the front windows. Someone is halfway through an oil painting of the valley on a much brighter day. Beyond that, in the window seat, watching the rain, is Celine Marchand.

She turns to face us, and it's like she's away with the fairies. She's beautiful ... but sort of ... haunting. And that's a nice way of saying scary. Not a face you'd forget in a hurry. Huge, round eyes, perfect pout, impossible cheekbones. But there's no

358

getting around it, she looks very, *very* sick. She's *much* too thin, her skin greyish and corpsy. A candy-pink knit hangs limp off bony shoulders.

'Celine,' Clara says gently, like volume could break her bones. 'It's good to see you, babes.'

Celine swings pipe-cleaner legs off of the window sill, too skinny to fill her skinny jeans. The two embrace a little awkwardly; that's the thing with models – a lot of clashing bones, not a lot to cuddle. 'You look good,' Celine says.

'You too, babe. Hon, this is Jana.'

She kisses me on the cheek. 'I see you on ze news.'

I'm not sure what to say to that so I just smile.

Madame Marchand pops her head around the door. 'Girls, the tea is served.'

We follow her into a magazine-spread rustic kitchen. Mum would *really* love this. A teapot waits on a sturdy oak table with a plate of homemade madeleines. 'I leave you to talk,' her mother says. '*Celine, mange quelque chose, s'il te plaît,*' she says pointedly. *Eat something, please.*

'*Maman! Allez, ouste!*' Celine rolls her eyes, slipping under the table almost like she's two-dimensional. 'God, she is making me go crazy, you know?' she says when her mother has left the kitchen. 'Always, "Celine, eat zis, Celine, eat zat."' Shunning food, Celine instead slides a cigarette out of a packet of Camels.

'How are you feeling?' Clara asks, taking a cake. 'I heard . . .'

'Zat I am going gaga?' Celine twirls a finger around her head.

'Well . . .'

'Last summer, I go to a clinic. Clarity Centre.'

'Did it help?' says Clara.

'Zey feed me, make me fat.' They absolutely didn't based on what I'm seeing now. 'I get clean off ze drugs, so is not bad.' She stares us down, sucking on her cigarette.

'Celine,' I say, pouring myself some tea so I don't have to look her in the eye. 'You know why we're here . . .'

'Yes.'

Clara finishes the sentence with all the tact of a demolition ball. 'What happened with you and Lucas Blo?'

She half-smiles, half-grimaces, and stubs out her cigarette. 'OK, I tell you ze story, but to you only. And only because Clara is asking. I remember you send, uh, ze flowers when I was out of clinic, so is to thank you.'

'Babe, of course. We was worried about you, hon. You were *everywhere* that season, and then you just *vanished*.'

'OK.' She pauses to choose her words. 'So. My birthday was last week. I was twenty years old.'

I'm not sure why that's important but then I look to Clara who seems to be running numbers in her head. 'I thought we was . . . we did our first season together, didn't we?'

Celine lights another cigarette and inhales before starting. 'Yes, yes. I was, uh, scouted in Paris when I was thirteen only. Ze photographer who saw me at Pompidou took me to agency and was saying to me, "Tell zem you are fifteen," and I am looking . . . older.'

With a nauseous churn in my tummy, I start to see where this is heading.

'I am doing my first Fashion Week when I am fourteen and zat year I shoot with Lucas.' She holds up a finger and heads back into the lounge. When she returns, she's carrying her agency book. 'Here.' She flips it open.

It's a typical Blo creative. Celine is wearing nothing but grubby-looking nude underwear and standing, inexplicably, in a paddling pool filled with spaghetti hoops.

'You were *fourteen* here?' I ask, astonished.

'*Oui.*'

'Did he . . . hurt you?' Clara asks.

'No! No, 'ee was my boyfriend!' She seems genuinely shocked. 'I was in love with him and I am thinking 'ee is in love with me!'

'You . . . dated him?' I ask uncertainly, glancing at Clara who looks equally horrified.

'I was his muse! That is what 'ee was saying. 'Ee said 'ee loves me and is going to leave his wife. I was crazy for him.'

Clara shakes her head. 'But, babes, you were a kid.'

'I know! I know zat now! But zen I was a baby! I knew shit!' I'm starting to think I might need a cigarette too at this rate.

'And did you . . .?'

'Fuck? Yes. All ze time.'

Clara and I look to each other and it don't really need saying, do it? Lucas Blo ain't just a pervert – he's a paedophile. Whether Celine consented or not is neither here nor there because a fourteen-year-old *can't* consent. That's the whole point. God, poor Celine. Oh, I can imagine how a man like Blo would have made her feel special, made her *feel* like she was in control. I expect men have been convincing little girls they're women since time began. Little girls are easier to convince, that's why they pick them. I feel sick.

'Shit,' Clara says.

'We got him,' I mutter, although it feels like a shallow-end victory.

'Celine,' says Clara. 'Will you testify about this? It's statutory rape. That's right, ain't it?' Clara asks, looking at me.

'I think so,' I say, although my legal knowledge is gonna need a google.

'I don't want to be in court.' Celine shifts in her chair. 'It was a, uh, long time ago.'

'Celine, c'mon.' Clara sits up straight. 'This is *it*. He's already being investigated for other stuff, you're not alone in this.'

'No. No, I do not want to make trouble.'

The kitchen falls quiet. Clara looks deflated. I know, though. I know, and have felt, all of the Less words: powerless; hopeless; speaking out felt pointless. But we've come so far. Too far to turn back. We might have dented his reputation, but for how long? It's like Clara said – sooner or later, he'll do his *mea culpa*, a couple of months in posh rehab, a few grand to a charity and then he'll be *back*. Lucas Blo must be *stopped*. For ever.

'Celine,' I say. 'Look at what we've done already. Have you ever seen anything like this before? We're so close . . . we could, like, change the industry. And, you know what, people spend fucking hours looking at us. We could change the *world*.'

Celine snorts. 'I don't know. I am finished with all this.' She gestures at the pair of us. I guess she means modelling. 'I don't want to be a doll for men to play with any more. I am tired, I am sick, I am poor.'

'I know,' I say. 'And I'm sorry about everything that happened to you. But we . . . all of us, can stop it from happening to any other girls.'

362

'And not just Blo,' adds Clara. 'All those other fucking skeezy men what think they can put their hands on girls in clubs; all those men what wind down their car windows to pass comment on our legs; all those men that think we're asking for it if we wear short skirts. Let's fucking cancel them.'

I look at Celine. She closes her eyes but then shakes her head. 'Nothing ever is different.'

'No,' I say, more forcefully than I intend. 'I'm sure a hundred years ago women said the same thing about the vote, or having jobs, or getting divorced, or having an abortion. Things *do* change. If someone like Blo goes to jail, then, I dunno, maybe these men will start to get the message.'

Celine sighs. 'Here. I give you this.' She gets up again and fetches an iPad.

'What is it?' Clara says.

'He made a sex movie of us. I will email it to you.'

Lien's smoking gun. 'Seriously?'

She's very French about the whole thing. 'We had a, how do you say, threesome? In LA. You want to see?'

'No!' Clara and I say together. Loudly.

'Can we give this to the police?' I ask.

Another sigh. 'Yes. Tell zem I was fourteen or maybe fifteen. I don't know how old ze other girl was. Another model.'

'The police will want to speak with you . . .' Clara warns.

Celine shrugs. She seems so tired, so threadbare. Chewed up and spat out. The girl, the child, in the portfolio in front of me is not the same girl that's sitting on the other side of the table.

Photoshop. Our lives are retouched. We've all been flattered and charmed by our agencies, groomed into thinking we're rare orchids, but the reality is we're on a conveyer belt and there are a thousand Elyssa Sayers, all around the world, just waiting to be discovered in Asda, or in the park, or on the beach. Five years ago, Celine was me. And now, without Photoshop, she's back home with her mother, starved sick and in recovery from god knows what. But no one's looking at her because they're too busy looking at me.

'Ze video,' Celine says, 'it is, uh, evidence?'

'Yes,' I say. 'Yes, it is.'

Got him.

SCRAPHEAP

A week or so after I get back from France, I go over to Sabah's. Her mum has gone to her aunt's house in Birmingham, so Sabah has to babysit her little sister. I go and keep her company and we get Deliveroo to bring us a cheeky Nando's. Hot peri-peri chicken and halloumi and fries to her front door in sixteen minutes.

Halima safely tucked up in bed, we spend about twenty minutes flicking through Netflix and get no nearer to finding anything neither of us has already seen. 'Shall we just watch *Jurassic World* again?' Sabah suggests, finishing off a piece of halloumi. 'Chris Pratt is so goddamn fine.'

'Yeah, but the bit where she runs away from the T. Rex in high heels? Just take them off, you wanker.'

'OK, you asked for it. I'm putting *Bridesmaids* on.'

'*Help me, I'm poor!*'

Sabah snorts and selects the film from the menu. We're sitting on the rug in front of the coffee table. Sabah lives in a modern ground-floor flat, two streets away from ours. It's kind of noisy, but they have a little patio out back. 'You want any more chicken?' She passes the box my way.

'No. I'm good. I'll burst if I have anything else.'

'OK.' She takes a slurp of her Diet Coke. 'If I tell you something, do you promise not to judge me?'

She won't look me in the eye. 'I promise. Go on.'

She buries her face in her hands. 'Oh, I can't! It's too shameful!'

I'm not sure if I should be worried or not. 'Sabs?'

'You've been honest with me, so now I should be honest with you.'

Oh, shit, what now?

She smushes her face into a leopard-print scatter cushion so her voice is muffled. 'I've been . . . sort of . . . seeing . . . Rob.'

What? I need a minute. 'Excuse me?' I pull the cushion away from her face. 'ROBIN Rob?'

'Yes, I know!' She shakes her head. 'But have you seen him lately?'

'No . . . pay attention. I've been in France hunting paedos. Keep up.'

'Well, girl, he is looking buffalo, buffet, Phoebe Buffay, buff.'

He *did* look kinda hench in the park, I guess. 'But . . . it's *Robin*?'

'He's joined the gym and the puppy fat is all turning to puppy fit.'

'Nice. See what you did.'

'When he takes off the shit checked shirts he has got all those lines going on!'

I smirk. 'You've seen Robin with his shirt off?'

'Oh, shut the fuck up! You fucked Westley Bryce, you whore.'

'Ouch! But fair. When did this start going on?'

'When you was off in Asia. With you being away and Laurel going over to the dark side, we sort of got closer. I feel safe around him. But, shit, I'm Muslim, he's Jewish. How is this ever going to work out?'

Wow. This has been going on a while. I'm a little wounded she ain't said anything until now, but I get it. 'Is it serious?' She shrugs. 'Worry about stuff like that in, like, ten years time. Enjoy it! Are you enjoying it?'

She smiles a sly smile. 'It's all very twenty-first century *Romeo and Juliet*. Don't tell *anyone*. It's forbidden. It's *haram*. He is quite literally *HaramBae*.'

'I won't. But don't you want to be out of the Robin closet?'

'I don't know. It's quite nice having it just for us without having the whole college know. But I guess I just told you, so the cat is out the bag.'

I give her a hug. 'You deserve it, hon. You both do.'

She throws her head back and exhales. 'Praise Allah, it feels good to get that shit out in the open!'

'No kidding,' I add wryly.

Sabah nods. 'So. Are we going to talk about Celine Marchand?' She puts on a French accent to do her name.

Damn. Thought I'd got away with it. 'Can we not?'

'No.'

I chuckle. 'OK. I just heard. Blo broke about a million laws by having sex with a minor in California. Looks like it'll go to trial. I don't know the ins and outs, to be honest. Clara has hired one of the best lawyers in America to handle everything.' I could tell her more, but every time I let the image of Blo into my mind, I feel nauseous.

'Good,' Sabah nods. 'I hope they fry him.'

'They don't have the death penalty in California . . .'

367

'Shame.'

'Sabs! Problematic!'

She grins. 'And I know you don't wanna talk about it . . .'

'But you're going to anyway, right?'

'*Vogue.*'

A huge, sad sigh pops out of my lungs. I honestly haven't made my mind up. 'I dunno. I'm retired at seventeen. How sad is that?'

'So you're just never modelling ever again?' Sabah frowns.

'Sabs, I honestly don't know.'

'OK, wait here.' Sabah pushes herself off the floor and retreats to her bedroom. She returns a moment later carrying a big spiral-bound notebook. 'Look at this.'

She moves our greasy plates to one side and sets it down on the coffee table. 'What is it?'

'Look.'

I open it up and gasp. It's a scrapbook bursting at the seams with my face. I flick through the pages: TANK, Coda, the Met Gala, *Elle*, dozens of catwalk pics printed from vogue.com and clippings about me and Clara and Blo.

'Wow, Sabs. What a creepy little stalker shrine you've made . . .'

She laughs and throws a cushion at me. 'Bitch! You'll thank me when your tits are by your feet!'

'This is nuts. I forgot about this one.' It's the editorial I did for a French magazine while I was in Paris. The one on the back of a row boat on the Seine at sunset, dressed in sunflower-yellow couture. It's romantic and soft and lovely. Of course, I know that faraway, dreamy look in my eyes was a mixture of Xanax, hunger and exhaustion.

'It's sickening,' she says. 'I wasn't planning on showing you this until we were forty, but it's a fashion emergency.'

'We're gonna be friends when we're forty?'

She grins. 'Babes, I've already booked us into the same retirement village.'

'Ha! Do I move in next week now I'm retired?'

'The point I'm making, fuckwitch, is that you're *bloody good* at this. There's not many people in the world who can do this.' She taps the portrait with an acrylic nail.

'Be tall?'

She kisses her teeth. 'You are not just *tall*. You never were. Little girls see you and want to be you.'

That feels ridiculous. 'Who on earth would want to be me?' I ask very quietly.

'Bitch, I see you. What you did was magnificent. You're the refugee off the estate what slayed a dragon.'

I physically attempt to crawl under the coffee table. 'Stop . . . talking . . . about . . . feelings . . . at . . . once . . .'

'We ain't scared to catch feels here, girl.'

I sigh another big sigh, hoping it lets the toxic gas cloud out of my lungs. It feels like there's a gurgling green swamp in my stomach. 'Sabs, what do I do?'

'It's *Vogue*. It's big.' Sabah shrugs. 'What do you *want* to do?'

I put my brain in gear. For the last year, I feel like I've been in a tumble dryer. My life and my body didn't feel like mine. My mind switched off, probably thanks to them pills, but also because I was too tired to string two thoughts together.

I wonder honestly if I've ever had a day in control of my life. I went from home, to school, to Prestige. I did as I was told.

Never really thought about what I wanted. I wanted Ferdy, I knew that, but now that I've got him back . . . what next?

'I suppose,' I tell her. 'Something that *matters*?'

'You done that already,' Sabah says. 'By outing Blo.'

She's right. But I don't think I'm finished. There's still work to do. My life, my story, will not be defined by Lucas Blo.

VOGUE

The stylist, a cute gaysian called Krishnan, tugs on the corset strings and I gasp for breath. 'Is that OK?' he asks.

No. 'It's fine,' I wheeze. Who needs internal organs anyway? He pulls the corset tighter.

'It looks amazing,' he adds, stepping back to admire me.

My ribs feel crushed. 'Is it *Vogue*?'

He smiles. 'Oh, it's *very Vogue*.' The whole day feels *Vogue*, somehow *sacred*, is that the right word? Hair and make-up people fuss over me in a respectful hush like I'm a virgin bride or something. This is everything I've been working towards. I see myself in the mirror and, yes, I look extraordinary, if I say so myself. I'm the Queen of Hearts, I'm Aphrodite, I'm living art. We already shot the cover this morning inside Hampton Court against a backdrop. I wore a red tartan Burberry trenchcoat. I was up at five-thirty to have my hair dyed brown again, so I feel like I've been awake for a whole day already. Ms Wintour didn't like the blonde with black roots combo.

Now, for the rest of the day, we have to shoot the fashion story to go with the interview. 'C'mon, I'll help you outside.'

He gathers up the layers and layers of red and black silk and taffeta. Vintage McQueen, so I'm told, all part of their piece about the contribution of British fashion designers. I'm not kidding, the dress comes with a security guard – it's on loan from the Met in New York.

Every once in a while, I remember Celine, Blo, the trial. My stomach gurgles. There ain't an anxiety drug strong enough, frankly. The skies might look blue right now, but there's a big old storm cloud on the horizon. The trial is scheduled to start in September. I shake my head. I can't think about that here. It's *definitely* not *Vogue*.

Amazingly, a golf buggy waits outside the palace – where they've set up a changing and make-up room – to take me to the maze where we're shooting this look. It's gonna be a looooooooong day. I have another three gowns after this one. I can't really *sit* in the gown, so I sort of have to cling to the back for dear life. It's a gorgeous August day – warm but not too hot. In the middle of the school holidays, children cheer and scream, chasing each other through the gardens, school dread still a long way off.

We're at the maze in about a minute. The photographer is shouting, in German, at his assistant. Gunter König *looks* very German. Arnold Schwarzenegger with white-blonde hair and piercing blue eyes. Now, I did French, not German, but I can tell he's not happy.

He did the cover shoot earlier, and it wasn't *easy*, but I suspect it might be downhill from here. Matilda from *Vogue* comes over. 'Gunter's having some trouble with light in the maze. We'll be ready for you in a minute, Jana. Are you OK here?'

'Sure,' I say, the corset digging into my ribs. I call the make-up artist over. 'Hey, could I check my phone?' I gave it to her for safekeeping.

She fishes it out of her pocket and I see I have a message from Ferdy: *One more shoot and then you're FREEEEEEEE! Love you.*

I smile and hand back the phone. I become aware of a woman and little girl edging closer. The park is open to the public, but for the next hour, the maze is closed to everyone except us. 'Oh, hello, sorry,' says the woman. 'Is it Jana?'

'Yes, that's me.' I step off the golf buggy, wobbly in the insane platform shoes they've put me in. I'm about seven feet tall right now. I must look terrifying.

'Hello! My daughter wanted to say hello and get your autograph, if that's all right?' The pushy mum thrusts the starstruck girl towards me. She's maybe nine or ten, with gappy teeth and glasses. She ain't grown into her features yet. People used to say that about me.

'Of course,' I smile. 'And what's your name?'

'Georgina,' she mutters, handing me a pretty pink notebook to scribble on.

'Georgina wants to be a model, don't you, Georgina?'

Poor Georgina's cheeks turn boiled-ham pink. Personally, I suspect Georgina's *mum* would like Georgina to be a model, but whatever. Now, do I lie, or tell the truth? 'Well, you're definitely beautiful enough,' I say with a smile and Georgina beams back at me.

Not a lie, but also not what I'd like to tell her about being a model. Not all that glitters . . .

'Jana!' Matilda calls. 'Gunter is ready for you.'

Flanked by assistants, we file into the maze. I gather up the skirts so they don't trail along the dirt paths. Apparently, we're starting in the centre of the labyrinth because there's more space for the lighting set-up. The walls of the maze are finely trimmed privet hedges and it's a tight squeeze in the gown. I've been before: Hampton Court is only about forty-five minutes from Clapham Junction. Dad once brought Milos and me and we spent hours chasing each other around this maze.

'Can we make a start, please?' Gunter calls. 'Quickly, before the sun comes out again and fucking ruins everything.'

We follow his voice, avoiding the dead ends. As we emerge from the maze, Gunter is pacing back and forth, camera in hand. What an asshole, honestly.

Hair and make-up make a couple of last-minute changes and we're off. 'You are Alice in Wonderland,' Gunter says. 'Come through the maze towards me.'

'OK!' I back up a few metres and start towards him.

He fires off a couple of shots. 'Look more lost!'

'OK!' I go back to the starting point and make my eyes wide with concern.

'Slowly!' he barks. 'You're too fast!'

'Sorry. Go again?'

'Yes. Go.'

Rude. I wander back and catch the dress on the hedges. 'Oh, shit, sorry.'

'Careful!' snaps the stylist, coming to free me. Gunter rolls his eyes and cocks his hip.

We try a couple more takes. 'This is not working,' Gunter says. 'Walk away from me and look over your shoulder instead.'

'Sure.' This time he follows me into the maze, snapping away. I look back at him, aiming for curiouser and curiouser with my expression.

'No!' he yells, flouncing off. 'This is awful. Look! Look at this!' He beckons the stylist over to his camera to show her the images. 'She looks huge in this dress! See? Fat coming out of the corset.'

The stylist hmms. 'Maybe I should loosen it?'

'Or maybe she is just too fat.'

Am I a ghost now? They do say Hampton Court is haunted, but not by me, the last I heard. 'Excuse me?' I say loudly, stepping into the centre of the maze. 'What did you just say?'

Gunter looks me up and down. 'You are too fat for that dress.'

I *could* cry. I think a year ago I might have. Now, instead, I smile. I exhale because I really want to enjoy this moment and remember it for ever. 'Tell you what, mate: go fuck yourself.'

Gunter's face falls.

Matilda hears my last words and rushes over.

I stoop down and hoist up the train of the dress. I turn on my heels and stride – oh, my walk is so good these days – into the labyrinth.

'Jana!' Matilda calls. 'You can't just . . . come back!'

But I'm already gone. I pick up pace, vanishing around the corners, twists and turns. I pull one shoe off and then the other, leaving them on the ground. And now I can run.

'Jana!' someone shrieks.

'Jana! Come back! That dress is priceless,' someone else shouts. Through the gaps in the hedgerow, I see them chasing through the maze, straight into the dead ends.

I break into a run. I start to laugh. I turn another bend and see the exit. I burst out into the palace gardens.

Turns out, I knew the way out of the maze.

I always did.

Just walk.

HIGH STREET GIANT
NOT TO BLAME
FOR FACTORY DEATHS

The Supreme Court of Spain, based in Madrid, yesterday dismissed an action by Amnesty International to prosecute Spanish clothing giant Coda for the deaths of two hundred and eighty-seven factory workers who perished in a Bangladesh factory blaze last January.

Coda, which has fifty-two stores in the UK, claimed they were not the only manufacturers to outsource to the factory on the outskirts of Dhaka, and cannot be held responsible for safety standards of external companies. The court upheld this plea.

Jennifer Glazer, speaking on behalf of CEOs Santiago and Alejandro Garçia, said: 'We are committed to improving the conditions of our factory workers and understand why our loyal customers feel let down by what happened in Dhaka. Across the entire industry, we must put ethics at the heart of everything we do.'

Last week, in an interview for *Stylist*, British model Jana Novak said she had stepped down as the face of the brand, expressing her concern over the devastating factory blaze.

KEYS AND FLAME SET TONGUES WAGGING AT FILM PREMIERE

Could the supermodel and rapper be more than just friends?

Celebritattle Online Exclusive

Last night, supermodel Clara Keys turned heads at the launch of her cosmetics line in London, arriving hand in hand with Baltimore rapper Mikita Flame.

Rumours about the pair have been swirling since they were papped last month frolicking in the Maldives. Keys (22) has always remained tight-lipped about her personal life, while Flame (34) has one child with her ex-husband, Detroit Tigers pitcher Amari Ennis.

Neither made an official statement at the launch, although insiders tell us the pair canoodled all night at the glitzy event in Selfridges which was attended by the glitterati and fellow models.

Next month, it is thought Keys *will* testify at the hotly anticipated trial of disgraced fashion photographer Lucas 'Blo' Blomfeld in LA.

KEYS X CLARA is a vegan-friendly, cruelty-free make-up line, which caters for all skin types and genders. The line is available now exclusively in Selfridges and is expected to sell out.

HONEST

My phone lights up and I see it's Cheska from Prestige. I turn it over so I can't see it. Since I walked away from the *Vogue* shoot I've had about a million missed calls a day from Trent in New York, Matilda from *Vogue*, Cheska – god only knows why Prestige are calling – but I'm ducking them all.

I'm listening to Blondie in my room, flicking through my issue of *Vogue* China, which just came in the post. *Atomic.* The portraits are quite stunning, I suppose, and, yeah, I do feel a bit proud. There's one shot where I'm bending over backwards, the sleeves of my salmon-pink Comme des Garçons kimono-dress-thing billowing metres behind me. You know what, it looks like *art*. Proper, legit art. I guess this makes up for the fact I won't be in American *Vogue* after all.

The end-of-movie feeling of triumph and glory only lasted until I got to the changing area. Once I got the corset off, I didn't feel nearly cool enough to pull off such a massive diva strop. They *begged* me to return to set. I refused. I just called Dad and he came to get me.

Dad being Dad, he said there was no excuse for being so rude and that I would personally email Anna Wintour to apologise. Awks.

My phone pings again. I have a new voicemail.

I guess I can't hide from the world for ever. I dial my messages:

'Welcome to Voicemail. You have ONE new message.

'Hi, Jana, it's Cheska DeBrett. I totally understand why you're screening my calls and, in your position, I would too. Listen, I've quit Prestige. Lots of reasons, really, but the way Maggie handled what happened to you . . . well. Jana . . . he did it to me too. I . . . can we please meet up? This week . . . next week . . . just whenever. You've got my number so . . . OK, take care.

'To listen again, press ONE. To save your message, press TWO. To delete, press THREE.'

I go to meet her, because how can I not after that message? That Thursday, I arrange to meet her in Soho House. Apparently she's a member and can sign me in. Fancy. I think it's a way rich people prove to other rich people they're rich or something. Inside it's quite dark, with lots of long, narrow corridors and nooks and crannies with important-looking people having hushed conversations in big leather chairs. I'm pretty sure I walk past Benedict Cumberbatch having a meeting, but don't like to stare. Hello, though! Fucking Sherlock!

Cheska's seated not far from the bar in an armchair near the fireplace, frantically typing an email on her laptop. 'Jana! Hi!' She embraces me and her perfume smells so good, like Parma Violets, I honestly might lick her. 'Thank you so much for coming.'

'It's OK.'

'Can I get you a drink? Tea? Coffee?'

'Yeah, um, tea?'

'Breakfast?' asks an impossibly handsome waiter and I nod. He's probably a model on the side, thinking about it.

Cheska snaps shut the MacBook and pays me her full attention. 'Sorry about that. Things are manic at the mo. Welcome to my new office!'

I look around Soho House, confused. 'Here?'

'It's not for ever, but, yes. You're in the temporary offices of Honest Models.'

The penny drops. 'You're starting your own agency?'

'Yes.'

I smile. 'Ah, I see. You want to sign me?' I'm not a little green kid any more, I know what I'm worth.

'Of course,' Cheska grins. 'Every agency in town wants to sign you.'

The waiter arrives with a plank of wood featuring a see-through teapot, cup and saucer. Trying a bit hard, to be honest. I wait for him to leave. 'There's a reason why I ain't signed with any of them, Cheska. I'm pretty sure I'm retiring. At seventeen. Do you think that's a record?'

'I doubt it. Jana, you can't. You're *too good*. Look. I was a Prestige model and I went from catwalk to office, so I can't speak for the other London agencies, but I can speak for myself. I want to do something different, Jana. As well as starting up the agency, I'm looking into launching a union for models, so we have proper legal rights when we're on jobs. They're trying something similar in the US at the moment but there's nothing quite like it here. Believe me, I know what it's like. I modelled for almost ten years, remember?'

I hold the cup under my lips and let the aroma float into my nostrils. Tea, I love you. 'What happened? With you and Blo?'

'Do you need to know the details?'

Actually, no, I don't. I shake my head.

'I tried to warn you. I've tried to warn a lot of girls. I thought if I was at Prestige I could keep an eye on you. But it wasn't enough.'

'It, like, *really* wasn't,' I say, more crossly than I anticipate.

Her shoulders crumple in. 'I know. God, Jana. I tried. I tried to make sure Maggie or Tom or someone went with girls if they were going to him. It sounds like bollocks, I know, but I sort of pretended what had happened to me was a nightmare. That it wasn't real. That maybe I'd imagined the whole thing, that it was all in my head. And every time I heard his name, I blocked it out all over again. I buried it away. And since you, and Clara, and all the others came forward, I just feel so guilty . . .'

A big tear rolls off her perfect cheekbones and plops on to her leather trousers.

'It's not your fault,' I relent. 'You didn't make him do those things.'

'Maybe if I'd said something . . .'

I shake my head. My eyes sting. 'Cheska. Fuck it. Maybe if you'd said something, you'd have been called a liar. Maybe you'd have been called a slut. Maybe columnists would have written bullshit about you and your family, and people would have sent you shit online. Maybe . . .'

'Jana, I'm so sorry.'

'When did he do it?'

Cheska dabs her eye with a napkin. 'About ten years ago. I was about your age, maybe a little older.'

'The thing is, Cheska, girls did speak out. It's just no one believed us. Or people like Maggie protected him.'

'She knew what happened to me.'

'So there you go. It's *not* your fault.'

'Well, thank you. I really don't think I deserve your forgiveness, but this is all I know how to do. For better or worse, I'm in this industry up to my eyeballs. Might as well see if I can make it better from the inside, right?'

I'm not convinced it's worth saving and tell her so.

'I've already signed Arabella Campbell-True and – and this is top secret – Clara's coming onboard too.'

'What?'

'Her contract with Prestige is running out and I've offered her a *really* good commission rate. All it takes is one big-money girl and, man, does she know it.' God, I love Clara. 'I'm starting small – boutique, as they say – but with Clara, the sky's the limit. I want to do it *differently*, though. No diets, no shitty model apartments, no underage girls, none of that. I'm thinking free-range, organic models!'

Even I have to crack a smile at that. 'Honest Models.'

'That's the idea. Jana, there are people out there who are *dying* to work with you. *Vogue* heard what happened with Gunter König and they're mortified. After the whole Blo thing, the industry is desperate to redeem itself. They're offering you the chance to finish the shoot with a different photographer.'

Huh. OK. 'I want Layla Palmer.'

'Done! They'll go for it! They love her. See, this is what I mean: we have more power than we think we do. We always did.'

I top up my tea because the first cup was too weak. Schoolboy error, didn't brew it long enough. Once, I can't remember when, I thought my life was like being on a rollercoaster. I wonder if the problem with rollercoasters is that you're not in control. You're stuck on a track, no way off, no way out, and by the end you feel like you've been through a cyclone. Maybe I can live life that fast, that exhilarating, but with the added bonus of a *steering wheel* and *brakes*.

Cheska continues. 'What if you could take all the bits you loved about modelling and get rid of all the heinous bits?'

'Is that even possible?'

Cheska leans in. 'That's what agents are for. We do the heinous bits. Or at least that's the idea.'

'I don't know . . .'

'Think about it! Take your time. What do you have coming up?'

'Despite everything, I've said I'll do Dermot's show at Fashion Week . . . and then . . . well, I don't know.'

She tilts her head inquisitively. 'So we can figure it out together.'

I close my eyes and sigh deeply. 'Just let me get through next week.'

'What's that?'

I open my eyes again. 'The trial. The trial starts next week.'

Cheska nods. 'What if . . . what if I come with you?'

– I see it now. This ain't a Cinderella story. Never was. It's *Little Red Riding Hood*. A *lot* of Little Red Riding Hoods, and a lot of Big Bad Wolves.

TRIAL

The sun rises higher and higher over Beverly Hills. Already there are buff guys sunning themselves in speedos like iguanas by the pool and it's not even ten o'clock. They look like briny frankfurters sizzling on a grill. The sky is blue, but there's a hazy smog over LA which makes everything feel like there's an Instagram filter over your eyes. I look out over the hotel complex from my balcony, wearing some of Ferdy's boxers and a vest.

I hear the door slide open behind me. 'I didn't wanna wake you,' I say without looking back.

We both tossed and turned all night. I don't know how much sleep either of us got really.

I ain't seen Lucas Blo since I ran from that hotel room.

Today I will have to look him in the eye.

'I was awake,' Ferdy says. He slips his arms around my shoulders and kisses my neck. 'You OK?'

I just shrug. Saving my words for when I need them.

Manuela Hernandez, our lawyer, struck a deal with the judge and district attorney that every 'alleged' victim would get a chance to speak in court. I ain't spoken to all of the girls, but having railroaded Celine into testifying, I honestly felt I couldn't say no.

'You got nothing to worry about,' Ferdy says. I know he means well, but I do. I have to be in a room with that man. He is gonna lie about us. 'Do you want breakfast?'

I shake my head. I'll speak when it's my turn.

It's almost as glamorous as the Met Gala. There are definitely as many rabid photographers camped outside the Stanley Mosk Courthouse in Los Angeles. A line of LAPD officers has to hold them back. They bark our names, spittle flying from their lips like hungry Rottweilers. I never thought when I finally came to Hollywood it would be to face off against a pervert in court, but here we are.

An unmarked car drops us off and an officer hustles me into the building as a trillion flash bulbs go off. Ferdy never once lets go of my hand. I've never gripped anyone so tightly.

Things are less mental inside. In fact, it looks and smells a bit like a public library. It's not as fancy as I thought it might be and I'm pleased. I don't feel *too* out of place or intimidated. My pits are already sweating in my Prada dress. I was sent about ten dresses by various designers. They're falling over themselves to clothe us for the event of the season. The eyes of the world are watching. It's bigger than the Oscars, so I'm told.

And it does look like a fashion show. I see Clara, Celine, Kami, Cheska and so many others. I count. There were twelve of us in total. All in a line, just like we're backstage at a catwalk.

'The People versus Lucas Blomfeld. Courtroom One. Please proceed to Courtroom One.'

'OK, that's us.'

Ferdy nods. He grips my shoulders and looks me dead in the eye. 'You're going to be fine. You hear me?'

Now I nod. Ferdy has to go into the public gallery and I fall into line with the other girls as an usher shows us in. We all sit FROW, just like Fashion Week.

'Please stand for Judge Gloria Rubin,' an usher says and just seeing the petite judge makes me feel a little better. Perhaps silly, but I tell myself I only have to speak to her.

Only then a side door opens and Lucas Blo enters with his lawyer, a chic black woman right out of the *How to Get Away With Murder* mould. Oh, clever little shit. See what he did there. He loves and respects women, right? How can she defend him? My blood boils. He don't even look our way as a police officer parades him past us. Somehow sensing my rage, I feel Clara take my hand in hers.

Blo's beard has been trimmed and he wears a very expensive-looking suit. He is paraded past us by a court official. Today, he walks the runway for us.

'You can sit down,' Rubin says, taking her seat at the head of the court. We all settle. The judge takes a sip of water and clears her throat. She has facelift-face, but so does any woman over forty I've seen since we got to LA. I wouldn't mess with her. She looks fierce. 'I have this morning met with the prosecution and defence attorneys. This is a highly unusual case and I'm taking the highly unusual step of allowing all of the complainants to speak in a class action of emotional damages before we explore the criminal charges of statutory rape. I think it's appropriate to hear all of the charges together.'

Next, Hernandez speaks, explaining that she intends to

prove Blo is a serial sex attacker who caused us all emotional distress and, for some of us, lost earnings. America is complex. I don't want a penny out of him, although I stand to gain if we win. I want him to pay, but in *time*, not money.

And then it's our turn.

Hernandez presents her case in chronological order, starting with a woman called Brittany who modelled for Blo at the very start of his career. Now she's in her thirties and works as a news anchor in Texas. 'He was very clear,' she says, 'that I would need to be naked, despite what we had agreed to . . . once I reluctantly agreed to do that, he fondled my breasts and my rear . . .'

Cheska. A late addition to the action. 'I don't know if my drink was spiked or if the drinks were very strong . . . but when I came to, he was having sex with me. I . . . I . . . there was no way I could have given consent in the state I was in.'

Kami Brennan. 'I mean, it was pretty clear what he meant. He would only book me for the job if I was prepared to give him oral sex . . .'

Celine. ''Ee knew 'ow old I was. I had lied about my age before, but Lucas, 'ee knew my real age.'

Clara. 'I didn't know that what he did was sexual assault or indecent exposure or whatever. I just wanted to get out of the shower as fast as I could . . .'

Then the others.

And then me. Hopefully the last victim of Lucas Blo. The walk to the witness stand feels like a hundred miles when it's only about ten steps. I place one hand on the Bible, although I don't believe in it, and the other in the air. I swear to tell the truth.

And, truthfully, I've never liked being looked at. I like being

390

listened to even less. I'm back at primary school, Nativity Narrator Number Three. How weird, that in the moment, I recall my lines: *The shepherds were guarding their flock when they saw a brilliant light in the sky.* I froze back then. Miss Skipsey had to prompt me.

Well, I can't fucking freeze now.

I see Ferdy sitting at the back of the gallery.

Speak. 'I was sent by my agency to a casting in a hotel room in Paris . . .'

VERDICT

Like the rest of the world, I see the verdict via the news. I didn't want to stick around in LA for three weeks while they picked over the evidence of the two charges of statutory rape.

Me and Sabah are on the Southbank, taking some pics for her Insta. I'm just getting us some hotdogs with ketchup, mustard and crispy onions from a van when her phone pings. A Google alert. 'The verdict is in,' she says, turning pale.

'Let's find somewhere to sit.' We find an empty bench outside the Royal Festival Hall. 'OK. Go on, then.'

She opens her phone and reads the BBC News article.

'Sabah? Seriously?'

'He got four years.' She looks up at me. 'Four years in county jail. And "unspecified damages" for all his victims.'

'Oh my god.' I collapse into her arms. That cloud of something bright acid green and toxic leaves my body like I'm her off *The Exorcist*. Sabah holds me tight. 'We did it. We actually did it.'

'You won.'

London spins around me. There's a lot going on in my head, and I know I ain't saved the world. But maybe, just maybe, I've *changed* it, just a little bit. All those men, getting away with it. Well, this one didn't. Not this time.

EXCLUSIVE: JUDGE GLORIA RUBIN'S STATEMENT TO CONVICTED RAPIST LUCAS BLO
SX9 Reporters

The trial of disgraced fashion photographer Lucas 'Blo' Blomfeld concluded today with LA County Judge Gloria Rubin sentencing Blomfeld to four years in jail over the statutory rape of underage models Celine Marchand and Raya Gutierrez. Blomfeld will also have to pay 'undisclosed damages' to ten other victims including supermodels Clara Keys and Jana Novak, who today said they would donate their payouts to a London crisis shelter for women.

Speaking from Stanley Mosk Courtroom in Downtown Los Angeles, Rubin told Blomfeld in her summation: 'It is clear to me and this court that you are a serial offender who used your unique position of authority and status to prey on teenage girls. There can be no excuses for this predatory behaviour. While my hands are tied regarding many of your historical offences, I fully intend to serve the most severe punishment I can in the criminal cases brought against you. It is my hope that this sentencing sends out a very clear message to those dangerous men who are hiding in plain sight within the fashion and entertainment industries.'

EIGHTEEN

The flat costs one million pounds exactly. ONE MILLION POUNDS. That's a fuck load of money. Unless, of course, you're flat-hunting in London, in which case it's fairly standard, it turns out.

It's a lovely flat too.

I stand in the living room by myself. It's a converted warehouse 'maisonette', whatever that means, slap bang between Hoxton and Old Street – stripped floors, open-plan living room and kitchen; exposed brick; roof terrace; big bedroom and little bedroom, which could be Ferdy's studio.

Mum and Dad don't want me to fly the nest, obviously, but it's time to be a grown-up. I'm eighteen now. I run a hand through my slightly greasy hair. It's getting long, grazing my shoulders.

I first saw the flat last week, and now I'm back to show Ferdy. The estate agent is up on the terrace, giving us some space. And, without any furniture in the whole flat, we have plenty of it.

Ferdy finishes his tour and pops out of the big bedroom. 'What do you think?' I ask.

'What do I think? I think this is the best student housing on the whole planet.'

I laugh. 'But could you live here? I don't want you to feel like a lodger or whatever. It's your home too.'

He crosses the lounge and cups my face in his hands. 'As long as you're in it, it's home.' He kisses me.

'Fucking hell. I'm gonna buy a flat.' I exhale loudly. I sit down, cross-legged on the bare floor.

Ferdy grins. He points out of the big windows. 'You seen that?'

I nod. I spotted it while he was in the bedroom. My Calvin Klein billboard, slightly peeling at the top left corner, is displayed over the road. Matty and me embracing each other, although looking very miserable, in the orange-red Death Valley desert. It was shot by Layla last February after the trial. That campaign is basically paying my deposit on the flat so it feels like a good omen.

Ferdy sits opposite me, mirroring my posture. I love his hair like this: short at the sides, long on top, pushed back off his face. Man, he's hot. 'This is gonna be so sweet, Jana. I can't wait to live with you.'

'I know,' I say – and mean it. I'm telling myself it's more of a permanent sleepover with Domino's, Ben & Jerry's and Netflix than it is like being wifey at eighteen. 'Me too.'

'So what's wrong?'

I shake my head. 'I don't know. This place is –' I lower my voice – 'a million quid. We're eighteen!'

'I know. But you've worked fucking hard, Jana. Holy shit, you *earned* this money.'

A tilt of the head. 'Oh, sure. No one has suffered like top models have suffered. The struggle is real.'

'You know what I mean.'

I lean back. The light flooding the apartment is so beautiful. Golden hour. It pours like honey across the floor. The warmth hits the side of my face and illuminates his. 'Do you think I changed anything?'

'Yes,' he says without hesitation.

It's almost a year since the trial. I've done some cool stuff: some massive campaigns, *Vogue* and *Vogue* UK, opened for Versace last Fashion Week. But sometimes, although Blo is sitting in jail, I still feel . . . grimy. I've been considering my next move. I think about some advice both Clara and Cheska once gave me. The name Jana Novak gets shit done. *I have more power than I think I have.* 'Ferdy, can we make a film?'

He grins a very sexy grin. 'What? You wanna spice things up?'

'Ha! Not like that, although I won't rule it out. I want you to make a film about me. I want us to make a film together. About what happened.' There. Now I've said it. I can't take it back.

Now he looks serious. 'For real?'

'Yeah. My name opens all sorts of doors. God, enough people have been asking if they can buy "My Story", but I'd rather we did it our way.'

'Jana, are you sure? It'll be really . . . putting yourself out there.'

'I know. But I trust you. I don't trust anyone else to get it right.'

He nods slowly. I can see his cogs are already spinning. 'Wow. OK. Let's talk more over dinner. You hungry?'

I grin. 'Famished. Apparently the Vietnamese places around

here are amazing. Suppose I should tell Grant he can come down off the roof.'

Ferdy hops to his feet. 'Wait.' He holds out a hand. 'Will you dance with me?'

'What?'

'It feels like something we should do.'

I blink at him like I'm tripping or something. 'You're insane. We can't dance. Not like *that*. Also, there ain't any music.'

He shakes his head. 'Yeah. So?'

'God, this is awkward.' Nonetheless, I take his hand and allow him to pull me up.

Ferdy gently wraps his hands around my waist and I drape mine behind his neck. I let my head rest on his shoulder. Out the window, the amber sun starts to set over London. I close my eyes and realise I don't have a single thing left to worry about.

'See?' he says. 'That's not so bad is it?'

We sway to non-existent music. 'It doesn't suck.'

'I love you.'

In the window I see our reflection. A man and a woman, I see, just a glimpse, a hint, at the adults we might become. 'Love you more, bumface.'

But not just yet.

– Jana, why did you want to make this film?

– Jana?
– I'm thinking.
– OK.
– Because . . . I found my voice.
– How do you mean?
– You know, it's an industry . . . a world . . . where a lot of people think girls should be seen, not heard. I mean, look at Blo. He took *pictures* of girls. Pictures . . . never films. We're things to look at. We're . . . visual, like, purely decorative. We're a commodity – bought and sold. And it's not just models . . . it's *girls*. If we speak up about anything, we're told we're noisy or stupid; wrong; naggers; liars; shrill; erm . . . hysterical; militant; bitchy or bossy. But people like Blo *need* girls to be silent. It's how they get their power – *don't tell anyone or it'll be worse*. I said something and, well, look at everything that happened. I guess I want other girls to know it's OK to speak up too.
– Sure.
– So that's why I want to do it. I won't be silent ever again. Never. I can do my job, but I can also have an opinion. I'm

not just a face or a body. I have a voice and I'm gonna use it. And you're gonna listen.

Jana and Ferdy would like to thank the following people for taking part in this film:

Sabah Sayeed is about to graduate from Nottingham University. In September she'll start a paid internship at Condé Nast, working as a fashion assistant at *Vogue* UK.

Kami Brennan-Winters is expecting her first child this December and is focusing on her new career in interior design.

Matty MacDonald is presently travelling the world with his husband. They married in Honolulu at sunset. When they return they plan to start a family.

Cheska DeBrett's Honest Models now represents over one hundred models, including Arabella Campbell-True, Elyssa Sayers, Jana Novak, Lexx and Clara Keys.

Dermot Deen was recently crowned Designer of the Year at the British Fashion Awards. He, and twenty other British fashion houses, have committed to using only healthy models over the age of eighteen.

Arabella Campbell-True is currently at RADA, training to be an actor. Her debut in *Carnage* at the Young Vic garnered rave reviews.

Westley Bryce won an MTV Movie Award for his breakthrough role in *Our Hearts Are the Color of the Sun*. Next up, he'll star as Gambit in the Marvel movie of the same name. He is currently dating actress Estella Fray.

Viktoria Jarasova retired from modelling and plans on enrolling at university. She lives in Paris with her boyfriend, an artist.

Lien Yim continues to model. She lives in New York and has just been announced as one of the faces of KEYS X CLARA Cosmetics.

Celine Marchand is writing an exposé about her time in the fashion industry and struggle with anorexia. It will be published next year by Hachette Books. She lives in Paris and is a freelance writer.

Clara Keys continues to model and fight for better conditions for those working in the industry. With Cheska DeBrett and Jana Novak, she runs Model Behaviour, a union which protects the legal rights of models. Her new cosmetics line KEYS X CLARA is the fastest growing make-up brand in the UK and specialises in make-up for women of colour. She lives in New York with her girlfriend.

Kai Ferdinand's debut documentary film, *Meat Market*, won best debut at the London Independent Film Festival. It will stream on Netflix this winter. He's studying Film Studies at UCL. His next film project, again working with Jana, will focus on the working conditions of garment workers in Bangladesh.

Jana Novak is in her first year at UCL, studying Law and Gender Studies. She lives in London with her boyfriend. She models when she wants to.

Acknowledgements

First and foremost, I'd like to thank the models, agents, photographers, scouts and editors who all spoke to me – off the record – about their experiences of working in the fashion industry. I don't think this book would exist without your insights and honesty. Your candour was at times hilarious and heartbreaking. I hope this book can, in some way, contribute to the much broader conversation on how we can improve working conditions across the entire industry, from factories to catwalks. I love fashion, but wish it didn't have to be a 'guilty pleasure'.

In the UK, models can join the Equity union. This followed pioneering work by Eva Fahler, Dunja Knezevic and Victoria Keon Cohen. In the US, Sara Ziff formed Model Alliance, a non-profit which devised the Child Model Act which reclassified models under eighteen as child performers and extended them protections, including provisions for educational requirements and maximum working hours. Leomie Anderson launched the LAPP website, giving women from all walks of life a chance to blog about their experiences of womanhood. Last year, Cameron Russell started the #MyJobShouldNotIncludeAbuse campaign to call out abuse within the fashion industry. All of these phenomenal women also happen to be, or were at one time, models, and inspired me to create the very fictional Jana Novak.

More personally, thank you to all at my agency, especially Sallyanne Sweeney, Marc Simonsson, Max Edwards and Ivan Mulcahy. To everyone at Hachette Children's and Quercus, thank you! Sarah Lambert, Kate Agar, Lily Morgan and Jenny Glencross: thank you for your patience. Ooh, this one wasn't easy!

To Unstoppable, your enthusiasm meant the absolute world. Can't wait to carry on the conversation under your guidance.

Thank you to the real Elyssa Sayers for bidding so generously in the Authors for Grenfell charity auction to have her name featured in this novel.

Thanks to Kerry Turner and Amy Swales for your help with China, South Korea and Japan. Thanks as ever to Sam Powick for her First Look, and to Kim Curran and Niall Caverly, founders of "Lookers": the fictional agency at Thorpe Park which started this whole voyage.

Finally, to all the girls reading this book: you are so much more than a body. Your body is a house for your brilliant brain, brave heart and powerful voice. It can do amazing things, so care for it, protect it, and – above all – have fun with it.

Also by Juno Dawson

Addiction, redemption, love and despair –
CLEAN will have you hooked from the first page.